# WHEN HE DARES
## The Olympus Pride Series, Book 6

SUZANNE WRIGHT

*To G,*

*I wouldn't have met this deadline without you, you're the best.*

SUZANNE WRIGHT

# PROLOGUE

*Quinley, aged sixteen*

*There he is.*

Her pulse racing with nerves, Quinley slipped out of the shadows at the side of the guest lodge. Zaire's step faltered at the sight of her, and his brows briefly knitted. It sucked that her own mate looked at her with zero recognition despite her having been in his periphery for years.

Her Alpha male Harlan was close friends with Zaire's father, Rodrick—an Alpha of another pride. Whenever Rodrick came to visit, he often brought his son along. And so Zaire had become friends with Harlan's children.

Quinley's pride was huge, as was its territory. The more important you were to the Alphas, the further inland you were situated. Her family was unranked and lived near the border, so she didn't move in the same social circles as the children of her Alpha pair, unlike Zaire. As such, she'd never had cause to *officially* meet him.

It was only two years ago, when he'd saved her from a tricky situation, that she'd been up close to him for the first time. As she'd looked directly into his eyes and taken his scent into her lungs, something deep and primitive had stirred inside both Quinley and her inner cat. They'd *felt* that he was theirs. When all he'd gifted her with was a blank, disinterested look, her stomach had roiled.

*He doesn't sense it,* she'd thought back then. It had been clear that something was jamming the frequency of the true-mate bond on his end.

She'd raced back home and told her sisters what had happened. They'd advised her not to approach him about it, saying it was best to give him time to sense the truth for himself. So Quinley had done exactly that, trusting that he'd eventually come to realize they were predestined mates.

But … he so far hadn't. Which was a special brand of torture. And after what she'd heard tonight, she couldn't stay silent any longer. She'd otherwise risk losing him for good.

Zaire gave her a severe glare. "You shouldn't be here." It was spoken with the authority of someone who actually *ruled* her pride.

Bold.

"I wanted to talk to you." She cleared her throat. "I'm Quinley, by the way."

He didn't react whatsoever. It was obvious that her name meant nothing to him and didn't poke at his memories. *Sweet.*

"You once intervened when I was surrounded by a group of my peers," she reminded him. Again, zero recognition. "In the woods," she added, but the words garnered no reaction. "Like, two years ago."

He continued to stare at her blankly.

Disappointment flooded her, but she flicked a blasé hand. "You don't remember. It's fine." *Lie.*

He sighed. "What do you want?"

She blinked at his rude tone. *Okay.* It didn't do much for her confidence, but she wasn't going to make her excuses and leave. This was too important.

She pulled in a preparatory breath and drew herself up to her full height, which wasn't anything close to tall. She parted her lips to speak, but the words got trapped in her throat. *Say it. Just say it.* "We're mates," she blurted out.

He stiffened from head to toe, his expression going tight. Not good. But still, there was relief in having *finally* spoken those words aloud. She'd held them in for what felt like way too long.

Zaire scratched his nape, looking uncomfortable. "Fuck," he muttered beneath his breath.

"I wasn't going to say anything. I was waiting for you to sense it for yourself. But you haven't, and then tonight I heard … I heard that you and Nazra plan to mate one day and run this pride together." Panic had squeezed her lungs so tight she'd struggled to breathe.

He dropped his arm back to his side. "Look—"

"I know there's a good chance my Alpha will make you sign a mating agreement even now. You can't, Zaire."

It wouldn't matter that he might not claim Nazra for many years to come. If he put his signature on those papers, it would be hard for him to back out without causing *major* insult to her Alphas—and it would break something in Quinley.

"You can't sign yourself away like that," she pressed. "*I'm* the one you're supposed to claim."

He pulled a face. "This is—"

"I'm no daughter of an Alpha, I'm not dominant, and my family as a

4

whole is unranked, so mating me will get you nothing—I know that. But we're *fated*, Zaire. That has to count for something."

"It would. If we were. But we're not."

Her inner cat flinched, her shoulders hunching. "We are," Quinley insisted, ignoring the pain that had lanced through her chest, cold and razor sharp.

He scrubbed a hand down his face. "Kid, I don't want to upset—"

"I'm not a kid," she bit off.

"You're, like, thirteen or fourteen."

His condescension was a slap. "I'm sixteen, two years younger than you. And I *am* right about this."

Disbelief plastered over his face, he shook his head fast. "You don't know what you're saying."

"Yes, I do. And I know I'm too young for you to claim; I don't expect you to do anything about this yet. But you can't sign a mating agreement, Zaire."

He slashed a hand through the air. "Okay, enough, I need you to listen to me." He pinned her gaze with his. "We're not predestined mates."

Her cat bared her teeth, the hairs on her back rising. "Yes, *we are*," Quinley upheld, sure to her bones that she was right.

"If you were mine, I'd feel it on some level. But I don't."

*Yeah, I noticed.* "Which means something's blocking the mating frequency on your end. We just have to figure out what it is." They could do that here and now.

"There's nothing to figure out. Whatever you're feeling … it's just a crush. Maybe you're too young to see that right now, but that's all this is."

Her spine snapped straight. Like she was naïve and didn't know her own mind? Quinley felt the edges of her temper fray. "A crush? You really think I'd confuse a crush with the pull of a true mate bond? I'm unranked, I'm not stupid."

He gave her an appeasing look. "I never said you were stupid, just mistaken. You'd be surprised how often it happens."

Quinley took a determined step closer to him and lifted her chin. "I *know* that we're mates. I *know* that this is real. And I *know* that if you sign a mating agreement, I'm going to lose my shit."

His eyes flaring with frustration, he stalked toward her. Dominant vibes rolled off him and beat at her skin.

Quinley was submissive—most black-footed cat healers were—so it was elementally instinctual for her to lower her gaze. She tried not to, but her eyes burned and watered from trying to hold his, so she dropped her gaze to the bridge of his nose.

"I was trying to let you down gently," he clipped, "but if I have to be harsh to get through to you I will." He leaned closer. "We. Are. Not. Mates."

The words were like bullets. She inwardly flinched, and a hiss sputtered out of her inner cat.

"I don't feel anything toward you that would suggest we're mates—not curiosity, not protectiveness, not even a pull to talk to you."

Fuck, he might as well have stabbed her right in the gut.

"Neither does my cat. He doesn't feel compelled to be near you or watch over you. That right there is a very telling point."

Her feline hissed again, now just as infuriated with his animal as she was with him.

"I don't go for submissive shifters, so it wouldn't make sense for my true mate to be one. Again, a telling point. I know this isn't what you want to hear. I'm not saying it so bluntly to upset you. I'm doing it because I need the facts to sink into your brain so that you'll let this go. We're not fated. What you're feeling is just—"

"A crush," she bit out, forcing her gaze back up to his. "I got it."

He studied her expression carefully. "Do you?"

"Yep. You're right. It's *all* clear now."

He didn't look convinced of her complete turnaround. And so he shouldn't. Because despite how deeply his claims cut and how much she wanted to slam her fist into his jaw, she knew as surely as she knew her own name that Zaire *was* her true mate.

But he clearly believed what he was saying. He wouldn't have otherwise rejected her so fiercely and with such finality. And she knew she could argue until she was blue in the face, but it would make no difference. For whatever reason, he wasn't ready to accept this yet. Maybe he never would be. Because if he couldn't sense it while she was *right here* with her scent surrounding him, if her claims weren't even making him consider they were fated, she wasn't sure what would.

His shoulders relaxed slightly. "I'll tell no one about our conversation here, and we'll forget it ever happened." His lips pursing, he gave her a considering look. "I will give you full points for risking Nazra's wrath. If she knew about this, she'd outright challenge you to shut this down. And, well, you don't look to me as though you have a chance of taking her on." With that casual put-down, he skirted around Quinley and walked away.

Her throat thickening, she rubbed at her aching chest. It felt like an ice-cold dagger had stabbed deep and was now lodged there.

Half-turning, she stared at his back as he walked into the nearby lodge without a backward glance—their conversation already forgotten. Her cat sulkily hunkered down, glaring at the small building in lieu of him.

She'd known he might refute her claim *at first*, but she'd thought she could convince him to consider she might be right. She hadn't expected the ugly condescension and sheer dismissiveness. Hadn't been prepared for just how agonizing it would be to have him turn his back on her like she was nothing and no one to him.

Her eyes stung with hot tears. She'd like to think he'd see the truth one day. Like to think he'd come for her, apologize, ask for forgiveness, and try to stake his claim. But she wasn't quite optimistic enough to let herself hope for it. Especially when he might just sign a mating agreement sometime soon.

A rustle of grass drew her attention to her far left just as a brunette stepped out from behind a tree, a smirk curving her mouth. "Well, that was interesting."

*Shit.*

# CHAPTER ONE

*Nine years later*

Having set his laptop on his thighs, Isaiah Hale switched it on and quickly logged in. He had a few things to do before attending a pride celebration later on, but he'd received a notification on his phone that he didn't want to ignore.

He brought up the web browser and selected one of the tabs he'd left open—the sign-in page for a website he'd recently become a member of. FindYourMate.com was a shifter-run site that aimed to pair up any who wished to enter an arranged mating. Its success rate was pretty high. Not many of its couples had later been forced to dissolve the mating.

After signing up, he'd had to complete an extremely thorough—not to mention invasive—questionnaire. What were his likes, goals, fears, hobbies, favorite books, moral beliefs, worst traits, sexual preferences? Did he have kinks? Did he want children? How was his relationship with his parents? What were his pet peeves?

On and on it went.

It hadn't been easy to expose so much of himself that way. But, no matter how personal the questions, he'd had to answer honestly. Otherwise, he would have been matched up with people who didn't fit him on every level.

Isaiah would have refused to complete it if there hadn't been a guarantee of secrecy. Not even members who were sent his name by the site would receive copies of his responses, just as he wouldn't receive copies of theirs.

It had taken him a long time to complete, but he'd managed to submit the filled-in questionnaire last night. An hour ago, the website had notified him via email that his account would now show a list of three potential matches. Isaiah was way too curious to hold off on checking them out.

on something, it was a rare occasion that they didn't catch it.

Even smaller than pallas cats, they looked much like a regular tabby. They were all about the simple things. Just wanted to eat, run, hunt, sleep, and eat some more.

Yes, they ate a lot. They would feast on anything—mammals, birds, insects, the living, the dead, the dying. As long as it was edible, they'd eat it. Hell, even if it wasn't edible, they would still try to eat it.

Whether in human skin or animal fur, they didn't seek trouble. But if pulled into a fight, they would battle fiercely and savagely until their opponent tired—which often occurred, because no other shifter was as high-energy as black-foots.

For Isaiah, their very existence flipped the finger at logic. Black-foots weren't built to take a beating in their feline form. Anyone could see that. But, as if blessed by shifter gods or something, they never seemed to die.

You stabbed one in the heart? Awesome for you. But they'd live. You set one on fire? Brave of you. But they'd survive. You drowned one in acid? Highly sadistic—and messed up. But they'd still live to tell the tale.

They did not brook the grim reaper's bullshit.

Or yours.

Maybe they'd kill you right there for making an attempt on their life. Or maybe they'd bide their time, sneak into your home one night and—in that very moment you woke up in bed, sensing you weren't alone—slice your throat while looking you dead in the eye.

It all depended on their mood.

But pallas cats had a healthy respect for ruthlessness, so Isaiah wasn't put off by any of it. None of his pride would be either.

*No, we have no issue welcoming other breeds*, he replied. *And you're a healer—healers are always welcome.*

There had been two in their pride until recently. Sam, somewhat heartbroken after a relationship went sour, had gone to temporarily stay with family in another pride.

Another message appeared on the screen: *Just to be clear, I'm not your typical healer. I can stop wounds bleeding, I can numb pain, I can speed along a person's recovery if they're injured, and I can give relief to those with chronic pain. But I can't close and heal wounds.*

Isaiah blinked. *I don't think I've met a healer who can aid with chronic pain.* He'd heard that some shifters could, but he'd yet to come across one. Until now.

*If you've got a bad back, I'm your girl. If you have a broken spine, I won't be of as much use to you. But I will hold your hand and sing soothing lullabies.*

Again, he felt his lips quirk. Before he had the chance to type a response, another message came through: *Does your pride know you plan to enter an arranged mating?*

*Yes.* He'd recently announced it. All were behind him. *Have you shared your plan with your pride?*

*My family knows, that's all for now.*

He twisted his mouth, wondering if maybe she was keeping it mostly to herself because she worried someone would give her problems—perhaps even her true mate. *Are they being supportive?*

*Yes, they think it'll be best for me to leave, though they wish that wasn't the case.*

*Is anyone going to give you any problems, try to throw up roadblocks, or outright contest?*

*No, why would they? If by 'anyone' you're referring to my TM, I don't anticipate that he'll react one way or the other.*

Good answer, because he didn't want to have to deal with anyone meddling.

*Is anyone protesting on your end?*

*No, they've made it clear they're behind me if this is really what I want.* He wouldn't have been able to say the same eighteen months ago—there were some who, irrationally still blaming him for something he'd had no hand in, would sooner see him forever miserable. But they'd thankfully switched to another pride.

*What about your cat?* Quinley asked. *How does he feel?*

Angry, in sum. Angry at Lucinda for committing to another man. Angry at her fiancé for claiming and impregnating her. Angry at Isaiah for never approaching her and telling her she was their mate—the cat still so sure she'd have chosen them if only she knew.

Isaiah grimaced as he typed, *I'll be honest, he doesn't care much one way or the other that I mean to take a mate.* He wasn't even paying attention to the online conversation Isaiah was currently having with Quinley. The cat had pulled away from the world. *He's still angry at the situation with my TM.*

Much as the animal felt betrayed by her commitment to another man and wouldn't accept her now that she carried said man's child, the cat wasn't ready to let her go.

Isaiah's recent attempts at dating had therefore amounted to nothing. The cat ignored the females Isaiah dated. He didn't see them, didn't want them, didn't like them on principle … because they quite simply weren't Lucinda.

It was why Isaiah had finally given serious thought to an arranged mating—something his father had initially suggested back before Lucinda was even pregnant.

If Isaiah claimed and branded a female, his cat would have no choice but to acknowledge her. He wouldn't ignore her the way he did those who Isaiah had dated. The feline would view her as his, protect her, engage with her. And just maybe stop obsessing over what had happened with Lucinda.

Isaiah couldn't see any other way of forcing his cat to let her go.

Not that that was the only reason Isaiah had chosen the arranged mating route. For him, there was plenty of appeal in it. But only if he could find someone on the same page as him.

He didn't want to mate someone who was only looking to form alliances or solidify a place for herself in his pride. He wanted a woman who was looking to build a future with him. Hence why joining the website had seemed the best idea. It would pair him up with someone who shared his wants and goals.

He knew there were some in his circle who, despite supporting his choice, were skeptical that it would work out. But his parents' mating had been arranged, and they were still tight all these years later.

His father Koen had explained that, though his inner animal hadn't emotionally connected to Isaiah's mother initially, it had thought of Andaya as under its protection once she was branded. The cat had acknowledged that she belonged to him and, like Koen himself, eventually bonded to her enough that an imprint connection had formed between them.

A shifter could form a metaphysical bond with someone who wasn't their true mate. Imprinting wasn't a process that was well-understood. It could happen to couples fast or slowly. It might spark to life even if they didn't harbor deep feelings for each other. It also might not happen at all, and it could even reverse itself if things went tits up.

Snapping out of his thoughts, he saw that he had another message from Quinley: *It's understandable that your cat would disengage, though it can't be fun for you.*

No, it wasn't. *What about your cat? Is she on the same page as you here?*

*She wants a mate, but I think it's more about filling a void than anything else.*

Isaiah knew a thing or two about voids. His cat's void was one huge gaping hole that might never be filled. Isaiah … he couldn't say if he'd ever manage to fill his own. His soul would never be bound to its other half; would always be incomplete. And it would also carry the open wound of being kept apart from his true mate.

But then … Quinley was in the same boat, wasn't she? They would have this in common. He liked the idea of that; of being *understood.*

Much as his head was kind of a mess, he did believe he'd be the best mate that he could be. He'd give it his everything, determined that imprinting would begin. He'd be loyal. Protective. Fully committed to the female he took as his mate, even as he might not be particularly possessive unless, or until, they bonded.

And as he looked again at the profile picture on his screen, he thought that maybe, just maybe, Quinley could be that female. The shadows in her eyes made him feel a sort of kinship with her, as did many of her answers and comments.

She ticked his boxes. She could relate to his anger. She *knew* his pain.

More, as a black-foot, she wouldn't feel neglected by how much of his time and attention was taken up with his enforcer duties and acting as bodyguard to his Alpha male. Quinley's kind weren't asocial, but they liked to have plenty of alone-time.

And … he was interested. More than he'd expected to be. So much so that he liked the thought of meeting her.

If nothing came of it, well, nothing came of it. He'd contact another of his recommended matches.

*Have you talked to any other shifter males on here?* he asked, wondering if maybe she'd met up with others but it hadn't worked out.

*No. I only logged in to find a list of potentials twenty minutes ago. I probably wouldn't have messaged you, though.*

He felt his brow pinch. *Why not?*

*You're tall. I'm kind of … height challenged.*

There was no stopping his lips from winging up. He'd noticed by the details on her profile that she was only five foot six—a good eight inches shorter than him. *A height difference means nothing when you're horizontal.*

*Hmm, valid point, I guess. I'm assuming, then, that you don't care about my not being tall.*

*It matters nothing to me. All I need to know at this point is that you wouldn't back out if things did move ahead.* He didn't want to waste time.

*There'd be no backing out.*

*Then I'd like to take the next step and set up a meet for us and our Alphas. You up for that?* Isaiah tapped his fingers on the edge of the laptop as he waited for a response, not liking how much a "no" would bother him.

*Sure. Do you have a preferred time or date?*

A breath eased out of him. *You choose. I can do it as soon as tomorrow, which I'd prefer if it's possible. I'm not interested in this being dragged out.*

*Me neither. I'll talk to my Alphas and then get back to you.*

*Speak to you soon.*

Isaiah logged out of the site, switched off his laptop, and did a long stretch. He'd taken the first step toward officially moving on with his life, and it felt good. Better than good.

Hopefully, he'd hear from Quinley again at some point today. The faster things moved, the better. Until then, he had errands to run and a party to attend.

# CHAPTER TWO

Hitting the reset button on life was a bitch, especially when you were only twenty-five years old, but sometimes shit called for an early intervention. And so you found yourself sitting across from your Alpha in his office, announcing that you'd pretty much arranged your own mating and simply needed him to help make it official.

Harlan blinked. "I've never even heard of this website." His pale-blue eyes slid to his Beta. "Have you?"

Leaning back against the wall, Astor nodded. "More and more shifters are using it."

In terms of appearance, the two males couldn't be more different. Harlan was dark, stout, and barrel-chested. Astor, on the other hand, was slim and long-limbed with hair so blond it verged on white.

Harlan's attention resettled on her as he sighed. "I suppose I should have expected that you'd want to be gone from the pride before Nazra and Zaire ascend."

Quinley didn't just want to be gone, she *needed* to be gone. She couldn't live under their rule. No way. Her cat wouldn't stand for it even if Quinley was prepared to do so.

It was hard enough for her to see them together—something that was thankfully uncommon, since they'd moved to his pride on claiming each other. Quinley suspected that Harlan had pushed for that transfer, worried that an imprint bond wouldn't form if Zaire was near his true mate. Because, although Zaire and many others had insisted it was all in Quinley's head, Harlan hadn't doubted her.

It was five years ago that Zaire and Nazra had finally mated. Harlan hadn't been willing to make them the Alpha pair straight off, however. He'd insisted they wait until they'd not only imprinted on each other but were solid enough that all could be certain the bond wouldn't crumble.

Imprinting could take weeks or years to start. Sometimes the process kicked in swiftly only to be dragged out for a long time; on other occasions, the bond formed during a short period.

Quinley doubted anyone had expected that Zaire and Nazra would take so long to be declared "solid." She sometimes wondered if maybe Harlan had delayed making the declaration for so long because he hadn't wanted to give up his position. Alphas generally didn't step down easily.

"I thought maybe you would ask me to organize a transfer," said Harlan. "You don't have to mate someone in order to have a place in another pride."

"I know that. I want to do this." Quinley had tried finding a mate the traditional way. She'd dated people from both inside and outside the pride, always open to having something more. But it either hadn't worked out, or the male in question had intended to wait for his true mate.

What she needed was someone on the same page as her. Someone from outside the pride, so she could transfer from hers. Someone who wouldn't want to move slowly. Someone who would fit her well enough that imprinting had a high chance of occurring.

Enter FindYourMatch.com.

And Isaiah Hale.

"You're certain of that?" Harlan asked her.

She gave a decisive nod. "Positive."

"And what about your cat?"

"She's on board. She wants a mate, kids, a bond, the whole shebang." What the feline didn't want was to be anywhere near Zaire or Nazra, let alone pledge her loyalty to them.

Yes, the cat was still furious at him. She didn't wish he'd made different choices, though. The animal thought him unworthy of her.

Quinley's fury had been dead a long time. She hadn't cried or raged when the pair had finally mated. Instead, a cold acceptance had settled over her. She'd made peace with the fact that she'd never experience a true-mate bond—something that bothered her more than his rejection at this point, because there was too much resentment there for her to pine for him.

But just because she'd made her peace with it didn't mean she had any intention of answering to him or his chosen mate. Much like her cat, Quinley was not prepared to owe either of them anything, let alone obedience. Nor would she allow them to have any control over her life. She certainly couldn't swear fealty to them—the words would be a lie.

Harlan leaned forward, resting his clasped hands on the desk. "People don't enter into an arranged mating lightly."

"I haven't made the decision lightly."

"You're only in your mid-twenties. You have years ahead of you; years during which you might meet and mate someone the old fashioned way."

"This way is faster." And the old-fashioned method had so far failed her. "It's not like this male is someone who I may have nothing in common with. The site only suggests pairings that suit."

"She has a point," Astor chipped in.

Harlan narrowed his eyes at the Beta. "And how can she know he answered his questionnaire honestly?"

Astor frowned. "It wouldn't have served him to be dishonest, since he'd want his mating to be successful."

Exactly. "You arrange matings all the time, Harlan. I don't see why you'd be trying to talk me out of one."

She hadn't expected him to be bothered by her decision. His mate wouldn't have, so Quinley kind of wished the woman wasn't off visiting relatives—Nel would no doubt have helped speed things along.

The staunch slipped from his shoulders as he sighed. "I didn't do right by you. I did right by the pride, by my daughter, by me. But not by you."

Quinley stiffened, knowing what he meant; remembering how he'd come to her the morning after she'd had her first—and only—conversation with Zaire. Harlan had asked her to accompany him on a walk, so she had. And she felt her lips tighten as she recalled the conversation ...

*"You know, hormones are funny things, Quinley. They can confuse an otherwise perfectly rational teenager into believing the object of their affections is their true mate."*

*She ground her teeth, infuriated by his insinuation. He was her Alpha. He was supposed to look out for her. Comfort her. Advise her. Support her.*

*"Now, the last thing I want is for Zaire to feel uncomfortable coming to our territory because one of my cats is insisting they're fated to be," Harlan went on. "He may not yet have signed a mating agreement, but it's pretty much a done deal that he will mate Nazra and, in doing so, tighten the alliance between our pride and his."*

*Quinley sensed that he expected her to duck her head, act all submissive, and go along with this shit. Instead, she asked, "Are alliances so important that true-mate bonds should be forsaken?"*

*He smiled, surprising her. "You're sticking to your guns?" He sounded admiring rather than annoyed.*

*Quinley shrugged. "Fact is he's my true mate. Another fact is that I can't force him to acknowledge it, or to choose me over being an Alpha one day. Status is everything to black-foots, and I don't have one. It wouldn't make him unusual to renounce his fated mate in order to pursue an ambition. But the situation is still a steaming pile of shit."*

*His smile kicked up a notch. "You have fire in you. Not many would try to tell me I'm wrong about anything—something you very expertly said without explicitly stating it." The curve to his mouth faltered. "The thing is, Quinley, whether the situation's fair to you or not isn't going to matter here. He's made his choice, hasn't he? He's not likely to change it."*

*Something in his expression made her sense …* "You want something from me."

*Again, his lips quirked.* "Sharp," *he praised.* "What I want is for Zaire to sign the mating agreement. His father and I have been planning a union between him and Nazra for years. It was always going to happen."

"You're telling me to back off?"

"It would be in your best interests. Rumors are spreading fast, aren't they?"

*Yes, thanks to Nazra's fucking bestie, Fila, who'd overheard Quinley's talk with Zaire. It was humiliating enough that everyone now knew that he'd rejected her. Worse, they'd been told a very twisted version of events: that Quinley had tried to kiss him, gone to bite him, even began to strip for him.*

*Though both he and Quinley had very firmly stated it hadn't happened that way, not everyone believed them. Each time she insisted she wasn't lying, it was taken as evidence that she was in fact a liar.*

"Nazra, well, she'll delight in making life hard for you and your family," *Harlan added.* "I'm literally the only person who has any sway over her."

*And then Quinley understood.* "You're saying you'll keep her away from me and my family if I stay away from Zaire?"

*A nod.* "Yes. I'll even make it clear to your peers that no one is to terrorize you on her behalf. But only if you agree to spread far and wide that, yes, it was just your hormones talking. So, what do you say? Do we have a deal?"

*Quinley cocked her head, confused.* "You could just order me to stay away from him."

"But you wouldn't, would you? You may be a submissive, but you're not passive, nor are you a quitter. It's admirable, but it won't help you here. So, deal or no deal?" *he pushed.*

*She wanted to say,* "No deal." *She wanted to tell him to stuff his offer up his ass. Wanted to tell him he was a shitty Alpha.*

*But then she thought of her sisters, of how hard it had been for them since their parents died, about how Adaline was pregnant and didn't need any stress right now, about how Raya would no doubt recklessly challenge Nazra to protect Quinley.*

*The whole situation had the makings of a clusterfuck. Whether Quinley liked it or not, this was really the only way to avoid it. So, for the sake of her family, she gritted out,* "Deal."

She'd never forgiven the motherfucker for pulling that stunt. She understood why he wouldn't have put her feelings first—they'd needed alliances back then, what with a few larger prides coveting their territory. Zaire's father had been friends with Harlan, true, but he wouldn't have placed his own pride at risk for mere friendship. Rodrick would definitely have helped protect a pride that his son would one day lead, however.

So yes, Quinley understood the larger picture. But that Harlan had not been in the slightest bit sympathetic, that he'd offered her no comfort, that his only concern had been ensuring she didn't interfere with his plans … no, she'd never forgiven him for that.

Nor had her cat. Even now it hissed at the memories, glaring at Harlan, having no respect at all for this male who'd failed her as an Alpha.

"You kept your word," said Harlan. "You never approached Zaire, never spoke to him, never even so much as glanced his way. In fact, you made a concentrated effort to avoid him as best you could. He didn't always make that easy for you."

No. No, he hadn't. There'd been times when Zaire just *happened* to be strolling around the area of pride territory where she lived. Times he'd uncharacteristically showed up at pride events for the unranked. Times he'd even unnecessarily been something of a shit to a male she happened to be dating.

"I think he was curious about you," said Harlan. "An eighteen-year-old boy's priority generally isn't finding their mate. But as the years tick on, it can become an itch under their skin. Even though he'd signed papers and was committed to one day claiming Nazra, he wanted to know for knowing's sake if just maybe he had found his mate. You saw that, didn't you?"

Quinley swallowed. "Yes." As had her cat, who'd been irate that he'd had the downright gall to go anywhere near her.

"It must have been hard for you to ignore it, but you did."

It hadn't really been about sticking to her word; it had been about protecting her family. Plus, she'd felt no desire to satisfy Zaire's curiosity when he had no intention of claiming her. He could go live with the mystery, the dick.

"I make difficult decisions all the time—some involve sacrificing a member's happiness for the greater good of the pride. Every Alpha does. It's my job to keep the pride strong and, by extension, safe. As such, I don't regret pairing Zaire with Nazra. But, Quinley, I would rather not reward your sacrifice by backing you in entering a mating with a complete stranger." Harlan paused. "I'd arrange one with a black-foot from another pride, but ..."

But she was unranked, so no one would be interested. Being a healer didn't give her status among the ranked. "I don't need you to do anything like that. I just want you to come with me to this meeting and, if all goes well, consent to having the appropriate papers drawn up. It's not like I'll be trapped in the mating. If there's no imprint bond within the first year, I get to leave." That was how it generally worked.

"I don't like that you quite clearly feel the need to leave. This is your home, your territory, your community. You should haven't a wish to—"

"He's from the Olympus Pride."

Harlan stilled, his gaze sharpening. "I see."

Astor chuckled. "You really should have led with that, Quinley."

Because the Alpha was so very obsessed with collecting alliances with powerful shifter groups, she knew. But … "He won't gain an alliance out of this, if that's what you're thinking."

"Pallas cat prides typically don't form them," Astor allowed, "but this particular pride is allied with some influential wolf packs."

A thoughtful look on his face, Harlan hummed.

Quinley felt her belly tighten. He was sat there wondering what he could use to wrangle an alliance out of the Olympus Pride. But she didn't have money or status or anything else. And she wouldn't put it past her Alpha to offer Isaiah someone more "worthy" in an effort to get an alliance.

She narrowed her eyes. "As you yourself admitted, you didn't do right by me when I was sixteen. I'm asking you to not fuck me over now."

Harlan had the nerve to look confused. "What is that supposed to mean?"

"It means you're thinking of throwing another of my pride mates at him to entice his pride into agreeing to an alliance."

Harlan's lips tilted upward as he glanced at Astor. "Told you—she's sharp, that one." He exhaled heavily. "Yes, yes, I considered it. I would be a fool not to. But I would like to, as my one last act as your Alpha, see to it that you are … compensated for what you lost out on with Zaire."

If he wanted to make himself feel better, fine—Quinley didn't care so long as he didn't mess this up for her.

"What did you say the name of the Olympus male is?"

She hadn't. "Isaiah Hale."

Harlan's gaze sliced to Astor. "Look into him, will you?" At the Beta's nod, Harlan returned his attention to her. "When and where does Hale want to meet?"

"The location has to be the website's HQ—that's a set rule," she explained. "Isaiah said that he wanted to meet soon, preferably tomorrow."

"Tomorrow? He doesn't hang about, does he?"

"I think it's a good thing. Why spend days twiddling our thumbs when we could just get the meet out of the way and find out for sure if we're compatible? It's best to find out as soon as possible. I don't exactly have the luxury of taking things slowly anyway for obvious reasons."

Harlan sat back in his chair. "If this is truly what you want, if this is a path you're certain is right for you, then I will support you. Arrange the meet for ten tomorrow morning."

Feeling the stiffness in her muscles leach away, Quinley let out a long, relieved breath. "I will."

"Am I right in assuming you'd prefer to keep working at the salon with your sisters?"

"Yes. Would that be an issue?"

"Not for me."

Quinley nodded, grateful. "Then that's what I'll do." She rose to her feet.

"Who else in the pride knows about this?"

"Only my sisters and their mates."

"You might want to keep it that way. At least until papers have been signed."

Understanding what he was getting at, she nodded. "That's the plan." Because Nazra's friends would otherwise hear of it, they'd pass it on to the soon-to-be-Alpha female, and Quinley didn't trust that the bitch wouldn't try to sabotage everything.

"Good." His gaze dropped to the papers on his desk.

Quinley nodded at Astor and then walked out of the office. It didn't surprise her that her older sisters waited there. Both petite blue-eyed brunettes looked so alike they could probably have passed for twins if there wasn't a seven-year age difference between them.

As their parents had died when Quinley was just five, Adaline—being not only the eldest but thirteen years her senior—had been her main mother figure growing up. All three of them were very close.

"How did it go?" Adaline asked without preamble.

Raya cast a brief frown at the office door. "I didn't expect you to be in there that long."

"Surprisingly, he didn't immediately agree because he wanted 'better' for me," Quinley explained. "Turns out he does feel just a little bad about how he put the pride before my right to be with my mate, though he doesn't regret it."

"Huh," said Raya. "Yeah, I wasn't expecting that."

"Me neither. He tried talking me out of it, but then eventually he agreed to support me. He warmed up to the idea once I told him that Isaiah's from the Olympus Pride."

The corners of Adaline's mouth tightened. "Typical."

Indeed. "I can't see him getting any kind of alliance out of this, which I warned him of. I don't think he'll try to screw me over if that turns out to be the case, but we'll see." He'd said he wouldn't, but Harlan had been careful not to give her his word on this.

"He's screwed you over before," muttered Adaline.

That he had. "Come on, let's get gone."

Together, they made their way through the Alpha's grand lodge toward the exit. They rarely ever came here. The unranked weren't invited to all pride events, they didn't eat meals in the large hall here at the lodge, and they didn't associate with the majority of the ranked. It was how most black-foot prides operated.

Stepping out of the lodge into the winter air, Quinley shivered and huddled further into her jacket. It was so cold her breath misted the air in little puffs. While December was one of her favorite months of the year, she often missed the summer warmth.

She halted to avoid bumping into two males who tromped right into her path carrying a wide and very tall arch of artificial flowers. Her cat narrowed her eyes at the female trailing after them holding a clipboard. Fila, Nazra's bestie.

Harlan had kept to his word, keeping Nazra and her friends in line. There'd been no challenges. No attacks. No harassment. But, thanks to Fila here, there'd been bullshit rumors. And with those had come insults, snickering, and a loss of not only respect but friendships.

Attacks weren't always physical.

Luckily, that crap hadn't come from every corner. A fair number of people—most of whom were unranked—had believed Quinley's version of events and had taken her side. But not vocally. They hadn't dared speak up in her defense, for which she couldn't blame them. Still, it hadn't felt good.

Unsurprisingly, Fila was playing a huge part in setting up all the decorations to celebrate Nazra and Zaire's return and ascension. Quinley sure hoped she was gone before the celebrations began, because attendance was compulsory—she absolutely could not be a part of them.

Fila cast her an ugly look. "What are you doing around these parts? If you're hoping to help out, the answer is no. I can't trust that you wouldn't try to wreck the decorations."

Quinley shot her a bland smile. "It's uncanny how well you read me." She glanced at Raya. "Don't you just love her?"

Raya grunted. "No."

Adaline guided Quinley away from Fila. "That woman is a trial."

Amen. "I really won't miss her."

Raya gently bumped her shoulder against Quinley's. "You'll miss me, though, right?"

"Probably."

Adaline snickered. "I'm still bummed that you're going to leave. Raya and I talked about moving with you. Our mates would—"

"Don't," Quinley advised. "I appreciate it. I do. But there's a chance that imprinting won't occur. If it doesn't, I may have to leave. There's no point in any of you uprooting when I might not stay in the pride."

"I know, but you're my baby sister—it's my job to look out for you."

Raya frowned at Adaline. "How come you don't look out for me anymore?"

"That's a full-time job that I don't have time for these days," said Adaline. "I love you to the depths of my soul, but I've never been more relieved by anything than when Lori claimed you—you're her problem now."

Raya huffed. "That's very nice." She looked at Quinley. "It'll be hard not having you live close by anymore."

It would. Mostly because they'd emotionally banded together so tightly after their parents died. It had even been difficult for them to live apart at first.

"You'll still see me almost every day," Quinley reminded them. "I'm not going to quit my job at the salon. Harlan said I could keep working there if I wanted to." She'd worked there since she was sixteen, and she loved it.

Blue Harbor Beauty Salon was owned by the pride and exclusive to shifters. A simple spell that Adaline had purchased from a witch was enough to repel any humans who might otherwise enter the salon. Black-foots hadn't stepped out of the closet yet, so humans were oblivious to their existence.

Blue Harbor provided several services—hair, nails, makeup, spa treatments, massages, and even pampering for their inner animals.

Shifters found the place relaxing because it accommodated their enhanced senses. The products weren't too strongly scented, the music was never too loud, and the lighting wasn't too bright. Also, no one had to keep up the pretense of being human since there were none around. They were free to be themselves.

"That is good news," said Adaline. "I figured he would."

Raya nudged Quinley. "What about Isaiah, though? You don't think he'll want you to give up your job, do you? I mean, he might not like the idea of you working for another pride."

Quinley frowned. "I stupidly didn't consider that." She inwardly cursed. "I'll make it clear in advance that it's important to me that I keep working at the salon with you two. If he won't accept that, I don't want him. I'm not interested in being with someone who won't care what's important to me."

Raya gave a pleased nod. "So, when's the meet?"

"Tomorrow morning, providing Isaiah's good with it." With that in mind, Quinley fished her cell out of her pocket and used the FindYourMatch.com phone app to message Isaiah: *Hi. My Alpha says we could do the meet tomorrow morning at ten. Would that work for you?*

It wasn't long before his reply popped up: *10am tomorrow is fine.*

Nosing over Quinley's shoulder, Raya mocked, "Very verbose, isn't he?"

"He's to the point, which I like." And he was not at all hard to look at. Very masculine with his rugged appearance.

His eyes were an unusual smoky grey that pulled you right in. Intriguing tattoos skated up his neck, ending below a strong jawline that was shadowed with dark scruff. The strands at the top of his black close-cropped hair stuck up slightly in a just-rolled-out-of-bed look.

His profile had only showed his face, throat, and shoulders. But she'd been able to tell he was broad, and she'd seen from his profile details that he was also tall.

Having him in her bed would certainly be no chore.

"I wouldn't have thought he'd contact me," said Quinley, pocketing her phone.

"Because you're unranked?" Adaline waved a hand. "That doesn't mean much to most shifter breeds."

True. It was easy to forget that, what with how obsessed black-foots were about it.

"If all goes well and you both decide to move forward," began Adaline, "do you think there's any chance this will all be done and dusted before Zaire and Nazra are appointed as Alphas?"

Quinley worried her bottom lip. "Isaiah made it clear he wants to move fast, so maybe. At the very least, there's a chance the papers will be signed, which is what's most important. There'd be no way Nazra could try to cancel the contract without offending the Olympus cats. Who'll want to do that?"

"Hopefully not her," replied Adaline. "She'll want rid of you eventually, but not for a while. She didn't get to torment you all these years because Harlan kept her in line. Once she's Alpha, she won't answer to him anymore. And she would just love you to have to owe her your submission and loyalty. That would be hell for you, and she knows it."

Nazra wasn't evil or anything. It was just that she would naturally have felt the urge to punish, challenge, or at the very least threaten Quinley for trying to "steal" Zaire from her. An urge that she had bottled up for *nine years*—that would only have made it worse. She would be *highly* unlikely to not finally act on it once Alpha.

Quinley sighed. "It's funny how so many people never believed Zaire's my true mate … yet she was not among them. It would surely have suited her to feel I was full of shit, but she didn't close her mind to my claim. She *called* me a liar. She never meant it, though."

"No, it was always a taunt to provoke you, not a claim she truly believed," Raya agreed. "I wonder how Zaire will react to you leaving the pride and mating someone else."

Quinley blinked. "Well, I mean … I'm sure he'll feel some relief at knowing I'd be out of his orbit."

Raya hummed. "Maybe."

"How he'll feel or behave isn't what's important," Quinley upheld.

Adaline eyed her carefully. "You really have fully let go of him, haven't you?"

"It was that or break," Quinley told her, hearing her voice harden. "No person will ever break me, least of all him."

# CHAPTER THREE

S tood in a crowded hallway of his old apartment complex, Isaiah couldn't help but smile at the sight of three Russian male wolverines blustering and shouting in their usual melodramatic way. He couldn't hear much of what was being said, thanks to the music blasting, but he suspected they were again complaining that their great-niece Aurora hadn't been given a Russian name.

Balancing a paper plate on one hand, Isaiah bit into his chicken wing. Pride events, especially parties, usually took place at the Tavern—their main hangout. But Bree and Alex had decided to throw an apartment-block party in order to celebrate the birth of their daughter. Isaiah suspected it was because the very anti-people Alex could then close himself in his apartment once his social battery ran out.

People were everywhere—the hallways, the open apartments, the stairwells, even the elevator. In fact, one of his fellow enforcers was manning a makeshift bar in the latter.

Some danced. Some drank. Some talked. Some chomped on finger foods.

Laughter regularly floated throughout the space, a balm to the pride's heart. It had recently suffered a few hits. One member had had to be executed, another was ostracized, and a third had temporarily gone to stay with family to heal from a breakup. As such, the birth of the baby wolverine had given some much needed light to the pride.

Unlike most breeds of shifter, pallas cats typically didn't claim territories. They did, however, live close together. There was strength in numbers, after all.

The pride owned not only three apartment complexes—including this one—but a nearby cul-de-sac and every business on both sides of the closest street.

His Alpha, Tate Devereaux, had reserved one of the other apartment buildings for lone shifters only, hoping to help with the growing problem of homeless loners. Such people were regularly targeted due to being without protection. All Tate's tenants had his protection.

Catching movement in his peripheral vision, Isaiah looked to see his fellow enforcer Deke approaching. Clinging to the tall male's broad back was his mate, Bailey, her silver hair looking exceptionally striking while pressed against Deke's short black strands.

Isaiah felt his brow crease, even as amusement pricked at him. "There a reason you're all the way up there?"

"Of course," she replied simply, but no explanation was given. Not a surprise. This particular black mamba did not live to please others. In fact, she set out to drive them insane … which made her an unlikely partner for someone as intolerant as Deke, but they fit in ways few people would have foreseen.

Isaiah's cat tended to glower at the newly mated couple, envious at what they had. Tonight, though, the feline did nothing—he was busy brooding, having withdrawn to a corner of Isaiah's mind.

Deke knocked back some of his beer. "Any progress with FindYourMatch.com?" he asked Isaiah.

Bailey's dark deep-set eyes lit with interest. "Ooh, yeah, what's going on with that?"

"I was sent the names of three possible matches," Isaiah told them. "Each has what you'd call a basic profile and a photograph on the website, so I checked them out."

"And?" pressed Bailey, impatient.

"One stood out for me." Isaiah tore a strip of meat from his chicken wing and chewed it fast. "I had River do a little digging, but he couldn't find more info on her than I already know."

"What kind of shifter is she?" Deke asked.

Isaiah felt his mouth bow up. "A breed that will never fear pallas cats, so I knew I wouldn't have to worry that she'd care what I am. I contacted her. We exchanged a few messages. She's agreed to meet with me."

Deke looked pleased. "When?"

"Soon." Providing her Alphas weren't difficult. "Tate will come along, as will her Alpha male. We'll probably—"

"*Dear God, will you never stop?*" yelled another voice from down the hall.

Isaiah looked to see Tate's youngest brother, Damian, scowling at his sister.

"*Until the world accepts that I'm right about you and brands you the monster you are, no,*" Elle bellowed back at him. "*No, Beelzebub, I will never stop.*"

Damian threw up his arms, his face red and splotchy. "*I can't with you.*"

Her insistence on him being the antichrist had never shifted, and Isaiah doubted it ever would. All pallas cats generally struggled to get along with their siblings as children if they were close in age. It wasn't even rare for them to attempt to kill one another. Tate and his other brother, Luke—who was also the pride's Beta—were perfect examples of that. But such siblings didn't always carry their grudges into adulthood. Elle was different in that respect.

His lips quirked, Deke looked up at Bailey, who'd quite clearly zoned out. "Are you in a mental world of your own again?"

She hummed as she snapped to the present. "I'm just wondering if colors look the same to everyone else as they do to me."

Isaiah felt his mouth curve. The female often came out with the weirdest stuff, though some of it could be described as insightful.

Deke frowned at her. "What?"

"Well … we can't know for sure that we all see the exact same thing when we look at a color, can we?" she asked. "*My* version of yellow could be different from yours, and we'd have no clue. And before you go thinking that our eyes can be trusted to see things exactly as they are, just note that leaves are not really green."

Deke stared at her for a long moment. "I'd tell you to look it up, but you don't like reading about anything that involves science."

"Because scientists lie." Bailey climbed down from her mate's back and skirted around him. "They shape our view of the world with bullshit from when we're young so we'll miss the truth even when older."

"I really don't think that's the case."

"Because they've successfully brainwashed you." She patted his cheek, all mock sympathy. "It's so sad."

Isaiah couldn't help but chuckle.

Deke fisted her sweater. "No one has brainwashed me, least of all scientists. They deal in logic—something I'm aware you fail to grasp."

"Preaching logic is another way to shape and control you. *Do what's rational, follow the rules, blend with the flock.*" She cupped his chin. "Don't let them trap and rule you."

His brown eyes glinting with exasperation, Deke insisted, "There is no trap."

"You have so much to learn, young grasshopper. Stick with me, kid. You'll be fine. I'll open your eyes to reality in time."

"My eyes are wide open."

"And seeing only what scientists tell you to see. *Hello, brainwashed.*"

Isaiah bit the last of his chicken from the bone to keep from laughing out loud.

Deke let go of her sweater and threw up a hand. "Okay, this conversation is just plain over."

"It's a good sign that my questions make you uncomfortable," she told him. "It means you're starting to believe I might be right but you're not ready to face it yet. I can work with that."

Done with his chicken wing, Isaiah walked over to the nearby portable trash can and dumped his rubbish into it. As he wiped his fingers with a napkin he'd earlier pocketed, he sensed someone approaching and looked up. His Alphas were on their way over—probably to check if Isaiah had heard from Quinley yet, since they'd said they would.

To be fair, she might have reached out again. It was so loud in here he wouldn't have heard his phone beep.

Having tossed his balled-up napkin in the trash, Isaiah dug his cell out of his pocket and checked his notifications. She *had* actually sent him another message. Reading it, he felt an unexpected sizzle of anticipation enter his bloodstream.

Isaiah had no sooner finished rattling off a reply than his Alphas reached him. "Just heard from Quinley." He closed the app and returned his cell to his pocket. "Her Alpha suggested we meet tomorrow morning at ten. I told her that'd be fine, since you said any day or time would be good for you."

Tate nodded. "Still is." The dark, well-built male cocked his head. "I wondered if you'd change your mind once it all became real. It's one thing to answer a questionnaire and contact someone online, it's another to take the next step. But you really are sure of your course of action, aren't you?"

Isaiah gave a slow but decisive nod. "I thought hard and long about it. Then I thought hard and long about it some more. And some more. This is the right thing for me."

"Then we're fully behind you," declared Havana, leaning into her mate as he stroked her long maple-brown hair. "Having a black-foot around could be interesting. I've met a few in the past. They seemed pleasant enough. They *always* seem pleasant enough"—mirth bled into her almond-shaped bluish-gray eyes—"but when riled ... Well, 'mean' often goes along with 'small' in the shifter world."

Very true. "Which is why she'll fit right in." Pallas cats could be mean as fuck, as could Havana's kind for that matter.

"I'll make an effort to befriend her so she doesn't get lonely," the Alpha female assured him.

"At no point does a black-foot ever feel lonely," Isaiah told her. "They treasure their alone-time. But I do appreciate the sentiment."

"Do you have a picture of her?" Havana joined her hands as if in prayer. "I want to see what she looks like."

"You'll have to wait."

Havana all but pouted. "What? Why?"

"I can't be bothered pulling my phone back out of my pocket." Well ... it was more that he didn't really want to show Quinley's profile to others. He felt protective of it. Didn't want to share it.

"You suck," groused Havana.

As tenacious as she was nosy, the devil shifter continued pestering him to show her Quinley's picture. When he didn't, she pulled both Bailey and Aspen—her best friends and bodyguards—into the matter.

Even as all three nagged him, he refused to share the profile. Mostly, at this point, to fuck with them. Their mates knew it, hence why Tate and Deke were biting back chuckles. Even Aspen's mate Camden was struggling not to smile, and the male tiger shifter rarely smiled about anything.

It was a few hours later that the party died down and people began returning to their homes. As one of Tate's bodyguards, Isaiah waited until the Alphas were ready to leave before making his way to the exit. Tate's other bodyguard, Farrell, did the same with his family, as did Bailey and Aspen with their mates.

As the crowded elevator began its descent, Isaiah caught sight of their pride's healer, Helena. Carefully skirting around one of the children, he sidled up to her. "Helena, you ever heard of healers who mostly specialize in numbing pain?"

She blinked. "I have, why?"

"The female I may take as my mate is that sort of healer," he told her.

Her eyes widened in delight. "Awesome. She'd make a wonderful addition. I can heal physical wounds, and the omegas are great with emotional drama. But we can't help the elderly with sore joints, or the migraine sufferers, or people who deal with constant pain from old injuries that didn't heal well."

Right then, the elevator stopped and its shiny doors parted.

As they stepped into the lobby, Isaiah scanned the parking lot via the large window and spotted no signs of anything untoward. Farrell did the same, his hand clasping that of his mate who carried their toddler. An enforcer always patrolled the lot, but it never paid to be too careful.

"You know," began Helena, "if she can help Aurora with her colic, Bree and Alex will love the woman forever."

Humming, Isaiah pushed open the main door. "Not sure Alex will allow a virtual stranger near the baby, even if it's my mate." The wolverine took hyper-protective to an entirely new level.

"He wouldn't let Aurora suffer unnecessarily, paranoid or not."

Isaiah held open the door for Helena and the others to file out. He then let it swing shut and moved to cover the rear of—

A series of loud sounds *cracked* the air in superfast succession.

*Bullets.*

Several people stumbled. One dropped like a stone. Voices cried out in alarm and pain. The heavy scent of blood peppered the air.

His cat lunging to the forefront of his mind with an enraged snarl, Isaiah grabbed Tate and ushered him back into the building as Bailey and Aspen did the same with Havana.

"Inside!" he yelled at the others, though it wasn't necessary—they were all fleeing as fast as possible, either dragging or carrying the injured with them.

The whole time, bullets kept flying.

He flinched as a hot fist slammed into his thigh and *exploded*. "Fuck." His cat roared its fury, raking at Isaiah's insides; wanting freedom to hunt and kill.

No, teeth and claws weren't a match for guns.

Isaiah was about to follow Farrell inside, but then he saw her—a small child crouched down, terrified, her hands plastered to her ears. Her mother was trying to get back outside to grab her.

His cat stilled, its heart stopping.

Isaiah made a move toward the little girl, but more bullets were fired near his feet, pinning him in place. Again, his cat roared—the sound so loud it seemed to bounce off the walls of Isaiah's mind.

Deke, Farrell, and Camden attempted to rush out, presumably to scoop up Emeline, but bullets peppered the door—which was thankfully bulletproof.

Tires screeched as a black, mud-slicked car came zooming toward the building. It halted, a rear door swung open, a slim male slid out wearing a clown mask … and he then darted straight for Emeline.

*Fuck, no.*

Isaiah acted fast, lunging at him. He crashed into the male, sent him toppling to the ground, grabbed his neck and—

*Snap.*

He went limp beneath Isaiah.

A bellow of pained rage filtered out of the open front passenger window. A masked head poked out, and it looked as if they'd leap out of the car. But then the vehicle started reversing fast as shifters began to converge on it from all directions.

The front passenger pointed at Isaiah. "You motherfucker! You're dead! You are *dead!*" Then the car was gone from the lot and speeding down the road. Several of his pride mates hopped into vehicles and zoomed off in pursuit.

Trying to ignore the hot throbbing pain in his thigh, Isaiah struggled to his feet just as people came tumbling out of the main door—some of who hurried over to little Emeline.

Tate came to him. "You all right?"

Isaiah gave a curt nod, unable to say the same for his cat—the feline was still raging. He looked down at the corpse at his feet and said, "He was going to take Emeline. He could have shot her. Didn't. He meant to *take* her."

As a bunch of others crowded them, Deke crouched beside the body and tore off the mask.

Gasps sounded. They knew that face. Knew the hazel eyes, dark scruff, scarred cheek, and deep brown hair. The shifter had recently made himself fairly infamous, along with his three brothers.

"Son of a bitch," Tate muttered beneath his breath.

"Knowing all he's done," began Bailey, "I kind of wish his death hadn't been so quick."

That was a relatable statement for sure.

Once Helena was done healing any wounds, Farrell escorted her and several others home. At Tate's insistence, the rest of them gathered at the house he shared with Havana in the cul-de-sac. His father Vinnie, who was also the pride's previous Alpha, had joined them. Luke and his mate Blair had arrived soon after. And now they were all spread around the spacious living area, varying degrees of all-out *pissed*.

Sprawled in an armchair, Isaiah cricked his neck. Of the people there, three had been shot earlier. Havana had taken a bullet to the upper arm, Tate had been shot in the shoulder, and Camden's calf was hit twice.

Isaiah suspected it was only Havana's injury that had kept Tate from rushing out of the building earlier to help Emeline. The guy was a nightmare for any bodyguard, because he was the first to risk his neck in the defense of a pride mate.

"It's definitely him," said Tate, stood near the fireplace, his hard blue gaze on the screen of his cell. A gaze that then lifted to Isaiah. "It's definitely Samuele Vercetti you killed." He turned his phone, flashing Isaiah a look at the online alert poster. A past photo of their dead guy was plastered right there.

The sight of it made Isaiah's cat snarl once more. He'd ceased raking at Isaiah's insides in some bid to claw his way out, but he wasn't yet calm.

The corpse had been taken away by Alex's uncles. The three wolverines were always happy to help get rid of bodies. Usually by eating them, but Isaiah decided not to think about that.

On the sofa, Bailey wore a bloodthirsty smile. "So many shifters worldwide are going to celebrate on hearing that one of the Vercetti brothers are dead."

More than likely.

Made up of several breeds, the Vercetti Pack had been pissing off shifters left, right, and center for years. They were so corrupt and conniving that not even jackals—a fairly cruel and shady species—would do business with them. Only humans, knowing no better, associated with them.

The pack didn't respect shifter laws, didn't take mates, didn't acknowledge the authority of Alphas, and didn't have any problem doing business with anti-shifter human extremists.

The pack didn't even have an Alpha. Four wolf-shifter brothers—Sebastian, Tommaso, Davide, and Samuele Vercetti—ran the group, acting much like a council. The rest of the members allegedly followed them blindly.

The pack had mostly operated in the shadows—trafficking drugs, cashing on bounties, dabbling in cybercrime, even running a shifter prostitution ring for humans who quite simply wanted to fuck a shifter.

But the pack hadn't made themselves true enemies of the shifter state until more recently. Their newest venture? Kidnapping shifter children—usually those of the Alphas—and either holding them for ransom or to force the aforementioned Alphas to commit acts they would never ordinarily do. Beat their mate, shoot their Beta, offer up another child in exchange for theirs, or even kill one of their parents.

It was totally fucked.

The ransomed children were usually returned uninjured. *Usually* being the key word. Sometimes they were missing a finger, ear, toe, or—in one case—a foot. Sometimes they didn't return at all.

The Vercetti brothers weren't really interested in money. They'd made enough cash over the years. What they liked was making Alphas submit to their whims.

There were bounties on their heads, and online alert posters had been sent around the shifter community complete with pictures of all four brothers. Hence why Isaiah and his pride mates had been able to so easily identify the now dead wolf shifter.

His expression grim, Tate looked at a silent but furious Havana, who sat on the other armchair. "If we'd had kids, the brothers would have taken ours. They won't have known whose child Emeline was, wouldn't have cared. It was about having me by the balls." He clenched a fist. "God knows what they would have done to her."

"It doesn't bear thinking about," Aspen murmured, snuggling into her mate on the sofa as he idly combed his fingers through her dark, choppy-layered bob. "What's known about the brothers? Their background, I mean?"

Stood between his mate and older brother, Luke stirred. Though he carried less muscle than Tate, the Beta was still well-built and closely resembled the Alpha male. "They were part of a prominent wolf pack," said Luke, sweeping his blue gaze over each person in the room. "Their mother died giving birth to Samuele, and their father passed on only days later. They were then raised by their maternal grandfather, who was Alpha."

"Giuseppe Vercetti," said Vinnie with a nod. "I met him once or twice. He had a cruel streak a mile wide. Seriously, he was one depraved son of a bitch. People who knew him well said that he treasured his mate and daughter but nonetheless beat them. Beat those boys, too. Often. Especially Samuele—Giuseppe blamed him for their mother's death, apparently."

Isaiah's cat peeled back his upper lip in contempt at the deceased shifter.

Mates and children should be protected, never mistreated.

"When Giuseppe stepped down, he didn't choose any of his grandsons to take his place," said Luke. "He instead gave the position to their cousin. The brothers killed Giuseppe, the cousin, and any who stood in their way as they then scampered."

Camden grunted, his brows sliding together. "A bit of an overreaction to being passed up for Alpha. Unless there's more to it?"

Vinnie explained, "It was said that Giuseppe had taken each of the brothers aside at one point or another when they were teens and—asking that they not share the news with their siblings—privately promised to give them the position. They did whatever he asked growing up, always thinking that their reward would be to lead the pack one day. Only he'd just been fucking with them."

Blair hummed, braiding her pale-blonde hair. "Sounds like Giuseppe had a profound effect on what morals they did and didn't establish. They're no less cruel than he was. I've heard that the eldest brother Sebastian is the worst; that he's committed every sex crime against women you can possibly imagine. Like he's addicted to deviance, you know? He takes it a step further every time, intoxicated on whatever high he gets; always trying to top the last high."

Isaiah splayed his hands on the chair's armrests. "Speaking of Sebastian ... I think he might have been the shifter in the front passenger seat. It's said that Davide is their getaway driver, so it won't have been him. Tommaso is the sniper, so he'll have been the shooter perched on a roof." Unfortunately, the enforcers hadn't been able to catch him before he vanished—only traces of his presence had remained.

"It'll have been Sebastian," Tate agreed, grim. "And now he's gunning for you." His jaw tightened.

"These fuckers need taking down," Havana declared, rage threaded through each word.

"Finding them will be the issue," said Tate. "Many shifters have tried. They still try. But for some fucking reason, no one can locate the pack."

Camden stretched out his legs. "It's said they live in the sewers."

"I heard they live in a campervan park," said Aspen.

Bailey piped up, "My intel says they don't have an address; they live on the streets."

Aspen looked at the mamba. "By intel, you mean whispers you overheard."

Bailey shrugged. "Same thing."

"Nope, totally different."

Blair folded her arms. "So, how do we go about locating them?"

"We may not need to hunt them down," said Camden, his ice-blue eyes pensive. "You ask me, they'll come back for Isaiah—he killed their brother."

Havana dipped her chin. "They won't see it as understandable that Isaiah defended and protected a child. In their mind, he's the big bad guy."

"Yes, they may come back," Tate agreed. "I'd like them to be found before that happens." He turned to his brother. "I want you, Farrell, and Camden on this. Ask Alex's uncles to participate, too—they make good hunters. I'd send you, Isaiah, but you have a mating to secure."

His cat's chest rumbled with an angry hiss. The feline wanted to be part of the hunt. Hey, Isaiah got it—it would be somewhat satisfying to track and kill the motherfuckers that had brought so much misery to the shifter community. But it wasn't more important than his plans to mate. And if he delayed things with Quinley, he risked her finding someone else. She was on a time crunch.

But, of course, his cat didn't give one fuck about that. The feline wasn't even acknowledging her existence.

Aspen bit the inside of her cheek. "Are you sure it's wise to bring someone else into the pride now, given it won't be a safe time for us?"

"Danger always shadows shifters," Blair reminded her. "There'll always be some threat out there. It makes no sense to wait until the coast is clear."

"Especially when we don't know how long it'll take before the brothers are found," Tate chipped in. "They've remained undiscovered for some time, so it seems pointless to delay Isaiah's plans." Tate raised a brow at him. "Unless you'd like to wait?"

Isaiah shook his head. "No, I'm not putting things on hold for the Vercetti Pack."

"Then we won't." Tate looked from his brother to Camden. "Find them. Find them fast."

"And when we do?" asked Luke.

"Don't bother bringing them to me," said Tate. "Just kill them outright. And make sure it hurts a hell of a fucking lot."

Camden's smirk was a little on the sadistic side. "Not a problem."

# CHAPTER FOUR

"You're not nervous, are you?" Astor cast a look at Quinley's tapping foot.

Quinley ceased the movement, unaware until right then that her restlessness was finding an outlet. She'd been cool and composed all morning, but that had changed once she'd arrived at the FindYourMatch headquarters.

"I wouldn't say I'm nervous," she told the Beta. "It's just that this is a pivotal moment. Depending on what happens here, a lot can change. Or nothing at all."

Her cat, too, was edgy. But that was mostly with impatience. The feline wanted to finally meet Isaiah, and she didn't like having to wait.

Seated on her other side, Harlan looked at her. "I have arranged many matings. They usually only fall through if terms can't be agreed on—some shifters don't like to compromise. But Isaiah made it clear that he wants to move quickly, so he won't want this meeting to be a waste of his time. That means he'll be less likely to be finicky about details."

*Hopefully.* There weren't really many terms that Quinley would refuse to budge on. But just because she found said terms reasonable didn't mean that Isaiah would agree, did it?

She took an idle glance around the reception area. It wasn't plain and clinical with rows of plastic seating. It had an earthy color scheme, comfy plush sofas, pine-scented air fresheners, and even played soft background music. Probably all in an effort to create a soothing atmosphere. Because tense shifters didn't make friendly shifters.

Others sat here and there, some appearing a little nervous about their own meetings while others seemed at ease.

"We can leave if you're not certain this is a route you want to go down," Harlan offered.

She frowned. "I am certain."

"Then why are you pulling that face?"

"I'm hungry."

Harlan snorted. "We'll go get pancakes after we're done here."

Quinley perked up. "You just read my—" She stopped talking as movement in her peripheral vision snagged her attention. Quinley looked to see a trio of males filing into the building. Her attention slammed on the one in front.

*Isaiah.*

Damn, he looked even hotter in real life than he did in his photo. Over two-hundred pounds of off-the-charts sex appeal stood *right there*, far more powerfully built than she'd pictured in her mind. And oh, sweet Lord, his large and muscular frame was packed with hard, roped muscle.

Those smoky dark-gray eyes scanned the room with a predatory focus. They paused on her, settled firmly. Heat flashed there momentarily, causing her gut to twist. And then he was stalking her way on those long legs, each glide-like step precise; lazy; confident. That dangerous prowl … damn if it didn't make her belly flutter.

He was essentially a walking sexual pheromone that went right for the ovaries. So it was no surprise that lots of bells and whistles and fireworks went off in her system.

She, Harlan, and Astor rose to their feet as he approached. Her cat unfurled and inched closer, watching Isaiah intently; noting the dominant vibes that flowed from him, potent and intense.

As a submissive, both she and her feline had always been attracted to dominants. The more powerful the male, the more drugging his dominance could be. A guy on Isaiah's level? Oh, they were catnip—pure and simple.

He slowed to a halt a few feet in front of her, a slight upward tilt to one corner of his mouth. "Quinley, good to meet you in person." His voice was deep with a pinch of smoke and just a little grit thrown in.

"Likewise. It's a relief to know I wasn't catfished or anything." She gestured at the males either side of her. "This is my Alpha Harlan and his Beta Astor."

"You must be Isaiah," said Harlan.

Nods, head-inclines, and brief words were exchanged between the five males as Isaiah introduced the cats he'd brought along with him. One was his Alpha, Tate. The other was an enforcer, Deke. Both were big, imposing, and watched her intently.

Isaiah tilted his head at her. "You sure you're five foot six?"

Astor snickered, the asshole. "I said I think she adds an inch to make herself feel better."

Quinley checked the urge to ram her elbow into the Beta's ribs. "I am *exactly* five foot six," she told Isaiah.

His lips twitched slightly. "Height doesn't matter, as I've already said." He paused, his eyes narrowing slightly. "Your cat is close," he noted, a hint of a question there … as if concerned that her feline might be on the defensive.

Quinley gave him a reassuring look. "She's always close." If one good thing had come from Zaire's rejection, it was that the bond between Quinley and her cat had strengthened. That shared awful experience had brought woman and animal closer; made them more protective of each other. Which also meant her cat was never far from the surface.

A line dented Isaiah's brow. "She's … agitated."

Quinley shrugged. "She doesn't like the music." Her cat was fussy.

Hinges creaked as a door to their right opened. A pretty dark-skinned female stood in the doorway, smiling. "Quinley Bevan and Isaiah Hale?" she called out.

"That's us," Isaiah told the woman before turning back to Quinley. "After you." His lips tipping up slightly again, he motioned for her to walk on ahead of him.

"Thank you." She crossed the reception area, shook the woman's hand— cheetah shifter, Quinley sensed—and entered a small room. A row of three chairs faced an identical row. To their left was an armchair and small mahogany table.

"Please sit," the cheetah invited once everyone was inside.

Quinley and her pride mates sat on one row while Isaiah and his fellow pallas cats claimed the other row. Directly opposite her, he sat tall, his thighs spread, his arms casually braced on the armrests—the image of at ease. He sort of *invaded* the space around him.

Having closed the door, the cheetah took the lone armchair and retrieved a clipboard from the table. "Now, it seems you all got the introductions out of the way in the reception area. Good. I'm Thalia, my role here is to draft up an agreement based on what you all discuss and decide. Should you fail to reach one, Quinley and Isaiah are of course free to contact any of the other FindYourMatch members."

Isaiah hoped there'd be no need for that. Because something about Quinley just pulled at him. Maybe it was that, being so petite compared to him, she called to his protective instincts.

Small she might be, but she didn't have a small presence. Would never go unnoticed in a room. Too striking. Too steady and sure.

And fuck, what an ass. It was round and tight and as perfect as her ample breasts.

Her cat was no easier to overlook. He could almost *see* her prowling beneath the surface, the light of her feline eyes coming and going behind Quinley's. It was fascinating to watch; even snagged his own cat's interest.

It was only then that his animal really *looked* at Quinley, immediately noting the shadows in her gaze and the cobwebs of sadness and resignation that clung to her.

Isaiah didn't speak. Neither did she. Nor did the others.

Often, a submissive would cut through silence as if to save everyone from any awkwardness. But as Isaiah stared at Quinley, she quite simply stared back; watched him with the patience of a hunter, reminding him that black-foots didn't always follow the script you expected.

"Quinley tells me you're an enforcer," Harlan said to him.

Isaiah inclined his head. "I am." He wondered if the Alpha knew that his son-in-law was Quinley's true mate or if it was something she'd kept from him.

"How long have been in your position?"

"Twelve years."

"And your bodyguard position?"

"That's a more recent development."

Harlan twisted his mouth. "I'd imagine, then, that you work a lot of the time."

"I do." Isaiah returned his attention to Quinley. "Would that be a problem for you?"

She shook her head. "I prefer being alone. People annoy me."

Isaiah smiled at her frank response. His cat wasn't sure how he felt by how intently she assessed them. Submissives did that. Read you. Studied you. Picked up on your unspoken wants. Heard the words you didn't voice. Anticipated your needs before even you did.

"And you're a healer, right?" Tate asked her.

She jiggled her head slightly, her nose wrinkling. "Of a sort."

"Yes, Isaiah tells me you specialize more in aiding with pain relief. It's a substantial gift." Tate slid his gaze to Harlan. "And yet, you are not straight-off attempting to negotiate a way to have that gift still at your disposal if she joins my pride. Most Alphas would. Do you have other members with the same healing ability?"

"No," replied the Alpha. "But any of my cats who need her aid will visit her at the salon I own and pay for her services like any other customer."

"I've worked there since I was sixteen, right alongside my sisters." She glanced from Tate to Isaiah and back again. "I don't wish to give up my job, so I'd prefer to know now if that would be an issue."

Tate pursed his lips. "The salon isn't on Crimson Pride territory, is it?"

"No," she replied. "It's near the train station not far from here."

That placed it at about a twenty-minute drive from where the majority of the Olympus Pride resided. "Then I see no issue," Isaiah told her. "If you wish to keep your job you should keep your job—I wouldn't object to it."

"Neither would I," Tate added.

Relief moved over her face. "Okay. Good."

Harlan arched a brow at Isaiah. "You understand that, should you take Quinley as your mate, it will give you no rights at all where the salon is concerned? It is my business and under my management."

"And when you step down as Alpha, will it still remain under your management?" asked Isaiah.

"Yes. I originally bought the salon for my mate; it was a personal purchase and not a property that will be passed along to the next Alphas."

*Thank God,* thought Quinley. She couldn't have worked for Nazra and Zaire in any shape or capacity.

Harlan turned to Tate. "You have alliances with both the Phoenix and the Mercury Pack, I'm told."

The Alpha pallas cat stilled. "I'm not here to form another one."

"Harlan." Quinley quietly dragged out his name, a warning there; hoping he wouldn't mess this all up despite his reassurances to the contrary.

"I didn't ask for one, did I?" her Alpha said, all innocence. "It was just a throwaway comment."

It was him being an opportunist. Focusing on the pallas cats, she said, "My family heard you're pretty inclusive, so they're worried they wouldn't be able to visit me if I switched to your pride."

Isaiah's brow pinched. "We're not so inclusive that we in any way attempt to limit contact between newcomers and their families or friends. They would be welcome in our home."

*Home.* She loved that word. "Where would we live?" She'd heard that the pride owned both apartments and houses.

Isaiah stretched his legs out a little. "I have a house next-door to my Alphas. Three bedrooms. Big backyard with woods just beyond it."

The latter appealed to her cat, who loved to wander and run and hunt.

"Do you have much you'd want to bring with you?"

"The basics, plus a few furnishings I'd rather not part with."

He gave a "that's fine" shrug. "The house has plenty of room. If I needed to remove some pieces in order to fit yours inside, I could do that."

He was just a little too perfect, really. Everything about him appealed to her.

A sense of such unwavering calm shrouded him. It was *powerful* in how safe and steady it could make a girl feel. This was a male who could be relied on, who'd be a rock in any storm, who absolutely had his shit together.

She licked her lips. "How do you make arranged matings official in your pride?"

"We hold a party that doubles as a celebration of the pairing and a welcoming to the pride. Mating ceremonies are later held if a metaphysical bond forms." Isaiah paused. "My next question may seem redundant, given your reasons for wanting a transfer, but I want to be sure: If we were to have

41

children—something you must want or we wouldn't have been paired by the site—would you wish to return to your old pride to raise them there?"

"Not at all." She heard Harlan's wince but couldn't find it in herself to feel bad. He was, after all, part of the reason she hadn't been happy there in a long time.

Isaiah didn't miss the wince, or her lack of reaction to the Alpha's discomfort. Didn't seem to really miss anything.

He so wholly focused on her. Still and watchful, he took in everything with that shrewd gaze—not just her appearance. Her expressions, her posture, her body language, what she said, *how* she said it.

She honestly felt like he saw through her right to the bone. Saw every strength, every weakness, every fantasy, every doubt, every scar. It was nerve-wracking.

"Good." He settled his gaze on Harlan. "Quinley doesn't think her true mate would be at all affected if she entered an arranged mating. Would you agree with that opinion? As his Alpha, you'll know him well."

Harlan's brow creased. "I'm not actually his Alpha. After he claimed my daughter, they moved to his pride with the intention of returning when my mate and I stepped down. As for your question, I'd have to agree with Quinley."

"Why?"

"I've known Zaire since he was a boy. He's a hard one to read, but it wasn't difficult to pick up that—despite how firmly he rejected the notion of them being predestined—he did later wonder if Quinley was right. Still, he did nothing about it. He claimed Nazra, and they fully imprinted. There's no reason he'd be affected if Quinley were to take a mate."

It shouldn't hurt that her true mate—the other half of her goddamn soul—wouldn't give one miniscule shit, but it stung nonetheless. It wasn't about Zaire as a person, just the situation itself.

"If you and Quinley were to enter a mating," began Harlan, "a year would be given for—"

"Two," Isaiah cut in.

Harlan blinked. "Excuse me?"

"I want us to be given at least two years to imprint," Isaiah elaborated. "We're not just two people who want an arranged mating to work, we're two people who chose this path because we've had to walk away from our true mate—that leaves a mark. We may need more time than the average shifter for imprinting to begin."

Harlan looked at Quinley. "Do you have an objection?"

She shook her head. "No. Two years is fine."

Isaiah nodded, satisfied. He would bet that the reason she hadn't hesitated to agree was that she was in absolutely no rush to return to her pride. By how very easy it would clearly be for her to transfer to his, she'd lost whatever comfort she might have once had in her pride. He didn't think that was merely due to her true mate's rejection. This wound seemed older, deeper.

"All right," said the Alpha before relocking his gaze on Isaiah. "Should you imprint but the bond dissolves, she will of course be permitted to leave your pride and take with her any of her personal belongings."

"Naturally," Isaiah agreed.

"Should Quinley expect trouble from your pride mates?" Harlan asked him.

He felt his brow crease. "Why would she?"

The Alpha hummed. "There are some who give *you* trouble, from what I heard."

Isaiah went still, knowing exactly what he would have heard. Tate and Deke had clearly reached the same conclusion, because both muttered curses.

Quinley looked up at her Alpha. "What does that mean?"

Harlan scratched his jaw. "Astor became aware that—"

"I was accused of arson and murder by a select number of pride mates when I was a juvenile," Isaiah blurted out, his gaze on Quinley; giving it to her straight. If she was someone who'd be put off by unproven accusations, it was best he knew now. "To this day, despite all evidence to the contrary, they continue to believe that I'm guilty. They also have no problem voicing this, hence the rumors."

She didn't bat an eyelid. "Then they're dicks."

A snort popped out of Astor.

She shrugged. "I only speak the truth."

Isaiah studied her face. She believed him, he realized. She wasn't just saying it, she *meant* it. She'd taken him at his word just like that.

A sigh slipped out of her. "I know a thing or two about toxic rumors."

That hooked Isaiah's interest right there, heightening his curiosity about her. Even his cat edged forward, intrigued despite himself.

"You don't believe the rumors are true, do you?" she asked Harlan. "His Alpha would hardly have made him both an enforcer and his personal bodyguard if he was capable of that kind of betrayal."

"I didn't say I believed what I heard. I just wanted to know if it will impact you."

"There's no reason it would," Isaiah told him. "Those cats are no longer part of my pride anyway."

Isaiah moved his attention back to Quinley. He'd always imagined that his mate would be as equally dominant as he was. He'd thought it was what he wanted. But here he was, drawn to this submissive in a way he never had been to any dominant.

She was candid. Decisive. Centered. Didn't make snap judgements.

All things he liked.

Despite the high-energy vibe she gave off, Quinley was pretty chill and airy. Restful in that way that only submissives could be, making a person feel they could breathe easier.

He could easily imagine having her settled in his home, making it *their* home. He could definitely imagine fucking her raw. That would happen a lot. He didn't have to worry that they wouldn't suit in bed—their sexual wants must have matched up for the site to have paired them.

As for his cat … the animal was intrigued by her but no more. Still, it was better than nothing. More than Isaiah had actually hoped for.

Isaiah leaned toward her. "Enough of the hypotheticals. Can we agree that we'll take each other as mates?"

Quinley's gut clenched, but in a *good* way. She hadn't realized how much she'd hoped he'd say that until the words flew out of his mouth.

When she'd signed up for the website, she hadn't held much hope that she'd find someone who would suit her well. But he did. At least in theory. Whether they'd manage to permanently bond she didn't know. The potential was definitely there, though.

He ticked her every box. As a submissive, she needed things in a mate that a dominant might not. A female dominant might *find* strength, power, and authority attractive in a male. But they wouldn't crave them the way a submissive female shifter would.

Isaiah's stabilizing strength and reliability came across in the confidence that all but poured off him. It seduced her like nothing else.

Her cat would accept him—powerful male shifters were its drug. She craved a strong and dominant mate who'd make her feel safe.

Quinley swallowed, knowing her life was about to change; exalted by the idea. "Yes."

His mouth curved. "Good."

Damn, he had a killer smile.

"Perfect," Thalia piped up.

Quinley blinked. She'd forgotten the woman was there.

"I want to make it official on Monday," Isaiah declared.

Harlan frowned. "That's in two days' time."

Isaiah flicked a brow at her. "Do you need longer than that to pack your things?"

"No." She'd rope her family in to help, if need be.

"Do you have an objection to going through with the mating so soon?"

"No, none. I see no reason to wait." Quite the opposite, really.

Harlan sighed. "This is all happening very, very fast. Are you sure you both wouldn't like to take a little time to think about it, or to at least schedule the mating for a time further in the future?"

"I'm sure," said Isaiah.

"As I said, I see no reason to wait," said Quinley.

Harlan puffed out a resigned breath. "All right. Monday it is."

# CHAPTER FIVE

After dropping Deke off at his apartment building, Isaiah drove straight to the cul-de-sac. Though they were only one week into December, the pride hadn't wasted any time in pulling out the Christmas decorations. Wreaths with red velvet bows hung on doors. Ornaments such as giant baubles or pre-lit reindeers were strewn on lawns. String lights and LED icicles were clipped to doorframes, rooflines, shrubs, fences, porches, and window frames. Nutcrackers, slim trees, or frosted snowmen bordered front doors.

Isaiah didn't own any such decorations—he'd always lived in an apartment until recently. So it had come as a bit of a surprise when he'd returned home a few days ago to find a wreath on his door, a pre-lit Christmas tree arch surrounding its frame, and garlands running along the rail of his porch and twined around the posts.

Before even entering the house, he had called his mother, knowing she'd be the culprit. She hadn't answered the phone with a greeting. She'd straight off asked, *"Do you really want to bring your chosen mate to a house that doesn't look the slightest bit festive?"*

Since the answer was in fact "no," he hadn't complained. He had, however, asked Andaya to at least not let herself into his house to decorate the interior.

Her response? *"Too late."*

An example of how submissives could be a law unto themselves just the same as any dominant.

As he right then pulled into his driveway, Isaiah cast a brief look at the male riding shotgun. "I appreciate you giving up your Saturday morning to—"

45

"Don't thank me, Isaiah," said Tate. "There's no need. You're not just one of my cats, or even just one of my enforcers. You're a friend. You need me, I'm there. Simple."

Isaiah inclined his head in appreciation.

"I like her. Quinley. I can see why the site suggested her as a possible choice for you. You're both compatible for sure."

Isaiah gave a slow nod. "She's calm. I need that. Havana, Aspen, and Bailey are a blast. But in a mate, I need someone a lot more low-key."

"Black-foots typically are calm." Tate's mouth quirked. "Until they're not. Try not to get on her bad side."

"That's the plan."

"You two being compatible doesn't guarantee an imprint bond, I know, but it gives the mating a better chance at working." Tate paused. "Kudos to you for what you're doing—and I'm not taking about entering an arranged mating."

Isaiah felt his brow pinch. "Then what?"

"It's not easy for us to dare reach for happiness when our state of mind is all fucked. You weren't in a good place for a while, but you climbed out of that dark pit and you haven't given up on the idea of still having something good. Not all shifters who've lost the chance of having their fated mate can say that."

They'd get no judgement from Isaiah—it had been a struggle to patch up his wounds when healing felt much like saying, "Hey, it's all good." Nothing had felt "all good" back then. And maybe nothing ever would, but he wouldn't know unless he dared reach for more. "Let's hope it pays off."

"My own hopes are high."

Isaiah grabbed his phone from the cupholder. "You should get home to Havana. I need to get inside before my mother comes out here to drag me in. There's no way my parents haven't let themselves into the house to wait for me—she'll want to hear exactly how the meet went."

Tate opened the passenger door. "Then you'd better go tell her." After exiting the car, the Alpha jogged to his own house.

Isaiah gave a nod to one of his other neighbors, who was jamming plastic candy canes along the border of his path, and then strode up to his house. He'd no sooner opened the front door than his mother materialized in front of him.

In terms of height, build, and facial features, he took after his father. But Isaiah had inherited his dark hair and gray eyes from his mother.

Her hands clasped tight, Andaya lifted her brows. "Well, how did it go?"

"Good," said Isaiah, stepping inside. "A celebration will take place on Monday to make the mating official." He closed the door behind him.

"Just like that?" she asked.

"Just like that." He slipped off his jacket and then hung it on the coat rack. "Why wait? Seems senseless."

She tilted her head. "I don't know whether to interpret this as you just don't care who you mate as long as it's done quickly … or if you're so at ease with moving fast because you've decided she might just fit you."

"The latter." Following the sounds of a football game, he walked into the living room to find his father sat on the sofa watching TV.

Koen looked up at him, an apology in his deep brown eyes. "I did tell your mom we should wait at home for you to call. She agreed, all smiles. Then she disappeared, and I had a pretty good idea of where she'd be, so I hightailed it here."

Slipping past Isaiah, she sniffed. "I was worried, that's all."

"You couldn't worry at home?" teased Koen, the glimmer of humor in his gaze.

Andaya cast him a haughty look. "Are you not even going to ask our son how the meet went?"

"I already know; heard him tell you." Koen refocused on Isaiah. "I'm glad it went well. I wasn't so sure if using the website was the best way to go, despite its success."

Isaiah took the armchair. "I had a few doubts as well initially." He'd signed up regardless because there had seemed no harm in giving it a try.

"But not now?" prodded Koen.

"No. She and I are definitely compatible."

"Tell us about her." Andaya sank onto the sofa beside Koen. "You've been stingy with details."

Because Isaiah hadn't seen the point in relaying them when he hadn't been sure the meet would amount to anything. "Her name's Quinley. She's twenty-five. A submissive. Works at a beauty salon. And she belongs to the Crimson Pride." Though not for much longer.

"Crimson Pride," echoed Andaya, her brow creased. "I don't think I've heard of it."

"What makes you think she'll fit you?" asked Koen.

"We're similar in some ways—blunt, decisive, determined, calm," said Isaiah. "We're on the same page, want the same things, and she has no issues with transferring to our pride. She also knows what it's like to find your true mate but be unable to have them." And also apparently understood the impact of toxic rumors.

Koen's brows inched up. "Is hers human like yours?"

Isaiah shook his head. "No. He's a shifter. He not only rejected her, he claimed and fully imprinted on her Alpha's daughter."

Andaya winced in sympathy. "So Quinley's had a front row seat to their personal show."

"To an extent." Isaiah sank deeper into his chair. "It seems that the couple moved to his pride for a while after the claiming. But they'll soon be back, and then they'll be appointed as the Crimson Pride Alphas."

Realization washed over Koen's face. "Yes, I can see why she'd be in a hurry to mate. No wonder she has no issues with a transfer. What breed of shifter is she?"

"A black-foot."

Andaya blinked. "Well, at least she won't bat an eyelid at how pallas cats are."

Speaking of eyelids not batting ... "She believed me when I told her the rumors about me were false."

His mother frowned. "You told her about them?"

"No. Her Alpha seemingly had his Beta look into me. He heard about the rumors and asked if those who spread them would give Quinley any problems." Isaiah crossed his feet at his ankles. "She dismissed the rumors; said the people persisting to believe that I was guilty were dicks."

Her frown smoothing out, Andaya smiled. "I like her already."

"I think she'll make a good addition to the pride," said Isaiah. "She's a healer who specializes mostly in easing pain. We don't have anyone like that."

Koen tipped his head to the side. "You know, I wouldn't have thought you'd choose a submissive for a mate. You never dated any."

"I've always been very self-focused, and care needs to be taken with submissives." Watching his mother bristle, Isaiah shot her a look. "Don't pull that face, you know what I'm talking about. You don't need to be handled delicately, but you do need someone who's attentive, mindful, and focused on you. I couldn't—and didn't particularly want to—give that much of my time and energy to someone I was dating. But Quinley will be my mate, so it's different."

"How did your cat behave around her?" asked Koen.

"At first, he didn't take much notice. But her cat is very bold and stays close to the surface, so that caught his attention." Isaiah didn't add that his cat had also been intrigued by her claim to be familiar with toxic rumors—he wasn't going to share her private business with others unless she gave him her consent.

Andaya pulled out her cell. "I'll contact the omegas and ask them to start getting the preparations ready for the celebration."

"Way ahead of you on that. I texted Bree earlier." As the primary omega, she took the lead in all omega-related matters. "She said to tell you that if you wanted to be involved just give her a call, so it seems she guessed that you'd want a hand in organizing the celebration."

A pleased smile graced Andaya's face. "I'll call her once I leave here." She eyed him carefully. "I know an arranged mating isn't what you initially pictured for yourself, and I know it might continue to hurt for a very long time that you'll never know what it is to be bonded to the other half of your soul. But that doesn't mean you can't be happy. You just have to be open to it."

Isaiah felt his brow pinch. "Why wouldn't I be?"

"Because some elemental part of you may feel guilty for allowing yourself to be happy with anyone other than your predestined mate," she explained. "And bonding with another can feel much like giving up all hope."

His frown deepened. "I already did give it up."

"There's a difference between being aware that it would be foolish to hope and being able to shake it off all the way. Sometimes, 'hope' is a defense mechanism. We hold onto it for our emotional sake."

"I don't believe I'm still doing that."

"Do you still keep tabs on Lucinda?" The question held a pinch of challenge.

"No." It had been hard to stop—he was so used to monitoring her activities, to watching over her in his way, that ceasing to do so had felt strange.

"Do you still dream of her?"

Isaiah stilled. "How did you ..."

"Your father used to dream of his. It stopped when we imprinted. But before that, she'd invade his dreams."

Isaiah rubbed at his nape, uncomfortable. "It doesn't happen as often as it used to."

"They'll occur less and less as you settle into your mating," Koen assured him. "Once a bond forms between you and Quinley, they'll cease altogether. Hand on heart, I don't regret not having been able to claim my own fated mate. Your mother and I have something very special. I can't imagine that I would ever have been happier with another woman. It's a ludicrous thought."

"That may seem hard to believe, but true mate bonds aren't the be all and end all, Isaiah," said his mother. "They certainly don't guarantee happiness. The only thing they guarantee is that your mate never has an out."

That was the thing about imprint bonds: they could reverse themselves if the relationship deteriorated, or if either of the couple or their inner animal withdrew from the mating.

"What we're trying to say is that you haven't missed out on the chance to have something special," Andaya continued. "It's just that you won't have it with the person you originally thought you would."

Isaiah liked to think he'd have a mating as solid as that of other imprinted couples around him—not only his parents, but Deke and Bailey, and also Bree and Alex. But ... "It'll be hard when I don't have my cat's support. For as long as he holds back from Quinley, it'll put a strain on our attempt to form a bond."

Koen nodded, sighing. "Like it won't be difficult enough to form one with a relative stranger. Imprinting is always harder for shifters entering an arranged mating, because they generally weren't a couple before then. They're usually two relative strangers thrust together, like your mother and I were. But if this FindYourMate website is as successful as it claims to be, you have a better chance than most at making it work."

Isaiah looked from one parent to the other. "It was four months before you felt the stirrings of imprinting, right?"

"Yes, which is fairly good," said Koen. "But don't be disheartened if you have to wait longer. I know you, son. You get annoyed if things don't move at your pace. You can start to believe you're wasting your time—something you hate to do—and then pour your energy into something else. Imprinting moves at a pace we can't control or understand."

Andaya nodded. "Don't lose hope or positivity if things drag out—that would only slow the process down. Be patient. Focus not on forming an imprint bond but on building a relationship. You can't have one without the other."

"I just don't like that I won't get a chance to meet him before the celebration," complained Raya, drumming her nails on the kitchen countertop. "I want to feel sure that you're mating someone who'll be good for you."

Quinley briefly looked away from the dish she was washing. "None of us can be sure of that. Isaiah and I don't know each other—"

"That's my point."

"This is just how arranged matings work. You know that." Her sister just liked to moan, especially if she felt left out. "*I* haven't even been in a room alone with Isaiah. Why should there be an exception for you?"

"I'm special. We all know that."

At the table, Adaline snorted. "Yeah. Special. We'll go with that."

Raya glared at Adaline, affronted. "You're insinuating I'm not?"

"It wasn't an insinuation."

Her lips thinning, Raya shook her head. "And you wonder why I insist that Quinley is your favorite."

"I don't have a favorite—I've told you this, like, a gazillion times."

"Because you're a liar."

"Or *you're wacked*. Which I say with love," Adaline added softly, her face serene. "Pure and unconditional love. That is what I feel for you."

"But you feel more of it for Quinley."

"That doesn't mean she's my favorite."

"*How is that not favoritism?*"

Quinley bit back a chuckle and plopped the clean plate on the drainer. The two women constantly teased each other in a way that would seem plain harsh to those who didn't know them. No real hurt was caused. They just each had a dark sense of humor.

Scrubbing yet another plate, she peered out of the window in front of her. Her nephews—Adaline's twin boys, Corey and Ren—were outside kicking a ball around with their father Will while Raya's mate stood aside cheering the little guys on.

After returning from the meet, Quinley had found all of them waiting on her porch with takeout food—a bribe for entrance so that they could grill her. She'd given them the rundown of what occurred in the FindYourMatch HQ, but she hadn't admitted just how enthusiastically her body had responded to Isaiah—her sisters would only tease her like idiots.

"Now stop whining at Quinley," Adaline reprimanded. "You said you'd support her in this."

"I will support whatever gets her away from Nazra and Zaire. But I still have concerns." Raya turned back to Quinley, folding her arms. "I should be allowed to talk to Isaiah; warn him to treat you right and stuff."

Quinley rolled her eyes. "You can do that at the celebration if you feel you must. Instead of complaining, could you maybe focus on the positives here? I'll be away from Twit and Twat. I'll get a fresh start. I'll have a mate. I'll still be working at the salon. And I won't be very far away." She set the clean dish on the drainer. "Isaiah made it clear that you're all free to visit whenever you want."

"Neither of you will be coming here to see us?" asked Raya, her brows dipping. "You should. Let those assholes Nazra and Zaire see that you've moved on and that they have no hold over your emotions."

"I'm not interested in doing that. I just want to be away from them. My cat will accept Isaiah, but that's not to say that imprinting will be simple for her. Having even minor contact with her true mate or the female who claimed him might get in the way."

"You don't want your cat to keep getting dragged into the past and end up focusing on her hurt rather than on what future she might have," Adaline understood.

"Exactly," Quinley confirmed, drying her hands on a small towel. "I want Isaiah to be the only male on her radar."

"Well, news of the arranged mating will be circling even now," said Adaline. "Nazra's friends will call and tell her. I wouldn't be surprised if she calls you, her father's warning to leave you alone be damned, because *this* is a huge deal."

Quinley shook her head. "She won't have my number."

"It won't be hard for her to get it," Raya warned. "So be braced for a call."

There was no call from Nazra that day, though. Or a text. Or an email. Or anything at all.

She also didn't send any of her friends to pay Quinley a visit on her behalf. So Quinley figured that either Nazra simply didn't care, or no one had actually told her.

It turned out she'd figured wrong. Something she realized the following evening, when Nazra turned up at her cabin.

*For fuck's sake.* Her grip flexing on the door handle, Quinley didn't say anything. She merely stared at the other female. Her inner feline slowly pushed to her feet, her hackles rising.

It was no mystery why Zaire had been—if the stories were true—attracted to Nazra right from the start. There was no denying she was beautiful. Slanted cat-green eyes, tight curls the color of caramel, prominent cheekbones, hourglass figure. That she was a born-alpha had only increased her appeal for him.

Nazra arched an imperious brow. "Are you not going to invite me in?"

"Nope, I'd rather have witnesses to whatever you do next." There was a couple standing not far away, their attention fixed on Quinley and her visitor.

Nazra exhaled heavily, suddenly looking … tired. "I haven't come here to argue. I just want to talk."

Quinley felt her brows draw together. This whole looking worn out thing could be a trick, but why use one?

"Really," Nazra persisted. "All I want to do is talk. If it makes you feel better, you can leave the door wide open."

Quinley poked her tongue into the inside of her cheek. "All right." She stepped aside for the other woman to enter.

Nazra strode into the cabin and glanced around. "You're all packed, I see."

Yup. Boxes full of her possessions were stacked here and there. Her reading chair had been pushed near the door, ready to be taken.

Quinley didn't shut the door. She remained right there, in full view of any who might pass or wander close. It paid to be careful when it came to Nazra.

The future Alpha female turned to fully face her. "I did think you might ask for a transfer. An arranged mating wasn't the avenue I expected you to go down. Once upon a time, I might have tried to ruin it for you."

*Once* upon a time? "But not now?"

"Don't get me wrong, a small part of me would get off on having you under my boot heel," Nazra bluntly admitted, unrepentant. "But the idea of having you gone from here appeals far more."

Quinley double-blinked, taken aback.

"That surprises you?"

"I think it'd surprise a lot of people." Even Harlan wasn't expecting it.

A sigh eased out of the woman. "Before, I liked that you had to see Zaire and me together. It made me feel better, I guess."

"About what?"

A hint of resentment blotted Nazra's eyes. "You have a soul-deep claim to the man I love. It does take some sting out of it that he chose me, but not *all* of it. Because I'll never know if he'd have made a different choice if the position of Alpha didn't come with mating me."

Ah. Huh. While some did suspect that his agreement to claim Nazra had been largely driven by ambition, it was also believed he cared deeply about her. And since they'd imprinted, Quinley hadn't really considered that Nazra might harbor doubts.

"So, yeah, I was always jealous that you have an inborn claim to Zaire. Knowing you were miserable made me feel better. Sounds cruel, yes, but I never claimed to be a nice person. I don't handle jealousy well."

*You're kidding,* Quinley inwardly deadpanned. "Most shifters don't when it comes to their mates—true or chosen."

"That's the thing, you see," said Nazra, her face hardening. "Whereas before I didn't mind you being in his periphery, now I do. The imprint bond changes things. It amplifies possessiveness to such an extent that it feels like a living force inside you."

"So you're actually glad I'm leaving?"

"Yes." Her eyes narrowed on Quinley. "What I want to know is if you're serious about this arranged mating, or if this is some ploy to get Zaire's attention?"

The woman couldn't *really* think that was the case, surely. But … she did genuinely seem to worry that it might be. Weird.

"It's no ploy," Quinley told her. "I don't want him. I don't see him as mine. He rejected me and chose someone else. I could never accept him as a mate. Neither could my cat."

"But you could be doing this because you want *him* to want *you*. I know all about hurting someone to make yourself feel better. And what better way to get back at me and Zaire?"

Quinley jerked slightly, totally baffled as to why the woman might think it would "get back" at him; that he'd at all react to *anything* Quinley did. "Has he given you some indication that my decision to mate bothers him?"

Nazra briefly looked away.

"He doesn't know," Quinley realized.

"No." It was a murmur.

Well, there was no reason that he needed to, so … "All right, but do you honestly worry he'll be bothered one way or another? Because truthfully, I don't."

Nazra cricked her neck. "There are things you don't know. If you did, you would understand why I have my doubts. I need to know that you're serious about mating the Olympus Pride enforcer; that any interest Zaire shows in this situation won't change anything for you."

"I've already told you, I don't want Zaire. You either believe me or you don't."

"I *want* to believe you. But in your position …"

"You find it hard to take my word for it because you love Zaire—you know you'd fight for him. I don't love him, and at no point would I ever want him."

Nazra stared at her for long moments. "All right. But let me warn you straight up: If it turns out that you lied to me today, if you make any attempt to take him from me, I *will* kill you."

Quinley let a slow, humorless smile curl her lips. "No, you won't. I'm not the easy target you imagine. But neither of us need to concern ourselves with what would happen if we came to that bridge, because it'll never come to pass."

"That had better be true." Nazra swanned out of the cabin, almost colliding into Adaline on the porch.

Quinley was guessing that one of the neighbors had called her sister, concerned that trouble might break out.

Adaline hurried into the cabin, closing the door behind her. "What did *she* want?"

"To be sure I wasn't just using Isaiah to get to Zaire in some way and that I'm serious about making the mating work."

Adaline's head twitched in surprise. "She's not going to try to stop it?"

"Apparently, she'd rather have me out of Zaire's line of sight." Quinley shrugged, still not getting why Nazra would be so invested in that.

"Huh." Adaline scratched her cheek. "It's good news for you, I guess. It makes me wonder why she'd be so behind having you gone from here, though. It never bothered her before."

"They weren't imprinted before. She said the bond accentuates possessiveness."

Adaline nodded. "True-mate bonds do—I can attest to that. If there was anyone near my man who had rights to him, I'd want her gone from my sight and—more importantly—from his."

"I can understand that much. But she seems genuinely worried about how he'll react to my mating Isaiah—*that* I don't get. She said there are things I don't know. I didn't ask her to elaborate because it was clear that she wouldn't."

"So he doesn't yet know?"

Quinley shook her head. "It surprises me, given how they're a gossipy bunch, that none of his friends from our pride have told him. I guess she might have made it clear through one of her own friends that no one is to contact him about it."

"That is odd," Adaline agreed.

"Let's just be glad she's not going to make any attempt to interfere in my plans. I doubt it would have worked, but Nazra can be ... enterprising."

"That much is true."

Hearing her cell beep, Quinley fished it out of her pocket. Her belly did a little tumble on realizing she'd received a message from Isaiah via FindYourMatch: *Hey, the celebration will start at 7 tomorrow, can you get to my place half an hour early so we can be ready at the venue for when the pride arrives?*

Her nerves sang a frantic song at the thought of the celebration. She wasn't having second thoughts or anything, she was just nervous. Quinley typed: *Hi, yes, six-thirty is fine with me.*

"I'm guessing that's Isaiah, because you're fidgety all of a sudden," said Adaline.

"It's him," Quinley verified.

Another beep came. The next message read: *Great.* He added his address.

"Huh. Apparently, he lives in a cul-de-sac." She'd worried he lived near a main road—Quinley's cat was used to space, lots of land, and being tucked away from the world. The cul-de-sac would hopefully re-create that feeling of being separate from the hustle and bustle. "He was just asking if I'd arrive earlier than the guests. He must want us to greet them as they enter wherever the celebration is being held."

"You all set for tomorrow?"

"Yup. Nervous, but definitely ready." Quinley pocketed her phone. "I have my duffel packed with everything I'll need until the rest of my stuff is delivered to Isaiah's house."

"It's *your* house now, too."

"Not until after the celebration. Want to see the outfit I bought for the event?"

Adaline's eyes lit up in interest. "Oh, yes indeed. Lead the way."

# CHAPTER SIX

The cul-de-sac was seriously cute, especially with all the Christmas decorations. Most were lit up, despite that it wasn't fully dark yet.

Not all shifters celebrated the holidays. Those who did generally didn't do so for religious reasons. Quinley's pride always went butt wild at Christmas.

And as of today, she'd no longer be a member of that pride.

*Cue belly flutter.*

While she lamented being in a position where transferring to another was necessary for her sanity, she had no doubts about what she would soon do. Not one. But, yeah, it would suck to not live close to her family.

As she brought her car to a halt outside Isaiah's address, Quinley noticed a bunch of people crowded together on the neighboring porch. His pride mates, obviously. Some were nosily looking at her car, probably guessing who she was. After all, not many strange vehicles were going to park outside Isaiah's place at this particular time.

Snagging her purse, she took a preparatory breath and slid out of the car. The chilly air danced along her back—the only part of her body exposed by her belted, ruby-red jumpsuit. With its diamante neckline and long mesh skirt at the back, it was a solid choice for an elegant party outfit in the winter.

Quinley did not do skirts or dresses during winter.

She gave a brief wave to the nosy parkers on the porch and then made her way to the back of her vehicle. She opened the trunk with her key fob … just as the sounds of hurried footsteps caught her attention.

Quinley looked to see three females approaching, all dolled-up in pretty dresses for what was likely the upcoming celebration.

The female in the center smiled brightly. "Hi, I'm Havana, one of your neighbors. Also the Alpha, so if you need anything let me know. These two tag-alongs are my besties, Aspen and Bailey."

"And her bodyguards—hence why we tagged along as she darted over here like her ass was on fire," added the female who'd been introduced as Aspen.

"Also, we're super nosy and wanted to meet you before everyone else," said Bailey.

Her lips twitching, Quinley grabbed her duffel from the trunk. "It's nice to meet you all." Her cat watched them intently, not too happy with how close they stood—she didn't tolerate it well from strangers.

Havana gestured at Quinley's jumpsuit. "I love your outfit. And your hair—it's so sleek and shiny, and those gold streaks … well, I want them."

Aspen cocked her head as she studied Quinley. "No one told me you were … not tall."

Hearing the creak of hinges, Quinley tracked the sound to see Isaiah stepping onto his front porch, his gaze landing straight on her. Damn, he looked *fine*. He wore a crisp white shirt, dark-gray pants that matched the shade of his eyes, and black shiny shoes.

He jogged down the steps and then stalked down the path, not once moving his attention from her. A corner of his lips hitched up, his gaze warming. "Quinley, you look—"

"Here," Havana butted in, snatching Quinley's duffel and then holding it out to him. "Take her bag inside while we have a natter."

His brow creasing, he took the bag. "I want to show her the house."

The devil waved that away. "You can do that later. We're having a conversation here."

The corners of his mouth tightened. "Tell me you're not planning to hog her."

"I wouldn't have to if you'd taken me to the meet on Saturday where I could have chatted to her, but you didn't, so …"

Coming up behind her, Tate sighed at her back. "It's tradition for Alpha males to arrange matings."

Havana tossed him a look over her shoulder. "It's also tradition for me to annoy anyone who doesn't give me my own way."

Tate gave Isaiah a helpless shrug and then nodded at Quinley. "Welcome. It's good to see you again."

"Thank you," said Quinley, closing her trunk. "And likewise."

"I'll show you the house later," Isaiah told her. "Let me take your bag inside, and then we'll all head to the venue." His gaze ran along his pride mates as he began backing up the driveway. "Just … maybe don't surround her. Black-foots don't react well if they feel cornered or crowded."

At that, all three females took a slow step back.

"Sorry, forgot about that," said Havana. "Have we made your cat uncomfortable?"

57

"Yeah," Quinley admitted.

Havana blinked and then barked a surprised laugh. "I love that you're honest. Most people would assure us it's fine and make excuses for us. They really shouldn't. We can be inappropriate and sometimes need reminding of that."

Bailey frowned. "When are we ever inappropriate?"

Aspen snorted, slamming up a hand. "Don't even."

Bailey sniffed and then turned to Quinley. "I hear you're a healer who can ease pain. That's sort of awesome. Not quite as awesome as me, but still."

Quinley felt her mouth curl. "You're a black mamba," she sensed.

The snake shifter's eyes widened in delight. "A lot of people don't recognize the scent of my kind; you must have rubbed up against one."

"Used to date one, actually." He'd been a total nut.

Aspen gaped at her. "Wow, I have to admire you for that. I genuinely don't know how Deke copes with this one."

"Hey," Bailey groused.

Aspen shot her an impatient look. "Oh come on, you know you're a pain in the ass. It's deliberate with you."

"Deke's your mate?" Quinley asked Bailey. "I met him briefly on Saturday. He didn't say much."

"He's one of those people who is talkative around those he knows well but otherwise says little unless he really has something to say." Bailey gestured at the porch. "He's on his way over with Camden, Aspen's mate."

Quinley glanced over to see a very hot specimen—who only seemed to have eyes for Aspen—at Deke's side.

"I have to say," began Havana, "my devil has taken an instant liking to you. You make us feel so calm. How do you—" She cut off as Isaiah reappeared.

He arched a brow. "Are we all ready to leave?"

"Yup." Havana threaded one arm through Quinley's and smiled at her. "I'll escort you to the Tavern."

Both Tate—who no doubt wanted to walk at his mate's side—and Isaiah frowned at that, but the devil shifter ignored it and strode away, taking Quinley with her while Bailey and Aspen flanked them.

"Havana," Isaiah drawled.

The Alpha female sniffed. "You had your chance to talk to her. I didn't. And once the celebration starts, she'll be treated to a sea of faces and it'll be hard for us to talk alone. Also, I'm still not happy with you."

Quinley tried and failed to stifle a smile. She hadn't been sure what sort of reception she'd get from the pride. Not all those who were transferred via arranged matings were welcomed, because not all shifters thought matings should *be* arranged. But so far, all seemed good.

Havana nattered away as they strode down the sidewalk. Lights from the lampposts danced along shallow puddles. Shadows moved in the apartments above the closed stores. Some pedestrians could be seen on the sidewalks, near the stoplights, or at the bus stops.

Though the stores' security shutters were down, Quinley could tell from the large signs above the doors that there was everything from a jewelry store and a deli to a coffeehouse and a book shop.

The streets were apparently busy during daytime, according to Havana. She explained that each business was owned by the pride and mostly employed its members, though some workers were humans or lone shifters.

"And here we have the Tavern," said Havana as she pulled Quinley toward a particular door. "We often hold celebratory events here."

Entering, Quinley could easily understand why the place would be used as the main party venue. It not only had plenty of seating, it wasn't merely a bar. It was also part-restaurant part-pool hall with a stage, arcade area, and widescreen TVs.

"The omegas took care of the decorations—they always do a grand job."

They hadn't failed this time either. A "Welcome" banner hung above the stage while a "Congratulations" banner was pinned above the bar. Clusters of white and gold balloons seemed to be everywhere. There were also lanterns, tinsel curtains, and tissue pompoms.

More, confetti and votive LED candles were set on every table and at each burgundy-cushioned booth. String lights dangled along the red brick walls, carefully avoiding the TVs and sports paraphernalia. There was also a white and gold balloon arch near the buffet table. A huge spread of food waited there, making her tummy rumble.

A pretty blue-eyed female with shiny chestnut hair approached, smiling. "Hi, you must be Quinley. I'm Bree, the primary omega of the pride." Her smile faltered as it landed on Havana. "Why are you clinging to her like a barnacle?"

"Two reasons: one, she makes my devil feel calm. Two, it's annoying both Isaiah and Tate." The devil slid a smug look at the males, who stood close.

Bailey sighed at Havana. "Don't you think you've annoyed them enough? It's kind of juvenile, isn't it?"

Havana gaped at her. "You annoy people constantly. On purpose. For fun. You're doing it right now."

The mamba grinned. "I know."

Isaiah shrugged his way through the females, his gaze on Quinley. "This is why I asked you to come here early. I knew the unholy trinity would do this." He looked at Havana. "I need to talk her through what will happen next, so …"

The devil exhaled heavily and released Quinley. "Fine."

Isaiah cuffed her arm and gently but dominantly drew her to him with an effortless strength that made her inwardly hum in delight. "You okay?" he asked, keeping his voice low.

She nodded. "Of course." She dealt with big personalities all the time, including her sisters. "Tell me what to expect. I'm guessing we're going to meet everyone as they enter?"

"Yes," he confirmed, not releasing her—which she liked. "I'll do the introductions when it comes to my pride. They'll welcome you to the pride and congratulate us on our mating. You'll obviously introduce me to your relatives when they arrive. Then we'll just enjoy the party."

"Heads-up: we have wolverines," Bree warned. "So when the buffet opens, grab food fast or it'll be gone."

"They're big eaters, I know," said Quinley. "My kind is just as bad, though. A guy I used to date was a wolverine. He was the only person who kept up with me." Black-foots could eat like there was no tomorrow.

Just then, a tall muscular male came from behind the bar with a bawling baby in his arms.

"Speaking of wolverines, here's my mate Alex and our daughter Aurora." Bree's face went soft with sympathy and concern. "She's colicky, so …"

"I drove her around in circles," Alex told Bree, looking somewhat harried; his dark eyes tired; his rich brown hair sticking up in places. "She stopped crying for a while but started again once I cut the engine."

Quinley licked her lips and lifted her hand toward the baby's back. "Can I …?"

Alex seemed to debate it for a moment. "Yes."

Quinley laid a palm on Aurora's back and pushed warm, soothing energy into her. She smiled when the little girl stopped crying. "There."

Bree gawked. "Wow."

"I didn't cure the colic. Can't. I just numbed the pain for her. It'll last a few days."

Bree's eyes widened. "A few days? Really?"

"It generally does."

Alex took a small but eager step closer to Quinley. "Can you move in with us?"

"No, she can't," Isaiah told him, his hand flexing on her arm.

The wolverine frowned. "It would be just for a little while."

Isaiah shook his head. "No."

Alex's jaw tightened. "You're so selfish."

"Would you let Bree live with me?"

The wolverine spluttered. "Yes."

"Lying bastard," Isaiah muttered.

Bailey held her arms out for Aurora. "Let me take her for a while."

His frown deepening, Alex held the baby closer. "Under no circumstances will you ever take my daughter anywhere. She'd come back with tattoos, piercings, and wearing a goddamn snake outfit or some shit."

Bailey dropped her arms. "That is so … accurate."

The front door swung open. An angelic-looking blonde strode inside, her fingers linked to those of a male who bore a close resemblance to Tate.

Isaiah cast Quinley a look. "These are the pride Betas, Luke and Blair." He gave them a curt nod. "Luke, Blair—this is Quinley."

Blair gave her a sweet smile. "Well, hi. Welcome to the pride."

Luke repeated the sentiment.

"Thank you." Quinley pointed at Blair, her eyes narrowing. "Bush dog, right?"

"Right," Blair confirmed, her smile kicking up a notch. "You're familiar with my kind?"

"Used to date one." He'd been a handful.

"She has the most fascinating dating history," Aspen commented.

It would be fair to say that Quinley had thrown herself into dating, searching for a partner, a mate, an *escape*. She hadn't found one until now.

Bree nudged Isaiah. "You'd better take your place over by the doors. People will start entering soon."

He planted a warm hand low on Quinley's back and guided her to a spot near the doors. Man, he smelled good. His scent was dark and woodsy and carried a hint of amber. Her cat rather liked it.

"Here we go," he murmured as the first few people entered.

Over the next hour, Quinley was on the receiving end of handshakes, chin-tips, nods, cheek-kisses, and welcoming comments.

When a particular couple approached, Isaiah smiled warmly. "Quinley, these are my parents, Andaya and Koen."

"We're so glad to meet you," Andaya told her, beaming. "If you need anything—anything at all—just give me a call. I left my number on the fridge, as well as our address should you feel like company."

Isaiah frowned. "She's a black-foot."

"Not *all* are asocial. She might be different." Andaya lifted a brow at her. "Are you?"

"No," Quinley admitted.

Koen chuckled. "As my mate said, we're here for whatever you might need. Isaiah works a lot. And it could be that, what with you being away from those you love, you do find yourself wanting someone to talk to. Should that happen, call my mate or pay us a visit. You'll always be welcome."

Touched, Quinley said, "Thank you so much."

"We'll talk more later," Andaya told her. "Welcome to the pride, and congratulations on the mating." With that, the couple melted away.

Quinley leaned slightly into Isaiah, once more letting her senses bathe in his scent. "They're really sweet. I was worried that maybe they'd be upset that you chose an arranged mating."

Seeming pleased that she liked his parents, he said, "Their own mating was arranged."

Quinley felt her brows hike up. "Oh. That explains it."

"Are your own parents coming?"

Oh shit, she'd forgot to mention … "They, uh, died a long time ago. But my sisters, their mates, and my nephews are coming." She could tell he wanted to prod for more information, but the door again opened as yet more pride members arrived.

A short time later, her family finally showed. Quinley introduced them to him. All greeted Isaiah warmly, their gazes somewhat studious.

"Thank you for coming," he said to them.

"We wouldn't miss it for the world," Lori told him. The curvy, olive-skinned female had proclaimed to Raya when they were just five, "*We're mates, you know.*" Raya's response had been: "*Well, duh.*" They'd been inseparable ever since. "You did good picking Quinley—she's a winner."

"And less trouble than her sisters," Will chipped in, his lips quirking when the two females in question cast him a glare.

Corey grabbed his brother's arm. "Ooh, an arcade!" The boys were the spitting image of their father, right down to the gray-blue eyes and red hair. "Can me and Ren head over there, Dad?"

"Your brother might not actually want to," said Will.

"He does, though," Corey insisted. "We want to play air hockey, then basketball."

Adaline tapped his shoulder gently. "Didn't we talk about how you should each let the other speak for himself?"

"We did, yes," Ren answered for his brother, making Adaline sigh.

"We're gonna need lots of quarters," Corey declared.

"I have quarters," said Isaiah. "What do I get in return for them?"

The twins exchanged a blank look then turned back to him. "Our unfailing allegiance," they said in unison.

Quinley barely held back a laugh.

While Quinley was deep in conversation with Helena and some of the omegas, Isaiah took the opportunity to corner Luke. "I know this isn't the time to have this conversation, but I need to know if you, Camden, and Farrell have had any luck tracking the Vercetti Pack?" He hadn't wanted to ask in front of Quinley—he'd lumber all that shit on her after the celebration."

The Beta's lips thinned. "No. They don't leave any kind of tracks, physical or electronic."

Isaiah's cat bared his teeth. "Do you think it's possible someone helps them hide?"

"Camden suggested that," said Luke. "It's a definite possibility. I just don't see who'd want to associate with them. Other than humans."

The sound of glass smashing drew Isaiah's attention to his left. Bailey was apologizing to someone for knocking over their drink but, knowing her, he wouldn't be surprised if she'd done it on purpose.

He took an idle look around. The place was now packed. Partygoers could be found everywhere—sat at tables, stood at the bar, tucked in booths, playing pool, spending money in the arcade area, shaking their asses on the dance floor, or even just standing in clusters talking and laughing.

So far, all was going good. Quinley and her family appeared to be enjoying themselves, and his pride mates appeared to have taken a liking to her.

"We will find the brothers, Isaiah," said Luke. "The minute we come across anything of note, I'll pass it on—considering they're gunning for you, it's only right that you're kept updated."

Isaiah inclined his head. "I appreciate it."

Just then, Blair and Elle approached.

"What are you two talking about?" asked Blair, her suspicious gaze sliding from him to her mate.

"Rainbows," both Isaiah and Luke replied at the same time.

She snorted. "Stop talking about work stuff. *You* should be focusing on Quinley," she added, pointing at Isaiah.

"Excuse me, I got shooed away by the omegas—they wanted to talk 'healer stuff.'" Isaiah had first checked with Quinley that it was fine; she'd been happy to talk to them alone.

"I really like her," said Elle. "She gives off this air of calm. It's like … like every bit of tension in me just eases away. Of course it comes right back when she walks away. Where did she go?" The redhead glanced around.

"You're not using her as a living chill pill," Isaiah told Elle.

"Why not?" Elle whined. "And what's it to you?"

"Everything. Once I've branded her, she'll officially be my mate. It'll be my responsibility to be sure she doesn't give too much of herself—submissives tend to do that. Healers are even worse for it, and I know she uses her gift as part of her job. I don't want her drained."

Elle smiled, pleased. "Good answer. I just wanted to be sure you're *all* in, because I can tell she is."

"How?"

"I just sense these things. Like magic."

Luke nudged him. "Valentina seems to have taken a shining to Quinley. That's a good sign."

Isaiah glanced over to see that the female wolverine and her brothers had in fact approached her. "Even the uncles are being nice to her." Good. He didn't really want to have to argue with a bunch of insane wolverines.

Knowing the uncles were an acquired taste and offended people all too easily, he said, "I'd better head over there to ensure they don't try giving her a Russian name or some shit."

He began to shoulder his way through the crowd toward her. His cat moodily retreated to his corner, having only come forward to hear Luke's news—or lack thereof—regarding the Vercetti Pack. The feline had been doing his best to ignore Quinley all night, though he hadn't been all too successful at it. She wasn't someone who anyone would find easy to overlook.

Two familiar females appeared in front of Isaiah, making him halt.

"Hi, again," said Raya with a little wave.

Adaline gave him a warm but stern smile.

Isaiah held back a sigh. "You've come to warn me that I'd better be good to your sister or you will slit my throat in my sleep."

They exchanged a look.

"We were actually thinking more along the lines of disemboweling you," said Raya.

Alllllll right. "I'm not going to hurt your sister," he assured them.

"Maybe not intentionally," said Adaline. "We just want to be sure she isn't going to be second best in your eyes. We get that you would have preferred to bond with your true mate—most shifters universally would. But we'd like to have the assurance that you're not going to be looking at Quinley wishing she was someone else."

Isaiah gave them a sober look. "That's not how it will be. She'll officially be my mate as of tonight. That's what I'll see when I look at her—my mate. I won't lie to you, it may take a while for us to form any kind of emotional ties. We're pretty much strangers to each other. A mating brand won't change that. But she'll be my priority."

A glimmer of surprised humor appeared in Adaline's eyes. "You don't anticipate that her wearing your brand will have any emotional impact on you?"

"No," he replied.

Raya's nose wrinkled. "You don't think it will make you possessive or anything?"

"Maybe a teensy bit, but … why are you both smiling?"

Adaline coughed into her fist as if to hide a chuckle. "No reason. We'll take you at your word and trust that Quinley won't be competing with the woman you were fated to have. But if we find out you hurt her …"

"Disemboweling will commence," he said. "Got it."

They both grinned, clearly satisfied.

Right then, Quinley materialized, her perceptive gaze bouncing from face to face. "Everything okay?"

"Of course," said Raya with a reassuring wave of her hand.

Quinley's eyes narrowed. "You two threatened to kill him if he upset me, didn't you?"

Adaline looked appropriately offended. "No."

Quinley sighed. "Let me guess, disembowelment was your choice of execution."

Adaline put a hand on her hip. "I'm just looking out for you. It's my job. Suck it up and deal."

Raya turned to Adaline. "I still don't see why you don't look out for me, too."

"As I said, you're Lori's problem now," Adaline told her with a flick of her hand.

Raya crossed her arms over her chest. "So, as of tonight, Quinley will be *Isaiah's* problem?"

"No."

"You're playing favorites. That's what's happening here."

Quinley toward Isaiah. "It's an old argument," she explained as her sisters began to bicker. "After our parents died, Adaline took over as the mom figure. I was only five, so she babied me in a way she didn't need to with Raya. That was when the whole 'Quinley's your favorite' began. As it irritates Adaline, Raya does it all the more. And due to being so irritated, Adaline makes teasing comments that imply Raya's correct." She shrugged.

Isaiah splayed his palm on her back. "I'm sorry about your parents."

She gave a half-smile. "Thanks."

He wanted to know more, but now wasn't the time or the place to ask. So, he instead said, "I like your family. Especially your nephews, even though they talk like they're one person." Like they knew each other's thoughts and feelings. It was eerie.

"They're quite aware that it freaks people out, and they like it." Quinley took a look around. "You know, your pride has more of a variety of shifters than I expected. I was surprised to see that your Alpha female isn't a pallas cat."

He tipped his head to the side, moving closer to her; liking how her pupils dilated. "Why?"

She licked those lips he wanted to nip. "Most shifter groupings are ruled by the same breed that forms the vast majority of the pack, pride, clan, or whatever."

"We aren't fussed about stuff like that," he said with a shrug. "I doubt Tate expected his true mate to be a devil shifter. She, Aspen, Bailey, and Camden were originally loners. They've known each other since they were children, and they still work at the rec center where they spent most of their time growing up."

Quinley edged a little closer to him. "Tell me more about the people here."

Liking her interest, he did exactly that.

# CHAPTER SEVEN

"I like it," said Quinley, taking in the spacious room.

Though the party wasn't yet finished, they'd left the Tavern once midnight hit. Isaiah had brought her straight to his house and given her a tour ... which had ended right here in the master bedroom. And she knew why; knew he'd saved this for last because his intention was that they wouldn't leave it for a while.

Quinley swallowed, nervous in a kind of ... delicious way. She was about to be claimed, and she just *knew* he'd take her, dominate her, in a way no other male had. And she had not one intention of fighting his dominance.

For Quinley, the idea of taking control in bed was a little off-putting. She wanted a dominant male who'd take the lead. It wasn't about kink or sex games, it was just part of her nature. She couldn't change it—nor did she care to—any more than he could alter how it was ingrained in him to lead, protect, shelter, and assume control. It just *was*.

Many humans had such a skewed perception of submission. Especially when it applied to *outside* of sex, as if they believed it weak to tend to the needs of another. She'd never really understood that. Was it not a good thing to take care of those who mattered? It wasn't as if the situation was unbalanced—he'd provide what she needed, and vice versa.

"If there's anything you want to change, anything you want to add, go for it," Isaiah invited, standing a few feet away. "It's your home now, too."

Liking the earthy color schemes that run throughout the place, she wouldn't go as far as to paint anything or haul in new furniture. But she'd put her own stamp on the place—it was what shifters did to claim their territory.

"That dresser is new and empty," he added, gesturing at it. "And one side of the closet is now clear."

"Thank you." She cast a look at the unused vanity dresser. "That's new as well?" Because if he'd originally bought it for a different female, Quinley would replace it.

"Yes," he replied. "I figured you might need it."

"You're good at this mate-thing."

Isaiah's mouth hitched up. "Pleased to hear it."

He stalked to her, every step unrushed and deliberate, making her pulse hiccup. And then he was *right there*, crossing over into her personal space without hesitation. His scent bounded into her and lured her cat closer.

Sexual tension arced between them, muggy and crackly. It made her stomach clench and her blood heat.

Isaiah gripped her jaw. "This face …" He dragged a blatantly proprietary gaze over her facial features, cataloguing each one. Male appreciation burned in his eyes. "It's probably good that Havana got in the way of us being alone here earlier."

"Why?"

"Because I would have fucked you for sure, and I want the first time I take you to be the same time I claim you as mine." Isaiah watched as need rose up in her gaze and swallowed her pupils. His body stirred and tightened in response.

He wanted to take her. Now. Hard. But before they got to that … "Let's make sure we're on the same page, I don't want any misunderstandings between us. My guess would be that, as a submissive shifter, you don't want to lead in the bedroom."

"Holds no appeal for me."

"All right." Releasing her jaw, he burrowed his hand in her hair, loving the silky feel of the thick mass. "In sexual contexts, I like to lead. The thing is … it won't be a case where I just give you orders to follow. Sometimes, there'll be no orders. I'll just come to you wherever you are, bend you over something, and take you right there."

Heat flared in her gaze, and the glimmer of her cat's eyes flickered behind her own. He liked that he had the animal's full attention as well as hers.

His own cat stayed back, moodily observing; a non-participant. He knew what Isaiah intended, and he was angry that Isaiah would think to brand a female who wasn't their fated mate.

"Consent is important," Isaiah went on, gently rubbing strands of her hair between the pads of his fingers. "I need to know I have it; that when we're here in this house, there is no need for me to request permission because it's already been granted. This is our space where, in terms of anything sexual, I lead and you follow. But if you ever say no, then it doesn't happen. Simple. That's all you ever have to say: No."

"But you won't ask, you'll just take," she understood.

"Only if you give me that consent here and now. You don't have to, Quinley. We can wait; give it time. There's no pressure. My ultimate goal is to have it eventually."

She licked her lower lip, her eyes diving deep into his; watching and searching. "You have it now."

His hardening cock twitched. "You're sure? You understand what that will mean for you? That no matter where in the house you are, no matter what you're doing, no matter if you're asleep or awake, you're my toy at all times? A treasured toy. One I'd never hurt or misuse. But one that will be there for me to fuck whenever I want it."

"I understand," she rasped.

"Can I trust that you will always speak up if you're not down for whatever is happening? You're a pleaser by nature, I get that. But it would never please me to realize you're not enjoying what's happening. I would sense it. I would know. I would feel like a bag of shit and, worse, so would you. My wants don't come before your needs, you understand?"

"I'm not someone who'd fail to speak up. If I don't like something or I'm just not feeling in the mood or whatever, I'll tell you."

Reassured, he nodded. "To be clear, you have the same permission where I'm concerned. Don't feel you ever need to ask to speak or touch me or anything else—I'm looking for you to give up control, not be a mindless participant. You want to struggle, struggle. You want to be passive, be passive. You want to make your own demands, make your own demands. Do whatever you want ... unless or until I tell you otherwise."

"Are we done talking now?" she asked, clearly eager to move things along.

That made him smile. "Not quite. I know some shifters in our situation wait until a bond forms before they brand each other. I get it. Brands are permanent. But to wait would be to start off this mating with doubts. I don't want to do that."

Also, putting that mark on her would be the only way to make his cat consider her his. "I want to brand you tonight, mark you as mine. I want you to do the same to me. But if you're not ready for that, I'll understand."

She swallowed. "I want us to do it tonight. I don't feel a need to wait."

Satisfaction flamed in his belly. "Good." He snaked his hand around her throat, taking a firm grip of it, power flooding his veins. He could do whatever he wanted to her. The knowledge of that wasn't merely a thrill, it was liberating. He could be himself. *Wholly* himself.

This extent of power wasn't something he'd had before. No dominant would give him that level of control—it just wasn't in their makeup. He got it. Because it wasn't in his.

But it was in Quinley's, and he fucking loved that.

Dipping his head, he tipped up her own and caught her bottom lip between his teeth; gave it a demanding tug. "Open." She parted her lips, and he delved right in. Licked into her mouth. Took her taste inside him, let it mark him.

He kept the kiss soft, lazy, and sensual. Fluid as liquid.

As she rose on her tiptoes for more, he flicked the tip of her canine with his tongue to stir up her cat, wanting her raring to bite. Quinley's lavender-and-vanilla scent took on a feral note; telling him her animal was very near the surface. It snagged his cat's attention.

Isaiah broke the kiss, drinking in the need-drunk look on her face. "Now"—he fingered the soft material of her jumpsuit—"take it off."

Quinley blinked, pulled out of her daze by the punch of dominance in his voice. She watched as he backed up a step and folded his arms, his expression molded into a mask of absolute authority. Her mindset shifted that easily—she took a mental step back, let her brain power down, and focused on only him as she lowered the side-zipper of her jumpsuit.

His gaze burned with approval. "Good girl."

Excitement tumbling in her belly, she peeled down the suit and let it puddle at her feet. Her bra went next, then her panties. His gaze tracked her every move, his focus steady and unshifting. Once she'd kicked off her heels, she used her foot to slide the pile aside.

She looked up at him ... and immediately became immobilized by the dangerous predatory heat that gleamed in his gaze. Sparks of tension prickled the air and skipped along her bare skin. She'd never felt more exposed, naked, or aware of herself.

He began to circle her, reaching out to let the pads of his fingers idly trace, press, glide, and tease. His touch was light but transmitted pure avarice and male ownership.

"So much to play with." There was more grit in his voice than usual, turning it throaty. "You are beautiful, do you know that?" A distracted question. He was busy shaping and palming her ass.

A shaky breath shuddered out of her. Already she was damp, anticipation winding her tight and gnawing at her patience.

Still behind her, he suckled on the crook of her neck. "I think I'll put my claiming brand right here. You're going to wear it with pride, just as I will yours."

"Isaiah." It was a plea.

"You never have to beg me, Quinley," he assured her. "I won't ever ask that of you. I want you to trust that I'll give you what you need ... even though I might not give it to you straight away."

Again, he circled her. This time, he didn't only explore with his fingers. He sucked on a nipple. Drew his teeth over the other. Nipped at her shoulder. Scored his blunt nails down her back. Briefly slipped a finger between her slick folds.

Basically, he teased her body into a state of such agonized suspension that her legs trembled. She couldn't be sure her knees wouldn't give out on her.

Finally, Isaiah came to stand before her once more. His arresting gaze held hers as he deftly undid the fly of his slacks and backed her toward the bed. He lowered his face closer to hers, pausing with his mouth mere inches from her own. "Get me wet."

She looked down to see his cock was now free, jutting upward. It was long and full. Thicker than she was used to.

Quinley sat on the bed and curled her fingers around the base of his cock. Warm and hard, it pulsed in her grip. She took him into her mouth and licked around his shaft.

"Eyes up, Quinley."

She lifted her gaze just as he flicked open the top button of his shirt. He didn't once break eye-contact as he tackled the buttons, and she never once stopped sucking him in and out of her mouth. She kept the suction tight, took him deep, and—noting he liked it—deliberately let the head bump the back of her throat again and again.

Finally, Isaiah shed his shirt and dumped it on her pile of clothes. Damn, his body was just sheer male strength. Flat abs, defined muscle, impressive ink.

His fingers burrowed into her hair gently. So gently. And then they grabbed a tight fistful of it and tugged. "Up."

Inwardly wincing at the sting to her scalp, she rose to her feet.

His eyes moved over her face, pure male greed simmering there. "Another time, I'm going to fuck this face." He let go of her hair. "And that pretty throat." He slowly twirled his finger, his expression one of expectation.

She turned to face the bed. He gripped her hips and—with an easy strength that made her toes curl—propped her onto her knees on the mattress. A hand landed between her shoulder blades and pressed down, bending her over.

And then two fingers plunged deep.

She sucked in a breath as he scissored them. He muttered what sounded like "Tight" and then began pumping his fingers, his mouth trailing suckling kisses up and down her spine. His fingers abruptly thrusted faster, deeper, harder.

And then disappeared.

"First time I clocked your ass," he began, wedging the fat tip of his cock inside her, "I imagined holding it tight while I fucked in and out of you." He grabbed two fistfuls of her ass, his fingertips digging in hard. "So that's what I'm gonna do." His hips sharply lurched forward, ramming his dick balls-deep.

She didn't have time to really *feel* the sharp burn that streaked up her inner walls, or to process how uncomfortably full she felt. Because then he was moving. Thrusting. All that power he kept contained quite simply spilled out.

Clenching his jaw, Isaiah kept punching his cock deep at an insanely savage pace. She was almost unbearably tight, and so fucking hot it near scalded him; made him need more.

So he took more. Rammed into her rougher and faster, filling the room with the sound of flesh slapping flesh.

She was small and slight with perfect curves. Like a living, breathing sex doll. Easy to lift and position her exactly as he wanted her. There was something intoxicating about that.

Power sang in his veins. She'd done that. Given him that. *Gifted* it to him.

Quinley didn't fully trust him yet—he saw that, wouldn't expect anything different. But she'd still surrendered control to him; had still agreed for them to brand each other here and now.

Even though she'd suffered a terrible betrayal, she wasn't holding back from him, she had the guts to put herself out there. Isaiah admired and respected the hell out of it. Out of *her*.

Looking at the faint score marks he'd put on her back earlier, he felt his balls tingle. Upping his pace a notch, he dug his fingers harder into the globes of her ass. His grip was going to leave bruises and they both knew it. But she didn't ask him to ease up, didn't complain, let him use her as he pleased.

He was fucking high on the thrill of it. So high that his release was almost on him.

Curling over her, he planted one fist on the bed beside her head and clamped his other hand on her nape. "Who's in you? My name. Say it." He needed to feel that she knew *exactly* who was about to claim her.

"Isaiah." It was a trembly rasp that licked up his shaft.

A growl rumbling in his chest, he sank his teeth *deep* into the crook of her neck. Skin broke, blood pooled—the taste tore a feral snarl out of him. He licked and sucked at the brand. "You're mine now."

A gasp flew out of Quinley as he pulled out, flipped her over, and slammed back inside. *Jesus Christ.*

An intemperate need thrashed in his eyes. "Bite," he said, the sound so guttural it was barely human.

He began frantically drilling his cock into her yet again, no restraint, no mercy. The pleasure was spiced by the rhythmic sting of the throbbing mark on her neck.

Clinging tight to his back, she reared up and clamped her teeth around his shoulder, driving them down deep until she tasted blood.

"*Fuck.*" He heaved his hips forward faster and faster, harder and harder, as she sucked on the brand. "Come, Quinley."

The build-up of tension that had been bubbling inside her finally boiled over. A hot, spinetingling supernova wave of pleasure crashed into her and ripped through her body.

She unlocked her teeth from his skin as a raspy scream tore out of her throat, her inner muscles squeezing and rippling around his cock; whips of hot come bursting out of him.

The strength vanished from her body, rendering her limp. Floating in a sea of bliss, she was barely aware of him lazily gliding his dick forward and backward; his every breath fanning the fresh bite on her neck.

Claimed. She was claimed. And that she'd been able to claim Isaiah in return, that he'd *wanted* what someone else had once flung back in her face, settled something inside both her and her cat—possibly that part of them that had felt so lost and alone for years.

All that was missing now was an imprint bond.

Finally, he raised his head. "Stay," he said, his face all soft and languid.

"Okay," she murmured.

He withdrew his softening cock, edged off the bed, and then left the room. He returned moments later with a damp cloth and cleaned her up, ignoring her offer to take over. Once done, he threw the cloth in the laundry basket and arched a brow. "You like sleeping naked or not?"

"Not. There's a long tee in my—"

"You like wearing tees for bed, you can wear one of mine." He snatched one from his dresser and tossed it to her.

Isaiah watched as she sat up and slipped it on. He felt his lips twitch. The tee dwarfed her, but she looked fucking cute in it. There was something far too satisfying about knowing his scent was now *all* over her.

He unconsciously dropped his gaze to the bite on her neck. It was red but no longer bleeding. It would heal, but the imprint of it would remain. A thought that comforted him more than he'd expected.

His cat had a mixed reaction to the sight of the mark. He was angry that Isaiah had branded her, but he was unable to dismiss its significance. The feline really *saw* her now; registered every detail, acknowledged her as under its protection.

Well, it was a start.

After flicking back the covers and settling her into bed, Isaiah lay beside her. He could sense that she was exhausted—it had been a pivotal day for her, and the emotional weight of that would have tired her out. But he couldn't let her drift off just yet.

Positioning himself on his side facing her, he gave her hip a little squeeze. "I want us to have one more talk, then you can sleep."

She blinked hard and stared up at him, giving him her full attention just like that.

"You and me … if we want to build something, we need to be forthcoming—starting now."

She nodded in agreement.

"This might be an arranged mating, but that makes it no less real. I don't expect you to trust me so soon—that can't be given, it has to be earned. But you *can* trust me. You can be sure that if you ever need me, I'm there. That if something's wrong, I'll do my best to fix it."

Caution flickered in her eyes. She made him think of a wounded animal who was hesitant to invest her full trust in someone. Who wouldn't be, when the person whose loyalty to you should have been absolute had let you down in every way?

"Your oldest sister has been your rock a long time," he went on. "You're used to turning to her, and I get that you won't naturally stop doing that. But know I'm a person you can rely on above all others. You're my priority."

"As you're mine," she said, her voice low.

He felt his lips tip up. "You can come to me about anything, day or night. If something's playing on your mind, run it by me. If you're unhappy about something, tell me. If you're sad or missing your family or feeling any regrets, say so. We can't get past something if we don't speak of it."

"Communication is important," she agreed. "Patience, too. We'll be learning each other's hot buttons, pet peeves, etc. on the fly. We're both gonna need some room to mess up in the beginning or there'll be unnecessary arguments."

"And let me state here and now that I don't consider you second best. It would be easy for both of us to worry that we're not the other's *real* choice. That isn't true. I chose you. You chose me. That's it now. It's done."

The finality in that statement soothed a jagged concern in Quinley that she hadn't realized was there. But of course it was there—she should have expected it. They'd both been denied the opportunity to bond with their true mate, but their situations were different. She knew hers would never want her, whereas he would live with the knowledge that his *might* have wanted him if things were different.

"You never have to worry you're playing second fiddle for me either," she assured him. "For me, entering this mating was never about finding a replacement, it was about moving *all* the way forward. I guess it was easier for me than it has been for you."

"Why would you think that?"

"Your TM doesn't know you exist. Mine does. He deliberately picked someone else over me; hurt me and my cat in a way we can't forgive. It wasn't like that for you."

His brow creased slightly. "That doesn't mean I'll get caught up in what-ifs, Quinley. I would have had no business claiming you or anyone else if my head wasn't on straight."

"But your cat isn't mentally where you're at," she said, recalling the messages he'd sent her through the site, explaining his situation.

"No, he's not. Not yet. In time, that'll change."

A shifter's inner animal craved a mate so much more than their human half did, so it was little wonder that his cat hadn't yet made his peace with everything. Even as she understood, it did sting that the feline wasn't invested in the mating. It felt too much like a rejection, and she'd had enough of those.

But … "I can be patient. I understand his pain."

At least she knew that Isaiah was fully invested. She really wanted to place all her trust in him; craved the security he offered, just as her cat did. They'd been without it for so long. They needed to feel they could rely on him in a way they'd never been able to rely on another.

And that, she thought, was a two-way thing. In his own way, he'd need to rely on her. And Quinley was determined that she'd give this mating her all. She'd pour into it everything she'd needed to hold back from Zaire, even as it terrified her a little that she'd be putting so much of herself out there.

"Your TM … what's his name?" Isaiah asked.

"Zaire. Why?"

"Because as of this moment, I'm not going to refer to him as your true mate anymore. *I* claimed you. The word 'mate' will never be applied to him again where you're concerned, not even as a reference to what fate intended him to be for you."

Hmm, she liked that. As did her cat. "Fair enough." She bit her lip. "What's her name?"

"Lucinda."

"Pretty."

"I like yours better. And mine is way better than Zaire."

Quinley chuckled into the kiss he slapped on her mouth.

He slid his hand from her hip to the small of her back and drew her closer. "Now sleep."

"'Kay." Feeling snug and warm and safer than she had in a long time, Quinley let her eyes close.

# CHAPTER EIGHT

A piercing blare penetrated Isaiah's dream, steadily clearing away the sleep motes. Flat on his back, he blindly reached out and slapped at his cell phone. As the alarm stopped, he let out a long sigh and rubbed at his face.

The sheets rustled, drawing his attention to the female who was using his other arm as a pillow. She lay on her side with her back facing him, one shoulder bare due to how baggy his tee was on her.

His focus darted straight to her brand. It was no longer raw, and the skin had reknitted. But the mark was no less distinct, and it would definitely scar.

Satisfied by that thought, Isaiah rolled into her, curling his arm around her. Her scent washed over him, and there was something ... comforting about it. That scent meant something to him now. It belonged to his mate.

She still smelled faintly of him even though they'd showered after the final time he'd taken her through the night. He supposed his tee was mostly responsible for that.

Isaiah nuzzled her neck. "You awake?"

"Hm."

He smiled. She had warned him that she wasn't a morning person. Neither was his cat, in truth.

The feline had calmed down some. It still wasn't happy that Isaiah had marked someone, but it did respect the meaning behind the brand. The cat understood that Quinley was theirs now.

Realizing he was idly tracing the brand with his fingertip, Isaiah felt his lips cant up. It was funny ... he hadn't thought he'd be moved by the bite. Not until they'd imprinted on one another. He hadn't thought it would pluck at his attention or stir anything in him. But, on a basic and elemental level, the sight of it was almost enthralling.

"You need more time to wake up, that's fine," he said, sitting up sideways. He got to his knees, shifted aside, and rolled her onto her back.

She lifted her head, her eyelids fluttering. "What are you …?"

It took some shuffling on his part, but he was soon lying between her legs, his face level with her pussy. He didn't respond to her question. Just got right down to eating her out.

She came fast. He'd learned the previous night that she didn't last long during oral. Which he didn't mind right then, because he needed to be inside her. Isaiah fucked her hard, not coming until she'd exploded a second time.

Wrung dry, he kissed her throat. "Morning."

"It is a good morning," she slurred. "Your tongue is a gift, your cock is a must-have, you fuck like a master, and your bed is the comfiest thing ever. I'm giving myself a mental pat on the back for mating you."

He felt his mouth curve. "Who wouldn't?"

A snort. "Don't be so humble," she deadpanned.

"I won't." He got out of bed, scooped her up, and carried her into the bathroom. "Come on, shower."

"I can walk."

"I like carrying you."

Once they were both clean and dressed, they migrated to the kitchen. As they bustled around the room making coffee and breakfast, it didn't feel awkward. He'd thought it might, considering it was the first morning they'd spent together, but no. Maybe it was that she was his, that this space was *theirs* now, that made the difference—he didn't know.

Sitting beside him at the breakfast bar, she waved her spoon around, gesturing at the space. "I really like this kitchen."

"Same. It was the only part of the house I didn't change when I moved in." Finished with his toast, he lifted his cup and shifted on the stool to better face her. "I haven't lived here long, but I put my mark on the place real quick. You'll no doubt want to do the same. Like I said last night, have at it."

She gave him a pretty smile. "Thank you."

"What time is the rest of your stuff being delivered?"

"Around six-thirty. There's not a whole lot of it, so it won't take long for me to unpack." Quinley shoveled a spoonful of cereal into her mouth. "I'll also have to let out my cat so she can leave her own mark on the place. She's also set on territorially marking the yard."

"She's welcome to do both." He took a swig of his coffee. "I want to meet your cat. Would she be up for that later?"

"Sure." Quinley cast him an odd, sideways glance. "I take it you'd rather wait before introducing your cat to me or mine."

Isaiah frowned. "There's no need to wait. He has no negative feelings toward you."

Her expression was soft but sober. "Don't lie. If he looks at me and resents that I'm not—"

"He doesn't," Isaiah stated, firm. "I wouldn't lie about that. I also wouldn't suggest you meeting him so soon if I thought he'd give you the cold shoulder."

Having been rejected by the one person who should never have overlooked or turned their back on her, she'd naturally be sensitive to any element of rejection. Isaiah knew he'd have to be mindful of that.

She eyed him for a moment. "Okay, if you're sure."

"I'm absolutely certain."

"Then I'll take your word for it." She ate the last of her cereal, dropped the spoon into the bowl, and then chugged down what was left of her coffee. "Gonna have to head out."

And ... he found that he didn't like that. Which took him off-guard, because he hadn't for a second imagined he'd be fazed by her doing something so mundane as going to work.

Her head twitched to the side. "What's wrong?"

Typical submissive, already so in tune with him. Being such a private person, he probably should have found it at least mildly irritating, but he didn't. "Nothing's wrong as such. I just unreasonably find that I prefer the idea of you spending the entire day here, where you're safe."

Her lips winged up. "You're cute."

"Cute?"

"Well ... there's no reality in which it would ever happen. I would never manage to spend the entire day indoors. And the beauty salon is not fraught with peril, so I'll really be fine."

Quinley could sense that, while he agreed with the latter, his instinct to keep her here wasn't shifting. He didn't intend to act on it, but he couldn't shake it off.

She twisted so she fully faced him. "I'll admit that you being Tate's bodyguard makes me nervous. Being an enforcer carries enough danger. That you're also the shield of the pride member who's the biggest target ... yeah, I don't much like it. Don't get me wrong, I'm not saying I want you to give up the position," she hurried to add.

He laid a reassuring hand on her knee. "I understand. We're in the same boat. I don't want you to give up your job, but I'm protective enough that I'll worry." He gave her knee a squeeze. "Thank you for that piece of honesty. I know you only confessed it to make me feel better."

*Busted.* "Did it work?"

"Yes. I like that there's a balance." He slanted his head. "What is your job at the salon?"

"It doesn't really have a title. People sometimes call it, 'the regular brush with near-death,'" she added with an amused smile, thinking he'd return it. He didn't.

"That does not make me feel better about you leaving for work."

"They're being dramatic."

"What is it you do that would make them give such a dramatic answer?"

Probably something he wouldn't like, actually, now that she thought about it. "The salon offers what has become a very popular pamper day package. So, basically, someone will come to the salon, shift so their inner animal can be bathed and groomed, return to their human form to receive a massage, and then go have their hair, nails, and makeup done."

He stared at her for a long moment. "Please don't tell me you bathe and groom their animals."

Yeah, he definitely wasn't pleased. "Would you prefer I gave massages?"

"Fuck, no." He lowered his gaze to her hands. "They're *my* hands now." He set down his cup. "And I don't want them getting bitten off."

"It's rare that I get bit or clawed."

He pressed his lips together. "Again, this isn't making me feel better about you leaving."

He truly was super cute. "Really, it's not dangerous. I use my healing energy to help relax and soothe them while I do my pampering part of the package. And shifters know that if their animals bite me they have to pay double, so they're particularly careful of ensuring the beasts behave themselves."

"*Still* not feeling better over here."

Snorting, Quinley slipped off the stool. "I'll be fine, I swear. And I really have to go, but I'll be back around five-thirty."

"You'd better come back unharmed or I'll be pissed." Rising from his stool, he dropped a kiss on her temple. "Have a good day at work."

"You, too."

"Drive safely, and call me if you need me."

She saluted him. "Will do. Watch your ass, not just that of your Alpha."

The drive to Blue Harbor beauty salon took only twenty minutes. She parked her car in the small lot across from it. The lot was used mostly by employees of the short row of businesses on that particular street.

The bell above the salon's door chimed as she stepped inside. The scents of fruity hair products, astringent nail polish, lemon cleaner, and chemical dyes washed over her—all of which were designed for shifters, so the smells didn't irritate her senses.

The small reception area was simple but stylish. Buttercream plush chairs were positioned near the floor-to-ceiling window, along with a round coffee table on which piles of glossy magazines rested. Products lined a glass shelving case pressed against the far wall. Among them were shampoos, hand creams, massage oils, and small bottles of nail polish.

Framed posters of glamorous hair models were hung on the white walls, not only in the reception area but between the large mirrors at the two individual hair stations.

Stood behind the curved, tidy white counter on which a computer, phone, and card reader sat, Adaline smiled at her. She was their main hairstylist, not the receptionist. But since having to fire their receptionist a few weeks back, they'd all pitched in with reception duties while they waited for the Crimson Alpha female to hire a replacement. Nel didn't come to the salon often, but she took care of the behind-the-scenes managerial side of things.

Raya was a master with more trendier haircuts and elaborate updos, so her clients tended to be younger. Lori was their nail technician, masseuse, and makeup artist. Quinley helped out Adaline where necessary by washing clients' hair when she wasn't otherwise busy. As a team, they made it work.

"Hey, you," greeted Adaline. "How's mated life?"

"The same as it was half an hour ago, when I replied to the text in which you asked that exact question," said Quinley.

Lounging on the padded swivel chair at her station, Raya looked up from her phone. "She just worries. About you, that is. Me, she couldn't give two fucks about."

"That's not true," Adaline objected. "I care. I just don't need to worry about you, because you have Lori."

"And *Quinley* now has Isaiah."

"I don't know him well enough to be sure he'll properly take care of her."

Raya jerked up her chin in challenge. "Just admit that she's your favorite."

Rolling her eyes, Quinley let the quarrel become background noise as she crossed the space. She said a quick hi to Lori, who was pottering around the hair washing station. Black leather chairs reclined toward the row of sinks behind them. Cubbies were stacked with burgundy towels and hair products.

She headed through an arch and to the pamper room on her left. The scents of herbal shampoo, fur, chlorine, and almond oil greeted her, familiar and comforting. She placed her purse in its usual spot in a corner cubby and hooked her coat on a wall hanger.

The large space was fitted with a grooming station, jacuzzi, leather swivel chair, supply cart, and a desk on which a heated lamp and other equipment rested. Different shifter breeds required different "luxuries," and she strived to cater for all.

Before long, clients began to trickle in. They were quick to notice her brand, especially her ex-pride mates. They nosily asked for details about Isaiah, the claiming, and the Olympus Pride. As always, Quinley was stingy with her answers.

Throughout the day, Isaiah popped into her mind often. Mostly because her cat wanted to know where he was and what he was doing. It left them both with a vague feeling of uneasiness that had no real *rational* source. It was just all tied-in to being bound to someone whom she hadn't yet imprinted on. It messed with your mind on an elemental level.

As such, she was grateful when the end of her workday rolled around. The sooner she got home, let her cat see for herself that he was alive—and, yes, gave herself that same assurance—she'd feel a whole lot better.

"Right, I'm off," she told her sisters and Lori, who were all gathering their stuff together.

Raya lifted her hand in a brief wave. "Later, sis."

"See you tomorrow," Lori called out.

"Say hi to—" Adaline cut off as her eyes darted to something behind Quinley.

In the process of zipping up her coat, Quinley turned … just as a tall figure pushed open the glass door. Her cat hissed, her hackles rising.

Zaire breezed inside, his face neutral, his body tense, a strange energy coming off him. His eyes locked on hers, and something flickered in their depths she couldn't quite name. He slowly planted his feet, his jaw tightening.

It was straight up weird being this close to him, having his attention so firmly on her. It hadn't happened since the night she'd tried to make him see what he'd refused to even consider.

He cleared his throat. "No one told me you were planning to enter an arranged mating." The words were low. Stiff. Emotionless.

She shrugged. "I guess they thought there'd be no need. It's not like we were ever friends or anything." Her cat thought him insane for thinking anyone should tell him anything that related to Quinley—he'd lost the right to know.

"True, but I'm due to be made Alpha soon. Harlan has been keeping me apprised of all pride business so I can slot more easily into the position when the time comes. *This,* though, this he kept quiet." There was a distinct bite to Zaire's voice that said he was not pleased to have been kept out of the loop.

"Maybe he thought it wasn't something you needed to be made aware of, considering he knew I'd be gone from the pride before you ascended."

"And you wanted to be gone because of me, didn't you?" Not a question, but rather a tightly spoken statement. "You wanted to be away from me." There was a sort of rueful resignation in his words.

God, she did not want to have this conversation. Really, what would be the point anyway? "I think you should go."

He arched a brow. "Do you now?"

"Nazra wouldn't like that you're here."

He grunted. "Since when do you care what she likes?"

"Since when do you not?"

He looked away, his lips flattening.

"I don't know why you came—"

"Because I shouldn't give a shit that some random pride member recently mated, right?" he clipped, his gaze flying back to hers. "No, I shouldn't care. I shouldn't care that, having transferred to another pride, she won't be under my protection or within my reach. But then, you're not a random member, are you?"

She went still, and she sensed her sisters and Lori do the same.

A smile of self-derision curled his mouth. "I fought that knowledge for a while. What you said to me all those years ago … it was true, wasn't it?"

Yes, but there was no sense in saying so. Their chance to mate had passed. "It was a crush."

"Now, *that* was what I kept telling myself. Whenever doubts nipped at me, I squashed them. The times I found myself deliberately seeking you out, I dismissed them. And any curiosity my cat felt about you, well, I just plain ignored it. But then I heard you were mated, and that kind of ripped off my blinders." He clearly wasn't happy about that; missed the bliss of ignorance. "What you claimed is true."

Quinley sighed. "It doesn't matter either way. We're both mated to other people. Both happy."

"Happy?" he echoed, his brows snapping together. "You don't even know the cat you mated. He's a fucking stranger to you."

She blinked, taken aback by the vehemence in his voice.

He took a step closer. "If you were really intent on an arranged mating, you could have chosen someone you knew. Do you know how rare it is for two shifters to imprint on one another when they have no foundations on which to build? You've practically set yourself up to fail."

Quinley inched up her chin. "I don't believe that."

"You didn't care who you mated, did you? So long as you were away from me, you weren't bothered."

Quinley frowned. "I wanted to be out of the pride before you and Nazra ascended, yes. But it wasn't the reason I took a mate." She'd done that for herself. "I could have transferred somewhere else without doing that. You're flattering yourself a little too much here."

His eyes dropped to her neck. "Did you let him brand you?" He reached out as if to move her coat collar aside.

Quinley jerked away from his hand. "That's none of your business."

"You did, didn't you?" His nostrils flared. "For shit's sake. If this mating goes tits up, you'll forever wear his mark."

And this was his business *how*? "I don't plan for it to go tits up. But if that happened, it'd be my problem. It's nothing you need to concern yourself with."

His expression tightened. "Just because I didn't claim you doesn't mean it'll be okay with me if you're unhappy."

"It never bothered you before," she couldn't help but snipe.

"Because I didn't before know what I know now."

"And you think that having such an epiphany means you get to seek me out? That you get to come here and express your thoughts on my decisions

SUZANNE WRIGHT

or actions?"

Unreal.

Her positively enraged cat honestly wanted to claw his eyes out. "You have *no say* in what I do or don't do, Zaire. Your thoughts on it don't matter. You have a mate. Concern yourself with her. I don't need to hear what you think or feel about anything."

Quinley skirted around him, careful not to let her body brush his, and pulled open the door.

"Must feel good," he said, his tone a taunt.

She glanced back at him. "What?"

"Being able to walk away from me like I once did you."

"That you'd think I'm so bitterly bitchy just goes to show you know nothing about me." Silently asking the universe to at some point throw him in a nest of fire ants, Quinley strode out of the salon.

"I don't think I've ever seen you this edgy," said Deke.

Dragging his gaze away from the neighbors bickering at the opposite side of the cul-de-sac, Isaiah looked at his fellow enforcer. "What?"

"You're antsy," said Deke, his hip propped against the lamppost. "So much so that just seeing two of our pride mates having one of their usual petty squabbles is putting you on high alert."

Tate nodded. "You've been like this all day, and it's only gotten worse as the hours went on."

Isaiah sighed. He *was* antsy. Had been since the moment Quinley drove off earlier this morning. And even knowing she'd soon be home wasn't improving his mood.

"If you're finding it uncomfortable to be out of contact with your little black-foot, that's normal," said Deke. "You two have no imprint bond, so there'll be an insecurity there that translates into a restless overprotectiveness. I experienced it with Bailey. Is your cat feeling just as edgy?"

Isaiah dipped his chin. "He doesn't like that she's out of his sight. He doesn't fully view her as his mate, but she's still on his mind."

"Which is what you wanted, right?" Tate checked. "You wanted for his mind to be off ... someone else."

"Yes. It's a good thing. Just unexpected." And hard to get a handle on.

"Did you brand each other?" asked Deke.

Again, Isaiah nodded. "I don't think he would otherwise have acknowledged her as ours. Right now, he mostly just feels protective of her."

Tate cocked his head. "Any regrets on your part? The arrangement went through so fast I worried you'd later wish you'd taken it slow."

"None," Isaiah told him. "Everything's going as well as can be expected."

He rubbed at his jaw. "It's stupid that I didn't see just how well a submissive would fit me. It's like something's clicked into place. Hard to explain."

"I get it," said Tate. "I had dominant females in my life before Havana, but none were a born-alpha. I *needed* that in a way I didn't see. And when I had it, things just felt right on a level they hadn't before. It bodes well for you and Quinley."

Deke pushed away from the lamppost. "I never pictured you with someone small. You could just tuck her in your back pocket and carry her around."

"I'd probably feel less anxious if I did," Isaiah muttered.

Tate's mouth bowed up. "That'll settle once you imprint."

"Maybe it would have been better to have waited before you branded her," Deke mused. "You wouldn't have felt so edgy while waiting for a bond to form."

Isaiah frowned. "No, it was—" Cutting himself off as a shadow loomed over them, he jerked his head up. A *mega* large bird was swooping down at them *fast*.

No, *at Isaiah*.

He ducked down as he lurched to the side. *Too late*. Talons dug into his shoulders and heaved him off the ground like he weighed nothing.

Then they were zooming through the air.

Hissing at the painful dig of talons, his cat in an absolute fury, Isaiah unsheathed his claws and stabbed upward—ramming them deep into the harpy eagle's stomach. It screeched, the sound piercing. He raked and stabbed and squirmed.

The avian shifter dropped him with a pained shriek.

Dropped him right into *incoming traffic*.

Horns beeped and tires screeched as he hit the asphalt *hard*. Bones cracked, and his breath left his lungs in a whoosh. A massive impact crashed into him, sending him rolling into his stomach.

He lay there, breathing hard—his head swimming, his heart pounding, his whole body hurting, his blood tainting the air, his cat going insane.

He was pretty sure fine bones in his spine were broken, and one of his legs was definitely fucked up. His skull … Jesus, he'd be surprised if it wasn't fractured, given the agony pounding through it.

Footsteps thundered toward him, and then Deke crouched at his side. "Motherfucking fucker."

"Get Helena *now*," Tate yelled to … someone—Isaiah couldn't see who. "Sorry, but this is gonna hurt."

Isaiah's vision flashed black as his Alpha and Deke scooped him up off the ground—the movement pulled at every injury, causing severe pain to rack his body. They carried him to the sidewalk, where they carefully set him down.

Within moments, pride mates gathered around him in a tight circle that protected him from any human eyes. They verbally fussed over Isaiah, assuring him that the healer would be soon with him.

They weren't wrong.

Helena appeared fast, her eyes glinting with dismay as she touched his leg. Healing energy crackled through him, shooting to every wound—reknitting skin, mending fractures, fixing breaks, making the pain gradually fade.

Isaiah sat upright and gave her a nod of thanks. He peered up at the sky, seeing nothing but gray clouds. "*That* attack I hadn't seen coming." Which pissed him off, but *how* could he have foreseen it, for Christ's sake?

"The harpy eagle shifter had to have been a member of the Vercetti Pack," said Deke as they both stood. "Though I doubt their plan was to throw you onto the road—the brothers would want to kill you themselves to avenge Samuele, not leave you to the mercy of traffic."

"The eagle was likely supposed to take you somewhere," hedged Tate. "You obviously proved to be too difficult for them to cart off, so they improvised."

And, in doing so, failed to kill him.

"Let's get you back to the cul-de-sac," said Tate. "You're gonna have to pretend to still be badly injured, just in case humans are watching."

It galled Isaiah, but he allowed it to look as though both the Alpha and Deke were helping him walk. Their gathering of pride mates stayed close, still doing their best to obstruct the view of nosy observers.

It was only when they were in the cul-de-sac that Tate and Deke released him. Isaiah walked toward his house on his own steam, reaching the driveway just as a car pulled up behind his own.

Quinley slipped out of it, her expression darkening as she took a good look at him. His injuries might be healed, but his clothes were dirty, ragged, and stained with blood. "What happened?" she asked, hurrying to his side. "Why is there blood on you?"

"I'm all right," he assured her, his cat's anger not quite easing back at the sight of her but losing some of its heat. "Helena healed me."

Her eyes flashed. "But you were obviously injured, which is *not* all right," she said, her voice tight. "What happened?"

Isaiah had to admit he liked that she worried. "Easy," he soothed, stroking her arm. "To sum up, I was picked up by a harpy eagle and thrown into the road."

She blinked. "You were *what?*"

# CHAPTER NINE

"Take her inside," Tate advised him. "You can fill her in there."

Isaiah had been about to do exactly that, since not only was she shivering but he'd rather they talked in private. "Come on, I'll tell you everything once we're in the house."

He ushered her up the path, through their front door, and into the living area. There, he guided her to the sofa.

She sat stiffly, her lips tight, her expression expectant. "Why would a harpy eagle come after you? And can I kill it?"

He wouldn't have thought he could want to smile at such a time, but the urge tugged at one corner of his lips. "Unfortunately, we don't have the avian shifter in our custody, so no, you can't kill it. As for why it came for me"— he sat beside her—"have you ever heard of the Vercetti Pack?"

"Yes. What shifter hasn't?"

Twisting toward her, he draped an arm over the back of the sofa. "They tried to kidnap a kit from our pride last week. I killed the youngest brother, Samuele, but the others got away."

She did a slow blink. "You killed one of the Vercetti brothers?"

"Yes."

Shock slapped Quinley, making her lips part on a silent gasp. On the one hand, it was great that a Vercetti was gone from the world—they contributed nothing good to it. On the other hand ... "The other three won't let that go, Isaiah. You're a target now."

Her inner cat stirred uneasily, her gut roiling. She already felt sick from the scent of his blood, *knowing* he'd been severely injured. That he then simply dipped his chin in answer, not seeming all too concerned about it, made her cat's eyes narrow in temper.

Agitation flared through Quinley. "And you didn't think to tell me this?"

85

The words came out on a hiss.

He winced. "I was going to tell you tonight. I assumed there was time for me explain everything before they made any overt moves. I shouldn't have waited."

*No shit.* "You think the harpy eagle is part of the Vercetti Pack?"

He tucked her hair behind her ear. "Yes. I think he was supposed to carry me to wherever the brothers waited. They'd want the kill to be up close and personal." Again, he didn't sound all that bothered.

*Quinley* was bothered. She scrubbed a hand down her face, muttering a curse. "This isn't good, Isaiah. Not at all. I knew that you were protecting a target, I didn't realize you are one. What's being done about it?"

"Members of my pride are doing their level best to locate the pack, as are Alex's three uncles. Until we know where the pack hides, we can't act."

She examined his expression, feeling her eyes go slitted as she sensed, "You're not too bothered that they came for you, because it might be the only way you can get to them."

"I want to completely erase the threat they represent, and I want it done as fast as possible. That might only happen if they make appearances, because they're somehow managing to evade detection. We have no idea how."

She swore again. "Your wounds are definitely healed?"

"All healed," Isaiah promised, resting a hand on her nape, not liking how pale she was. "I'm sorry I didn't tell you before now about the Vercetti Pack situation. I know it had to have been a fuck of a shock to come home and see me like this."

She rubbed at her arms. "You're not supposed to get hurt."

He leaned forward and pressed a kiss to her hair. "Don't worry, I'm not going anywhere."

"But they *will* come back for you, won't they?" She bit down on her bottom lip. "Maybe you shouldn't act as Tate's bodyguard for a while. Maybe you should instead have a guard of your own."

His cat bristled. "Not necessary."

"Because dominant shifters can protect themselves, right," she said, her voice dry. "It's arrogant to think that you're invulnerable just because you're a dominant."

"I don't think I'm invulnerable, I just believe I can protect myself better than anyone else can." But, yeah, it was partly an ego thing.

"Not if you're too busy worrying about watching someone else's ass."

Isaiah frowned, pensive. "You do make a good point there. It might be worth Tate having me temporarily replaced so that he isn't caught in any crossfire."

She sniffed. "Much as I am concerned for Tate, I'm more bothered about *you* getting caught up in anything. It isn't wise for someone else's safety to be your priority at a time when your own is at risk."

He tapped her chin with one finger. "*Your* safety is my priority, but I completely understand what you're saying. I also agree. I'll talk to Tate about it tomorrow. For now, I just want us to relax and have dinner before your stuff gets delivered."

"Okay." She drew in a deep breath. "First, you might want to know that Zaire stopped by the salon."

It took a few moments for the words to penetrate. "Say that again."

Her gaze slid to the side. "Uh …"

Outrage. Contempt. Jealousy. A dark territorialism. All of it blended inside Isaiah. Boiled in his blood, hot and thick as lava. "Seriously, say that again."

Quinley nibbled on her lower lip. "Zaire stopped by the salon."

*Unbelievable.* "When?"

"Just as I was about to leave."

His cat flexed his claws, his upper lip quivering in an ugly snarl. He didn't want Zaire anywhere near her.

Isaiah very nearly snarled himself. The fucker had no right. He'd given her up, he'd bound himself to a different female, he'd stayed away from Quinley all these years. He didn't get to turn up now that she was claimed by another. "What did he want?"

"He'd heard I mated you and, uh"—she scratched at her cheek—"he said it tore off his blinders."

Isaiah cursed, pushing off the sofa, unable to sit still while so many dark emotions scratched and bit at him. "So he's claiming he believes you two were fated?"

"I denied it at first; said it was just a crush. He didn't buy that. Funny, really, because *he* was the one who originally stated it was a crush," she mused, though she seemed to be speaking more to herself than Isaiah. "Back then, I'd been the one to argue differently."

"You should have called me."

Her brow pinched. "What for? He wasn't insulting or abusive. Just annoying. I was due to head home anyway."

She seemed so blasé about it. Like it was no biggie for the other half of her fucking soul to show at her place of work and finally, after so many years, acknowledge that they were fated. It wasn't "nothing" at all. In fact, depending on what Zaire wanted from her and just how much she might—consciously or subconsciously—be willing to give him, this could mean a lot.

Isaiah set his hands on his hips. "Did he try to persuade you to leave me?"

"No. He actually seems pissed off that the blinders are gone. I think that, while a part of him might have once been curious to know if I was right in what I once declared, he would rather not have known for sure."

"Because then his mind wouldn't play the *what if* game."

She shrugged, seeming not to care either way. "Maybe."

"What are his intentions?"

"He doesn't have any. He doesn't now want me. The only thing that really bothered him other than no longer having the bliss of ignorance is that I've entered an arranged mating with someone I barely know. He believes it won't work out. I told him he was wrong and then left."

Isaiah narrowed his eyes. "And how do you feel about all this?"

"Annoyed, mostly. What he did was super shitty. For all he knew, I was holding onto hope that I'd one day have him. He didn't do me the courtesy of staying away just in case. And Nazra, his mate, is hardly going to like that he showed up if she hears about it. More, it isn't fair to you that he did that."

*Nazra, his mate.*

Those words smoothed over Isaiah's hackles like warm syrup. They were so casually spoken—no bitterness or hurt had laced her tone. It had been a matter-of-fact remark. She didn't view Zaire as hers in any sense.

Her head tilted. "You thought I'd, what, be all flattered and excited?"

"It would have been understandable if some part of you had felt hopeful that he'd walk away from her to pursue you."

She frowned. "No part of me hopes that."

"Yes, I'm getting that impression."

"It's not an impression. It's a fact." Quinley stared up at Isaiah, genuinely surprised at just how bugged he was by Zaire's visit. Oh, she'd known he'd be pissed. Such a visit was bound to pluck at any possessive strings in Isaiah that had come to life after they branded each other. But she hadn't expected him to get *quite* so wound up about it.

She also hadn't thought he would worry that any part of her pined for Zaire. She'd been very clear that that wasn't the case. He hadn't seemed dubious at any point before now, so she'd assumed he'd taken her at her word.

Resolved that he'd have no doubts, she leaned forward and added, "Even if I didn't have you, I wouldn't want Zaire. I couldn't accept him. Neither could my cat. Just as you couldn't accept Lucinda now that she's preg—" Quinley cut herself off at his flinch.

Her blood ran cold. Well, that explained why he doubted she'd fully let go of Zaire. He couldn't imagine it was true because, despite his claims, he hadn't been able to do the same with Lucinda. *Ouch.*

Logically speaking, it was understandable. But—stung at knowing that the male she'd claimed still hurt at being unable to have another woman— Quinley wasn't feeling very understanding right then. Nor was her cat—a growl rumbled in the feline's chest.

Quinley slowly pushed to her feet. "What I said was true, Isaiah. I can't *make* you believe me. Maybe you will in time." She began heading for the kitchen.

And a hand snapped around her wrist.

"Stop." The order was low but firm, and there was a tender note in it that surprised her.

Grinding her teeth, she stayed still as Isaiah approached her left side and stepped fully into her space.

He placed his mouth near her ear. "You saw me flinch," he began, his voice soft, "and you're thinking I haven't let her go. You're wrong. I flinched because my cat dug his claws into me. He doesn't like thinking of her pregnant—for him, it's the ultimate betrayal."

Oh.

Isaiah took her by the shoulder and gently turned her to face him. "Listen to me. It isn't that I don't believe you. I just wanted to be sure where your head is at."

Quinley sighed, knowing she'd overreacted a little. The truth was that a lifetime of having to defend herself against false rumors meant she was too used to not being believed. When people who mattered to her doubted her word on something, it always hit harder than it needed to. Add that to her assumption of why he'd flinched and, yes, she'd clammed up.

"And yeah, what Zaire did is fucking with me a little," Isaiah continued. "I don't want him anywhere near you. My cat would like to slice his throat."

Her brows knit in surprise. "I didn't think your cat would be bothered."

"Oh, he's bothered. It's part of why he reacted so badly when you brought up Lucinda's present condition—he's already agitated from Zaire's behavior, and he wasn't exactly calm before then thanks to the harpy eagle. Do you have the little shit's cell phone number?"

"No. Why?"

An innocent shrug. "I'd like to talk to him."

Her nape prickled at the *far* too casual note in his tone. "If you mean to warn him off, that's not necessary. He won't turn up again. There was no real point to him showing up today—I think it was just a spur of the moment thing driven by a realization that knocked him off-balance. He'll regret it when his thoughts are clear."

His eyes searched her face. "You seem sure of that."

"He never wanted me, Isaiah. Never will. He made it very plain years ago."

"How old were you at the time?"

"Sixteen."

*So young*, thought Isaiah. To be sent away by your fated mate at any age would be difficult. But to be only a juvenile—someone who was in the vulnerable stage of still growing into their own skin and developing a sense of self—it had to have hit that much harder, cut that much deeper. "What happened exactly?"

"You sure you want to hear this story?"

He gently rested his hands on her upper arms. "I'm sure."

She nibbled on her lower lip, hesitant.

He'd done damage here, he realized. She was now so worried he'd think she pined for Zaire on some level that she'd prefer not to speak of him. Isaiah didn't want that. He needed for her to feel she could talk to him about anything.

"Maybe it's better if we just forget he exists," she said.

Isaiah curled his arms around her and held her close, protectiveness filling him at how small she was in comparison. "There's no need for that. He's not so important that we need to convince ourselves he never entered your life. The fact is he did, and whatever happened after that placed you on the path that eventually led you to me. I'd like to hear about it."

A resigned sigh slid out of Quinley. "Okay, fine." She gently placed her hands on his chest. "When I was fourteen, I got cornered by some male pride members. They wouldn't really have assaulted me, they just felt confident they could toy with me because I was unranked."

*Fuckers.* "What does a lack of status have to do with anything?"

"It has *everything* to do with it where black-foots are concerned. Only ranked members and their families are considered important. The rest of us live near the perimeter of the territory and don't really socialize with them."

Outrage speared through Isaiah yet again. "So, in the event of an attack, you're the first line of defense?"

"More like sacrificial pawns, but yes. We're all taught combat, but that's really only so we can keep intruders at bay long enough for the ranked to get prepared."

*Son of a bitch.* "That's fucked up. The more vulnerable members should be protected." It infuriated his cat that she'd been so at risk all these years.

"Black-foots don't really operate that way," she said with a careless shrug. "My kind have always had an obsession with status. I've never really understood it, but that might be because I'm a submissive. Ranks generally only mean something to dominants."

To black-foot dominants, maybe, but it didn't apply to all shifters. In Isaiah's opinion, her breed had serious issues. But then, many would say that same thing about his own. "Anyway, back to your story ..."

"Yeah, so, Zaire intervened and chased the boys off. Looking into his eyes, picking up his scent, I just knew in that moment that I was staring at the person who fate had selected for me. It hit me like a brick. The knowing was crystal clear—there's no mistaking it, is there?"

"No, there isn't." It was a realization that hit soul-deep.

"But he didn't have the same reaction. Just visibly checked I was fine and then walked off. I was so shocked I didn't say anything to him. I ran home and told my sisters. They suggested I give him time to pick up on what I'd sensed. I think they knew he would have rejected me if I said anything. I followed their advice."

"But giving him time didn't amount to anything," Isaiah guessed.

"I would have held out longer, but when I was sixteen I overheard that he might sign a mating contract. I knew Harlan hoped to pair him with Nazra, and I knew Zaire was ambitious enough to go along with it if it meant being Alpha. He also cared about her, I could see that. So I panicked."

"And you told him."

"Picture it. There I was, an unranked submissive, telling a born-alpha who was also the son of an Alpha pair—someone who'd therefore be considered way above my reach—that we were fated; insisting he couldn't sign a mating agreement that would grant him both Nazra and the right to one day rule my pride." She shook her head, sighing.

He personally didn't see how Zaire being a born-alpha *or* the son of Alphas should place him out of Quinley's reach. He was about to say as much, but then she spoke again.

"Maybe he just thought I was ridiculous, maybe he just cared so much for her, or maybe he was so focused on his becoming-an-Alpha-goal that it was to the exclusion of all else. But he wouldn't consider that I might be right."

"Was he harsh in his rejection?"

"At first, he tried letting me down gently; tried convincing me I was just crushing on him. I insisted he was wrong. I wouldn't let it go. He got pissed at me and, in a bid to make me really listen, he hit me with what he thought were 'hard truths.' Said he didn't feel the slightest pull toward me; that his cat had no interest in me; that he wasn't attracted to submissives so it made no sense he'd be paired with one." She puffed out a breath. "I wasn't hopeful that he'd later change his mind, which is good because he never did."

"Did he tell Nazra what you said?"

"No. But her friend did. Fila overheard it all. She told everyone but twisted it—said I threw myself at him, tried to force a claiming bite on him, and even made an attempt to strip. None of it was true, I swear."

He palmed the back of her head, pinning her with a reassuring look. "I believe you."

"Not all do. I stated loud and clear that Fila was talking tripe. The more I insisted I wasn't lying, the more of a liar I apparently was in the eyes of some. Harlan believed me, though. But he was also worried that I'd push Zaire to see the light, so he put me in a corner."

Isaiah felt his skin prickle in unease. "What does that mean?"

"He promised he'd keep Nazra and her cronies from coming for me and my family if I stayed away from Zaire and spread the word that I'd been wrong and it was just a crush."

His cat bared his teeth, her words rekindling his anger. An Alpha protected their pride members; they didn't fucking manipulate them into silence. "Harlan is as much of a goddamn letdown as Zaire." He understood now why she hadn't seemed all that comfortable with him at the

FindYourMate HQ. "Did Nazra and the others leave you be?"

"They never came at me *physically*, but rumors do damage of their own. And people also slung insults my way or snubbed me or whatever. Aside from my family, those who believed me rarely spoke up for me, not wanting to draw negative attention their way."

Jesus, her pride almost as a whole was as big a disappointment as both its current Alpha male and the one who'd soon take over. "What about Zaire? Did he defend you?"

"He did say the rumors weren't true, but I find that people who—for whatever reason—want to hate or ridicule someone will believe just about anything to give them an excuse to be a shit to that someone."

A grim sense of understanding snaked through Isaiah. "You're right about that."

"You've dealt with bullshit rumors too," she remembered. "Will you tell me about what happened? You don't have to."

No, but it wouldn't be fair of him to hold back when she'd opened up the way she had. He'd be throwing it back in her face.

Isaiah pulled in a breath. "There was a kid in the pride who I never got along with. Jenson. We butted heads constantly. I was supremely pissed when I found out he'd been slapping my ex around. I threatened to make him pay. That night, someone set his house on fire with his family in it."

"And he was the only one who died?" she asked, her voice a mere murmur.

"Yes. A few people jumped to the conclusion that I was the arsonist, including his parents. But my mom and dad swore I was home at the time; that it couldn't have possibly been me."

"That wasn't enough for people to drop it?"

"It was for most. But Jenson's parents, Cherrie and Kristopher, insisted my parents were lying, and they did their level-best to ensure everyone else thought the same. They basically embarked on a hate campaign. They even tried pressuring my old Alpha Vinnie to kick me out of the pride."

Her upper lip quivered slightly. "Fuckers."

He grunted. "It was hard to do something so mundane like go to the deli. I'd hear people whispering; see them looking at me weird. I could sense that some truly believed I'd done it." For a short time—as he'd vacillated between fury, humiliation, and hurt—he'd pulled back from the majority of the pride and avoided socializing.

She slid her hands up to clasp her fingers behind his nape. "Did you ever find out who really did it?"

"It turned out to be Jenson's cousin. Apparently, Eddie had confided in him that he believed a member of our pride was his true mate. Jenson's response had been to start dating her."

"*What?*"

"He was a shit that way."

In that case, he'd probably pissed off a fair few people, so it seemed particularly unfair to Quinley that some of the pride had immediately suspected Isaiah. Then again, there was the whole threatening-to-make-Jenson-pay thing. Still, pledges of vengeance were tossed out all the time; they were mostly just said in the heat of the moment.

"Trusting that Vinnie wouldn't declare Eddie guilty unless confident it was true, most who'd suspected me then backtracked," said Isaiah. "But Jenson's parents didn't."

"They couldn't admit they were wrong."

"By that point, they'd invested so much negative emotion and energy in the belief that it was me that they just couldn't let it go. On top of that, they blamed me for their nephew being 'wrongly punished;' said Eddie was just a scapegoat."

Quinley shook her head, furious on his behalf. "I get that they must have badly needed someone to blame. But to latch onto you when there was no proof, and then to refuse to believe—even to this day—that what you've been saying all this time was true … What possible peace can they find in holding onto their beliefs this way?"

"I'm not sure they want peace. They certainly didn't want me to have it." He paused. "There were times when I considered embracing the rumor, since defending myself sometimes only made people seem less likely to believe me. I think it's in some people's nature to enjoy seeing others torn apart or ruined or hurt."

She nodded, grave. "I think that, too."

"My parents suffered for it. Cherrie would constantly knock on their door, rant at my mom, accuse them of being terrible parents. Kristopher would turn up to drag his mate home, but he'd always end up in an argument with my dad."

Practically able to feel the emotional wound throb inside him, she leaned into him and rested her head on his chest. "I'm sorry that happened."

His arms tightened around her. "I thought maybe it would limit my chances of becoming an enforcer. Don't get me wrong, I was aware that Vinnie believed me to be innocent. But it's important that the pride feel they can trust the enforcers, and a handful of them didn't. I think he thought the problem would resolve itself eventually, but it never did. Jenson's family persisted in their beliefs."

"Do they still give you or your parents trouble?"

"No. They spent the last few years pretty much pretending we don't exist. That suited us fine. It suited us even better when they left the pride." Nuzzling her hair, he hummed. "But I'd rather we didn't talk about them anymore. Especially when I can hear your stomach rumbling."

"I'm so hungry it's about to eat itself," she confessed.

He snorted. "Then let's get you fed. Your stuff will arrive soon, and you'll want to have finished your dinner before it does."

It was literally ten minutes after they'd eaten their evening meal that her family arrived. Isaiah and Will did most of the heavy lifting so the females could focus on unpacking the boxes. Meanwhile, little Corey and Ren chased each other around the house.

She'd been telling the truth when she'd said she wasn't bringing much. And yet, having her things among his seemed to change the "tone" of the house.

His living room now featured throw-cushions, her knick-knacks, new coasters, and framed photographs. A tall mirror was hung in the hallway, plants were sprinkled around various rooms, her coats were placed on the rack, and her kitchenware was added to his own.

She had some Christmas bits and bobs—baubles she put on the tree, LED candles she placed on shelves, a garland she set on the fire mantel, and some ornaments she spread around.

At her request, he and Will set her reading chair and books in the bedroom while the females placed more of her personal belongings throughout the space—filling the dresser, vanity, and closet. Other bits were taken to the en suite bathroom.

Once they were done, they took the empty boxes to the large van Will had borrowed to deliver her stuff. Her family stayed long enough to have a quick coffee, but then they left.

Quinley did a long stretch. "I'm tired after that, but resting isn't gonna happen right now. My cat is itching to get out and do some marking."

"So let her out," urged Isaiah, eager to meet the little feline.

Quinley went to the patio door and opened it enough that her cat would be able to squeeze through. "I'm not getting undressed outside," she explained. "It's too damn cold."

He watched her as she stripped—a show he enjoyed despite how quickly it was over. Clearly to escape the chilly air filtering through the open patio door, she shifted instantly.

Isaiah smiled down at her cat. Light-green eyes took him in, curious. She looked much like a tabby or Bengal cat. Black spots and tiger-like stripes decorated her tawny fur. Thick dark bands surrounded her long tapering tail.

"Hey, there," he murmured, going down on his haunches. "Come over here," he softly coaxed.

Her small pointed ears pricking forward, she cautiously padded toward him.

"Good girl."

Pausing near his thigh, she prodded him with a paw he knew would be black—hence where the name of her breed came from. "Want a stroke, do you?" He petted her gently, focusing mostly on her head and neck, since she seemed to prefer being stroked in those areas.

His own feline watched her every movement, admiring her grace; feeling a little left out.

Apparently done being stroked, she wandered off. Isaiah hung back as she rubbed herself over furnishings, leaving a few claw marks here and there—marking their territory as partly hers.

He followed her into the yard and remained on the patio while she darted around, fast as fucking lightning. No, faster.

She sprinted. Climbed. Jumped. Rolled. And then found herself a goddamn spider, which she promptly ate.

Isaiah grimaced. "To each their own, I guess."

His cat pushed for supremacy, done being an observer.

Isaiah returned inside long enough to shed his clothes and leave them in a pile beside hers on the floor. *Be gentle with her*, he told his cat.

The animal sniffed, insulted that Isaiah would think he'd do otherwise, and then lunged to the surface.

Settling into his fur, the pallas cat padded into the yard. The other feline jerked up her head, spotted him, froze. He slowly sat on the deck, not intending to play, only to watch.

She eyed him closely for long moments before turning away. He watched as she ran, played, clawed trees, hunted.

After a while, they returned to the house. She shifted first, and her human half looked down at him. Her mouth curving, she said, "Hi." Like her cat had earlier, she remained still, just watching him.

He still wasn't too sure he liked having another person in his space, but it didn't matter. She was his to protect. So the cat held back a moody growl and shifted.

Isaiah pushed to his feet, relieved his animal had been so well-behaved. "That went well enough."

"It did," she said, clearly relieved.

"Your cat sure has a lot of energy."

"Dude, that was nothing. She can run for literally hours."

He frowned. "But she won't, right? I know black-foots are roamers, but we're not like the Crimson Pride—we don't have lots of land where she can run free without worry of being attacked."

"She won't go too far," Quinley assured him, snatching her panties from the floor.

"What are you doing?"

"Uh, redressing?"

"No point in that." He took the panties from her hand. "I'm about to fuck you, and I'd rather you were naked for that."

"Oh. Well. Okay, then."

# CHAPTER TEN

S tudying the Alpha pair's Christmas tree, Quinley tossed another salted chip in her mouth. "I don't think I've ever seen a zombie tree topper before."

Beside her, Aspen smiled and put a hand to her chest. "It was a gift from me."

"I don't like to use it," said Havana, drawing Quinley's attention back to where the devil sat on the sofa with Bailey. "But Aspen kept switching the topper, knowing it'd eventually reach a point where I couldn't be bothered changing it back."

"How can you not like it?" demanded Aspen. "Look at it. It makes a statement."

Havana stared at her evenly. "Yes, it says, '*The person who bought this is a fucking nut.*'"

A sniff from the bearcat. "I resent that."

"Go forth and resent. It won't make it untrue." Havana swigged some of her soda. "*You're* the one who loves zombies, I don't know why you didn't buy it for yourself ..." She trailed off at Aspen's shifty expression. "Oh my God, you bought it for yourself. Camden wanted no part of it, so you regifted it to me."

"You're only just considering that?" Bailey asked the Alpha. "Wow."

Havana tossed a piece of popcorn at her, but the mamba moved fast and caught it with her mouth.

Chomping it down, Bailey grinned with pride.

"I want to hate you," Havana told her. "I tried in the beginning. Really hard. It didn't work."

Still smiling, Bailey shrugged. "I'm just so utterly loveable."

Aspen blinked at the mamba. "Yeah, that's not what it is."

Quinley stifled a smile and ate another chip. In the short time she'd been part of the pride, she'd come to learn that the three females were incredibly tight. A lot of shit talk went on, and Aspen's bearcat often got into it with Bailey's mamba. But the love and loyalty between the trio was set in concrete.

They often checked in on Quinley when Isaiah wasn't home, inviting her to hang out at Havana's house. Much as Quinley liked her alone time, she wanted to get to know her new pride mates—especially those who were part of Isaiah's immediate circle.

He and Quinley had only been mated five days now, but it somehow felt like longer. They'd started to brush up against each other's quirks and pet peeves; were learning where and where not to step so no hot buttons were pressed. They'd developed a rhythm that worked for them and managed to share the same space just fine.

Quinley returned to the armchair. "Isaiah said you three work at a rec center for loners."

"We do." Havana knocked back more soda. "The place was our haven when we were younger. The guy who runs it, Corbin, took us in."

"I seriously considered becoming a lone shifter," said Quinley, "but my sisters were dead-set against it and begged me to find another way out of the pride."

Aspen gave a nod of understanding. "Loners are easy targets. We encountered a lot of trouble growing up. It'd be so much more dangerous for a submissive. Not that I'm saying you're weak—"

"I know what you're saying," Quinley assured her, unoffended. "And you're right. By nature, we're vulnerable to dominants. Their vibes can oppress us enough that it makes it hard for us to fight back. We learn tricks to get around it, but they don't always work. Hence why my sisters freaked at the idea of me becoming a loner. They asked that I just seek a simple transfer."

"But you wanted a mate," said Aspen, taking the other armchair.

"Yes. I also didn't want to go to another black-foot pride." In between more bites of her chips, Quinley explained about the whole ranked and unranked division in such prides.

Havana gaped. "Oh my God, that's ludicrous."

Bailey nodded, her brows drawn together. "I usually admire brutal, but no, not in this case."

Quinley gave a loose shrug. "It's our normal, we don't think much of it. But when new unranked members join, they're toyed with by the ranked until boredom kicks in."

Aspen squinted. "Because they want to get across *exactly* where you stand in the hierarchy—which is nowhere."

Quinley dipped her chin. "I knew other breeds of shifter were protective of submissives. I wasn't looking for protection, just peace, you know? So when I was filling in my FindYourMatch questionnaire, I made sure to note that I didn't want to be paired with another black-foot. My preference was *some* kind of feline, but it wasn't a necessity."

Havana's mouth curled. "Bet you didn't have a pallas cat in mind."

"They've been called everything from demonic to psychotic, but I always thought it was unfair. They don't go looking for trouble, they're just set on being the ones to end it. I can respect that." Quinley chomped down another chip. "Ruthlessness is fine so long as there's no targeting those who are vulnerable. Pallas cats don't do that."

"They're very protective of their own, particularly the vulnerable—whether that's children, the elderly, healers, omegas, or submissives," said Havana. "It's how it should be."

"But the vulnerable often struggle majorly as loners," Aspen cut in, "so I'm glad you didn't go down that route, Quinley. Most especially because you really do suit Isaiah. Far more than I thought you would, actually. That website really does its job well. I'm glad it exists, because it's a real good option for those in your position."

Chewing on the last of her chips, Quinley balled up the packet. "Suiting on paper isn't always mutually exclusive with suiting in real life—you see that all the time with dating sites. But things are going really well with me and Isaiah."

Havana set her glass on the coffee table. "I saw his cat watching yours play—yes, I was nosing out of the window; go sue me. Anyway, I know it might have seemed sad that he didn't interact much with her. But it's a good sign that he wanted to be in her company and watch over her."

"Does he ever play with her?" Aspen asked.

Quinley shook her head, hiding her disappointment. "There's rarely any physical contact between them at all. She leaves him be, sensing that he needs to be the one to close the distance." She rose, plopped her empty chip bag in the trash can, and took a napkin from the table.

Bailey tipped her head to the side. "Does he let you stroke him?"

"No," replied Quinley, wiping the salt from her hands. "He's never mean or snarly, though. I'll take what I can get. Though I doubt I'd get any of it if it wasn't for the brand."

Aspen gave a slow shake of the head. "It's amazing how much power a claiming brand can have over the mental dynamics of shifters, isn't it?" she marveled. "It takes whatever you're feeling toward a person to *entirely* new levels. Especially emotions like protectiveness and possessiveness."

"They automatically kicked in once Isaiah and I claimed each other." Quinley threw the napkin in the trash. "To be truthful, it can be kind of a pain."

Havana smiled. "Isaiah does not like you being away from him—it's this elemental thing he can't control."

"I'm in the same boat, so I get it." Quinley returned to her seat. "Things will eventually settle."

"I'm surprised he hasn't at least asked you to cut back on your work hours," said Aspen.

Quinley crossed one leg over the other. "The thought has probably crossed his mind, especially since he doesn't particularly like my job. But if so, he's fought the temptation to ask."

Havana's mouth curved again. "Yeah, I heard about the pamper day package. I must admit, I'm seriously tempted to try it."

"You should," Quinley told her. "The salon isn't exclusive to my old pride. Any shifter can enter. Lots do. The scents, smells, and lighting are designed to accommodate our enhanced senses, so it really is relaxing." She hoped to eventually treat Isaiah's cat to her usual pampering treatment, but she knew it wouldn't happen in a hurry.

Aspen stretched her legs out. "Surely there are some shifter species where you're like, *hell no, I'm not touching their animal.*"

Quinley had occasionally considered it, but … "I've never turned anyone down."

"What breeds have you groomed?" asked Havana.

There were too many to count. "Everything from minks and badgers to lions and hyenas."

Aspen blinked. "So you don't have a sentimental attachment to your hands, then?"

Quinley snickered. "Honestly, the animals most likely to get nippy or scratchy are the smaller ones."

Bailey cocked her head. "Would you turn away a snake?"

"Nope." They rarely got fang-y. "I mean, most don't require me to groom them in any way. But they like to sit in the mini hot tub with the heated lamps bearing down on them."

Bailey's face went all soft. "Oh, that sounds amazing." She looked from Aspen to Havana. "We should definitely go."

The Alpha gave an enthusiastic nod. "We could make it a girl's day out. And then we'd also get to see where Quinley works—I'm nosy enough that I want to check the place out."

"I half-expected Isaiah to try sending you all there every day after the Zaire incident." Isaiah had made the entire pride aware of it, passing around Zaire's photo and asking that they keep a look out for him.

Havana's nose wrinkled. "Isaiah *might* have suggested you have a personal guard, but I pointed out that you're in no physical danger from Zaire. He seemed mollified by your later promise not to engage with the guy if he reappeared."

Quinley knew about the whole suggesting a guard thing; he'd told her about it afterward. She'd said exactly what Havana herself had seemingly said to him. He'd actually conceded that they were both right; hadn't tried pushing anything on Quinley. But it had been clear that the thought of Zaire returning to the salon had concerned him.

She understood that his emotional reaction was massively driven by the insecurities existing between them due to their lack of a bond. It was a visceral thing that neither of them could quash, not even when they knew their thoughts or reactions weren't entirely rational.

Since she wouldn't much like Lucinda approaching him and didn't want Isaiah feeling all knotted up inside, she'd given him peace of mind by swearing that if Zaire did reappear—which was highly unlikely, in her opinion—she'd retreat to the rear of the salon and call Isaiah straight away. He could then make his way there and have a chat with Zaire.

Hearing her cell beep, she dug it out of her pocket. Speaking of Isaiah, she had a text from him: *Where are you?*

Apparently, he was home. She typed: *Hello to you, too. I'm next-door.*

*With the unholy trinity?*

*You know, they like that you all call them that.*

*I do know.*

"That Isaiah?" asked Havana.

"Yes, he's home." She pocketed her cell as she pushed out of the chair.

"That doesn't mean you have to leave," said Havana.

Quinley felt her nose wrinkle. "No offense, but I've hit my social limit."

Aspen chuckled. "I'm honestly surprised you didn't hit it sooner."

A knock came at the front door.

"That'll be him," Quinley predicted, slipping on her thick coat. Swinging open the door moments later, she discovered she was right. And just seeing him there—so tall and steady with that tiny upward tilt to one corner of his mouth that made her want to lick it—was enough to make her smile.

"Hey," she greeted as her cat slinked closer, drawn as ever by his scent; finding it both comforting and enlivening. "I was just about to head home."

"Now I can walk you there." He called out his hellos to the girls in the living area, who returned the greetings and told them both to enjoy their evening.

Once Quinley shut the door behind them, he dragged up her coat zipper—such a small thing, but it was so sweet it made her smile again.

He did little things like that all the time. Considerate things. He placed her gloves on the radiator in the morning so they'd be warm when she left for work. He secretly slipped her favorite snacks and candy bars into her purse. He helped around the house with chores, never leaving the bulk of anything to her.

Her cat was totally seduced by how he took care of Quinley in such ways. Seriously, the feline melted into a pile of goo often around him—the sweet, protective treatment so foreign to her. Her trust in him grew every day. Quinley could say the same regarding the latter.

He dabbed a kiss on her mouth. "Hmm, you taste like chips."

"I was hungry."

His lips tipped up. "It's rare that you aren't."

The dude was not wrong.

Taking her hand in his, he led her down the porch steps. "How was your day?"

"Fine, yours?"

"Busy."

All the enforcers were right now, since they were having to pick up the slack while Farrell, Luke, and Camden were tracking the Vercetti Pack. Isaiah would typically have been focused on guarding Tate, but the Alpha had temporarily had someone else take over—he'd agreed with Isaiah that it would be best. Like her, Tate didn't want him distracted as it would make Isaiah a more vulnerable target. She appreciated that, and she'd thanked the Alpha in private.

"Have you heard anything from Alex's uncles?" she asked.

The corners of his mouth turned down. "No. They're still not taking or making calls. Not even Valentina or Alex have heard from them."

"Do you think they're dead?"

"No. Satan protects his minions."

She snickered.

"It's not unusual for them to stay out of touch when hunting. But Sergei had assured Tate that he'd check in with him regularly."

Hopefully they called sometime soon. Not wanting to talk any more about the Vercetti bullshit, she asked, "Anything in particular you feel like eating for dinner?"

Slowing as they reached the bottom of the Alpha pair's path, he replied, "I was actually thinking we could eat out."

She felt her brows lift in surprise. "I'm up for that. Where do you want to go?"

"The pride owns several eateries," he reminded her. "We could choose one of those."

"Works for me." She'd prefer to stay close to the pride, given he had a target on his back. "I'm good with whichever restaurant is closest."

"Hungry again?"

"Oh my God, *starving*."

His lips curved again. "Then let's get you fed."

As the waitress left with their order, Isaiah set the steakhouse menu back in the holder. Quinley sat across from him, nattering away to one of the omegas who'd stopped by their table.

People often did that. Paused to speak to her. Asked her this or that.

He suspected that they were naturally put so at ease by the calm she gave off that they felt comfortable confiding in and consulting with her. She had that same effect on him.

Isaiah didn't slip himself into the conversation, content to just listen. It was amazing how much more settled he felt now that she was in his line of sight. The same applied to his cat, who'd been antsy all day right up until she'd opened the Alpha's front door.

Isaiah had initially thought it would get easier to be apart from her; that he'd somehow get used to how uncomfortable it felt. But there was no becoming accustomed to it, no managing to ignore or block it out.

He supposed that made sense, though. The longer they went without a bond, the more their natures would demand they spend time together in order for that to be rectified.

His father had cautioned him to be prepared for this, but Isaiah really hadn't expected it to be quite so difficult. Hadn't expected there to be something both comforting and arousing about looking at the brand on her neck. Hadn't expected that those same emotions would come from seeing the brand on his shoulder.

His protectiveness toward her had grown, as had his sense of proprietorship. No, "grown" wasn't the right word. They had *deepened*. Become less a mere result of the claiming; become more about Quinley as a person.

It seemed strange when he'd only known her a week—yes, he counted the day they'd had their first exchange of messages. But some people you could come to know quickly, especially when they were so open with you. Others? You would never really feel that you knew them, no matter how much time you spent around them. The latter didn't apply to Quinley.

Unfortunately, he couldn't say that his cat had made any further progress. He still kept his distance from her in many ways. But he hadn't backtracked, which was a relief.

Isaiah had worried that his cat, despite viewing Quinley as theirs, would come to feel that she was taking up space that should have been Lucinda's. But the feline didn't want Quinley to leave; felt she was where she should be. That was something.

Just then, she and the omega rounded up the conversation. With a respectful nod at him, the omega then strode away.

Quinley's full attention fell on him. "Sorry about that. She's been having—"

"You never need to apologize for taking time to talk to one of my pride mates." Fuck knew they approached him often enough about random things—she never did anything but smile. "It pleases me to see you settling in so well and making friends."

"Oh. Good."

He leaned forward, placing his lower arms flat on the table. "You got plans for tomorrow?" She often worked Saturdays, but not this weekend.

"I do, actually. I'm going shopping with Blair, Elle, and Bree."

Tension gripped his gut and threatened to stiffen his muscles—and all at the mere thought that she'd be away from him yet again. It was ridiculous. The fact that his cat reacted in much the same way made him feel less of an idiot.

"When was this arranged?" he asked, careful to keep his voice casual.

"When I stopped by to see Aurora on my way home from work. Bree said her colic was bad again." Quinley's brow pinched slightly. "What's wrong?"

He shrugged, but he suspected that the movement was a little too stiff to come off as nonchalant. "Nothing."

She twisted her mouth. "I'd invite you to come shopping with us. I mean, it's a *ladies* trip, but we'd all pretend you had no penis so that you could be there. We're shopping for Christmas gifts, though. I don't want you to see what I buy you."

He felt his lips twitch. "I wouldn't horn in on your 'ladies only' time. That would be a dick move. I'm just battling the irrational urge to somehow convince you to stay at home."

She hummed in understanding. "You know, it would be easier for us all to travel there together than use separate cars, but one trunk probably won't be enough to contain all the bags we'll have. So I was wondering if maybe there's a chance you could drop us off in one of the pride's SUVs and then later pick us up?"

Isaiah's chest went warm. She didn't really need that from him. She could easily borrow one of the SUVs herself, as could Elle, Blair, or Bree. But Quinley knew that letting him feel like he was taking care of her in such a way would ease his tension a little. "Trying to make me feel better again?"

Her eyes twinkled. "Did it work? Again?"

"It did. Again. And yes, I'll take you and pick you up later."

A passing pride mate, Leia, paused near the table to let a waitress pass. Noticing him and Quinley, Leia gave them an awkward smile and then hurried off.

"She always acts like that around us," Quinley noted. "An ex-bedmate of yours?"

Yes. "There aren't many in the pride."

"Why?"

"I was so set on finding my true mate that I kept any bed-buddy arrangements short and sweet and shallow. I only ever slept with females *outside* the pride, because I didn't want my mate to feel uncomfortable when I brought her here. But then I realized she was taken. That was when I started dating pride members, thinking to mate with one, but it didn't work out. I was never really much good at relationships."

Quinley's brow knitted. "That surprises me. I mean, I have no complaints about ours."

Pleasure unfurled in his stomach. "It's different with you. We're mated. Before you, I held back from people. Found it too difficult to trust that another would be one-hundred percent loyal—a lot of people initially turned on me after Jenson's death, and seeing Lucinda with another male felt like another betrayal. You could say I have trust issues."

"I sensed that. I have the same issues, though. It's not only about Zaire's rejection or even how many of my old pride mates reacted to the rumors. It was how guys I'd later get involved with from outside the pride would eventually hear those rumors and not always fully believe my account of what happened. It got to a point where I held back, constantly braced for someone to walk away because of those lies. Some didn't; they believed me. But those relationships just didn't go anywhere."

While he lamented that she'd been so unhappy, he couldn't regret that those relationships had failed; not when she might otherwise have not been his to claim. "Did you mention the rumors on your questionnaire?"

"Only in the part where it asked, 'What are things you hate?' I put stuff like 'toxic rumors,' 'injustices,' and 'when people don't consider both sides of a story.'"

"I typed similar answers. I suppose it's part of why we were paired."

"The site sent me, like, seven suggestions."

He felt his brows flick up. "Seven? They only sent me three."

"Apparently, you're harder to please or something."

He smiled. "Want to know why I chose to contact you first?"

"I do, actually."

"It was your eyes. I saw the shadows there. I have those same shadows. I wondered if maybe we had similar wounds."

"Which we do. And it's helped us, I think. I've never before talked to anyone who could really relate to all that happened in my life. Our situations aren't the same, but they're similar enough to count."

They were. And yes, it had helped. Threads of kindship had formed almost immediately.

Just then, the waitress appeared with their food. He and Quinley talked more as they ate. Mostly about their pride mates, because she liked to hear stories about them, liked getting to know them through his eyes and memories.

Once they'd finished their meal, he bundled her up into her coat and pulled on his own. Hearing his cell ping, he checked it. "It's my mom," he told Quinley. "She somehow knows we're here—my guess is one of her friends reported we're on a date." Andaya kept a close eye on anything Isaiah-related. "She's asking if we'll stop by on the way home."

Quinley grinned. "So she can make sure I'm treating her baby boy right?"

"It's *you* she's worried about," he said, pocketing his phone. "She's not only a submissive mated to a dominant like you are, she entered an arranged mating just the same. She knows what comes with both situations." He began guiding his mate toward the door. "I've been warned by her several times not to screw this up."

"I like her. And your dad."

"They like you." The door opened just before they reached it, and a familiar couple waltzed inside. Isaiah nodded their way. "Valentina, James."

James smiled and went to speak, but his mate beat him to it—as per usual.

"Ah, it is good to see you both," Valentina declared, a hint of a Russian accent to her voice. "Quinley, I wanted to thank you for how much you have helped our Aurora. She was in terrible pain. My Alex and Bree were heartsore by it, and so exhausted." She raised a hand, all imperious. "Do not tell me there is no need to thank you. There is. And I have done it."

Quinley smiled fondly. "You really are supremely bossy."

"You don't know the half of it," James muttered.

Ignoring that, Valentina cocked her head at Quinley. "I heard your cat terrorizes your neighbors."

His mate pulled a face. "Would we call it terrorizing?"

Valentina blinked. "She stands on top of their fence and stares down at them, irritating their animals to extent that they shift to chase her off. Except it is as if she vanishes into thin air. They can never track her."

Quinley shrugged. "She's really just trying to make friends."

"Bah. She does not want friends. She wants to make it known to those around her that she will not make easy prey. I approve."

So did Isaiah. The neighbors who'd tried shooing her cat off by hissing or yelling at her often shortly afterward found "gifts" on their pillows, such as legless barely-alive spiders—something Quinley denied knowing anything about. But everyone knew her animal was to blame.

There was pallas cat mean, which basically involved trying to eat your face.

And there was black-foot mean, which typically meant circling back and sneaking into your house to either slit your throat or leave you icky stuff to freak you out.

Valentina's eyes narrowed. "It does make me curious about whether or not—"

"No," Isaiah cut in, sensing where this was going.

"What?" asked Valentina.

"You're wondering if your wolverine would be able to catch her. No way are we conducting that experiment," he stated firmly. "I like my mate alive and breathing." Wolverines were fucking vicious, and they didn't stop fighting until someone was dead.

Quinley let out a sound that was something between a snicker and a snort. "She'd *never* catch me."

Isaiah glared at her. "You're making this worse."

"My wolverine is wonderful tracker," Valentina warned.

Quinley smiled placidly. "Super. Also irrelevant. She'd never find my cat."

James stirred. "I agree it would be dangerous, but I admit to being curious myself—"

"No," Isaiah again interjected.

His mate looked up at him. "You have no faith in me?"

He pointed at her. "Don't twist this."

She only smiled again.

"Have you tried tracking her?" James asked him.

"Yes." He'd done it last night when he'd returned home from work to find her phone and keys in the house, indicating she'd gone for a run in her cat form.

James lifted a brow. "And?"

Isaiah ground his teeth. "And I may have failed."

Quinley snickered. "I warned you. You wouldn't listen."

She *had* warned him. More than once, actually. But he'd had faith in his abilities as a hunter to trace her location. It turned out he shouldn't have.

Valentina hummed. "Camden, I believe, is very good tracker."

Isaiah slashed a hand through the air. "We're not testing this with his tiger either." His inner feline was equally against her being hunted down that way.

Valentina's shoulders dropped. "You are so boring."

"I'm not boring, I'm protective. I've also met your wolverine many times. She's a menace who gets caught up in a hunt and plans only death for whatever she catches. Am I wrong?"

"No, but—"

"He's right," James told his mate, "it would be too risky."

"No, it wouldn't," Quinley piped up. "Because she'd fail."

Isaiah growled. "Quinley, for fuck's sake. You know exactly what you're doing."

She only chuckled.

Valentina shook her head. "I swear, Quinley, I did not realize he was so boring. I would have warned you before you mated him." The wolverine slid her gaze back to him. "A woman needs some adventure in her life. Thrills. Excitement."

"Being hunted by a wolverine isn't something anyone would term 'exciting,'" he insisted.

"*I* would," said Quinley.

He groaned, his head almost falling back in exasperation.

"There, you see," Valentina said to him, triumphant. "Dominant males and their overprotectiveness. *Yawn.*"

Quinley started to laugh, the minx.

# CHAPTER ELEVEN

B lair pulled a face at the complimentary pot of ketchup. "That's not something that would count as any kind of gift, let alone a Christmas present."

"Oh, I know," said Elle, bopping her head to the music coming from an idling car in the mall's parking lot.

"Wait, you don't *want* it to count?"

The redhead plopped the ketchup into one of her shopping bags. "No."

Blair turned to her. "But he's your brother."

"Half-brother."

"You and Damian have the exact same parents."

"Same mother," Elle corrected. "*His* father is Satan himself."

Quinley smiled against the inside of her coat collar, her face half-buried inside it to protect her skin from the cold.

Blair gave Elle a flat smile. "Hmm, Damian kind of looks like your dad."

"The Antichrist can take any form he chooses," said the redhead.

"Okay, how is it you think your mom came to have sex with Satan?" Blair challenged.

"He obviously fooled her into thinking he was my dad."

"Fooled her how?"

"The Devil can take any form he chooses."

Exasperation flickered across the bush dog's face.

Bree snickered. "Give up, Blair. Give up now. You're only hurting yourself."

The music faded away as the once-idling car drove off, adding to the traffic sounds of engines running, horns honking, brakes squealing, and wheels spinning.

The mall was incredibly busy, so the lot was a current hub of activity. Her cat didn't like it; wasn't fond of the assault to her senses. Streetlights flashed. Bushes rattled with the breeze. Puddles rippled. Laughter came from kids using a curb as a balance beam.

Thank God it was an indoor mall, because the weather was abysmal. Windy, cloudy, cold, and rainy. The rain had now died off, but the smell of ozone remained, overlaying the scents of car exhaust and wet pavement.

Quinley felt for the long cue of people stood at the taxi rank, exposed to the elements. Quinley and her pride mates were huddled under a shelter near the drop-off/pick-up area, waiting for Isaiah. He was on his way to collect them.

Shopping wise, it had been a productive day for Quinley—as evidenced by the amount of bags she was carrying. Her gloves provided a nice buffer between the skin of her palms and the dig of the bag handles.

Bree danced on the spot. "My feet are freezing."

So were Quinley's, courtesy of the cold concrete—the icy temperature was seeping through the soles of her boots. "We'll be gone from here soon, thankfully."

Bree grimaced. "Do you think I have time to pee before Isaiah gets here?"

"I doubt he'll arrive for another ten minutes or so," Quinley predicted. "The shit weather slows traffic down. Go, it's no biggie if he gets here before you're back. We won't mind waiting."

The woman apparently didn't need to be told twice, because she swiftly disappeared.

Watching her leave, Elle said, "Those bags have got to be heavy. She walks around with them effortlessly, like they're lighter than air. There's no lugging or heaving."

"Mom hands," said Quinley. "I swear, my mother used to easily carry armfuls of bags like they were empty." It was one of the few clear memories she had of her mom. Most weren't notable, just general things.

"I still can't quite believe Bree is a mom," Elle remarked, shaking her head. "It's so cute how much she's missed Aurora today."

"I miss Luke being at home more often," began Blair, "but it's imperative he locates the Vercetti Pack for Isaiah's sake. Those fuckers cannot be found soon enough."

"Amen," said Quinley, her cat in full agreement.

"I really do think someone's helping them hide," Elle commented. "Someone with influence, land, and power. Maybe anti-shifter extremists even."

Quinley pointed at her. "I hadn't considered it might be them, but yeah they'd *totally* help out any shifters who targeted the rest of our kind. Of course, they'll also stab the Vercetti assholes in the back eventually."

"Let's hope we manage to find them before that happens," said Blair.

"Luke will sulk if he doesn't get to have a personal hand in ending their lives and ... Oh my God, I almost didn't see you there."

Tracking the Beta female's gaze, Quinley noticed a tall, very good-looking blond slow to a halt several feet away as his eyes clashed with Blair's. Definitely a shifter, going by his fluid walk and how he carried himself.

He was quite a specimen, and he sure dressed well. Tailored suit, long cashmere coat, shoes that looked to be Italian leather. The shopping bag he carried featured the logo of a very expensive designer store. The dude obviously had money.

Blair walked over to him, leaving the shelter. With all the noise, there was no way to hear what they started to talk about. His cool-blue gaze briefly flicked to where Quinley and Elle stood. And that gaze paused on the redhead, narrowing in ... recognition?

Quinley looked at her, only then noticing that the female pallas cat had pinned her gaze on something straight ahead, her cheeks flushing. "Who's that?"

Elle blinked. "What? Who?"

"Oh, are we playing the, *I don't know who he is* game? I can go along with that, if you want."

For long moments, Elle continued to stare straight ahead. But then she sighed at Quinley. "You don't push," she complained. "You're supposed to push so it'll be easier for me to get it all out."

Stifling a smile, Quinley nudged her. "Elle, offload; you'll feel better, I promise."

Elle rolled her eyes. "All right, if you're going to badger me about it." She turned to fully face Quinley, probably so that the guy wouldn't be able to read her lips or anything. "You know Enigma?"

"The shifter club?"

"Yes. That guy, Gabriel, co-owns it. He's a silent partner."

"Really?" Interesting. The club was not only exclusive to shifters, it was a place where they could go to ... well, get laid. Like *anywhere* in the club, even on the dance floor.

"He's also a childhood friend of Blair's," Elle continued. "They were part of the same pack until he went to live with his human uncle as a kid after his parents were killed. He lives as a human now. Enigma seems to be the only connection he has to the shifter world."

"How do you know him?" Because it was obvious that they knew each other to some extent.

Elle poked her tongue into the inside of her cheek. "I met him at the club. We fucked, no exchange of names. But I knew who he was because I recognized his photo—it was passed around the pride back when Luke thought Gabriel might have been the person stalking Blair."

"Someone *stalked* her?" What the fuck?

"Don't worry, they're very dead. Forget about that. Focus on me. I'm more important right now."

Quinley snorted. "Okay. So, does Blair know you slept with him?"

"Nope. And, uh …"

"What?"

Elle cleared her throat. "I didn't tell Gabriel that I knew any of what I just told you. I acted like I didn't know anything about him."

"I see." Quinley flicked a look at him. Going by his expression … "Well, I'd say he's fast figuring out that that might not be true."

"Yeah," muttered the redhead.

"I doubt he'll be pissed that you know all that, though. Do you think he will?"

"Maybe not pissed, as such. But I think Gabriel likes to not be *seen*. Likes shifters he sleeps with to not know his name or anything else about him. So it might irritate him that I knew him. And he probably won't like that I played dumb. It meant he was at a slight disadvantage when we met, and no one likes finding stuff out *after* the fact."

True. "Why would he not want to be seen?"

"It was just the feeling I got. I've met people at Enigma before who just want a fast, emotionless fuck—it's not uncommon that names aren't exchanged. But it was different with him. I can't really explain it. Though it may just be that he's only that way with shifters, given he's intent on living as a human—I don't know." Elle paused. "He's not like anyone I've ever met. He's sort of, I don't know, *flat*."

"Flat?"

"Emotionally, I mean. He doesn't much react to anything. Which I find inexplicably appealing. Apparently, he was always 'different'. Blair's word, not mine." Elle puffed out a breath. "I really didn't expect him to come onto me."

"Why?" The female pallas cat was gorgeous.

"He has a type. Submissive leggy redheads. I'm not a submissive shifter."

"But you're not very dominant, so maybe that counts for him."

Elle gave a lazy shrug. "Maybe."

"When did you have your little encounter with him at Enigma?"

"About two hours after Joaquin broke things off with me a few weeks ago." Elle hummed at whatever she saw in Quinley's expression. "You heard about that, huh?"

"A little." The pride's grapevine worked at top speed. "I didn't ask for details. I knew you'd tell me yourself if you ever wanted to." Quinley grimaced as wind blew under the shelter, slapped at her face and ears, and whipped up her ponytail.

"You're supposed to push," Elle reminded her, annoyed.

Amused, Quinley's cat twitched her tail. "Oh, yeah, sorry. Elle, will you just tell me already?"

"All right, fine, don't go getting yourself all wound up." Elle sighed. "I've had a thing for Joaquin for years, but he's a close friend. I didn't want to cross that line in case it all went south and messed up our friendship. But then I saw how Aspen and Camden are. Did you know they were friends for years before they mated?"

"Aspen once made a passing reference to it."

"They held back, kept things platonic—both worried they'd otherwise shit all over a friendship they treasure. But they took a risk and it paid off. So I decided to do the same. Only it didn't pay off for me."

If what Quinley had heard was accurate, Joaquin had called it off, claiming that they were better off just being friends. He hadn't used the word "regret," but he might as well have done. And wouldn't that sting like a bitch?

"He wants us to still be friends. So do I. But it's *hard*."

Sympathy squashing her chest, Quinley crossed to the redhead, put her bags at her feet, and then hugged the woman tight.

Elle grunted. "Fucking submissives."

"A hug won't kill you." The woman was practically *screaming* for one.

"I want to shove you away but then I'll feel bad because it's like kicking a puppy."

"We can pretend I'm forcing the hug on you if you want."

"I'd appreciate that."

Quinley eventually stepped back but kept one palm on Elle's back. "Trust me when I say that I know it sucks large to want someone you can't have. Especially when you can't completely distance yourself from that person. But it does get easier."

"It stopped being hard for you to be away from your true mate?"

"Yup. Now it doesn't bother me at all. Maybe things will be better for you once you've moved on. But you can't do that fully until you let go of Joaquin."

Just then, Bree reappeared. "So what are we talking about?" Her gaze sharpened as it danced from Quinley to Elle. "It looks like it might be interesting."

"Not really," mumbled Elle. "I was just telling her about what happened between me and Joaquin. I didn't want to talk about it, but she wouldn't let it drop—she's so nosy. I figured she might as well hear the full story from me."

Bree exchanged an amused look with Quinley, obviously knowing her friend well enough to know that no such nagging had been necessary to make Elle spill.

"Where's Blair?" asked Bree.

Picking up her bags, Quinley looked the bush dog's way, realizing ... "On her way over." And she wasn't alone.

Her mouth curved, Blair said, "I just wanted to introduce you three to an old pack mate of mine, Gabriel. We were friends as kids. Gabriel, this is Elle, Bree, and Quinley."

He inclined his head in greeting, his gaze settling on Elle. "You look familiar." It didn't appear to be a genuine comment, more of a taunt. Like he was fucking with her.

"As do you," said Elle. "Weird." Apparently, she'd decided to fuck with him right back.

At that very moment, a familiar SUV pulled up at the curb.

Quinley felt her pulse jump. "Here's Isaiah." *Thank the Lord above.* She was freezing. She joined the others in walking straight over.

Leaving the engine running, he unfolded from the vehicle, as always looking far too gorgeous to exist. Her cat, pleased to see him, eagerly got to her feet.

"Isaiah, this is my old pack mate, Gabriel," said Blair.

The male bush dog stared at him steadily. "Now I can put a name to the face of one of the cats who used to watch my building when they thought I might have been a danger to Blair."

Quinley's cat wrinkled her nose. There was something about his voice. It was just so toneless. So lacking in emotion. Now Quinley got what Elle meant by "flat."

"I appreciate any part you played in finding out who her stalker was," Gabriel added.

"No thanks necessary." Isaiah turned to Quinley, took in the sight of all her bags, and then his mouth curved. "So you don't like shopping, then," he mocked.

"Idiot."

He smiled. "Your nose is all red."

"I'm cold."

He pressed a kiss to her mouth, his lips delightfully warm, and then tipped his chin toward the SUV's front passenger door. "Hop inside, I switched on the heated seats."

Oh, he was a gem. As he swiped her bags from her, she pointed at him, "Do *not* peek in them."

"Would I spoil my Christmas surprise that way?"

"Yes. Patient though you are, the fact is you don't like to wait for anything."

"I find it's a dominant male thing," remarked Bree.

They exchanged goodbyes with Gabriel, who gave Elle one last long look before striding off.

"You're right," Quinley whispered to the redhead, "he's very detached. Like he's dissociated from life."

"He's had it hard," Elle murmured, "but I don't think trauma made him that way. As I said earlier, Blair swore he was always different."

Finally sliding into the SUV, Quinley sighed in pleasure as the warmth of the vehicle washed over her. The heat coming from the seat was an added bonus. By the time Isaiah had dropped her shopping buddies at their respective apartment buildings, she was feeling cozily warm.

Inside the house, she went straight upstairs to put away her purchases. She also stashed Isaiah's gifts somewhere he'd never find them.

Returning downstairs, she went to the kitchen, intending to make a hot drink. She was about to call out to Isaiah and ask if he wanted one, but then his scent breezed into the room. A half-smile curved her mouth, and she parted her lips to speak. The words didn't come out, replaced by a gasp as his hand fisted the back of her hair.

He roughly spun her to face the kitchen island and shoved her forward, pinning her front flat to its surface. Her hands shot out in surprise—one gripping the end of the island on her right, the other gripping the edge above her head.

*Well.*

His body heat pressed into her back as he curled over her and put his mouth to her ear. "Don't move. Don't speak. Don't come until I say."

Sheer dominance looped through every harshly spoken word, planting hooks in her mind, compelling her to obey, snaring her cat's focus. It also triggered a chemical reaction that woke up Quinley's nerve-endings, revved her sexual engines, and made her body relax for him.

She'd never be able to adequately describe how such expressions of dominance could seize her focus and have such a physical impact on her. It was just so instinctual, so automatic. Like a preprogrammed response encoded in her DNA. She suspected only other submissives would really understand.

Isaiah released her hair, snapped open the fly of her jeans, and dragged both them and her panties down to her knees. Then suddenly one of her legs were free, he kicked both apart.

And plunged two fingers inside her.

*Oh, fuck.*

Every pump of his fingers was hard but shallow, delicious but teasing. Having no way to find purchase with her feet, since the tips of her toes barely brushed the tiled floor, she held tight to the edges of the island.

Isaiah roughly shoved the back of her sweater all the way up to her nape. His fingers whispered over patches of her flesh, and she knew he was tracing the bites, bruises, and scratches there. Every touch was gentle but so damn *entitled.* Her cat loved it.

He drove the fingers inside her deeper with a growl. "Your skin is painted with my marks. My own personal masterpiece."

Her feline melted under the force of his dominance, so drawn by it she edged forward. Quinley felt the brush of fur just beneath her skin, smelt the feral edge in her scent signaling her animal's closeness.

A long, drawn-out snarl came from Isaiah. Both his hands disappeared. A zipper lowered. Something hard, hot, and long slapped her ass.

He glided the head of his cock between her wet folds. "All day I've been thinking about this pussy. Filling it. Using it. Feeling it drench my dick when you come."

Isaiah clamped a hand on her hip and ruthlessly slammed his hips forward, forcing her to accept every inch of his cock. *Needing* her to take it. Her tight pussy spasmed around him and, fuck, he could come right then.

But he didn't.

He planted his free hand on her nape to hold her in place. "This is gonna be fast." He rode her hard, his pace almost rabid.

He hadn't lied. Throughout the day, his thoughts had so often drifted to fucking her that they'd bordered on obsessive. His instincts—again powered by the absence of the bond—had driven him to hunt her, bring her back to their den, take her over and over and over.

He'd texted her several times, unable to resist; needing that connection; trying to let the exchange of messages be enough. The chaos in his mind and body had eased off once he'd picked her up from the lot, his system satisfied now that she was back in his possession.

Still, he now had her bent over the island as he plowed into her. Why? Because he needed it. Not because they lacked a bond, not because primitive instincts were fucking with him. But because he'd come to crave this—how she yielded to him, how her pussy felt around his cock, how he could finally *be*.

He upped his pace, brutally pounding into her, urged on by her soft, trembly moans. "You needed this, didn't you?" he gritted out. "I did. Needed to shoot my come where it belongs."

She whimpered, her inner walls heating and tightening.

Sensing she was close, he squeezed her hip, letting her feel the prick of his claws. "Go on, you can come. Do it now."

She did. Her head snapped up, a rough scream grated her throat, and her pussy all but strangled him.

A growl escaped through his gritted teeth. "Good. Fucking. Girl." All finesse, control, and rhythm disappeared as he fucked her harder, pursuing his own release.

Then he found it.

The thrashing current whipped through his body and shot up his shaft as he exploded, filling her with all he had.

When his release finally subsided, he pressed a kiss to the back of her shoulder. "You good?"

Panting, she made a committal sound. "Feel free to do that again any time you want."

He smiled. "That's the plan."

# CHAPTER TWELVE

Jerking away from the woman sniffing her, Quinley frowned. "What are you doing?"

"You smell like Isaiah, but it's not that his scent is embedded in your skin like with imprinting," said Raya. "It's more like he rubbed himself over every inch of you before you left the house."

Quinley returned to scrubbing the bath of her grooming station, which she'd just used to bathe a wild-dog shifter. "I didn't get a shower this morning, since I had one last night. He likes me to wear one of his tees for bed, so ..." And yes, there'd been some rubbing.

It had been subtle—his cheek grazing hers, a nuzzle to her neck, a long stroke of her hair. But it had been obvious that he was scent-marking her.

She hadn't minded. Her cat liked it a lot. In fact, the animal had wanted to return the favor. But Quinley hadn't had enough time to shift and let her cat spend time with him.

Raya leaned back against the wall. "You all done with your Christmas shopping yet?"

"Pretty much." Quinley gave her the side-eye. "Are you still sulking that I went without you last weekend?"

"Well, it wasn't fair."

*Eye roll.* Considering it was now Wednesday, you would think that the woman had gotten over it by now. Particularly since ... "I asked you *and* Adaline to come. You were both busy."

"I know, but I feel left out." Raya pouted. "And neglected."

"I've already said that the three of us should go shopping together sometime soon. You sniffed and said, 'No thank you.'"

"It's not like I really meant it."

Quinley sighed at her. "Can you not be happy for me that I've managed to make friends within my new pride?"

Raya lifted a finger. "Okay, first of all, it was inevitable that you'd make friends. You do that without trying. Like it's your super power. Second of all, yes, I'm happy for you. It's a huge relief to me that you're settling in so fast so well."

"But?"

"But I like to whine. It makes me feel alive. You know this already."

Quinley plopped the scouring pad at the side of the bath, teasing, "And you wonder why Adaline loves me more."

Raya gaped. "Hey!"

Quinley chuckled. "I'm kidding, I'm kidding. You *know* I'm kidding. You're just taking the opportunity to whine. Again."

"Can't help it."

Wiping her hands on a small towel, Quinley said, "That's me done for the day. My last client had to cancel."

"She was also meant to have her hair and nails done, so we're all finished. But Lori's taking the opportunity to have her roots sorted while Adaline's got time. You might as well head out, though. No point in you hanging around for no reason."

"I can sweep and stuff."

"Already done. I'd leave, too, if I wasn't waiting for Lori." Raya pushed away from the wall. "Now go. Shoo. Spend some quality time with your pallas cat."

"He won't be home yet, he works enforcer shifts. But I'm not going to fight leaving early. My cat could do with a run."

So Quinley put on her coat, grabbed the snack that Isaiah had earlier slipped into her bag, and hooked the strap of said bag over her shoulder. Once she'd said her goodbyes, she headed out, biting into her candy bar as she did.

Crossing the road to head for her parked car, she noticed a group of males were hanging at the nearby corner of the road. They appeared to be merely talking among themselves, minding their own business ... but something about their body language was a little *too* casual.

Her scalp prickled, and a sense of unease wrapped around her lungs. She didn't tell herself she was being paranoid, she paid closer attention to the group. They seemed to be pointedly avoiding looking her way ... as if they were trying not to set off her internal alarms.

As she reached the curb, one male edged to his left slightly and she got a clear view of another face. A face she recognized from the warning posters that had been passed around.

Her heart slammed against her ribs. *Fuck.* It was Sebastian Vercetti.

The pack must have somehow seen her with Isaiah and decided to target her in lieu of him, because it was just too damn coincidental that they were loitering near her place of work.

Her car was too far away, as was the salon. The guys would reach her and drag her into their vehicle before she could get to either. And if she *did* somehow make it to the salon, they'd only barge inside and potentially hurt her family. She couldn't have that. So, as Sebastian's attention locked on her, she did the only sensible thing.

She shifted.

Panicked, the little cat leaped out of the puddle of clothes and sprinted toward the parking area.

"*Get her!*"

She heard growls and snarls and the thundering of paws. Heard boots pounding and voices yelling. The cat kept running, too fast for them to catch.

But they kept coming.

She galloped passed the parked cars and sprinted down an alley. A chain-link fence waited there. A well-timed jump had her halfway up the fence. She scrambled up the rest of it and jumped down into a grassy area.

Curses and growls came from behind her as she darted across the stretch of land. She heard the fence rattling, heard boots thumping the ground, heard those same boots chasing after her again.

A crack of thunder split the air.

Bark flew off a tree.

*Bullet.*

The cat weaved through bushes and trees, making herself a difficult target as bullets showered the area.

Hot fire punched into her back leg. She staggered. Ignored the pain. Kept running. Sped her pace.

More fire whizzed across her ear.

With an inner hiss of fury, she sped her pace.

*Badger hole.*

The cat crossed to it fast and dived inside. The tunnel was narrow, but her small body easily made its way through the—

Thuds peppered the ground above the tunnel.

*More bullets.*

She hurried through the channel, confident the other shifters couldn't fit into the slim passage but still not wanting to slow down.

The cat came to a junction. Turned left. Ran and ran, still ignoring the pain in her leg.

Home. She needed to get home.

I saiah sighed at his mother. "Will you stop fussing? There's no need. All is good."

Sniffing, she moved aside to let a pedestrian pass. "I'm not fussing."

He ushered her near the wall, out of the way of the people walking up and down the sidewalk. "Yes, you are. You're fretting over how there's no imprint bond yet. *You're* the one who told me to be patient; that you can't rush it."

"I know. And I'm not worried the bond won't form. I'm just eager to see you settled."

Sensing by her shifty expression that there was more to it, he folded his arms. "What's going on?"

Andaya absently pulled at her earlobe. "I bumped into Cherrie."

Both he and his cat went motionless.

Distress lining her face, Andaya continued, "She knows you're mated. I don't know who told her, but you can be sure she's not pleased about it. She wants only misery for you."

"What did she say?" Because the woman had obviously said *something* that had his mother all wound up.

"That she feels sorry for 'the girl' for having unknowingly bound herself to a cold-blooded killer." Andaya wrung her gloved hands. "Cherrie 'suggested' maybe someone should tell her. What if she makes it her business to find out who Quinley is? What if she approaches her?"

His cat's upper lip quivered at the idea of it. "I'll be seriously fucking pissed if Cherrie goes near her." So pissed he'd want to burn shit down. "But there's nothing she'd be able to reveal that Quinley doesn't already know. I gave her the full story."

"Yes, but Cherrie wouldn't give her the *real* story; she'd talk complete rubbish. She can be convincing. You know that. She had a whole bunch of people on her side until Vinnie revealed he'd identified the culprit as Eddie."

Tate caught his eye from further down the street, where he stood with Deke and JP. The Alpha lifted an *Everything okay?* brow.

Isaiah gave a subtle nod of reassurance.

"I told her that your mate is well-aware of everything. Cherrie said, 'She might know *his* version, but not the truth.'"

"Mom, I get why you'd worry that Cherrie could cause problems for me— she's damn good at it. But I don't for a second believe that she'd make Quinley come round to her way of thinking."

Andaya tilted her head. "What makes you so sure?"

He hesitated. "I won't give you the full story—it's Quinley's to share or not to share. But she's been the subject of bullshit rumors herself. She's wise to what such liars are like. Wise to how manipulative they are. Cherrie would not find her whatsoever easy to fool."

Andaya's face went soft. "I'm sorry to hear Quinley had to deal with that. No one should have to. And Cherrie ..." Trailing off, she sighed.

He settled a reassuring hand on his mother's shoulder. "I don't actually think that Cherrie will go near her."

"You don't?"

"No. Her Alpha male is tough, but he fears Tate—he'd be furious with any pride member who caused trouble for one of ours. She'll know that. She has probably even been warned to keep her distance from us, given our history. If I was her Alpha, I would have issued such a warning. My guess is that Cherrie just wanted to mess with our heads—it's kind of her thing."

Andaya frowned, thoughtful. "You're right. She probably just took the opportunity to bitchily make us worry."

Hearing his phone begin to chime, Isaiah told her, "I have to take this. Now, don't go stressing yourself out over what Cherrie said. All will be fine."

She gave a weak smile and nodded. "Okay."

He walked off and pulled his phone out of his pocket. *Quinley*. He tapped his thumb on the screen and answered, "Hey, you good?"

"Isaiah, this is Adaline."

He stopped in his tracks at the shake in her voice. "Why are you using Quinley's cell?" he asked, dread taking root in his belly. "Why doesn't she have it?"

"As she left work to go to her car, I noticed her shift across the road and flee," replied Adaline, her words coming sharp and fast. "A group of guys chased her. Some shifted into wolves."

Isaiah's blood ran cold, and his cat froze. *Fuck*. He bolted down the street, heading for the cul-de-sac.

"She sprinted past the lot opposite the salon. She seemed to be heading in the general direction of the park behind it ... but after that I don't know. She *will* have gotten away, Isaiah. Whoever they are, they won't have found her. There's no way they'd have managed that."

"I'll call you back when I find her." He hung up, running faster, panic powering every step.

"Hey," Tate called out as he, Deke, and JP caught up to him, "what's happening?"

"Quinley's on the run in her cat form," Isaiah replied, turning into the cul-de-sac. "Fucking shifters are chasing her."

A curse burst out of Deke.

"Where about is she?" asked Tate, his face hard.

"No clue." Nearing his car, Isaiah unlocked it with the fob. "She ran past the lot where she leaves her car and seemed to be going in the direction of the park behind it—that's all her sister knows." He ragged open the driver's door and hopped into the seat, unsurprised when the other three males slid into the vehicle with him.

Isaiah dumped his phone in the cupholder, gunned the engine, and then sped out of the cul-de-sac. His cat hissed at him, insisting he go faster; intent on getting to the feline they'd claimed as theirs. Because yeah, Isaiah might have been the one to do the branding, but his cat had come to mentally claim her—he just hadn't realized it until that moment.

"Either Zaire's mate targeted her, feeling a little bitter," said Tate, riding shotgun. "Or it was the Vercetti Pack."

Isaiah had already considered both possibilities.

"If it's the brothers," began Deke, "they might have done this to lure Isaiah into a spot where they're better able to get to him."

Isaiah felt his grip tighten on the steering wheel. "Or they mean to either kill her or offer a trade—her for me."

"I don't think they'll have her," said Tate. "Black-foots run at the speed of fucking light. I've seen Quinley's cat run—she's no exception."

No, she wasn't. His woman was like a goddamn blur when she went at full speed. "But the pack carries guns," Isaiah reminded him, sharply taking a turn. "They could've shot her."

"More than bullets would be needed to take down a black-foot and you know it," said Tate, his tone firm, insisting Isaiah *think*, not panic.

But how the fuck could he not panic, especially when ... "Bullets could have slowed her down enough that they—"

"Don't go there. We don't even know they're definitely armed. Let's operate on the assumption that she got away. We won't be able to track her, but we can track whoever chased her."

That was exactly what they did, following the scents of wolf and gunpowder—and yeah, the latter made the bottom fall out of his stomach— eventually ending up in the park that Adaline had mentioned. There was grass, bushes, trees, an old rusty kids playground. But there was no Quinley.

Isaiah clenched his fists. "Where the fuck is she?"

"The wolves seemed to have paused here and then backtracked," said JP, studying the ground.

"Maybe Quinley's cat disappeared down there," mused Deke, pointing at a hole. "It would explain why someone seemed to have been shooting at the ground here. It might have been some desperate attempt to hit her with a bullet, hoping it would penetrate the earth."

His cat hissed, furious that she'd been shot at. Isaiah crouched near the hole and shouted, "Quinley! Quinley!"

Nothing.

Squatting beside him, JP sniffed. "I don't scent her."

"You wouldn't. Her scent trail disappears as fast as she does." Isaiah shot to his feet. "It's fucking uncanny."

"Nature tends to give the smaller breeds cool defenses to compensate for how vulnerable their size can make them to bigger creatures," Tate reminded him.

Deke set his hands on his hips. "Our cats are just a little too big to make their way through that tunnel. It's a shame Bailey ain't with us. She would have fit."

"Why didn't Quinley run back to the salon?" asked JP as he stood upright.

"The pack would have just chased her inside and then possibly killed everyone in there," said Tate. "She did the right thing by shifting and taking off. She had more chance of losing them than she did of taking them on."

Isaiah's phone started to ring. He pulled it out of his pocket and saw that it was Havana. "Yeah?" he answered, his tone clipped.

"Thought you might want to know that your mate just appeared at my door," she told him.

Isaiah went very still, the knots in his gut beginning to loosen. "She all right?" he gritted out.

Havana hesitated. "Uh …"

And like that, the knots inside him went tighter. "*Is she all right?*"

"She's been shot, but she's okay."

*Motherfucker.* His cat clawed at Isaiah's insides, needing an outlet for his anger.

"Helena's on her way to my house as we speak—Aspen just got off the phone with her. Quinley will be healed by the time you get back."

Isaiah drew in a breath that did nothing to calm him. His mate was alive, she was out of the pack's hands, but she'd taken a fucking *bullet*. "Put her on the phone."

"I would, but I haven't managed to coax her cat to shift back yet."

He cursed. "Don't leave her side, Havana." He needed to know that someone he trusted was with her.

"She will remain under my watchful eye until you get back, I promise." The line went dead.

Isaiah looked at Tate, who was fast approaching him. "She's at your house. Just arrived."

"And?" prodded the Alpha, falling into step beside him as Isaiah hurried back the way they came.

"And she took a bullet."

Tate swore. "She's alive, Isaiah."

"Yeah," he bit out, wanting to feel relieved but all he could taste was fury.

As they reached the car, Tate spoke, "Deke, JP—track the scents of the pack, find out where they went. Me and Isaiah are gonna go and check on Quinley."

As they both slid into the vehicle, Isaiah gave the Alpha a sideways look. "You don't have to stay with me, I'm not going to do anything stupid."

"I'm not leaving you on your own while you're like this."

Isaiah started the engine and pulled out onto the road. "Like what?"

"Mentally all over the place. You think I don't know how you're feeling? Havana was once shot out in the open, remember? I was ready to blow by the time I got to her."

Isaiah remembered. It was he and Deke who'd sensed the danger and yelled at her to duck. They'd also watched over her until Tate had arrived.

"I'm not going to blow." Because Quinley needed him to be calm.

"But you're probably going to start blaming yourself for this. Don't."

*Too late.* "I should have waited before mating her," muttered Isaiah. "I should have made sure we'd dealt with the Vercetti Pack first."

"If you'd have waited, she'd have mated someone else," Tate pointed out.

The thought of that made Isaiah's breath catch and his pacing cat halt.

"Quinley wasn't in a position to give you time. You didn't do anything wrong. *The pack* is in the wrong, not you."

"Why is it so hard to find them?"

"I don't know," replied Tate, his voice dark. "But they can't hide forever."

It wasn't long before Isaiah was once more parking in his driveway. He all but leaped out of the car and then jogged to the Alpha pair's house. The front door opened before they got to it, revealing Havana. She waved them inside, saying, "She's in the den."

Isaiah stalked into the room, and his belly roiled. Quinley sat in an armchair in clothes a little too big for her, her skin far too pale. *Blood loss,* he thought.

She stood as she saw him, her expression going soft. "Hey."

Isaiah made a beeline for her, ignoring everyone else in the room. He took her face between his hands, a growl rumbling in his chest at the faint smell of blood that clung to her—a growl that came from both him and his cat.

"You were shot?" The words came out guttural.

She placed a palm on his chest. "In my cat's hindleg. Bullet went straight through. Helena healed me."

He skated his hands up to her hair, pinning it back to fully expose her face, needing to just *look* at her. "Who shot you?"

"I'm not sure who held the gun, but it was someone from the Vercetti Pack."

His teeth snapped together. *Bastards.* "What exactly happened?"

"As I was heading to my car, I noticed a group of guys and … I just knew something wasn't right. Then I recognized one of the faces. It was Sebastian Vercetti. I shifted and ran, knowing it was my best chance of escape. They followed but couldn't catch up to my cat. All the shots went wide bar one. She disappeared down a badger tunnel."

"We figured your cat used it to escape. We noticed it when tracking the wolves."

"When she got out of it, she tried getting into our house but it was all locked up tight, so she came here."

He carefully let her hair fall back to her shoulders and topple down her back. "The wolves seemed to have backtracked after your cat did her disappearing act."

"Not surprised. They had no way of knowing where she'd pop out. Did you track their scents to see where they headed afterward?"

"Deke and JP are on it."

"I called Deke about ten minutes ago," Bailey cut in from the sofa. "He said the scents vanished in an alley. Looks like the pack left in two four by fours."

Isaiah felt his nostrils flare. The fuckers had gotten away yet again, and so now the threat to Quinley was still very real. Curving an arm around her neck, he hauled her closer.

"I'm okay," she said, leaning into him.

"Not the point," Isaiah bit off. "I thought they would come for me, not you."

She lightly pinched his arm. "Stop feeling guilty. This isn't your fault. Dominants are strong, but they aren't all-powerful. You can't control other people's actions. The pack did what they did because they wanted to, and because they're assholes—plain and simple."

"What she said," muttered Aspen, pointing at Quinley.

"Listen to your mate, Isaiah," Tate ordered. "Don't take the weight of this."

*Easier said than done.* He tightened his hold on Quinley and spoke against her hair, "I'll kill them. I'll fucking kill them."

Her arms looped around him. "I know you will. I know."

# CHAPTER THIRTEEN

Waking to her alarm the following morning, Quinley leaned over and turned it off. Letting her head loll to the side, she saw she was alone in bed. Her brow knitted at the very unusual occurrence. And then, just as she was extending her senses to detect if Isaiah was in the attached bathroom, memories of yesterday rolled over her.

Quinley felt her lips flatten. That goddamn sorry excuse for a pack needed executing *fast*. She couldn't lie, it had given her a little scare to have them come at her that way—guns, claws, teeth, and all. But as she'd sat in the Alpha's house waiting for Isaiah to return from trying to locate her, fury had settled in. And it hadn't left.

It had, however, eased under the warmth of Isaiah's attentiveness. He'd stayed at her side all evening, broody and quiet. He'd showered her, cleaning every inch of her himself. He'd then dressed her, carefully brushed her wet hair, and sat her at the kitchen island with a mug of tea while he made dinner.

A mini argument had ensued when she'd tried stacking the dishwasher—he hadn't wanted her to lift a finger. She'd subsided, sensing he not only needed to feel he was taking care of her, he needed to feel *in control*. And it had allowed him to give all the protective anger tumbling around his system some release.

Several people had come to check on her, including his parents and both her sisters—who'd also kindly returned her bag and clothes—but he hadn't let any of them stay long, insisting she needed to rest. None had argued, all sensing the *real* problem was that his protective instincts were in a tailspin and driving him to keep everyone at bay.

When he'd finally taken her to bed, he hadn't fucked her; just held her close. She might have protested, but she'd sensed he hadn't trusted that he wouldn't lose all control. She actually wouldn't have minded if he had lost it, but *he* would have minded. He would have later regretted it and been upset with himself. She hadn't wanted that, so she'd let it alone, planning to wake him in style come morning.

Except … he wasn't here. And if her senses could be trusted, he wasn't in the attached bathroom either.

It surprised her that he was awake. He hadn't slept well. She'd woken several times due to how restless he'd been, too in tune with his moods to sleep through it.

Her own cat had been just as restless. She still was, as it happened. Fleeing for her life wasn't exactly a common occurrence in her world. That the danger to both her and Isaiah hadn't yet been taken out … yeah, the feline *really* wasn't happy.

Making a decision that brought the animal just a *little* relief, Quinley took her phone from the nightstand and rattled off a quick text to Adaline. She then sluggishly sat upright, yawning. Her sister's response came fast. Satisfied by it, Quinley left the bed and then went on about her morning business.

Finally presentable, she padded downstairs and tracked Isaiah down to the kitchen. He stood near the sink, his gaze on whatever he could see through the window above it. His shoulders were stiff, and his body was a mass of tension.

Turning on sensing her presence, he frowned on seeing her in her sweats.

"I'm not going into work today," she explained.

His shoulders lowered, losing their stiffness, and his eyes drifted shut. "You don't have to stay home just because my protective instincts are going nuts." He opened his eyes, both relief and conflict swirling in their depths. "I was planning on going to the salon with you and hanging out there to keep an eye on things. Tate already okayed it."

"I figured you'd have that in mind. But my cat is a little too wound up to deal with a lot of company today. I'm not sure she'd want strangers near her."

Isaiah crossed to her, his gaze delving into hers, searching. "Yeah, I see her looking all agitated and edgy."

"A day at home where she feels safe should settle her down."

He skated one hand along her upper arm, over her shoulder, up her neck, and then skimmed it over her ear as he sank his fingers in her hair. "I'll stay here with you."

Loosely gripping the sides of his tee, she opened her mouth to protest, not for a moment expecting him to neglect his responsibilities just to keep her company.

"I won't be able to focus for shit if we're apart today, not even knowing you're here at home. Your cat isn't the only one feeling edgy."

Quinley bit the inside of her cheek. "Okay."

He cruised the pads of his fingers over her scalp in a slow, circular, soothing motion. "I'll be coming with you to work tomorrow. I won't get in your way. I just want to stand guard."

"That's fine. I don't think the pack will strike in the same place twice, but I'd rather not take chances. I really don't feel like getting shot again."

His expression turning sober, he caught her face with his hands. "That won't happen."

She ran her fingertip along the shadow beneath his eye. "You didn't sleep well."

"No," he readily admitted in a murmur. With a sigh, he pressed his forehead to hers. "I didn't think you'd matter this much to me this quickly. Didn't even realize how much you'd come to matter until yesterday."

Her chest squeezed, warming. Before she could share that it wasn't a one-way street, he was talking again.

"You should know that my cat is now fully on board." Isaiah righted his head. "He doesn't just consider you his because I branded you. He considers you *his*, brand aside."

Relief, delight, and affection flowed through her. Her lips curved. "You know how to cheer a girl up."

"Oh, you shouldn't be smiling. You thought he was protective before? It's just gone up several notches. He's also gone from slightly possessive to full-on territorial. To the point where if I were to let him out now, he'd bite you to leave his own mark. And if I was to let him and your cat have time together, he'd bite her too. Probably fuck her at the same time."

"Stop, you're turning me on."

His lips twitched into a smile. "I never quite know what you're gonna say."

Her stomach chose that moment to rumble, annoyingly breaking the soppy spell that was brewing in the air.

He released her face. "Sit. I'm going to feed you."

"I can do—" She stopped when he raised a bossy brow, clearly intent on still babying her for a while. "All right."

Satisfaction lit his gaze. "Better answer."

They ate at the breakfast bar as usual, both taking their time, in no rush to get gone. They then stacked the dishwasher and made their way into the living room.

"I say we have a lazy day," Isaiah proposed, weaving his fingers through hers.

"It really does sound intriguing, but I'm not good at being lazy."

"I'll fuck any excess energy out of you."

She smiled. "I like where this is going."

Isaiah chuckled. That he could even feel amusement when his system was so chaotic was a testament to just how soothing her very presence was to him. "My plans are simple. We relax, watch TV, fuck …" He let his sentence trail off as loud voices came from outside.

"Neighbors arguing again?"

"Maybe." But maybe not. Still wound tight from the fuck-up yesterday, he wasn't going to dismiss any disturbance. He released her hand and strode to the window, intending to check. What he saw made his jaw harden. "Motherfucker."

"What's wrong?" asked Quinley, sidling up to him. "Isn't it … You've *got* to be kidding me. What the hell is he doing here?"

Good question. The last place Zaire should be was the bottom of their driveway arguing with Deke, who was blocking his path. Isaiah hadn't seen the guy before in real life, but he recognized him from the photos he'd circulated among the pride when warning them to keep a lookout for the male black-foot.

His cat unsheathed his claws, eager to draw blood. The animal was already in one hell of a shitty mood after the attack on Quinley. He wanted to badly track, maim, and kill those who'd dared shoot her. The asshole outside would *definitely* make a good alternative.

Unfortunately, it would be considered an overreaction unless Zaire was here to challenge Isaiah for Quinley—that wasn't likely. But Isaiah would certainly have his say and order the asshole to get gone and never return.

"Stay inside, Quinley." Isaiah stalked into the hallway, determination in every step.

She hurried after him. "Wait, you—"

"Baby," he began, turning toward her, not missing how her expression softened at the endearment. "I need you to do as I say. He's obviously here to see you. That ain't happening."

"I wasn't going to go outside, only stand in the doorway and tell him to go; make it clear this was a wasted journey."

"But it won't have been a wasted journey if he gets to interact with you. If he even so much as sees you, he's effectively being rewarded for hauling ass *to our home*—somewhere he has no right to be."

She blinked. "I didn't think about it like that."

Sensing her acquiescence, he gave the side of her neck an appreciative squeeze. "I won't be long." Isaiah left the house, closing the door behind him.

The sound made Zaire's gaze snap to him. A gaze that didn't once shift from Isaiah as he descended the porch steps and then prowled down the driveway. The black-foot scrutinized him closely, taking his measure; working to detect his level of dominance.

If the asshole thought Isaiah would lower his eyes he was out of his mind.

Isaiah sidled up to Deke, saying nothing; communicating with his steady gaze alone that he couldn't be intimidated. Glaring at the male who might have claimed their mate if certain things had been different, Isaiah's cat snarled and flexed his claws.

Zaire continued to stare, his body stiff, his neck corded, his jaw clenched. Lines of tension were etched into his face, giving him a pinched look. He was absently drumming his fingers fast against his outer thigh, as if filled with a restless energy that he couldn't quite contain. "You must be Isaiah."

"I must be." Isaiah slid his fellow enforcer a sideways look. "It's all right, Deke. I got this." And Zaire needed to *see* that; see that Isaiah didn't need backup. Something that became clear when Deke stepped aside without hesitation or argument, showing he had faith in Isaiah's ability to protect himself and his mate.

"My name is Zaire Daniels," he said, his chin inching up. "I'm Alpha of the Crimson Pride."

Ah, so he'd ascended, then.

"I heard what happened to Quinley."

"And?"

"I want to see her, I want to know she's all right," said Zaire, his voice stilted. The concern lacing his tone held a begrudging note, and there was a strain to his words ... as if speaking them aloud vexed him.

The guy didn't want to be here, Isaiah thought. Not really. He didn't want to be so affected by the situation. But he—probably largely driven by any concern his cat might feel—had been unable to ignore the urge to check on her.

"Quinley is fine," Isaiah told him. "If you heard what happened, you'll know that, too." He cocked his head. "How did you know where we lived?"

His shoulders stiffly rose and fell. "I heard Harlan mention the cul-de-sac. I knew there was one near the stores run by your pride. I drove here, noticed Quinley's car, figured out this is your place."

"*Our* place," Isaiah corrected. "Mine and Quinley's."

The black-foot ground his teeth. "I want to see her."

"I'm unsure why you'd think I care what you want," said Isaiah, keeping his tone bored.

The corners of Zaire's eyes tightened. He opened his mouth but didn't speak, either intent on choosing his words carefully or struggling to find the right ones. Finally, he settled on asking, "Did she talk to you about me?"

"You were mentioned."

"So you know who I am to her."

Anger pricked at Isaiah and wrenched a growl out of his cat. "You're no one to her. The woman you imprinted on? She's yours. Not Quinley."

Zaire's nostrils flared. He drew in an impatient breath and then exhaled slow and heavily. "If you don't want to let me in your house, fine," he clipped. "Just call her out here. Five minutes is all I need." Authority vibrated through his voice, thick and oppressive.

"Throwing your Alpha weight around isn't going to work here. You're not my Alpha, or hers."

Zaire swore. "You can't stop people from seeing her."

"I don't keep people away from her. I'm just keeping *you* away from her."

A taunting brow hiked up. "Why, worried I'll lure her from you?"

"Not at all." It was the truth. "Even if you weren't mated, neither she nor her cat would ever accept you."

Zaire's flinch was minor, but Isaiah saw it.

Taking a slow yet aggressive step forward, Isaiah felt his face harden. "That being said, I'm *really* not fucking okay with you showing up to see Quinley whenever you feel like it. That's never going to be something I'll tolerate, or something she'd want even if I okayed it."

The black-foot's face scrunched up, his cheeks reddening. But then his expression smoothed out as all emotion washed away from his face. "I looked into you."

"Did you now?"

"You had nothing to gain from entering an arranged mating. And you're not so far ahead in life that you're running out of time to start a family. That tells me you did this because you found your true mate but can't have her."

Isaiah didn't allow his expression to change, giving the cat nothing.

"Put yourself in my position for a minute. Let's say you heard she got shot and pursued by a pack of fucking wolves. Would you not want to know she's all right?"

In truth, yes. But Isaiah wouldn't seek Lucinda out; wouldn't try to check on her even from afar. To do so would shit on the promises he'd made to Quinley. Worse, it would not only disrespect this female he'd come to care for, it would hurt her. That wasn't something that Isaiah would ever intentionally do.

"You already know that Quinley's fine," Isaiah pointed out. "And as it happens, no, I wouldn't be stood where you are right now if our situations were reversed. You shouldn't be here at all. I get that it can't be easy to keep your distance from Quinley now that you've faced reality. But it's too late for you to do shit about it. Focus on the woman you chose to mate. She needs you. Quinley doesn't."

"You're really gonna stand in the way of me seeing her for two fucking minutes?"

"I wouldn't care if you only wanted to see her for two fucking seconds. The answer would still be no. You're not getting near her. Not now, not ever again."

"You have no right to—"

"I have *every* fucking right," Isaiah asserted, a growl edging his voice. "You look at me, and you see someone who has no real claim to her. But it's actually the other way around. You gave up what you could have had. You hear me?

You *had* a right to her soul, but you gave it up. And I then took it. Claimed it. Wrote my fucking name on it. She is mine."

"Won't make you her true mate," Zaire sniped. "That'll always be me."

Which bothered Isaiah on one level, yes, but … "That doesn't mean anything, really. *I* take care of her, not you. *I* come inside her, not you. *I* wear her brand, not you. And she wears mine, always will. You're just a walking, talking road her life might have gone down but didn't."

Zaire's face turned so red it gave a whole new meaning to the term, "Crimson Pride Alpha."

"Now get the fuck away from here," Isaiah ordered. "And Zaire, don't come back. If you do, I'll take it as a challenge—you'll walk away from that bloody and broken … if you walk away at all."

Zaire hissed. "You son of a—"

"You heard Isaiah," a new male voice cut in. *Tate.*

Isaiah had sensed both his Alphas step out onto their porch, so he didn't start in surprise. Zaire did, though.

Go," Tate bit off. "That or challenge my enforcer here and now. Though you'd then have a lot of explaining to do when you got home."

The latter comment made Zaire's eyes flicker. Yeah, Nazra wouldn't like it much to hear he'd got into it with Quinley's mate.

Rolling his shoulders, the black-foot pinned Isaiah with a resentful glare but backed away. He angrily stalked to his car and jerkily hopped inside, slamming the driver's door behind him. Then, after flashing Isaiah one last hateful look in his rearview mirror, Zaire was speeding out of the cul-de-sac.

Deke rubbed at his nape. "I thought he imprinted on someone."

"He did," Isaiah confirmed.

"How can he care that much about what happened to Quinley? I mean, if I knew who my true mate was and heard she'd been shot, I sure wouldn't like it. But I wouldn't feel any need to track her down to look in on her. *Bailey* is my mate. The imprint bond exists where a true-mate bond might have been—it leaves no room for that kind of emotional response to anything happening to whoever was predestined for you."

"But the imprinting process can reverse itself, can't it?" said Tate, approaching with Havana at his side.

Isaiah glanced at him. "You think maybe that's happening to him and the woman he claimed?" He'd been close enough to Zaire that he could have sensed if the bond was only partial, but he hadn't thought to check.

"Possibly," said Tate. "I don't see how he'd otherwise have sensed that Quinley is his true mate. The imprint bond should have acted as a block between the realization and him."

Havana nodded. "People who are imprinted generally don't recognize their true mate."

"Like with Mila and Joel," said Tate, referring to Alex's sister and her fated mate. "He's protective of her, and he wanted to be near her sometimes until he realized they were predestined—then he knew it was best they keep their distance from each other. But anything he felt, and still might feel, toward Mila is totally platonic. His commitment to the female he imprinted on drowned out everything else."

"Exactly," said Havana. "But it isn't drowning out everything for Zaire."

Deke puffed out a breath and turned to Isaiah. "It was ballsy of him to come here. He had to know you weren't going to step aside and let him talk to Quinley."

"Actually, I think he did expect it," said Isaiah. "Maybe he assumes she doesn't mean anything to me, or maybe he thought she'd insist on talking to him and that I'd then back down." Sighing, he gave Deke a nod. "Thanks for stopping him from coming to the door. If he'd gotten that close, it would have been hard for me not to kill him."

"Wouldn't have been a huge loss if you had," muttered Deke.

Havana dipped her chin. "Fucking A."

Isaiah backed toward his house, sweeping his gaze along each pride member. "Later." When he entered, he found Quinley stood by the living room window, her arms folded.

"I'll admit," she began, "I cracked the window open just enough to overhear the conversation. I also overheard what you and the others were just discussing."

Isaiah headed straight to her. "And what do you think?"

"I think it doesn't matter whether he's tightly bonded to Nazra or not—that's for them to worry about. I'm only bothered about you. Are you okay?"

Fuck, that got to him. Like a fist of warmth punched into his chest. "Yeah."

She sighed, her arms slipping to her sides. "I really didn't think he'd come back."

"Because it didn't occur to you that the imprint bond might not be solid."

"If it isn't, it would explain the stuff that Nazra said to me."

Isaiah felt his brows draw together. "What stuff? When did she talk to you?"

"She came to see me at my old cabin the night before you claimed me."

"You never mentioned that."

"Forgot about it," she said with a blasé shrug, clearly so utterly unmoved by it that it had completely slipped her memory.

Undeniably pleased that this woman she could rightfully have been jealous of simply wasn't on Quinley's radar, he asked, "What did she say?"

"She wanted my assurance that I wasn't mating you to get a reaction out of Zaire, and that I would definitely send him away if he approached me. She also said there were things I didn't know. Maybe this is that; maybe they're having problems. But if that's the case, why would Harlan let them ascend?"

Isaiah twisted his mouth. "He could be hoping that it would help mend things between them; that if they're focusing on ruling the pride together, it would help unite them and distract Zaire from you."

She let out a long sigh. "I suppose it could be that." She looked out of the window. "It will have cost his ego to leave before he was ready. But it was a good sign that he didn't insist on staying—your points must have hit home. Let's hope he doesn't come back."

"You wouldn't want to watch him get his ass handed to him by me?"

She gave another loose shrug. "Not really. I don't have any interest in what happens to him, good or bad. What I definitely don't want is to watch you brawling—not that I think you'd lose, I just don't want to see you injured."

Feeling his lips tip up, Isaiah looped his arms around her and pulled her flush against him. "You genuinely don't give a hot shit that he's finally sensed the truth, do you?"

"Nope. It doesn't make any difference to anything. As you pointed out, *you* claimed me; it's your mark I wear—he's no one to me. And I don't wish the situation was different." She fiddled with his collar, avoiding meeting his eyes. "Did you mean what you said out there? That you wouldn't go to Lucinda if she was hurt?"

Isaiah used his finger to tip up her chin so he could fix his gaze on hers. "I meant it." Even his cat wouldn't demand it. Not now, because it wasn't torn where Quinley was concerned anymore. She'd won her way into his affections, pushing Lucinda's memory out.

"Really?"

"Really. *You're* my mate, not her. My commitment to you is absolute. That's what that brand on your neck means."

Quinley swallowed. "Okay."

"Okay." Isaiah lowered his head and took her mouth, sipping and tasting. "Now ... I say we forget about them and everything else but us. I say we concentrate on our original plans. You ready to start our lazy day?"

She grinned. "More than ready. Bring on whatever you have in mind."

# CHAPTER FOURTEEN

Returning home from the convenience store the following day, Isaiah walked straight into a wall of warmth. There were times when Quinley setting the thermostat so high drove him nuts. But entering the house after a walk in the freezing cold was not one of those times.

He put down his plastic bag and shrugged off his coat, listening for sounds of his mate. She'd been wrapping presents in the living area when he'd left, but he couldn't hear the snipping of scissors or crackling of paper now.

Having hung his coat on the rack, he nabbed the bag from the floor and walked into the living area. She was no longer sitting near the tree, but a new bunch of gift-wrapped boxes were now positioned beneath it.

As he strode further into the house, he caught a fresh lungful of her scent. There was a *shift* to it; a feral edge that told him she was currently in her cat form. And she had to be close, or her scent would likely have dissipated.

His own animal stirred, eager to see the little female again. He'd wanted time with her last night, but Isaiah had vetoed it, knowing the antsy feline would have marked her with every fang in his mouth.

His cat was calmer now, refreshed from having spent all day yesterday enjoying quality time alone with his mate. Then, today, they'd accompanied her to the salon and stood guard while she worked. The lack of separation, the ability to stay close to her, had soothed the feline enough that his agitated state had eventually evened out.

No issues had cropped up while they were at the salon. The Vercetti Pack hadn't returned. Similarly, Zaire hadn't made a reappearance. Isaiah had thought the male black-foot might try reaching her at the salon since he'd been denied access to her, but he hadn't.

Entering the kitchen, Isaiah glanced around. He found the little cat near the back door facing the corner wall, her furry butt up in the air. He set the plastic bag on the island. "What are you doing?"

She turned to face him ... a huge-ass fucking spider dangling from her mouth. Dangling *alive*, its legs curling and uncurling.

He jerked his head back. "Jesus."

Then she bit into it.

He grimaced. "Oh, the fuck no. Not here." Especially when the spider wasn't even fucking dead yet. He opened the back door. "You want to eat it, take it outside and do it."

It was amazing how a single look from a cat could call you dramatic. Even more annoying, his own animal thought he was being unreasonable.

"Nah, this is where I draw the line." Okay, so he'd drawn various lines with this feline, but it had to be done. Because her idea of "acceptable" didn't generally cohere with his own.

She tossed the insect up in the air, let it drop to the floor, and then pounced on it—killing it in one, smooth merciless move. His cat approved.

Isaiah grunted. "Better." He kicked the dead insect outside. "You going or staying?" he asked her.

She sat down and started licking her paw.

He took that as a "staying" response. Isaiah closed the door, swiftly cleaned up the spatter of spider blood, and then squatted close to her. "Do I get to pet you?" he asked, holding out his hand.

She sauntered over, walking beneath his palm, leaning into his touch. He petted her over and over, focusing on her favorite spots—mostly her chin, neck, and forehead. All the while, he murmured sweet nothings to her, smiling whenever she scent-marked him.

His animal pressed close to his skin, pushing hard; wanting out. Caving, Isaiah stripped off his clothes and gave his feline freedom.

The female cat stilled in surprise. Not wanting to startle her, the pallas cat walked toward her slow and easy. She stayed still, not moving her gaze from him.

He bumped her nose affectionately. She startled but then bumped his right back.

The male cat slid his body against hers. Again, she mimicked his move. Their tails tangled—one slender, one bushy.

Once done rubbing themselves all over each other, they played. Tussled. Climbed. Ran around the house for over an hour.

Finally, pressured by their human halves, they returned to the kitchen and subsided, giving over the control.

Her skin hot from the shift, Quinley shuddered as the air whispered over her flesh. The house wasn't cold, but the air felt cool in comparison to her body temperature. She pulled her clothes on so fast it was a wonder she didn't clumsily trip over.

Isaiah—who seemed to burn hotter than any fire, the lucky bastard—lazily pulled up his jeans, his lips curling in amusement at how quickly she'd dressed.

"Your cat is super cranky," she groused. The feline had played, but he liked to control the game. And if he hadn't been winning a chase or able to herd her cat in the direction he'd wanted her to go, he'd gotten all moody.

Isaiah fastened his fly. "He doesn't like that your cat won't obey him all the time."

"He also doesn't like to lose, but he'll never beat her in a race."

"We're never going to talk about that out loud, though."

She felt her lips bow up. *Dominants and their egos.* "Oh, right, okay."

He snatched his long-sleeved tee from a stool and slipped it on. "So ... we're gonna make a new rule."

She groaned. "*Another* one?"

"No eating spiders in the house. And it isn't my fault your cat needs rules."

"And it isn't her fault you're squeamish. You overreact about the littlest things. Like when she caught the mouse. I mean, she's a cat; it was a mouse. These things happen."

"I didn't freak because she'd caught a mouse. I freaked because she buried it alive, though not before breaking its legs and taking a bite out of its tail."

"Squeamish," she sang low.

He shrugged, snagged her hip, and drew her close. "Call it what you want." He pressed a long kiss to her mouth that she couldn't help but hum into. "On a whole other note, have you finished wrapping?"

"For tonight," she replied, curving her hands around his shoulders. "If there's any stuff you want me to wrap for you, let me know; I'll do it." She liked wrapping. There was something soothing about the mindless activity, especially if she stuck on a Christmas movie to half-watch while doing it.

He nuzzled her hair. "Thank you."

She glanced at the bag on the island. "Are there snacks in there? Because I'm feeling peckish." He'd only gone to the store to stock up on bread and pastries, she knew, but he had a habit of coming home with snacks for her.

"I did in fact buy you a candy bar."

She smiled. "You shouldn't spoil me, you know."

"I like spoiling you." He scraped his teeth over the brand on her neck. "And if it turns you into a brat, it just gives me excuses to spank you."

"Since when do you need excuses to do that?" she grumbled.

A wicked laugh came out of him. "Don't act like you didn't enjoy it."

Just then, a knock came at the front door.

Isaiah tensed, his amusement fading as tension slipped into his muscles.

Quinley sighed. This was a "thing" now. They'd had a few visitors today.

Each time they'd realized someone was at the door, his mind had automatically flicked to the possibility of it being goddamn Zaire.

She still couldn't quite believe that the ballsy bastard had come here yesterday morning. He had some real nerve to even *think* about seeking her out, all things considered.

What pissed her off most about it was that him turning up now and then could very well interfere with the forming of a bond between her and Isaiah. Zaire's presence not only dredged up bad memories for her and her cat, it evoked some seriously negative emotions in Isaiah ... none of which was conducive to starting off the imprinting process.

Also, she didn't want her mate worrying that Zaire might somehow win her to his side if he ever chose to try. It would never happen, but she wouldn't be able to blame Isaiah for worrying about it.

He raised a finger. "Wait here."

Uh, no. "I like to nosily peek out of the window. That's as far as I'll go if it's Zaire." She didn't want to award the shithead with her acknowledgement or attention—he deserved neither.

"You swear it?"

"I swear it."

Isaiah grunted and said, "Fine." His protective instincts demanded he be cautious, but he knew he had to be careful not to let his protectiveness become oppressive.

Plus, he could insist she remain here but, knowing Quinley, she'd head to the window anyway and then later claim ever so innocently that she could have sworn she'd heard him say, "Go nose, it's good with me."

It wasn't Zaire at the door, or anyone who'd be similarly unwelcome. It was Isaiah's parents. They hurried inside to escape the cold.

"We were just on our way home after having a late dinner at the diner," said Andaya before dabbing a kiss on Isaiah's cheek. "We thought we'd pop in and say hi. Where's Quinley?" She was gone in a flash.

Watching as his mother and mate greeted each other warmly, Isaiah spoke to his father, "They bonded fast." It pleased both him and his cat.

Koen grinned. "Son, your mother would take her home with us if she could."

"Well, she can't. It ain't happening." Too many people had the bright idea to do it—including Alex, who hadn't given up on convincing Isaiah to consent to Quinley being his and Bree's live-in nanny. "I like having her right here where she is." Where she belonged.

His gaze darting from Isaiah to Quinley, Koen noted, "Something shifted between you two."

"Hearing your mate got shot has a way of making you face a few things." Like just how much said mate was coming to mean to you. Like just what it would do to you to lose them.

Koen gave a slow nod. "I suppose it doesn't help that the new Crimson Pride Alpha came around. It can't be easy for you or your cat having her true—"

"Don't call him her true mate," said Isaiah, his tone flat. "That term will never be used to describe his association with Quinley. That's not what he is to her."

"Fair enough." Koen slanted his head. "Do you think he'll be back?"

Unfortunately … "If his imprint bond is crumbling, probably. The breaking of such bonds are hard on shifters. It would be instinctual—both consciously and subconsciously—for him to seek out the one person who'll fill the void and make everything better."

Koen's gaze moved to Quinley, who was still talking rapidly with Andaya. "She won't leave you."

"No, she won't. I know that in my bones." She had never let Isaiah doubt her commitment to him. Not once. "Doesn't mean I'll ever be good with him showing up here or anywhere else she might be." Isaiah paused. "But I doubt you came to talk about him."

"Your mother wants to know what your plans are for Christmas day. She's probably persuading Quinley to join us for dinner that day as we speak. While they're distracted … I did want to ask if you've heard from Alex's uncles yet?"

Isaiah gave a grim shake of the head.

Koen frowned. "I would have thought they'd have found the Vercetti Pack by now. Luke said that he, Camden, and Farrell have still had no luck with it."

"A whole lot of shifters have been hunting the pack for quite some time. None succeeded. So I wasn't expecting this to be a quick or simple hunt."

"You want to be out there tracking them," Koen sensed.

"Part of me does, but the rest of me wants to stay with her. Besides, I don't think I'd be much good out there. I'd only keep wondering if she was all right; if they'd come back for her. I wouldn't be able to focus well." He stopped talking as his mother and mate approached.

Andaya gave him her prettiest smile—the one she always tossed his way when she wanted something. "I was just saying to Quinley that, if you don't already have plans, you should join me and your father for Christmas dinner."

"You also said we should do it even if we did already have plans," said Quinley, her lips quirking.

"Well, it makes sense," Andaya told her. "Your sisters and their families would be welcome, too."

"Thanks, but I doubt they'd come. My old pride throws a feast and has music and dancing—it's wildly popular among the unranked. The ranked members have a separate celebration that's more prim and proper, of course." Quinley rolled her eyes. "I've never envied them that. Sounds boring."

"The whole ranked and unranked business is just galling and *wrong*," stated Andaya. "At least you're away from all that now. You two *will* come to dinner, won't you?"

Isaiah sighed. "Stop pressuring her, Mom."

"Stop leaving me hanging, boy."

Quinley gave him a "I'm up for it if you are" look.

In that case … "We'll be there."

Andaya predictably beamed in a triumphant delight.

Once his parents were gone, Quinley said to him, "Your mom's pretty bossy, but she's so sweet about it that I could never call her on it. It's sneaky in a way I admire."

"You sure you don't mind us eating at their table Christmas day?" Isaiah asked her.

"Positive."

"All right."

She put a hand to her belly, grimacing. "All this talk about dinner has made me hungry."

Typical. "When are you not hungry?"

"Rarely. But you don't get to complain—I warned you before you claimed me that my appetite rivals that of a wolverine. You knew what you were getting into."

"I thought you were exaggerating."

"Little late to whine about it now. I *own* your ass."

A smile pulled at his mouth. "Yeah, you really do." And he found himself completely fine with it.

# CHAPTER FIFTEEN

A nick of fire blazed along her inner walls, piercing Quinley's sleep and snapping her awake … just as Isaiah's cock bumped her cervix.

A shocked gasp burst out of her, and her cat woke up with a start. Above her, he groaned deep in his throat, so much grit in the sound. His thick shaft pulsed against her inner walls, stretching her until it stung.

Her lips parted, Quinley planted her palms on his back, blinking hard. It was only then she realized he'd shoved up her tee, baring her breasts. Her sleepy cat rumbled a pleased growl, liking that he would take what he wanted in such a way.

Male possession stamped all over his face, Isaiah pitched his hips a little further forward, forcing his cock even deeper. "You can go back to sleep, baby," he said, his voice low and molten and laced with raw dominance. "Just need to fuck you."

Oh, like she'd ever manage—or *want*—to sleep through that.

He pulled back in a slow retreat, rasping his shaft over supersensitive nerve-endings. Then he rammed deep. Again and again he did it—pulled back slow, drove in hard, went balls-deep.

Keeping her legs curled tight around him, Quinley clung to his back. His weight, his heat, the ripple of his muscles, the pressure of such *fulness* … it all swept her away and rendered her cat a puddle of seduced mush. "Isaiah."

He took Quinley's mouth, the kiss reeking of so much sensual finesse it made her toes curl. One lower arm braced on the mattress beside her head, he explored all he could reach of her with his free hand—stroking up her side, plumping her breast, pinching her nipple, giving her throat a little squeeze, diving his fingers into her hair.

His touch inflamed her every nerve-ending and treated her to a hormonal cocktail that made her head go fuzzy. The warm and lazy air ebbed as his thrusts became harder, but he didn't speed up, leaving her approaching orgasm just out of reach.

A growl poured down her throat just as a thread of greed wove itself into the kiss, ramping it up. He hungrily ate at her mouth like he'd never tasted anything better. The kiss—so hot and deep and urgent—was pure sex magic.

He tore his mouth free. "Before you go to work in the morning, you're going to suck me off. I want my come in your belly while you're walking around all day."

She whimpered. "Faster."

"Give me your throat."

Isaiah's balls tightened as she tipped her head to the side without hesitation. Just the same, a pleased growl came from his cat. That immediate surrender, that demonstration of trust, didn't just shoot to Isaiah's cock, it stabbed right into his chest in the best way. The high that her submission gave him wasn't merely sexual anymore, it warmed his insides.

Nothing had made him feel good about himself in a long time. Not emotionally. Until Quinley.

Possession roaring through him, he zeroed in on her claiming brand. Licked it. Suckled on it. Grazed it with his teeth. Swirled his tongue over it.

All the while, he took her with slow and sure strokes, spurred on by every moan, gasp, whimper; every ripple, flutter, spasm. He blew cool air over the wet brand, and a mini shiver rode her spine.

"You're torturing me," she rasped.

"Not torturing you," he said with a swivel of his hips. "I'm not doing anything *to* you. None of this is *for* you. It's for me."

He took her that little bit harder, drilling his cock deep. Swear to Christ, nothing had ever felt better. She was so tight and hot and wet and *his*.

He gripped the skin of her shoulder with his teeth but didn't bite down—which annoyed his eager-to-mark-her-again cat. A frustrated sound crawled up her throat and she arched, pushing into his teeth.

He didn't give her what she hinted for. He just kept fucking her slow and steady, keeping her pinned in place with the gentle holding bite. But then she dragged her claws from his nape all the way down his back—breaking skin, drawing blood.

And he lost it.

Isaiah bit down and violently powered into her. He was lost in the heat and tightness of her, the taste and scent of her blood, her breathy cries and gasps and demands for more.

He snarled into her ear. "You belong to me, Quin. Never forget it."

She came just like that, her pussy contracting around his dick, her mouth open in a silent scream, her claws slicing into his back yet again.

His own release hit him, then. The onslaught of mind-numbing bliss rushed at him at full-force. He exploded with a growl, grinding and flexing his hips, wanting his come as deep as it could go.

He collapsed on top of her, shoving his face in her hair, breathing in the scent of her shea butter shampoo. The throbbing sting of the rake marks on his nape and back made him feel nothing but pure satisfaction—much as they did his cat. The slices were deep enough that they'd scar. Isaiah fucking loved that.

When he'd finally scrounged up the energy to move, he raised his head. She dazedly blinked up at him, the image of sated. He gave her a soft kiss. "I'd say I'm sorry I woke you, but I'm not."

She gave a weak shrug. "No apologies necessary," she all but purred. "I'd say I'm sorry for making you bleed a little, but I'm not."

Smiling, he pulled out of her. "No apologies necessary." He retrieved a cloth from the bathroom, cleaned her up, and then tossed the cloth in the hamper. Once he'd righted her tee, he lay beside her again. "Go back to sleep," he coaxed, dragging the bedcovers over them.

"Will do." She was out seconds later.

Isaiah carefully drew her to him, keeping her burrowed into his side. Yawning, he closed his eyes. Sleep took him in moments.


"You gonna walk round with that look on your face all day?"

His elbows on the counter, Isaiah peered at her over the rim of his mug. "What look?"

"Pure male smugness," replied Quinley, stood at the opposite side of the breakfast bar.

His lips curling, he lifted and dropped one shoulder. "Probably."

On the one hand, Quinley *adored* that he was so pleased she'd left permanent marks on him. It was a relief, and it hit her in the feels that the brands so clearly meant something to him. Just the same, her cat was delighted.

On the other hand … "My sisters and Lori are gonna ask why you look so smug. My clients are gonna ask why. Any pride mates we come across are gonna ask why. What are you going to tell them?"

"That you clawed my back to shit and the marks are going to scar."

Yeah, she'd figured he wouldn't lie. Shifters *loved* to be marked by those they were possessive of; loved showing off the marks and bragging about it. Normally, she wouldn't care. But these brands were deep and long and gah she was gonna get teased mercilessly.

"People will notice them anyway."

Some peeked out the back of his collar, so people wouldn't miss those. But that wasn't so bad, because no one would realize they spanned his *entire* back unless he told him. Which he clearly intended to do. "I can't convince you to keep it to yourself?"

"Nope."

She was afraid of that.

"What shifter male wouldn't be proud that their mate is so territorial she carved permanent grooves into the full-length of his back?"

"I'm good with you being proud, I'm just not good with everyone knowing." She rolled her shoulders. "Raya and Adaline will tease me something fierce."

His head twitched slightly to the side. "Why?"

Quinley hesitated a moment before admitting in a fast mumble, "Because I did it to them whenever they got brand-happy."

Mirth shimmered in his gaze. "Ah, karma has come calling."

Basically, yes. "They'll also tease me for losing control. And there'll be catcalling from pride members. Lots of it, because every bit of news travels through this damn pride at warp-speed."

"I know," he said, smirking.

Quinley sighed. "You're no help at all." Her cat lay down with a yawn, no more bothered by the situation than he was. The feline wanted other females to know that he was well and truly taken—the brands served to warn them away.

"Are you ashamed you did it?" he asked, his face falling. "Is that what it is?"

She shot him a look of disgust. "Don't even try to kid me that you're all hurt and insulted."

He chuckled and took a sip of his coffee. "Honestly, I find it fucking cute that you're so embarrassed you lost control in bed."

She hadn't merely lost control, though, she'd shredded his back.

"Why be embarrassed, though? I'm not. Your entire body is decorated in my brands."

"But people don't know that, because I don't tell them."

"They'll eventually find out. Your clothes cover many of them now, but they won't come spring when you're wearing lighter layers."

It was clear by the satisfied look on his face that ... "Knowing some of those marks will soon be visible really doesn't bother you at all, does it?"

"Not in the slightest."

She cocked her head. "What about the letter 'I' you carved into the slope of my breast while I was so deep in an orgasm I didn't notice until afterward?"

He gave a nonchalant shrug. "What about it?"

Sighing again, Quinley flicked a hand. "Forget it. Just tell me you won't add the rest of the letters of your first name."

The little shit only grinned.

"You're lucky I kind of like you."

His eyes danced with laughter. "You more than *kind of* like me," he oh so confidently stated.

"Arrogant bastard."

"But not wrong."

"No, not wrong," she confessed, and it was worth admitting it just to see the warm and lazy look he then gave her. She checked the time on her phone. "We need to head out. You ready to leave?"

He slipped off his stool and chugged back his coffee. "I am now. Tomorrow is your last day of work before the salon closes for the holidays, right?"

"It is." Some salons were open for Christmas Eve, but Blue Harbor always closed the twenty-third day of December. They didn't reopen until the second of January. "I'm going to use the opportunity to do some last minute Christmas shopping."

Frowning, he set his cup next to the sink as he said, "You went shopping yesterday with your sisters."

"But not at the mall I want to go to." They'd hit the local Christmas market—it took place each Sunday of December, but she'd been so busy it was the first chance she'd gotten to go there. "I need to pick up a few things." Grabbing her purse from the island, she dropped her phone into it.

"I'll come with you." He paused, one brow sliding up. "Unless you've already arranged to go with some of our pride mates."

Quinley felt the set of her mouth soften. She knew that, preferring to be with her, he hadn't wanted to add that last bit. But he'd done it anyway, knowing he could be greedy with her time and attention.

It worried him that she'd find him too much. She hadn't realized that at first—he'd hidden it well. But he needn't worry. The level of his dominance was tempered with how thoughtful, caring, and attentive he was. It made her cat that much more comfortable with, and trusting of, him.

"No arrangements have been made," she told him as they left the kitchen. "I was hoping you'd come with me. Your presents have been bought and wrapped, so there's no reason you can't be there."

A smile lit his eyes. "Then we'll go together."

Knuckles drummed on the front door.

His step faltered, his expression predictably cooling. "Wait here." He strode to the window, peered outside, and his shoulders relaxed. "It's Virginia," he said, referring to one of their pride mates.

Quinley followed him to the door. He opened it wide, keeping his body slightly in front of hers. Their visitor shot them a trembly smile, looking both sheepish and distressed.

"I'm sorry to bother you so early." She focused on Quinley. "Especially when I know you probably need to leave for work any minute now. But my daughter is having a really severe migraine, and I was wondering if you could help."

"Absolutely." Quinley pulled her cell out of her purse. "Let me just text my sisters to let them know I'll be a little late."

Once she'd done that, Isaiah bundled her up in her coat, scarf, and gloves before putting on his own coat. All three of them then hopped in his car, and he drove to Virginia's complex. Inside the building, she led them to her floor and, finally, to her apartment.

Isaiah kept his palm splayed on his mate's back as she followed Virginia to a bedroom. The woman quietly opened the door. All the lights were off, the curtains were shut, and the scent of pain tanged the air.

Despite the dark, Isaiah could see just fine with his shifter-enhanced vision. He made out the juvenile lying in the bed and saw that her face was lined with agony. Her eyes opened to mere slits, darting from her mother to him and then to Quinley.

"Marnie," Virginia whispered, "I have Quinley with me. She's going to help you."

Isaiah remained in the doorway as his mate padded into the room, keeping her tread light. Without a word, she crouched near the bed and rested a hand on Marnie's head. He watched as the lines in the juvenile's face gradually smoothed out one by one.

Pride washed through him and his cat as they observed their mate use her gift. She was powerful. Rare. A gem to the pride.

"There." Quinley stood, smiling.

Marnie sat up in bed, her lips parted, gently probing her head. "It's really gone. People said you numbed pain, but I wasn't sure if they just meant minor hurts."

"How often do you get migraines?" asked Quinley.

"Once a month, usually."

"Whenever it happens, have your mother call me. I'll come straight away."

Marnie beamed. "Thank you. Thank you so much."

"Not a problem." Quinley reeled off her number to Virginia, who saved it in her list of phone contacts, and then returned to Isaiah. "Ready?"

"Ready," he confirmed.

Following them to the front door, Virginia studied him. "Why are you looking so smug?"

Quinley stilled. "Don't ask."

Well, the woman already had, so ... "Thanks to Quinley, my back looks like a grizzly went at it."

A pretty blush stained his mate's face. "Isaiah! Don't be an ass!"

"But it's okay," he continued, still speaking to Virginia, who was stifling a smile. "It makes us even, because *her* body looks like she had a run-in with a nest of vampires."

Quinley gawked at him. "For God's sake, will you stop talking!" She stalked off.

He exchanged an amused look with Virginia and then trailed after his mate, following her to the elevator.

Her mouth tight, she cast him an indignant glance. "I can't believe you just did that. Actually, no, I can believe it. But it was totally unnecessary." She jabbed the button to call the elevator. Jabbed it a little *too* hard.

Amusement trickled through his cat. Like Isaiah, he wanted all to know about the brands. The feline was smug as a motherfucker right now, more content than he'd been in a while.

Isaiah took a lazy step toward Quinley, earning himself a narrow-eyed look. Deciding not to tell her she looked seriously fucking cute right then—he figured it wouldn't go down well—he gave an innocent shrug and instead said, "I was just answering her questions. It's rude to ignore people, you know."

"Be rude. *Be. Rude.* Especially when it comes to my sisters." She again jabbed the "down" button on the wall panel. "Do not say anything to them that's even remotely similar to what you just said to Virginia."

Humming, he let his face mold into a troubled expression. "It doesn't seem right to lie to them, baby. I mean, they're family. You don't bullshit family. It's wrong."

Oh, her cheeks were now on fire. "That's it," she fumed. "That is *it*."

"What's it?"

"I'm not biting or clawing you ever again."

He chuckled under his breath and advanced on her, swallowing up her personal space; watching her pupils dilate. "Oh, you will, Quin. You won't be able to help it. Just like I can't help but brand you."

She spluttered. "Yeah, well."

"Yeah, well what?"

"I don't know. That's all I've got right now."

Smiling, he planted a hard kiss on her mouth. "Good comeback," he deadpanned.

He wasn't in the least bit surprised when she splayed her palm over his face and shoved him back a step. In fact, he probably deserved it.

# CHAPTER SIXTEEN

"A t least let me carry a few."

Isaiah slid her a frown and kept walking. "I've got it."

*Typical dominant male shifter*, she thought, catching up to him. If you offered them a helping hand with anything, it seemed to offend them. "You don't have to look at me like I'm attempting to unman you."

"Quin, I'm fine. The bags aren't that heavy."

Her hormones went all gooey whenever he abbreviated her name that way. No one else called her that. She liked it. Liked that only he did it. "But there are plenty of them."

"That there are," he acknowledged, casting her a quick look. "I thought you only needed to buy 'a few things.' There's more than a few here."

She pulled a face at what she could admit was in fact an understatement. "I may have downplayed it a little. Or just gotten a bit carried away while shopping. Or both." It wasn't her fault the storefront windows had such amazing Christmassy displays that they sucked her right in. "At least we're heading to the last shop now. Then we can go."

"You said that about the previous two stores we went to."

"You weren't supposed to remember that."

He snorted. "Hard to forget when each promise had filled me with hope both times."

Quinley chuckled. "What a big baby you are." She gave a polite "No, thank you" smile to a worker who tried offering her a free beauty cream sample.

Much as she teased Isaiah, she could totally understand his eagerness to leave. He preferred to shop online, and they'd been at the mall for hours. Her cat was just as fed up.

The building was all glass, tiled floors, bright lighting, and fake foliage. It was also decked out for the holidays. Fairy lights flashed and danced. Tinsel curled around plants. Inflatable Santa's and snowmen were perched here and there.

This mall was different from the one she'd ventured to with Blair, Elle, and Bree. There were plenty of stores, kiosks, coffee shops, and juice bars, but this mall was somewhat smaller and not so much about big brands.

It was also closer to their neighborhood and less busy. Well, *usually* less busy. It was currently more hectic than it would typically be due to it being the holidays.

An endless amount of shoppers carted around bags of all sizes that bore various logos. A jumble of voices, laughs, and cell phone chimes echoed throughout, barely overridden by the Christmas music. Lots of squeaking and clicking came from the soles of wet shoes that left damp trails in their wake on the tiled floor.

Though she was enjoying herself, she'd be glad to leave. Her feet were sore, every shop was jampacked, and the lengths of the cues at counters were ridiculous. She kind of felt sorry for the workers—they had to be both shattered and frazzled.

Of course, she hadn't told Isaiah that her feet hurt. Overprotective as he was, he'd either carry her around or pressure her to leave. She wanted to grab just one little last gift for her nephew Ren first.

She hadn't been able to find this particular toy anywhere—no mall, no market stall, no public street store, not even online. There was only one toy shop here that they hadn't yet searched. She had her metaphorical fingers crossed that the place had the item in stock.

A teenager preoccupied with scrolling through his cell almost bumped into her. Isaiah's arm shot out wicked fast, protectively acting as a blockade.

The teen's head whipped up, and his eyes went wide at the sight of Isaiah.

"Move, kid," her mate ordered.

Oh, the kid moved. Quickly.

She smiled. It had to be said that the dude came in handy. And there was something about him acting as a living shield that made her all tingly.

"Just to let you know," she began as he dropped his arm, "I'm thinking of always taking you shopping with me from now on."

He cast her a sideways glance as they resumed walking. "Why?"

"Because I don't have to weave my way through the throngs of shoppers when I'm with you." They naturally parted for him. Maybe it was his large frame, or maybe it was that they sensed the predator in him. Either way, it worked out nicely for her because it meant they also moved out of *her* way.

His lips curled. "It has to be hard to be sma—"

"Height-challenged."

His smile grew. "Yeah. That."

*Ass.* "You're not going to protest to being my shopping buddy?"

"No," he replied, raising his voice slightly to be heard over the sound of water pattering the base of a fountain. "Unless it's a day when I can't get time off work. I usually can, but sometimes it's necessary that I stay local to the pride or that I accompany Tate somewhere."

Whereas, since he was effectively *her* bodyguard at the moment, he could focus on her. "Do you miss not working as much?" She knew he prized his position.

"If you'd asked me in advance if I would, I'd have said yes."

"But you don't?"

"No. I like that we've been able to spend the extra time together. It's made it easier for us to get to know each other. And it would have frustrated me to have to trust someone else to watch over you lately. I wouldn't have trusted them to be as vigilant with your safety as I am."

"In all honesty, I wouldn't have either." She turned her head at a loud, "*Ho, ho, ho.*" It came from a guy dressed as Santa who was striding around with a bucket, collecting money for a charity.

Returning her attention to Isaiah, she saw that he was staring at her, his expression soft and warm. "What?" she asked.

He shrugged. "It's just nice to know that you trust me to keep you safe."

She wasn't sure when exactly that trust had solidified in her gut, but it was there. This man would never purposely harm or neglect her—Quinley believed that with everything in her. Her cat agreed, the animal's faith in him an unshakable thing. "I thought you already knew that."

"I was pretty sure you did, but I wasn't certain until now. It's nice to have it confirmed." A wicked little glint lit his eyes. "You could confirm something else for me."

She felt her brows pull together. "What?"

"I noticed a store bag in our closet earlier. It had fallen off a shelf, and its logo was of a lingerie brand. I didn't peek inside it, but I would like to know if I'm right in guessing there are some kind of Christmas-themed underwear in there."

It took effort to keep her expression unreadable. "Why would you guess that?"

"I heard bells jingling when I lifted the bag and placed it on a shelf."

*Busted.* "You'll just have to wait and see," she said with a haughty sniff—a mistake, because it drew the scents of meat, pizza, spicy foods, and fresh bread that were wafting from the nearby foot court right into her lungs. "Those smells are making me hungry."

His brow furrowed. "We ate dinner half an hour ago."

"You always seem to think that will make a difference to my appetite. I don't understand."

Sighing, Isaiah faced forward again. He squinted and then tipped his chin at something up ahead. "Is that the store you want to go to?"

Tracking his gaze, she smiled. "That's the one."

They made a beeline for the toy shop. Its door was wedged open, so they stepped straight inside. A woman heading in their direction did a double-take at the sight of *all* that was Isaiah. Very common. The attention of both genders often got snared by him.

Hell, a woman had almost tripped over her kid's stroller earlier in an effort to get a better look at him. Quinley's cat had hissed at her, unimpressed.

"Which way are we headed?" he asked, situating himself in front of her—again protecting her from the crowds, the sweetheart.

"East," she replied, hooking a finger around the loop of his jeans waistband. Regardless of how crowded the store was, there was no skirting and pausing and sidestepping with Isaiah—just a smooth, purposeful walk that said people moved to let him pass.

Quinley couldn't help but smile at the sight of a little girl trying to drag her mother to a mountain of plush bears—she was so tiny that the mom didn't move an inch, but the kid didn't stop pulling.

"That little girl over there reminds me of—" An *oof* flew out of Quinley as Isaiah abruptly stopped dead, causing her to bump her nose on his back. "Ow."

Rubbing at her nose, she frowned. He'd frozen. Frozen from head to toe.

Skirting around him, she peered up at his face. It was hard as stone. She followed the path of his gaze to see what he was so focused on. A couple stood several feet away hemming and hawing over a padded baby playmat, and the woman was resting a hand on her slightly swollen belly.

A painful realization crept up insidiously on Quinley, making her stomach roll and clench hard. *Lucinda.* It had to be Lucinda and her fiancé.

Her inner cat went ballistic, hissing and pacing. The animal was furious that the woman was close to him. Furious at having to be so near to her. Furious by the hurt that came over Quinley.

Breathing through her cat's turmoil, Quinley concentrated on Isaiah. She curled her fingers around his bicep and tugged. "Come on, let's go." He didn't protest, he let her lead him out of the store.

Examining his expression, she saw that it had lost its hardness. Now, it was blank. Utterly unreadable. "So. That was her, huh?"

He didn't meet Quinley's gaze as he urged her forward. "Yeah." A curt response that invited no questions.

It hadn't for one moment occurred to her that they'd bump into Lucinda here. Or anywhere, for that matter. "Is this where you first saw her?" Because if so, she would have appreciated the heads-up; they could have then gone somewhere else.

"No." Again, his voice was sharp.

Arriving at a little lounge area, she halted. "Stop."

He did, frowning, his gaze finally dropping to hers. "Why?"

She nudged him onto the carpeted lounge area and curved her arms tight around him. He went still at first, maybe in surprise. But then his arms—still loaded with bags—loosely came around her. She thought about guiding him to the sofa but, going by the tension in his frame, there'd be no getting him to sit. His instinct was to just leave.

He rubbed the side of his face against hers and placed his mouth near her ear. "I'm good."

No, he wasn't. And neither was she.

She could honestly have gone her whole life without ever having to know what Lucinda looked like. The human was beyond beautiful. Tall and blonde and elegant.

Quinley's complete opposite.

And his reaction to seeing Lucinda … It was understandable. It was. *Of course* he'd find it majorly difficult to see her again, especially given that she was pregnant. It was one thing to *know* of her condition and another to have that visual of it.

And yet, it hurt Quinley that the moment had had such an impact on him. Her cat was equally wounded by it.

Little rattled Isaiah. Little caused him to freeze. And never in a public setting so damn crowded would he not protest to Quinley leading as they waltzed through a store. But he hadn't said a word when she'd drawn him outside.

Understandable. Completely. Utterly. But it still hurt.

"Let's go home," he said, his lips grazing her ear.

Sighing, she pulled back. Neither of them said another word as they made their way to the nearby elevator, or as they descended to the underground parkade.

With every step they took, she pretended her chest wasn't aching. Pretended her eyes weren't burning. Pretended her throat wasn't thickening.

Reaching the car, he unlocked it with the key fob. "Get in, I'll put these bags in the trunk."

Mutely, she did so and then clicked on her seatbelt. She heard his phone chiming as he rounded to the driver's door. Opening it, he answered the call.

He kept his phone volume lowered enough that shifters couldn't overhear his caller's side of the conversation even with their enhanced hearing. But she sensed from Isaiah's responses and queries that it was Deke regarding an enforcer-related matter. It seemed that he intended to update Isaiah on incidents he'd missed.

Isaiah paused the conversation long enough to link his phone to the car's Bluetooth, and then he continued the call as he drove. His voice was slightly stiff, but he otherwise sounded remarkably normal.

The phone conversation didn't end until shortly before they arrived at the cul-de-sac. She opened her mouth to speak … but didn't really know what to say. She couldn't relate to his pain; wouldn't have felt the same depth of it in his shoes.

But she didn't think it wise to just pretend it away. That wouldn't help either of them. And she didn't want him holding his feelings inside.

Once they'd parked the car in their driveway, he scooped the bags out of the trunk and carried them inside. As they hung their coats on the rack in the hall, she asked, "Are you okay?"

His gaze snapped to hers. "Yeah." He looked genuine. *Sounded* genuine. But she wasn't convinced. She didn't see how he could possibly be "okay."

Following him into the living area, she said, "I don't want to pretend that that didn't just happen; that we didn't see her. Let's not do that."

He shrugged, setting down the bags near the armchair. "I confirmed it was her. What else is there to say?"

Maybe nothing. Or maybe he just didn't want to speak his thoughts *to Quinley*, worried it would make her feel bad. He wouldn't want to hurt her.

She appreciated his sensitivity, yes, but she didn't like the idea that he might be ignoring his own pain. Didn't like that he'd refuse to process it in order to dance around her feelings. "Do you need some space?"

His brows flew together. "Fuck, no."

"I can go on a run," she offered, "or spend some time with—"

"No." He came right to her, his expression sober. "The one thing I'll never need from you is space."

"I wouldn't mind," she assured him.

"*I* would." His gaze sank into hers, uber serious. "Really, I'm good."

"You're mad. You're hiding it pretty well, but I *feel* it."

"Yeah, I'm mad. Mad because you and me were having a good day, and life decided to throw a glass bottle in our faces. Now you're upset, and I don't like it. I know how it is to stare at the person who would have claimed your mate if circumstances had been different. It isn't fun."

"No, it's not. But seeing her had to have been harder for you than it was for me."

He gave a slow shake of the head. "Remember Zaire came here but you were more bothered about how I was feeling? It's the same situation right here."

"You went *so still*."

"Shock."

"Right."

Isaiah tensed. The softly spoken word hadn't been sarcastic, but it was laced with resignation. As if she'd decided to give up on trying to reach him. Like she thought he'd simply clammed up.

In hindsight, he could have handled the moment better at the mall. He'd just been so caught up in his battle with his cat that he'd been careless with her. Shock had contributed to that, yes, but it wasn't an excuse. *She'd* been rocked by it all, too. Rocked and upset and dismayed.

Yet, she hadn't pulled away from him at the mall. She'd hugged him. Comforted him. Put him first. Even now, she was still more concerned about his feelings than her own.

That was his Quinley. That was who she was.

He hadn't thought she'd assume that he'd be so impacted by the sight of Lucinda and her fiancé together. He had figured that, given how she reacted whenever Zaire was near him, she'd understand that Isaiah's only thought would be for Quinley.

He'd figured wrong.

And now he could almost *see* her taking an emotional step back, putting distance between them. He placed a finger beneath her jaw to tip up her head, catching her gaze with his own. "Don't retreat from me."

"I'm not. I just find it hard to believe that you're fine. And I'm cautious of saying or doing the wrong thing here. If I saw Nazra pregnant with Zaire's baby, I wouldn't care. But you—"

"It didn't hurt me to see Lucinda. It just took me off-guard."

She gave him a tired, dubious look. "You more or less checked out. I had to guide you out of the store."

"It wasn't that I checked out. I was focused on trying to calm down my cat so he didn't shift right there."

Her brow pinched. "He wanted to savage the fiancé?" It was more of an assumption than a question.

Isaiah frowned. "What? No. He wanted to get to you."

Her head flinched back in surprise. "Me?"

"He was pissed that she was near you, just as your cat is pissed whenever Zaire is in my general vicinity. It's normal. Our animals each perceive them to be potential threats to the forming of an imprint bond. Then he sensed you were upset; sensed that your cat was mad. He did not like that, did not like that he couldn't get to either of you to offer comfort, and so then he got more pissed."

She didn't appear totally convinced. "You didn't say a word to me as we walked to the car, or as we were driving home. You dragged out your phone conversation with Deke—don't deny it."

"I did, yeah. I was still concentrating on calming down my cat. Hearing about mundane enforcer shit was distracting him."

"He was really *that* mad?"

"Yes." Isaiah caught the top of her ponytail in his fist. "The first time I saw her and her fiancé together, it was a hot stab to the fucking chest. But it was different this time."

"How?"

"The only person on my mind was you." He skimmed his fist down her ponytail, allowing it to slip through his grasp. "I wasn't aching to follow her. I wasn't feeling the need to pound her fiancé's face into the ground. I wasn't hurting to know she's pregnant with his child. Because I have you."

Quinley looked away. "You don't have to say that."

"Hey." He curled one arm around her waist and pulled her close, curving his body around her. "It's true," he said as he swept his free hand up her back. "If you can look at Zaire and not be hurt, why can't the same apply to me with Lucinda?"

"It's not that I don't think it *can*. It's just that I've had a long time to get used to the situation with Zaire. You haven't had that same length of time to make your peace with your situation with her, and she didn't reject you the way he did me."

"Doesn't matter. Know why?" He palmed her nape tight. "Because I let her go. And somewhere between claiming you and hearing that you got shot, my cat did the same. *You're* ours. Not her. I have no regrets, Quinley."

She leaned into him, hugging him tight again. This time, though, it seemed that she just wanted to hide her expression from him. Maybe didn't fully believe him. Or was *scared* to fully believe him.

"I wouldn't say any of this if I didn't mean it, Quin. I wouldn't fill your head with lies, not even to make you feel better." He stroked his fingers over her nape, doing a little foray over a bite mark there. "Ask yourself honestly, taking into account everything you know of me, do you truly think I would do that?"

She tipped her head up to look at him, pensive. "No," she finally answered.

"Then there you go."

"It's just … we can convince ourselves of something to make it easier to deal with."

"So you think I could be lying to myself? No, baby." Releasing her nape, he brushed his palm along the side of her face and into her hair, pinning back the stray strands that were too short for her ponytail. "I'm too self-aware for that."

"She's your other half."

"Doesn't feel like it. She's not the person who makes me laugh, who brought my cat out from under his cloud, who lets me take care of her because she knows I need it, who gives so much of herself to me while expecting nothing, who eats all my snacks and leaves IOU notes that never fail to make me smile."

He slid his hand down to palm the side of her neck. "*You* fill that space inside me. Not her. I chose you. And if she was suddenly single and I was given the choice between you and her, I'd still choose you." He breezed his thumb up the column of her throat. "You're all I want, Quinley. You hear me?"

She swallowed hard, the doubt gone from her expression. "I hear you. But I need you to be quiet now or I'll cry."

"You're already crying."

"No, I'm not."

His lips twitched. "My mistake."

Her heart aching in a good way now, Quinley stayed still as he gently thumbed away her tears. He touched his lips to her forehead, pressing a feather-light kiss there. He pressed another to the outer corner of one eye ... then to the outer corner of her other eye ... then to her nose ... then to the curve of her mouth.

His lips brushed over hers in a butterfly kiss. Again. And again. And again, adding a little more pressure each time.

His tongue sank into her mouth—just a shallow dip, flicking the tip of her own tongue. The kiss was light and easy and sensual. It went on and on, only pausing as he peeled off their clothes. Then he gently lowered her on the rug in front of the fireplace and took her right there.

It wasn't slow and hard like the other night. It was *soft* and lazy. He touched her with an aching tenderness, a hint of reverence there. And possession. So much possession, reminding her who'd claimed her. When she came, he pounded into her like a savage until he finally exploded inside her.

Afterward, he collapsed over her in that way he always did. His face buried in her neck, he licked and blew over the brand there.

Softly dragging her fingertips over his back, doodling patterns, she became aware of something. Something that had made her cat sprawl to the floor with a satisfied purr.

Quinley tensed about the exact same time as he did. Ever so slowly, he lifted his head, his gaze captivating in its intensity. She licked her lips. "It isn't my imagination, is it?"

He shook his head. "No. No, it's not. We're wearing each other's scent."

Which meant imprinting had officially begun. A thought that made her chest go tight and pulled a smile from her very soul. It just ... there were no words to really describe what this meant to her; what it did to her insides.

His eyes flashed with satisfaction, but then they darkened. Heated. Fairly glowed with possession as his cock hardened inside her.

"Again?" she asked.

He rumbled a growl. "Again."

This time, he fucked her *hard*. Held nothing back. Took everything, gave the same in return. And he bit right over her claiming brand as they both came.

# CHAPTER SEVENTEEN

"It doesn't matter how many times I watch this movie I never get sick of it," said Quinley.

With her sat between his thighs on the sofa as he pretty much wrapped himself around her, it was easy for Isaiah to dip his hand into the bag of chocolate drops she held. That she didn't bite his fingers was a testament to the level of comfortability they had—black-foots didn't share food with just anyone.

He threw two chocolate drops into his mouth. "So it's a favorite, then?"

"Yes, but I only ever watch it in December—and usually only on this very evening each year." Tipping her head right back to meet his gaze, she asked, "How do you usually spend Christmas Eve?"

"I don't really treat it differently than any other day."

She grimaced. "Oh, you poor soul. That's just sad."

He felt his lips curve. "And you do this every year?" he asked, his gaze sweeping from the movie to the wide selection of snacks on the coffee table.

"Watch Christmas movies and pig out? Yup."

Typically, Quinley didn't do well with sitting still for long periods, so he was honestly surprised she'd been content to laze about for several hours straight. Then again, the abundance of candy, cookies, and other snacks were probably responsible for that.

They'd spent the whole day together, aside from the hour she'd disappeared upstairs to finish wrapping the gifts she'd then stuffed under the tree with the others.

"You're free to leave me to my own devices and go do whatever you want," she said. "I don't expect you to lounge about with me."

157

"I like lounging about with you." He nabbed another chocolate drop and threw it into his mouth. "There's beer at hand, more snacks than even you could eat—"

"Don't be so sure."

"—and I get to feel you up." He cupped her breast over her sweater and squeezed. "What's not to like?"

"How come *I* don't get to feel *you* up?" she groused.

"Because I said so."

"*Lame.*" She righted her head, returning her attention to the TV.

Smiling, Isaiah nuzzled her neck and pulled her closer. She fit against him just right. Fit there like she'd been born to. He couldn't imagine that another person would suit him better than she did.

His father had said the same of Andaya, just as Deke had said the same of Bailey. Originally, Isaiah hadn't really understood how a shifter could feel that way about anyone other than their true mate, the *literal* other half of their soul.

But Quinley ... she was like a puzzle piece he'd been missing. She made him feel alive and chased away the numbness. She'd restored the balance he hadn't realized he'd lost.

It had cut him deep that he'd never have his true mate. But each time Quinley had given herself over to him, had trusted him so implicitly, had let him in that little bit more, she'd increasingly closed over that wound. It now no longer bled. More, she was a balm to the jagged scar there.

Both he and his cat were elated that imprinting had begun. They were also less edgy, satisfied that their claim to her was taking metaphorical shape. But neither man nor animal would relax completely until the bond formed. Both were resolute that it would; both determined that said bond would never turn brittle or break.

There had been a slight change in her since yesterday. She was more relaxed. More sure of him, of *them.* As if the beginning of the imprinting process had given her the reassurance she'd needed that they were on the *exact* same page.

It was just as much as a relief for him. He was actually glad they'd come across Lucinda yesterday. Because it had been the subsequent conversation between him and Quinley that had fully opened up the possibility of imprinting.

He'd assured her in the very beginning that she wasn't some kind of fallback mate; that she would never play second fiddle. She'd seemed to have believed him, but maybe a part of her had needed some extra reassurance. He hadn't seen that. Should have.

Once the bond formed, she wouldn't be able to—consciously or subconsciously—hide such doubts from him again. He'd *feel* them. The thought of that pleased him. He would then be able to better monitor her emotional welfare. He didn't like the idea that she might hold shit in and torment herself with it.

They hadn't yet told anyone that imprinting had started, because they knew that they would be thereafter swarmed by nosy well-wishers. They wanted this time alone; wanted to spend their first Christmas Eve as a mated couple alone.

On the table, her cell phone began to ring.

She leaned forward to peek at the screen. "It's Tina again."

Annoyance sizzled through him. He'd always liked Tina—she was a friend of his mother's, and she'd been one of those who were *adamant* that Isaiah had not killed Jenson. But she could be a bit of a diva at times. Like now.

Quinley again tipped back her head to look at him, worrying her lower lip.

"The answer is no," he told her.

She sighed. "I'm a healer, I'm supposed to help those in pain."

"But as we've established, she's being unreasonable. All she has to do is let Helena heal her wound, but she won't. She'd rather suffer than accept the aid of someone she's currently unhappy with." It was all part of the diva thing.

"I know, but—"

"Worse, she's been coming to you morning and night for pain relief. She doesn't even need it that often. The slightest twinge and she calls." Again, it was part of the diva thing.

"Not everyone has a strong pain threshold."

Isaiah exhaled heavily. He didn't like saying no to Quinley. Didn't like seeing her face fall in disappointment. But he couldn't support her ignoring her limits.

He wanted to be everything to her. He wanted to lift her up. Be her strength when she needed it. Make her feel safe and secure. Spoil her in what ways he could. But shove aside what was best for her? No. That he wouldn't do.

He stroked a hand over her hair. "Baby, I get that you want to help people. That's a good thing. But it's important to have boundaries and ensure others don't cross them. It's important to take care *of yourself.* Tina isn't being fair to you. She knows that coming to you so frequently for that level of relief will make you feel drained. She's doing it anyway. It's not right, and it's stupid when she could rid herself of the pain easily by accepting Helena's help."

"It's hard for me to ignore when someone's hurting."

"I know. But your wellbeing comes before healer instincts. It has to, if only because you'd otherwise be too worn out to be of help to the rest of the pride."

The lines of distress in her face smoothed out. "You're right."

"Of course I am."

Even as her eyes shimmered with humor, she gave him a dirty look. "You've been very bossy today. I can't take Tina's calls. I'm not allowed to cook because you want to make dinner for us. And I'm not allowed to touch you until we're in bed." Huffing, she cut her gaze back to the TV. "Sounds like a crap deal to me."

He licked at her brand. "Let's not pretend you don't like when I give you an order to follow. You like the challenge. You like the tension. You like to hand over control." He grabbed his beer from the small shelving unit beside the sofa. "You also like when I make you wait for what you want."

"Uh, the latter? No. You're wrong there. I'm no better at waiting for things than you are. On that note, stop eyeing the stocking, you're not opening anything until tomorrow."

He *did* occasionally eye it. She'd hung four on the fireplace—one for him, one for her, one for his cat, and one for hers.

He, of course, had piled small gifts into the stockings belonging to Quinley and her feline. She hadn't asked for hints or peeks, content to wait until Christmas morning. But Isaiah and his cat were far more curious and impatient than their mate, so they both wanted to know what she'd bought them.

He swigged back some beer and complained, "You're supposed to cater to my every whim."

"Ha. You're funny."

He caught her earlobe with his teeth and tugged. "I'll make it worth your while."

Her breath hitched. "No."

Isaiah returned his bottle to the unit. "Or I could torture your agreement out of you." Wicked fast, he slipped his hand—cool and damp from condensation—under her sweater and tickled her bare skin.

She let out a little squeal, squirming like crazy. "Don't, your fingertips are cold!"

"I know." He continued for a good five seconds before stopping.

"That was cruel."

"It's your own fault for not giving me my own way."

"I'm curious, are you going to be like this every time there are occasions when I buy you gifts that you don't immediately get to open?"

"Yep."

So this was her life now. Rolling her eyes, Quinley leaned back against him. Watching movies was much more enjoyable when she had him virtually curved around her like this, making her feel all snug and cocooned, his scent *the best* kind of blanket.

A scent she now wore on her skin.

She *loved* that. Her cat preened each time she thought of it, smug as all shit that she had Isaiah for a mate. He was everything the animal would have wanted. Everything *Quinley* would have wanted. So it seemed nuts that her predestined mate didn't have much in common with him.

But then … Zaire's rejection had changed Quinley. She'd been just a teenager at the time. Barely grown, her identity not quite fully developed. Having her true mate turn his back on her, enduring years of bullshit rumors and having to watch him get closer and closer to Nazra, had all gone towards shaping Quinley into the woman she'd become.

So if those things hadn't happened, maybe she would have grown into a different person. One who would click with Zaire well. A person who therefore *wouldn't* click so well with Isaiah.

God bless FindYourMatch.com. Because without that site, she was pretty sure she wouldn't have found Isaiah.

And thank the high heavens that, of the women on his list, he'd chosen to reach out to Quinley. Because it seemed highly likely to her that *any* of the potential matches would have resulted in a claiming—he was just too easy to like, so any of the women would have agreed to sign a mating contract. Then again, she was totally biased.

As the movie credits came up, she said, "I'm so glad you're smart."

"What?"

"Well, you could only contact *one* of the females who FindYourMatch recommended. You picked me. That was smart. I'm an absolute winner."

He chuckled. "You are, baby. You are. And you're just as smart for agreeing to the meet without hesitation. I would have otherwise had to hound you."

She snorted. "You would have just moved onto another female on your list."

"I don't think so. The messages we exchanged weren't deep and meaningful. But the tone, the easiness, the kinship there … it all gripped me. And I think it gripped you, too."

"You know something, you're right."

"You always sound so surprised by that. Eventually, you'll get used to the fact that I'm never wrong."

She let out a *pfft*. "I wouldn't say *never*."

"You should, because it's true." Keeping an arm tight around her waist, he stood, easily lifting her. "Need to use the bathroom. I'll be right back."

As he left the room, she put down her empty bag of chocolate drops and did a long, languid stretch … which was right when a double-knock sounded on the front door.

Oh, that had better not be Tina. Isaiah would *freak*. And much as it wasn't easy for Quinley to ignore a person's pain, he had been right in all he'd said.

"Check who it is before you open the door!" ordered Mr. Cranky from the half-bath.

Like she hadn't already planned to do so. "Yes, sir!" She cautiously walked to the window. Relief worked through her. "It's just Havana!" Smiling, she strode to the front door and opened it. "Hey, everything okay?"

Shuddering with the cold temperature, the Alpha replied, "As okay as everything can be when I'm doing all my wrapping at the last minute." Havana bent to itch her knee, adding, "I won't come in, I just wanted to ask if—"

Quinley jerked as white-hot fire blazed across her temple, shaving off skin. Her hand automatically whipped up to touch the spot as she hissed in pain. Becoming aware that something had thudded into the wall behind her, she fast realized what had just happened.

She'd been shot at.

She ducked, yelling, "Get in!" But it was unnecessary, because the devil was already all but diving into the house. They both slammed the door shut as more bullets flew, all peppering the door but not penetrating it.

"What the hell?" Havana burst out.

Straightening, Quinley probed the wound on her temple—it was wet and warm, and she could smell blood. "Are you okay?"

"That was going to be *my* question." The Alpha pulled out her cell just as Isaiah came striding into the hallway, his brow furrowed.

"Why did you slam the—" He stilled, his nostrils flaring. "You're bleeding."

"Tate," Havana said into her phone, "we've got a sniper somewhere."

"*Sniper?*" Isaiah echoed.

"Someone just shot at me, but the bullet only grazed my temple." Quinley watched as his face turned hard, red, and menacing.

"*Motherfucker.*" He glared at the bullet that was lodged in the wall behind her. He gently but firmly dragged her into the living room. "Wait here, Quin. Do not move from this house."

"Like I planned to go for a stroll, you weirdo. *Be careful.*"

He planted a hard kiss on her mouth and then vanished, disappearing out of the patio doors.

She blew out a breath and peeked at the living room bulletproof window. There were no marks to indicate that it took any hits. She wondered if maybe her shooter had known that every house and apartment complex owned by the pride was built to withstand such an attack, because why else would they have waited for her to open the front door?

"Right," began Havana, walking into the living room, "I texted Helena; she's on her way. I'll wait with you while our mates and a bunch of others deal with who shot you."

"The bastard's probably in the wind."

"Oh, I'm sure that he intended to be. But we knew one of the Vercetti brothers was a sniper, so we were prepared for such a move. I'll be surprised if he isn't being detained as we speak."

S tanding on the rooftop of the pride's bookshop, Isaiah glared down at the wolf shifter pinned to the concrete floor like a butterfly by several enforcers. His stubbly face was red and splotchy, and there was a manic glint in his hazel eyes that said he knew he was *fucked.*

The enforcers had been stationed on nearby rooftops, unhidden. They hadn't noticed the stranger in time to prevent him from taking shots at Isaiah's house, but they'd spotted him swiftly enough to subdue him when he tried fleeing.

Rage flamed in Isaiah's blood and took over his cat. This motherfucker had made his mate bleed. Had attacked her from afar when she was in her own damn home, the one place she should feel safe. He'd taken that from her.

More—and far worse—he'd tried to *kill* her. He'd tried to take her from Isaiah.

And the wolf would goddamn pay for it.

"So you're Tommaso Vercetti," said Isaiah. "You look a lot like your baby brother." Same colored eyes, same brown hair, same chin dimple. "Samuele was his name, wasn't it?" It was a taunt; a reminder that Isaiah himself had killed the youngest Vercetti.

Tommaso peeled back his lips, revealing gleaming white, slightly crooked teeth. "Do not speak of him."

"Why not?" asked Isaiah with a slight shrug. "It isn't like he'll know, being dead and all."

A deep growl rattled the wolf's lips.

Tate looked at Isaiah. "You were right in thinking he'd come. I didn't believe he would."

"Neither did I," said Luke, stood slightly behind his brother with Deke and Camden.

"It's said that Tommaso here is a bloodthirsty hothead." Isaiah met manic amber eyes once more. "You're the reason a lot of the ransom victims either went home injured or not at all. You like to hurt people. And once you start, you don't like—maybe don't even know how—to stop. So yeah, I figured you'd make this move."

It was likely that Isaiah had been Tommaso's primary target. Likely that, tired of waiting for him to show, the wolf had tried executing Quinley instead. After all, the death of a shifter also meant a death of sorts for their mate—if it didn't kill them literally, it would at least destroy a part of their soul. That would definitely have counted as vengeance for Tommaso.

But that Quinley might have been a secondary target made no difference. The fact was she'd been grazed by a fucking bullet while standing in her own damn house.

"My pack will be on you any second," Tommaso warned.

"No," Tate contradicted. "Apart from your getaway driver—who's already dead, by the way—you're alone."

It had been disappointing to learn that the aforementioned driver hadn't been Davide, another of the brothers. He typically drove during "jobs."

"My guess is that the others don't know about this," Tate continued. "Especially not your big brother. Much as your pack doesn't have an official Alpha, Sebastian more or less calls the shots, doesn't he?"

Isaiah cocked his head at the wolf. "You've been wanting to come here for weeks now, but Sebastian vetoed it, didn't he? He knew the move was too predictable. He knew we'd be prepared for it. You were aware of the risks. But you just couldn't help yourself, could you?"

In a way, Isaiah understood it. He didn't have siblings, but if he had and their life was cut short, he'd ache to avenge their death.

"You're wrong," Tommaso swore with a snarl. "He knows. He's in your house fucking up your mate as we speak."

Isaiah tensed, his gut twisting in panic. But then it loosened, because … "No, he wouldn't sacrifice one of his brothers, especially when he only recently lost another. But when he realizes you're missing, I'm sure he'll suspect that our pride killed you. It won't be a stretch to assume you went against him and then died just as he'd likely warned you would."

Luke hummed. "Bet you're wishing you'd listened."

Tommaso kept his gaze locked on Isaiah. "It was worth it just to make her bleed. Again."

Isaiah didn't rise to the attempt to bait him. "Oh, that's part of why you came tonight, is it? You hated that she got away from you; that she survived the hit."

Deke snickered at the wolf. "You don't know shit about black-foots if you were expecting her to be an easy target."

Tate scratched at his jaw. "Much as it pisses me off that you tried putting a bullet in Isaiah's mate—a bullet that was *far* too close to my own mate, come to that—I can't be sorry that you're pinned to this roof right now. It means we get to kill you."

"Congratulations," Camden drawled. "You've made your pack smaller and weaker just like that. We appreciate it."

Tommaso's cheeks darkened. "Don't bother asking me where they are. I'd never tell you."

"I know that," said Tate. "I know that, because I have brothers. I wouldn't give up their location either. Someone could cut me up a piece at a time and I'd still say shit. So I'm not going to waste my time trying to torture the information out of you. That said … torture is still on the table just because."

The wolf went motionless.

"If you feel like throwing in some helpful info to make it stop early, you do that. If not, well, we'll just stop when we're bored." Tate arched a brow at Isaiah. "Want to be the first to draw blood?"

Oh, Isaiah would have insisted on it. He advanced on the wolf, his cat growling its eagerness to gut him open. "You shot my mate. Twice. I'm going to enjoy every minute of this, I really am." Isaiah sliced out his claws. "Happy fucking Christmas to me."

# CHAPTER EIGHTEEN

The one thing that Isaiah hadn't expected to find when he returned home was the sight of a black mamba looped tight around a bearcat as they rolled around his living room, biting each other and crashing into furniture.

The noise level was horrendous. So much growling and hissing and yowling and objects hitting the floor with a thud.

It wasn't remotely uncommon for Aspen and Bailey's animals to get into a tussle, or for those tussles to go so far. But normally, Havana would order them to stop. Tonight, however, she sat on his sofa munching on chips while watching them dispassionately.

He knew why, though. Because it was distracting Quinley. She was so engrossed in the brawl—not to mention preoccupied with picking up fallen objects and setting furnishings to rights—that she wasn't anxiously awaiting his return. Hell, she hadn't even noticed him yet.

The bullet graze on her temple was healed, and she'd cleaned the area so there was no blood. But it didn't unravel the knots inside him, because he could still see the image of her wound in his mind's eye.

So close. She'd come *so close* to having a bullet in her brain. Had Tommaso's shot been more accurate, she'd be gone now. Isaiah would have lost her; lost this person who'd found a way to live in his blood and filled his every empty spot. So no, those knots in his gut weren't going anywhere.

His cat's insides were roiling and tightening. Mauling Tommaso to death had given the animal an outlet for his rage, but it hadn't made him feel any better—let alone calmer.

As if she sensed his presence, Quinley's attention snapped to Isaiah. Her gaze jerkily roamed over him, as if searching for injuries, as she approached.

"I smell blood. It's not yours," she added with some relief.

"It belongs to Tommaso Vercetti."

Havana let out a low whistle.

"That's who shot at me?" asked Quinley.

"Yes." Isaiah rested a hand high on her upper arm. "He acted alone; only had a getaway driver with him. Both of them are dead now, and their vehicle is on fire." One of the enforcers had dumped it in an isolated spot far from here before setting it alight.

Havana went to speak, but then her phone rang, and she scrambled to answer it.

Isaiah turned back to his mate. "You're good?" he asked, lightly palming the side of her head and breezing his thumb over her now healed graze.

"Helena came." Quinley fisted his long-sleeved tee. "You're not hurt?"

He shook his head. "I wasn't part of the struggle to capture Tommaso. Other enforcers nabbed him before I got there. He was the one who shot your cat."

"Bastard," she tossed out.

Havana stood upright, pocketing her phone, and then clapped twice. "Right, Frick and Frack, time to go."

Like that, the two brawling animals went still.

"*Now,*" pressed Havana.

When the animals hurried over to their prospective piles of clothes, Isaiah again turned to Quinley. "I noticed the front door took some bullets. Not the window, though. Either they guessed our security is so tight it'd be bulletproof or they somehow learned of it."

"That's what I was thinking," said Quinley.

"Why does your snake hate my bearcat so much?" Aspen demanded of Bailey, both females now almost fully dressed—they only needed to slip on their shoes.

"There's no hate," objected the mamba. "Just love. The purest, purest love."

"I have more puncture wounds than a goddamn pin cushion," Aspen bit off.

Bailey inched up her chin. "Blame Havana."

"Why would I do that?"

"She didn't tell my snake to stop."

Aspen all but jammed her foot in her sneaker. "Havana shouldn't have to. *You* should have told your mamba to stop."

Bailey flicked out her hand. "I don't interfere in her business; she doesn't interfere in mine. That's how we roll."

"*Roll. Differently.*"

"Why?"

"All right, enough," Havana cut in. "It's time to go, so let's *get gone.*"

167

Her faux fur ankle boots now on, Bailey turned to Isaiah. "I dug the bullet out of your wall. I'd give it to you as like, you know, a memento or whatever. But Aspen's bearcat stole it and shoved it down my snake's throat. She barfed it back up pretty quick, thankfully. Quinley then trashed it."

"Unnecessary story." Aspen shoved the mamba aside and beamed up at Isaiah. "Congratulations on the start of the imprinting process, by the way."

Bailey's lit up. "Ooh, yeah, congrats!"

Havana smiled. "We're thrilled for you."

He looked at each of the three females. "*Don't* say anything of it to anyone."

"We would *never*," Bailey assured him.

"Ever, ever," Aspen added, tugging on her other sneaker.

Havana gave a solemn nod. "It's your news to deliver."

Isaiah sighed, sensing … "You've already told people, haven't you?"

Aspen pulled a face, sheepish. "Only Blair."

"And Elle," said Bailey.

Havana cleared her throat. "And Bree. Oh, and—"

"Go," he told them, pointing at the door.

All three said quick goodbyes to Quinley as they melted out of the room and then promptly disappeared out of the house.

Rolling his shoulders, he let out a long breath and refocused on his mate. "Come here," he coaxed, opening his arms.

She all but fell into them, her own arms winding around his waist.

He held her close, rubbing his chin on the top of her head; needing the contact and sensing she needed it too. His cat pushed against his skin in an effort to be closer to her.

"I was worried you'd get shot the moment you went outside," she said against his chest. "I thought maybe the shooter was trying to lure you out of the house."

"It wouldn't have been Tommaso's plan. Not when he'd be aware that we'd quickly work out his position. He needed to take a few shots and then run—plan successful or not."

"I can't believe he really came here, *knowing* the pride's security would be stepped up and that we'd naturally be alert for a sniper. It's reckless."

"His pack has escaped consequences for so long it's likely made them arrogant."

She let her head fall back, revealing a pensive expression. "Huh. It would explain why they came after this pride in the first place. Only absolute dumbasses would target pallas cats."

"I think the pack views it as pitting their strength against ours. The more powerful and dangerous the shifters they target, the more invulnerable they feel. But they're *not* invulnerable, and they've forgotten that."

"Samuele's death should have served as a reminder."

"It did to some extent, because the pack hasn't tried swarming our pride. His death probably shook them a little. Then they came at me, but that didn't work out. So they went after you, which also resulted in nothing. Each failure would have been unexpected and shook them that little bit more."

Quinley really hadn't thought about it like that. It made sense, though. The pack weren't accustomed to being thwarted. Bending Alphas to their will over and over, evading detection and consequences, had made them cocky. It had really only been a matter of time before they became careless.

"I don't suppose Vercetti told you anything helpful," she said, lifting a brow.

"No. We didn't bother questioning him. He wouldn't have given up the location of his brothers." Isaiah paused. "He did have the option of making the pain stop by telling us something, but he didn't."

Further proving that, no, he wouldn't have blabbed under pressure.

Isaiah touched his forehead to hers. "He should never have gotten to you. Let alone here, in your own home. I promised you you'd be safe here."

*Oh, dominant shifters and their propensity to shoulder unnecessary guilt.* "First of all, to state the obvious, this was not your fault. Second, I'm as safe here as it's possible for me to be. Nobody is completely safe in any one place. You never heard of home accidents?"

"This wasn't an accident."

"No, but I'm making the point that being inside these four walls doesn't give me some kind of magical immunity against all forms of danger."

His gaze sank into hers, searching *behind* it. "Your cat's all worked up, I see."

Quinley nodded. "She's tired of me and her getting shot at. And she was fretting like crazy that you'd be hurt, too. It only made her more cranky that your mom was mad at me."

His brows flicked together. "My mom was here?"

"News of the shooting reached your parents pretty fast. They only left here about twenty minutes before you walked through the door. They're elated that we're imprinting, but it didn't make Andaya any less mad."

"Why was she angry at you?" he demanded, clearly outraged on Quinley's behalf.

"For opening the front door when Havana knocked." Quinley shrugged at his baffled expression. "She was a little shaken, I think. Fact is I should be able to answer my own front door. *I* didn't do anything wrong tonight. *The shooter* did. *I* didn't put myself in danger. *He* was the threat. Which was what I told her."

"And her response?"

"Tears. Lots of them." It had been one heck of a show. "I ended up apologizing for opening my door just so that she'd stop crying."

His lips twitched. "She's good at making you feel bad even when you've done nothing wrong."

"Speaking up in my defense, Bailey pointed out that if *I* hadn't opened it, you would have. The idea that you might have then been shot made Andaya cry even harder. Which, honestly, didn't seem to bother the mamba at all. I think she enjoyed it."

"So, the unholy trinity took care of you, huh?"

"They did their utmost best to distract me. Out of appreciation, I pretended I didn't know it was their game. And really, they *are* distracting. Have you seen the mamba and bearcat go at it before?"

He nodded. "I have."

"I panicked at first because I know mambas are highly venomous. But Havana said bearcat shifters have peptides that make them immune to snake venom, 'so it's okay.' Her words. I didn't really agree that it was okay, considering those bites had to still hurt. But the bearcat's just as vicious."

"She's just as merciless, too. Last week, they had a brawl in the Alpha's house. At one point, she sat on the mamba's head and then unleashed her anal glands."

Quinley gaped. "Oh my God, that's awful. *Beyond* mean."

"Thankfully Havana has some kind of spray that neutralizes the smell."

Quinley puffed out a breath. "I tell you, this has been the weirdest Christmas Eve I've ever had. Call me strange, but I've enjoyed it. Not the bullet-graze part, but the rest."

"*I* haven't enjoyed it." He cupped her head, sobering. "I came far too close to having to know what it'd be like to live without you."

"Let's not stew on what *could* have happened. Let's focus on the actual situation. I'm okay. You're okay. Our pride's okay. Tommaso Vercetti? Dead and gone. That's two brothers down, two to go. Their messed-up pack is on its way out. Karma is catching up to them fast, and it's using our pride to do it. Don't you think that's ace?"

"Well—"

"Me, too. I also really don't want to talk about that pack anymore— they've commandeered enough of our time and attention tonight. Can we put them out of our heads for a while?"

He sighed. "Yeah. Yeah, we can do that."

"Good. Because I'm hungry again, and Havana ate most of my snacks so I need to dig out more."

"I'm surprised you let her have any."

Quinley had actually refused at first, which had only made the Alpha laugh. "We made a deal."

"Which was?"

"I'd let her have some, and she'd replace it all—with interest."

"'Interest' being an additional bunch of snacks?"

Quinley beamed. "Ding, ding, ding, we have a winner. Congrats."

He shook his head, mirth creeping into his eyes. "You're a nut."

She could live with that. "A nut who's hungry, so let's get that fixed."


Slipping on her gloves the following afternoon, Quinley walked to the bottom of the stairs and called out, "Are you having a number two up there or something?"

There was a muffled thud. The closing of a door, maybe. "No!" Isaiah yelled from presumably the bathroom.

"Then what's with the hold up?"

No sounds of footfalls preceded his appearance at the top of the stairs. For a dude his size, he was seriously stealthy.

"There's no hold up," he said, making his way down to her, taking the stairs two at a time. Reaching the bottom, he stared at her, the epitome of cool and casual. There was a glimmer of heat in his eyes, though.

Feeling her lips flatten, she set her hands on her hips. "You peeked in the lingerie store bag, didn't you?"

He gave an innocent shrug. "It's Christmas day. There's no more need for purchases to be surprises."

She ground her teeth. "Yes, but I specifically said that what's in the bag is a surprise *for later tonight*."

"I never heard that last bit."

"*Sure* you didn't," she mocked. God, he was unbelievable.

His lips canting up, he inched closer. "I actually regret looking in the bag, because now all I'm going to think about is having you under me while you're decked up like that."

Ha. "Serves you right." She let her gaze drop to his sweater. "You're not really gonna wear that, are you?"

His mouth curved a little more. "Yeah. Why not?"

Well … it read, "*Property of Quinley. All Rights Reserved.*" A joke gift she'd had made which, ironically, appeared to be his favorite of all she'd bought. "I thought you'd laugh and then maybe stuff it in a drawer and leave it there." It wasn't exactly manly, despite being black and gray, and it was truly more of a gag gift.

"You thought wrong."

So it appeared. "But … we're leaving the house."

"Yes. And?"

"And that's something you wear when having lazy days at home—*if* you're going to wear it at all—not for Christmas dinner at your parents' table."

He grabbed his coat from the rack and shoved his arms into it. "They'll love it, trust me."

That wasn't really the point, which he *had* to be well-aware of. "This is like with the rake marks on your back, isn't it? You want to show off the display of possessiveness?"

He pursed his lips. "Pretty much, yeah."

She supposed she really should have seen this coming.

He picked up the gift bag that she'd set on the floor—it contained the presents they'd chosen for his parents. "Let's go."

When they stepped out onto the porch deck and the winter air fanned her face, she shuddered. "It's a shame it didn't snow."

He arched a curious brow. "You, hater of all that is cold, likes snow?"

"I like *looking* at it."

His lips curled. "Right." He took her hand and led her down the porch steps.

As Christmas mornings went, well, she'd never had one better. She'd woken to his mouth on her pussy, received a spectacular orgasm, and then been brought to yet another powerful release when he fucked her in the shower afterward.

The sex hadn't been hurried or short on foreplay. He'd lavished her body with his attention, touch, and skills. He'd focused on her to the exclusion of all else, which her cat had loved.

Once dressed and ready to face the day, they'd exchanged gifts downstairs in the living room. Her favorite was definitely the charm bracelet she'd subtly cooed over in Valentina's jewelry store weeks ago.

Obviously, she hadn't been as subtle as she'd thought. Or maybe she had. Because the fact was that Isaiah paid attention to her on such a level that he rarely missed anything.

As they right then left the cul-de-sac and began walking toward the pride's apartment buildings, her mate scanned every rooftop, studied every car, scrutinized every individual near or far. So she didn't speak, not wanting to distract him.

Finally, they arrived at his parents' complex. They went up the elevator and got out on the correct floor, wishing any pride mates who they came across a merry Christmas.

"I thought your cat would be more at ease today, but I can sense how tense she is," he said to her as they neared their destination. "She seemed fine earlier."

"She *was* fine until now. It's not that she doesn't trust you to keep her safe while we're out and about, if that's what you're thinking. It's that she *only* trusts you. We're going to be around lots of people today. She's a little too shaky to be chill about it."

"We could go back home," he offered.

"Not happening. And she doesn't want to lock herself indoors anyway. She's just on edge, that's all. She'll relax at some point."

Isaiah frowned, wishing he'd considered that her cat might be so antsy once they left the house. The feline had just been so at ease all morning that he'd assumed she'd be fine throughout the day. His own cat hadn't been concerned either. Now, the animal wanted to scoop her up and take her back home, loathing that she was uncomfortable.

Isaiah was about to suggest they go back regardless of Quinley's assurances, but she right then knocked on his parents' front door.

"If she gets worse, we'll make our excuses and leave," he made clear.

His mate waved away his concern—not being dismissive but reassuring. "She'll be fine in an hour or so. Don't worry."

*Don't worry?* He almost snorted. Next, she'd be telling him not to breathe.

The front door creaked as his mother pulled it open, beaming. "Merry Christmas, you two."

They returned the sentiment as she hurried them inside. The welcoming scents of hot meat, vegetables, and gravy laced the air and went right to his belly. His cat rumbled a hungry growl.

Andaya hugged them both and treated them to air kisses. She gratefully took the gift bag from him, and her smile went to a whole new level of bright when he removed his coat and she saw his sweater.

"Oh, I love this. I should get one made for Koen." Andaya's smile faltered as she took his mate's hand. "I'm sorry for last night, Quinley, I shouldn't have—"

"You got a scare, it's fine; I understand," Quinley assured her, hanging her coat on a hallway hook. "You can make it up to me by feeding me extra dessert."

Andaya grinned, clearly relieved. "That I can do." She looked at him. "I can sense the beginnings of the bond. I passed on my congratulations to Quinley last night. Congrats to you, too, sweetheart."

"Thank you," he told her. "Where's Dad?"

"Probably in that ugly armchair he won't part with."

"I've had this chair longer than I've had you!" Koen yelled from somewhere in the apartment.

"That doesn't change the fact that it's ugly and ratty-assed!" Andaya shouted as they began to make their way toward the living room.

Isaiah leaned into Quinley and lowered his voice as he asked, "You're really going to exploit her guilt to get yourself some extra dessert?"

Quinley frowned at him. "It'll make her feel better and it'll make my belly fuller. How is that not a win-win situation for us both?"

He shook his head. "You can be so sweet it's easy to forget you're also devious as fuck."

Her lips bowed up. "I know, I like it that way."

In the living room, they exchanged greetings and well-wishes with Koen. Andaya and Quinley then disappeared into the kitchen so his mother could show her the appetizers that were almost ready to be served. And he would bet everything he owned that his mate would start snacking on food before it was brought out.

Returning to his chair—which, Isaiah had to admit, *was* ugly as fuck—Koen said, "I'm real glad you both came, son. I know you might have preferred to spend your first Christmas alone."

Isaiah sank onto the sofa. "I also want Quinley to feel part of the family. This helps."

His father gave a satisfied nod. "Before the ladies reappear—because God knows your mom will kill me if she hears me talking about it—I have to say I couldn't be happier that another Vercetti is gone from the world."

"You and me both."

"How long do you think it will be before the last two brothers decide we're responsible for Tommaso and his driver's death?"

"Not sure. There are enough bounties on their heads that it won't be immediately assumed we're the guilty party. Not unless others in the pack knew of Tommaso's plan to come after me."

Koen glanced at the kitchen. "Did Quinley tell her family about last night?"

"No. She doesn't want to spoil their Christmas, so she's going to tell them tomorrow."

"They'll be furious that she was targeted a second time."

"Not more furious than I am." Isaiah flexed his fingers, his cat hissing at the memories of last night. "He almost got her, Dad. If she'd been stood just a few inches to the—"

"But she wasn't. She's alive, and she's fine."

"But not safe. And I hate that." Isaiah cricked his neck. "I hate the idea of her living in fear."

"She's a tough one, your black-foot. Not in a feisty, confrontational, in-your-face way. It's a quiet strength. It's part of what makes her soothing to be around." Koen paused. "Personally, I think the only one of you letting their worries get the better of them is you."

Isaiah sighed, loathed to admit his father might be right.

"Forget all that for now. Enjoy your first Christmas with your mate."

He set about doing exactly that.

Appetizers were eaten. Gifts were exchanged. Dishes were served. Christmas crackers were pulled. Visitors came and went. Evening snacks were passed around.

And yet, when the evening was almost over, his mate was *again* shoving food in her mouth. It didn't seem possible that anyone could eat so much that regularly throughout the day.

Beside her on the sofa, his belly so full he felt like he'd burst, he watched in fascination as she devoured a sticky toffee pudding. "I don't know how you're still eating."

She sniffed. "You're just jealous that you have no room left for extras."

"I mean, you're not wrong. But I still have no clue how you aren't full yet."

Koen laughed under his breath. "I heard that you and Alex are going to go head to head in a burger-eating contest," he said to her.

Isaiah felt his brows draw together. "A what?"

Quinley spooned more of her pudding. "It was Bailey's idea."

He sighed. "Why am I not surprised?"

"Alex stupidly thinks he's going to win," said Quinley.

At the other end of the sofa, Andaya slanted her head. "How do you know he won't?"

"I've gone up against a wolverine in an eating contest before. I won." Quinley shoved her spoon of dessert into her mouth. "Trust me, I have this in the bag."

The doorbell rang for about the thirtieth time that day.

Andaya stood. "I'll get it." She disappeared.

"I'm going to answer a call of nature," said Koen before walking toward the bathroom.

Isaiah turned his attention back to his mate. His gut clenched as she idly licked the back of her spoon. A frisson of heat worked its way through his blood and surged to his cock.

She stilled. Blinked. Met his gaze. "I felt that."

"Felt what?"

"*You know*. It was just a flicker of heat, but I felt it."

Another sign that imprinting was starting. "You'll be feeling a fuck of a lot more when I get you home later."

It was honestly killing him that they hadn't yet left, his mind filled with all sorts of plans. Going by her expression, she sensed it just fine.

He let out a pained groan.

Her lips kicked up. "You really shouldn't have looked in that bag."

"I know," he mumbled.

She chuckled, low and wicked.

# CHAPTER NINETEEN

Hearing the bathroom doorknob squeak, Quinley warned, "I'm not quite done yet." *Give a girl a second, would you?*

But the door swung open anyway, and then Isaiah stood right there—his feet planted, his face cold, his eyes hot.

She stilled, feeling a little like a deer caught in the headlights at the sheer sexual intent in his expression. Her pulse jerkily jumped, and her skin prickled as teensy little bumps rose.

His gaze dropped to her red-velvet bra, tracing over the white-fur trim and honing right in on the little bell that dangled from a bow between her breasts. His attention dipped lower, taking in the matching, diamante-buckled mini skirt—it was so short it left her ass pretty much bare and just about covered her clit. And then his eyes coasted further down, lapping up the sheer red stockings that featured tiny red bows on the lacy tops.

She hadn't yet pulled on the skimpy red thong that came with the outfit. The impatient bastard hadn't given her enough time, despite that she'd told him she'd return to the bedroom once ready.

His eyes skated back up to pin her with an unblinking stare, his focus absolute and unwavering. Her cat froze. The look in his eyes wasn't human. It was too feral. Too hungry. Too predatory. And positively indecent with how much carnality it transmitted.

Droplets of excitement rained down on Quinley. She was gonna get royally fucked and she knew it. Welcomed it.

A muggy tension simmered in the air, turning it thick and static. He didn't move. Just stared, his inborn air of dominance sharper and more intense than usual. Almost electric. Her cat reveled in it.

Quinley realized he had something balled up in his fist. Something white.

But she couldn't make out what it was.

And then she didn't care, because he was coming toward her, a sense of purpose in every step.

Her heart lost all sense of rhythm. Anticipation sizzled across her nerve-endings. Her fingers flexed with a delicious nervousness.

He halted in front of her, lightly brushing his nose over hers, nuzzling her face. His attention zipped to something over her shoulder, and she knew he'd be checking the rear of her outfit through her reflection in the mirror there.

He let his stubbled cheek rasp against hers and kneaded one globe of her ass. "Utter perfection," he said, a gritty rumble to his voice.

She swallowed hard, lifting her hands to touch him.

Isaiah gave a shake of his head and stepped back. He then lifted his balled-up fist and loosened it, allowing what he held to uncurl and dangle in front of her.

The silk tie from her robe.

Her pulse skittered.

"Hold out your wrists together in front of you." The dominance embedded in his tone settled on her bones, seized her compliance, and steadied her mind even as it sent her hormones into meltdown.

She allowed everything else to fall away as she centered her world on him, them, this moment. As she followed his instruction, she saw a sheen of pride in his eyes.

"You can't know how much it pleases me that you let go this way." He knotted the tie around her wrists, securely binding them together but not so tight it hurt. "If that starts to get uncomfortable, I want to hear about it."

She gave a firm nod.

His tongue eased out and licked along her bottom lip. "Good girl."

He swooped down and took her mouth. The kiss was fevered in its intensity and laced with pure entitlement; a kiss so heady she didn't notice he was herding her backwards until her skin met the cool tiled wall.

Isaiah freed her mouth, grabbed her joined hands, lifted them up, and attached them to the hook high above her head using the silk tie.

*Well, now.*

Satisfaction rippled across his face. "All mine to do with what I wish."

She gave a light, testing tug on the knot. No give. It sent her excitement soaring and stirred her cat up in the best way.

He trailed a finger down the column of her throat and between the valley of her breasts, flicking the bell there. "So *that's* what I heard the other day."

Quinley watched as he planted a hand on her stomach, spreading his fingers wide to claim as much skin as he could.

"My babies are going to grow in here, you know." One fingertip roamed downward until he reached her skirt. He flipped it up, and his eyes flared as they went from hot to scorching. "Bare."

Her heart thumped in her chest as he went to his knees. Again, her skirt was shoved up. She gasped as his tongue did an idle swirl around her tight bundle of nerves.

"Now," he began, his pitch lowering, "we both know you don't last long when I go down on you. But tonight, you're going to hold out until I'm done." Notes of dominance, compulsion, and sexual power were all threaded through his voice. "Is that understood?"

Was it understood? Yes. Was it possible? Likely not. "And if I fail?"

"I fuck you, but I don't let you come." He shrugged one shoulder. "Call that an incentive to help you hold out."

"I'm not sure I can."

"You can. You will. Because I told you to."

Isaiah threw one of her legs over his shoulder, the stocking incredibly soft but still nowhere near as soft as the luscious thigh he then gripped. Having her hanging right there on that hook, his own personal plaything completely at his mercy, was like a hot fist around his cock.

The earthy scent of her pussy drew him closer. He nuzzled her with a hum. "Already slick. Good."

He wanted to fucking devour her, but she'd come too fast if he did. So he stuck to featherlight licks of his tongue, barely-there nips of his teeth, and shallow dips of his finger.

He loved eating her out. Loved her taste. Her scent. The little noises she made.

Quinley tilted her head back and tried arching into his mouth. He didn't let her, keeping his grip on her ass firm so he could hold her hips at the exact angle he wanted them.

Stifling a smile at her low hiss of irritation, he took her clit between his lips and suckled over and over. She gasped, her leg pressing against his back. He went motionless, keeping his tongue pressed on her clit with the barest amount of pressure—enough to tease, madden, and inflame.

Then he shoved two fingers inside her.

She moaned, her inner walls beginning to spasm.

He pulled back and withdrew his fingers. "Oh no you don't."

She whimpered in frustration, sagging against the wall. "Why don't you like me anymore?"

He didn't bother holding back a chuckle. "Let's try that again, shall we?"

Isaiah went back to eating her out. Not soft or light this time, though. He dug right in and feasted.

With firm licks, suckling bites, and thrusts of his tongue, he drove her up high yet again. He knew her. Knew she was raring to come. But he didn't ease off.

He swiped his tongue up, down, left, and right; dragged it over her slick folds in a zigzag fashion; rubbed it along the side of her clit. But even as her thigh muscles quivered and her pussy quaked and her breathing went to shit, she held out for him.

"Such a good girl," he praised. "You can come now." He tugged on her clit and bit into her inner thigh hard, making his cat—drunk on her scent—growl in approval.

She came with a rasp of his name, her head falling back.

Isaiah surged to his feet and lowered his zipper, needing to be in her more than he needed to fucking breathe. He caught her ass again, lifted her, angled her hips just right, and nudged the broad tip of his dick inside her.

Her fuck-drunk eyes fixed on his, the gleam of her cat's gaze moving just behind them. The sight drew his own cat closer.

"Come whenever you want." He roughly rocked his hips upward, slamming deep, taking what was his.

Her breath hitched, her body jolted, and her pussy spasmed around him.

Isaiah groaned through gritted teeth. "Feel how deep I am, Quin. Feel me use you." He railed her hard, the drive to once more stake his claim beating in his blood and throbbing in his soul. The little bell on her bra jingled with every dig of his cock.

He looked down, watching her tits bounce in the red velvet cups. Tits that were as perfect as the rest of her and looked even prettier all covered in his marks.

Feeling her pussy start to heat around him, he snarled, "Who owns you?"

Once more, those sex-drunk eyes locked with his. "You."

He fucked her harder, jacking his hips upward again and again, his senses feasting on her—the spicy scent of her need, the carnal picture she made, her breathy moans and gasps, the hot viselike clasp of her pussy.

He let one fingertip whisper over the bud between the globes of her ass. "I'm taking this tonight, Quin. I'm gonna fuck it until you scream."

Her pussy fluttered, rippled, tightened, squeezed. And then she fractured with a rough cry, her head tipping back.

"Fuck, baby." He punched his cock faster, deeper, *brutally*. His release smacked into him like a battering ram, all but flattening him as her inner muscles milked him dry.

She went limp in his hold, breathing as hard as he was. He planted a kiss on her temple, sated and replete. Worried her wrists or shoulders might be hurting, he glided his cock out of her, put her on her feet, and then freed her hands. "You okay?"

Her only response was a gratified hum. She rested her body weight against his while he massaged the full length of her arms from her fingers all the way up to her shoulders.

"Thank you," she pretty much purred.

He cleaned her up with a wet cloth and helped her remove her outfit, knowing she wouldn't want to sleep in it, and then guided her into the bedroom. He slipped one of his tees on her and then ushered her into bed. She flopped on her front with a sated sigh.

Isaiah settled beside her and snaked his hand under the tee to palm her ass. "Christmas wasn't shaping up to be all too good this year. Then came you."

She smiled. "Right back atcha. December is usually my favorite month. The closer it gets to Christmas, the giddier I get. But not this time." Her smile dimmed. "There was too much dread around the thought of Harlan and Nel stepping down. Too much uncertainty about what lay ahead. I was sad and mad and stressed out. Then came you."

He pressed a kiss to her shoulder, not liking that she'd spent months in that state; feeling as if—irrational though it was—he should have been there for her. But he hadn't known she existed back then. Neither of them had even signed up for FindYourMatch.com or been ready for this step.

"I had a really great day," she said. "Your parents are the shit."

A fond smile curled his mouth. "They are." He paused, his lips pursing. "You never mention your parents."

Quinley didn't tense. It had been an observation, not a complaint.

"I didn't want to ask, because I have no wish to make you talk about something that's painful to remember," he went on before she could respond. "But if the imprinting is to progress, we can't keep things from each other. Secrets act as blocks to the bond."

It wasn't so much that she was being secretive, just that it was habit to not raise the subject. "It's not really as painful to talk about as it should be," she admitted. "Obviously, it's devastating that they died. I wish with everything in me that I hadn't lost them. But I don't remember either of them well enough for it to hurt whenever I think or talk about them."

"That's only to be expected. You were a kid when they died."

"Just five," she confirmed.

He idly dragged his fingertips down her bare arm. "How did they die?"

"My dad had a heart attack. He'd always had a weak heart. It was a birth defect that no healer could fix." It sadly worked that way sometimes. "My mom wasted away within a week of him dying."

"It's not easy for shifters to survive the breaking of a bond," he noted.

It was, in fact, exceedingly difficult. Still, some managed it, though they were allegedly never the same afterward. "Adaline said that Mom fought the pull to let go, but I don't get the sense that that's true. My opinion? My sister lied because she didn't want me to think our mom gave up and willingly left us."

His brow pinched. "What makes you feel it was a lie?"

"Adaline wouldn't meet my eyes, and Raya got all fidgety and turned away. Plus, they avoid talking about Mom. And whenever I'd ask questions, they'd keep their answers short and sweet. Like it hurt them to think of her. But when I'd ask about Dad, they'd smile and tell me all sorts of stories."

"Ah," he said, understanding. "It's normal for some to feel betrayed if a parent made no attempt to cling to life for their sake in such situations."

Absolutely. "I totally get it. That's why I don't push for them to talk about her and why it's become habit for me to just not mention my parents at all. It's not like I need to hear more. I know enough, and I remember some things."

"You said Adaline raised you. Didn't anyone else in your family attempt to step in?"

"My dad's parents were already long gone from the world—they died before I was born. He had no siblings, and we didn't know his extended relatives well. According to Adaline, his uncle from another pride did offer to take us in, but she didn't like him much. Apparently, Dad hadn't liked him either."

"What about your mom's family?"

"She wasn't in contact with them, not even her parents. They all live in another pride."

Unable to envision a reality in which Isaiah wouldn't be in touch with his parents, he asked, "Why the gulf between her and them?"

"They hadn't wanted her to mate with my dad because it was well-known due to his heart defect that he might not live a long life—it's typical for shifters with that condition, because the life we live and the amount of shifting we do causes too much strain on a weak heart. But she didn't care. She wanted to be with him."

"Were they true mates?"

"Yes, so it's pretty unreasonable that they expected her to walk away from him."

Very. It wasn't exactly a simple thing to ignore that you'd discovered your true mate. Yes, you could move on and still be happy—he and Quinley were examples of that. But not many shifters would abandon their fated mate over something like a health issue.

"Then her father challenged mine in protest, *knowing* what a duel could do to his health; probably hoping my mom would be put off on seeing how physically weak my dad was. It backfired. My mother appealed to Harlan to object to the duel, which he did. She then apparently disowned her parents, for which I can't blame her."

Neither could Isaiah. As something occurred to him, he narrowed his eyes. "So she always knew he might live a short life compared to other shifters, then."

"Yes. I think that's why my sisters are so mad she didn't fight. She'd had years to prepare for the day his heart might give out—it wasn't a shock to her. But she just let go."

Yeah, it made sense why Adaline and Raya would therefore be so upset.

"What about you? Are you mad?"

"No, I get it. Just as I get why my sisters *are* mad." She bit her lip. "From what I do remember of my parents, they were *so tight*. He was her entire world and doted on her. She lived for him. But then she couldn't, because he wasn't here anymore. So I understand why she might not have felt able to go on without him."

"It's easy to say a person should fight."

"It is. But you don't know if you'll have the strength or will to do it. Not really. I don't think *I* would if you …" She trailed off, swallowing.

Warmth flooding his chest, he nuzzled her shoulder. "I don't think I'd be able to do it either. Or that my cat would want me to." The animal wouldn't want to be without her any more than Isaiah would.

"I have to be honest, I didn't expect him to become so … invested. I believed he'd eventually come to consider me his mate, but I guess I always thought—given how wounded he was—that our connection wouldn't be airtight."

"How wrong you were."

She snorted. "You didn't expect it either."

"Initially, no, I didn't. But I'm not at all surprised that he is so attached to you and your cat. You fit us in a way that would be scary if we weren't determined to keep you."

"Totally get you on that one. I hope we won't be one of those couples who has to wait years before the bond makes itself fully known."

"I don't think we will."

She gave him a pointed look. "You *want* to think that, so you think that. But we can't *know* it, because the process of imprinting isn't easy to understand or predict."

"No, but I still feel confident that the process won't be dragged out." He squeezed her ass. "Don't worry so much."

"I'm not worried, just impatient."

"You're worried," he asserted, having already sensed it.

"Only because it would devastate me if everything went tits up. Being rejected by Zaire broke something in me. It took a while to mend. But to lose you would break *all* of me, and I don't think I'd ever heal."

His lungs burning with emotion, he pressed his forehead to hers. "You'll never have to know if you're right on that. We *will* imprint all the way, Quin. Our bond will be solid and vibrant. And it's never going to weaken or break."

"I hope not. Because you gave me you. No takebacks."

His lips curved. "Same goes for you." He lifted his forehead from hers and kissed her. "Nap."

Her brow arched. "Nap?"

"I told you I was taking this ass tonight," he said, sweeping his finger between the soft globes. "I wasn't kidding." To claim every part of her was a craving so primitive it badgered him constantly.

"You're letting me 'nap' because you like startling me awake by touching my no-no places," she accused.

He grinned. "Not one part on your body is a no-no place for me. I get to touch, taste, and take whatever I want."

"Well, yeah, there is that."

"Hmm, so nap."

"Okay." A put-out response, but she closed her eyes and let sleep pull her under.

# CHAPTER TWENTY

The following afternoon, Quinley cast an affronted look at the female sitting across from her in the diner. "I don't know why you keep glaring at me like that." It wasn't called for.

Adaline angrily plucked the shaker from the center of the table and sprinkled salt over her meal. "I specifically told you not to get shot again. I was very clear on that."

Oh, well if she was clear on that …

"But did you listen to me? *Noooo.*" Adaline sprinkled a little salt over the twins' fries and then put the shaker back down with a thump. "It really wasn't too much to ask."

*Sigh.* Of course, Quinley wasn't at all surprised by Adaline's behavior. She'd known that both her sisters would be furious on hearing of the second shooting. Adaline was prone to overreacting when super angry or extremely worried—the sniper incident was bound to make her feel both.

That was why Quinley had chosen to spill the news in public. Her oldest sister was less likely to wave her dramatic flag around if they weren't alone. An obvious choice of location had been one of the pride-owned eateries, since it would be safer. So she'd invited her family to meet her and Isaiah at the diner, and they'd happily accepted the invitation.

While they'd waited in the wide booth for their orders to arrive, Quinley had brought them up to speed. She hadn't had to be mindful of her wording for two reasons. One, the twins—who were snugly seated between their parents—wore headphones; their attention glued to the screen of their tablets. Two, because the only people around them were Olympus Pride members; there wasn't a human in sight.

Her plan had proven to be a good one. Rather than flying off the handle, Adaline had instead spent a whole ten minutes stewing in silence. Meanwhile, the others had posed questions at both Quinley and Isaiah, looking for more information.

Apparently, Adaline's period of silence was now over.

"You said it wouldn't happen again," the woman snapped. "I took you at your word."

Quinley exchanged a look with Isaiah, who sat as close to her as it was possible to be without them sharing clothes. It was clear to see by the tight set of his jaw that he did *not* like her sister's tone. Her inner cat wasn't too fond of it either.

Neither were the nearby Olympus Pride members, if their impatient expressions were anything to go by. Adaline's words were loud enough that they didn't get lost beneath the squeaking of stools, the clinking of cutlery, the sizzling of meat, and the music playing low.

The diner was as busy as always. Some patrons sat at booths while others were positioned on stools at the long counter. Waitresses moved back and forth, the rubber soles of their pumps making slight squeaking sounds against the checkered tile floor. Various food smells dominated the space, particularly that of hot oil, coffee, and frying onions.

"You're not even listening to me, are you?" clipped Adaline.

Will sighed at her. "You can't actually hold her responsible for what happened, Ade."

"Oh, I can."

"Not *rationally*," Quinley insisted, forking some coleslaw. "Look, I know you're upset—"

"'Upset' is a minor word for what I'm feeling." Adaline angrily bit into a slice of cucumber.

"But that doesn't give you the right to speak to Quinley that way," said Isaiah, his voice cool and calm and laced with a velvety warning.

Will predictably stiffened, his protective instincts ruffled. But he didn't try defending Adaline, likely because he knew she was in the wrong.

"Yeah, you're being a total drama queen, Ade," said Lori, sitting beside Quinley as she dug into her spicy chili. "When Raya got shot by my cousin years ago, you held *him* accountable. Maybe do the same here with Quinley's shooter."

Adaline blinked, her brow wrinkling. "Raya was shot?"

On Lori's other side, Raya gawked. "You don't even remember? A serious thing like me once having a bullet in my back just *slipped* from your memory?"

Adaline spluttered. "No. It was just a long time ago." She paused. "Right?"

Her jaw hard, Raya shook her head. "Oh my God, you don't remember. See, you totally love Quinley more."

185

"Would you stop with that shit? I love you both equally."

"I don't know how you manage to keep a straight face when you say that."

Waving the comment off, Adaline looked at Isaiah. "I do thank you for playing a part in killing the bastard who held the gun, but I can't deny being angry that Quinley hasn't been better protected. I know that isn't fair or rational—"

"Oh, *now* you know you're being irrational?" asked Quinley.

"—it's just how I feel," said Adaline, ignoring her interruption. "Your pride is doing the best it can to locate the Vercetti Pack, I know. But they came at her twice, Isaiah. *Twice*. That's, like ..."

"Two times?" supplied Quinley.

"*Unacceptable*," Adaline stated.

Setting down his iced water, he looked at Adaline soberly. "Trust me when I say you can't make me feel more pissed at myself for that than I already do."

Her brows snapping together, Quinley looked at him. "What? So now you're both going to be irrational?" Her agitated cat whipped her tail. "You're not at fault for them targeting me."

"No, I'm not," he allowed. "But I did know that I was bringing you into the pride at a dangerous time. I did it anyway."

*Oh, Lord.* "There's always *some* shit going down in the world of shifters. We're never totally safe."

"Which is why I wasn't going to let the situation get in the way. But I could have at least warned you before we mated. I didn't even do that much, not thinking they'd go after you."

"Any such warning would have made no difference. I wouldn't have considered it a reason to not take you as a mate. So unless you would have delayed things nonetheless, the result would be the same. And if you *had* needed such a delay, I would have chosen a different guy to ma—"

"We're not going to talk about that," Isaiah asserted, lowering his face closer to hers, possession etched into his features. That look made her cat all tingly.

"Okay. But you get my point." Quinley paused to drink some milkshake through her straw. "I'd rather be in the sights of the Vercetti Pack than be all safe and sound while bound to a different male."

His expression softening, he dabbed a kiss on her forehead. "I know you would. And I don't regret that I claimed you. How could I? But I can still acknowledge that I was selfish to do so when I had the Vercetti Pack gunning for me."

Sliding his headphones backwards so they were hooked around his nape, Ren lowered his half-eaten patty melt to his plate. "Dad, can you pass the ketchup?"

"Sure, son." Will handed the condiment bottle to him. "Liking your food?"

There was a bubbly squirting sound as Ren squeezed red sauce onto his plate. "It meets with our approval." He offered the condiment to Corey, who paused his movie.

"Boys," began Adaline, her tone all maternal patience, "remember we spoke about how you don't need to speak for each other?"

"We remember," said Corey, heaping ketchup over his fries.

Adaline exchanged an exasperated glance with Will.

Lori gently bumped her shoulder into Quinley's, saying, "Recommending the chili was a good shout, it's amazing. I'd totally eat here again."

Raya hummed. "Same. We should make it, like, a weekly family meetup. Only without Adaline."

"Hey," Adaline complained, her frown deepening when the boys giggled. She snatched one of Ren's fries in retaliation, and the kid promptly coughed all over it. "Ew, no!" she groused, dumping it back on his plate.

Corey gave her the sweetest smile. "Mom, can me and Ren have a strawberry sundae for dessert?"

"Don't ask on behalf of your brother. He might not want a strawberry sundae."

"I do," Ren told her.

"Well, you coughed on me, so you don't get one," she teased.

"Speaking of desserts," Raya piped up, "I'm *so* having pie after this. Maybe blueberry. Or lemon meringue. Maybe both."

Right then, a figure appeared at the table. "Ah, Quinley, such cute little boys," said Valentina. "These are your nephews, yes?"

"They are," Quinley confirmed, smiling. "I tried introducing them to you at the party in the Tavern weeks ago, but they frequently disappeared to the arcade area."

"What are your names?" the wolverine asked them.

Ren pointed at his brother and said, "He's Corey."

"That's Ren," Corey told her, tipping his head at his twin.

"I am Valentina. How old are you?"

"Eight," they replied at once.

"And you are black-foots?"

"Uh-huh," they again answered in unison.

Valentina's mouth twitched. "You make me think of my Mila and Alex when they were younger. They are twins, too. They would finish each other's sentences and would swear they knew what other was thinking. They always seemed to know when one was hatching plan to kill other."

Corey giggled. "We like you."

"And so you should." Valentina pointed at Quinley. "Do not eat too much or you will be too full for hamburger eat-off tomorrow."

Quinley smiled, putting a hand to her stomach. "Oh, a black-foot can never eat *too* much."

Valentina barked a light laugh and disappeared.

Raya looked at Quinley. "You're competing in a hamburger eat-off? With who?"

"Valentina's son, Alex. Like her, he's a wolverine."

"Which means there is a chance he'll win," said Isaiah. Every head at the table swung his way and treated him with a pitying look. He lifted his shoulders. "What?"

They only sighed.

Isaiah went back to his meal, his hackles lowering now that Adaline had calmed down. He got that she was concerned for her sister, and he understood why she'd be so upset on hearing what had happened—she wasn't the only one. But he didn't like her taking any of that out on Quinley.

His cat, equally annoyed by it, would have swiped a paw at Adaline if Isaiah had allowed him to shift and warn her off. Though she'd now eased back, the feline still watched her closely.

Thankfully, though, the rest of the meal went smoothly. Everyone enjoyed their food, and his mate's family suggested they eat at the diner again soon. Afterward, they walked back to the cul-de-sac, where both sisters had parked their cars.

Quinley wasn't content to merely wave goodbye to her nephews, she grabbed them both, pulled them into a huge hug, and peppered their faces with kisses. He liked watching her with her nephews. She was so good with them, and he could all too easily imagine her with their own children.

After waving off her family, he and Quinley went inside the house. They spent a couple of hours lounging around, watching TV. And, in her case, snacking.

It was just as their movie finished that his cell rang. "It's Tate," he said as he looked at the screen of his phone.

"He probably wants to discuss enforcer stuff," Quinley predicted, pushing off the sofa. "I'll let my cat out for a run while you two talk."

Isaiah frowned at her back. "Don't let her go far," he said even as he pressed the "answer" button on his phone.

"I won't," Quinley promised, heading for the rear patio doors. "She'll stick to the backyard."

Snorting, Isaiah put the phone to his ear. "Yeah?"

"Why did you just snort?" asked Tate.

"Because Quinley assured me that her cat wouldn't go further than the backyard."

An equally dubious snort came out of the Alpha. They both knew that her cat considered every backyard in the cul-de-sac to be an extension of her own. She wouldn't pass the rear perimeter of any fence, but she *would* hop from yard to yard.

As always, it would annoy their neighbors that her cat had the nerve to prowl along their fences while looking them dead in the eye. These days, though, they didn't try chasing her off. Partly because they liked Quinley too much to get annoyed by her cat's antics at this point. But also because they didn't want to find more icky "gifts" in their house.

Tate went on to relay several pride matters—some minor, some more serious. It was his way of ensuring that Isaiah still felt a close and vital part of the inner circle regardless of how he no longer spent as much time with the Alphas. Isaiah appreciated it.

After twenty minutes or so, the conversation reached its end. There was no sign of Quinley yet, though. Isaiah was about to go outside and release his own cat so that the animals could have some quality time together, but then his phone beeped. He saw that it was a message from Havana: *Zaire's back.*

Feeling his jaw harden, Isaiah strode to his front window. Sure enough, the black-foot stood near the bottom of the driveway arguing with Tate, who was flanked by Farrell and JP.

Isaiah's cat jumped to his feet, his fur puffing up in anger. Spitting out several curses, Isaiah headed outside, slamming the door closed behind him. He'd seriously had enough of this motherfucker.

Zaire's gaze zipped his way at the slamming of the door. He rounded on Isaiah, his eyes whirling orbs of fury. "She was shot *again*? I overheard what happened, I couldn't goddamn believe it had occurred a second time! You're supposed to keep her safe!"

"Calm the fuck down," clipped Tate.

Zaire scowled. "You expect me to be *calm*?"

Shaking his head in disbelief, Isaiah said, "You have got some real fucking nerve to act like Quinley's wellbeing means anything to you." It was honestly astounding.

Zaire actually appeared offended—which was quite frankly just as astounding. "Of course it's important!"

"Yeah?" Isaiah squinted. "For years she dealt with all kinds of bullshit when part of the Crimson Pride. Everyone knew you'd one day rule it alongside Nazra; you had enough influence over them that you could have made it all stop. But you did *jack*."

Zaire snapped his mouth shut, visibly floundering. "I told people that the rumors weren't true."

"That wasn't enough, though, was it? They didn't leave her alone. You could have done more. You could have ordered them to back off. You could have shut all that shit down. But you didn't." No, he'd done the bare minimum … and then gone about his life without a qualm.

Zaire looked away, his jaw clenching.

"You sat back while a bunch of your peers—all dominants, all high in the hierarchy—bullied an unranked submissive who'd done *nothing* to deserve it.

And then you fucking *mated* one of them. You claimed a woman who'd wanted to make Quinley miserable." How exactly the black-foot could ever have brought himself to do that was beyond Isaiah.

"Back then, I didn't know Quinley was my—"

"From the start, you let her down in every way possible," Isaiah went on, striving to keep his cool when his cat urged him to rip this motherfucker apart. "And now you don't even have the fucking decency to stay away and let her live her life."

"I would if she was safe in this pride, but she clearly isn't!"

"If that was the case, it would have not one thing to do with you." Isaiah smoothly stepped forward. "Does Nazra know you're here?"

Zaire's eyes flickered.

"Thought not." At this point, Isaiah would have felt sorry for her if it wasn't for how she'd treated Quinley over the years.

"I want to know why the hell no one in this pride seems to give a shit about Quinley's safety. Is it because she's a black-foot? Or is it that she's a submissive?"

"Unlike black-foot prides, we don't think 'submissive' means 'weak.' She's a valued member of this pride, and she's under the protection of every single dominant. The only one standing here who's ever looked down on her is *you*."

Zaire's head flinched back. "I have never looked down on Quinley."

He was *seriously* going to claim that? "That's bull, and we both know it. You've never viewed her as your equal. You see submissives as lesser shifters. Most dominant black-foots do."

"How the hell would you know?" he sniped.

"Because she told me. She explained how it goes. Explained how obsessed you all are about status. Told me how the unranked and more vulnerable pride members reside near the border of your territory—they'd be the first to be slaughtered in the event of an attack, and everyone else seems fine with that."

Shocked mutterings came from his pride members who were nosily observing from porches or front yards.

"The unranked are considered expendable, plain and simple. So maybe you get why I'm thinking you have some balls to act concerned over the idea that *this* pride might not be making her safety a priority. It was never a priority in *yours*."

Zaire swallowed. "Black-foot prides operate differently—that is true," he said, the words stiffly spoken. "But all our members are considered important."

Havana huffed from her position a few feet behind Tate. "You sure have a weird way of showing that."

Agreed. "The fact is, Zaire, that you never gave Quinley's wellbeing a second thought before—"

"I didn't know she was meant to be mine," the black-foot upheld. Isaiah shot him a skeptical smirk. "I don't buy that. Not anymore."

# CHAPTER TWENTY-ONE

I saiah inwardly smiled at how Zaire stiffened. *Bingo.* "Hearing the shit you say and the *way* you say it … I think you figured out some time ago that she was right. But I also think you did your best to ignore it, because you cared about Nazra and were too set on being an Alpha of a pride."

It was what the guy had strived for growing up, what he'd likely been groomed to be, what his inborn nature would have demanded of him. And with the way black-foots operated, he could never have ruled with a submissive at his side.

"Not true." The hard protest held a shaky note that betrayed its lack of genuineness. "I didn't know."

His cat snarling at the lie, Isaiah forged on, "You bonded with Harlan's daughter instead, who I think you do love. You thought you'd be happy with her; happy to rule alongside her. And maybe you are to some degree. But there's a strain on your relationship. I'm standing close enough that I can tell your imprint bond is chipped at the edges. What caused it?"

Zaire's eyes flared. "That's none of your—"

"Let me take a guess." Really, it seemed pretty obvious. "At some point, you realized your personality is better suited to a submissive than a born-alpha."

The black-foot pulled in a sharp breath.

"You and your cat need things from Nazra that, being the complete *opposite* of a submissive, she simply can't give. In the beginning, you may have been able to gloss over it. But it steadily began to eat at you and your animal, and you soon started to wonder if maybe you should have made different choices. Still, you stayed on the path you'd put yourself on."

As someone who'd never been able to exercise the full extent of his

WHEN HE DARES

dominance until Quinley, Isaiah knew how it felt to have to hold back. It was like boxing away a part of you. It meant leaving certain needs unmet. It stopped you from feeling completely fulfilled. And there eventually came a point where that lack of fulfilment nagged at you.

Isaiah suspected it had been nagging at Zaire for some time. The black-foot had likely ignored it, sure it would disappear once the position of Alpha became his; sure *that* was what he needed.

"My relationship with Nazra is none of your fucking business," Zaire hissed.

"And my relationship with Quinley is none of yours. Doesn't stop you from coming here and expressing opinions I don't give a shit about."

"The only reason I'm here—"

"Is that you're hoping you can push me into starting a brawl," Isaiah finished. He'd picked up on that pretty much straight away. It was why he hadn't planted his fist right in the black-foot's face. Isaiah was feeling no inclination to give Zaire anything he wanted. "Then you get to have an excuse for why violence broke out—you were just defending yourself."

Zaire's nostrils flared. "I'm not here to challenge you."

"But you want a full-on duel. So does your cat. I can feel his rage. He wants to gut me open. I have what he thinks belongs to him. Only he's wrong. Quinley's mine."

Zaire's eyes briefly flashed cat as an animalistic growl eased out of him. "If you give such a damn about her, why has she been shot twice while under your watch?"

Isaiah didn't point out that the second shooting had resulted in a bullet-graze, not a full-on shot. He didn't owe this male anything, regardless of what the dick seemed to think. "Pride business is pride business. You're not entitled to know shit. You never were, where Quinley's concerned. And yet, you've kept an eye on her through others."

Surprise rippled across Zaire's face.

"It was an easy enough guess," said Isaiah with a slight shrug of one shoulder. "You 'overhear' far too much. Having people report back to you anything interesting regarding her all these years—that's where you fucked up. By indulging your need to know what happened in her life, you kept her in your mind's eye; in your cat's mind's eye. It would have been better for you to go on as if you'd never met her."

Not that it would have been simple. Isaiah knew that personally—he'd kept watch over Lucinda, unable to help himself. The difference here was that he had stopped once he claimed Quinley. Zaire hadn't done the same when he claimed a different female.

"You really didn't know about her plans to enter an arranged mating, though," Isaiah mused. "My guess is that your sources kept it from you—probably at the bidding of Nazra, who worried you'd otherwise put a stop to it." He slanted his head. "She was right to worry, wasn't she? You would have stopped it."

Zaire ground his teeth. "I wouldn't have wanted Quinley to bind herself to a stranger, so I would have found her a different mate."

Isaiah snorted. "You couldn't even bring yourself to stop monitoring her. How could you have given her to another male? You definitely wouldn't have consented to her leaving the pride. It would have suited you and your cat to feel that you had some control over her. You hate that you don't. You hate that I have her. But what you hate more is that you have everything you thought you ever wanted ... and it *still* feels like something's missing. Which, you've come to realize, is Quinley. You're here to vent all your shit on me."

"No—"

"I'd warned you last time you showed up here that I'd take your return as a challenge, so you were banking on me attacking you instantly. Your mistake was in thinking that I wouldn't pick up on it."

"*I'm here because I need the dreams to stop,*" Zaire burst out. "That's what happens when I fight any urge to see her, or I know she's in danger. I dream about her." He paused, his eyes narrowing perceptively. "You know what that's like."

"Yeah, I do. It sucks. But it doesn't change that you have no right to be here."

Hearing the dick claim that Quinley featured in his dreams, it was hard for Isaiah not to lunge forward and claw the fucker's face right off his skull. The only thing that stayed Isaiah's hand was knowing it would give Zaire the reaction he wanted. Why else admit to a man that you *dreamed* of their mate?

A shuffling sound came from his left. Isaiah looked to see Quinley's cat edging out from under a car. He tensed, not wanting her to be exposed to this.

He expected her to snarl at Zaire or swipe out a paw in warning, but she didn't. She deigned the guy with a disinterested look and padded over to Isaiah. She then scrabbled up his side to settle on his shoulder like she belonged there, paying the Alpha zero attention.

It hit Isaiah, then. Hit him hard. Right in the chest. And it was the best kind of punch. Because it was apparent that she felt no need to warn Zaire away since, as far as she was concerned, he presented no threat to her and Isaiah's bond.

His raging cat ceased pacing, soothed by just how much she evidently trusted that the connection they were building couldn't be sabotaged. It settled something in Isaiah as well, making some of the tension leach from his shoulders.

He reached up to stroke her head, his eyes on Zaire; watching the emotions that drifted across the Alpha's face. Pain. Jealousy. Anger. Conflict. Resentment.

The thing was … those feelings weren't really about Quinley as a person. They were visceral reactions; came from the elemental heart of Zaire and his inner cat, *not* from their emotional heart.

Her little feline continued to pay the guy zero interest. She was all about scent-marking Isaiah, rubbing the side of her neck against his head.

Zaire's gaze flicked back to his. "My cat was like that with Nazra in the beginning. Not so much now. That's how it goes with imprinting." It was a taunt.

"Only when the bond becomes brittle. That won't happen with me and Quinley. And if you had put all your focus on Nazra instead of selfishly keeping tabs on Quinley, it might never have happened to *your* bond. Maybe you could fix it—I don't know. Don't care. I'm done here."

"But—"

"Admit it or don't, but we both know you came in the hope of provoking me into starting a fight. I'm not going to give you that. I'm not going to give you any damn thing." Not even his cat, despite how much he'd enjoy mauling this son of a bitch, would grant him any such satisfaction. "You can either challenge me, or you can *get the fuck* out of here."

Zaire wanted to challenge him. It was evident in his expression and body language. He wanted to give his inner animal the release it desperately sought; wanted to punish Isaiah for claiming Quinley.

The male's gaze again bounced to her cat, who'd tucked herself into the crook of Isaiah's neck—something she occasionally did at home to nap. She was purring, content. And something about it made the anger in Zaire's gaze fade, only to be rapidly replaced by pure turmoil.

"Do you see how settled she is right there?" Havana asked the Crimson Alpha, sidling up to Tate. "There you are, fronting off against her mate. But she's not pacing and hissing or tense as a bow. She's perfectly relaxed, trusting that he'll protect them both if necessary."

Zaire slowly swerved his head to look at the devil shifter.

"To her, *he's* her mate and you are quite literally irrelevant," Havana bluntly stated. "Fighting with Isaiah won't make you relevant to her. Nothing you do would mean anything to that cat. You rejected her, you turned your back on her, you did nothing to protect her when she needed protection, and you went and claimed another female."

"I know what I did," Zaire gritted out.

"It's like Isaiah said before," Tate cut in. "You hate him for having her, but you hate more that the choices you made years ago didn't bring you the contentment you were sure they would. Do you really want to make Quinley pay for that?"

Zaire glared at him. "I'm not making her pay for anything."

Havana cast him a *Come on* look. "Dude, you're stood here trying to goad her mate into a public brawl. How can you think that won't impact her? You can sense that they're imprinting on each other, so you know she cares for him. If you were to hurt him, it would hurt her. Haven't you done enough of that?"

Zaire averted his gaze again, swallowing hard.

"Go," said Isaiah, pulling the black-foot's attention back to him. "There's nothing for you here. You won't get a duel, you won't get contact with Quinley, and you won't have a shot at fixing your bond with Nazra unless *you move on.*"

Zaire drew in a long breath, his attention zipping to Quinley's cat.

Isaiah peered up to see that she was now staring at Zaire, a warning in those eyes.

The Alpha's own eyes turned cat again, his animal looking right at her. She went back to scent-marking Isaiah—making it clear where her affections and loyalties lay.

A low growl oozed out of the male cat. Zaire's eyes abruptly became human once more, and he squeezed them shut as he shook his head hard.

Tate folded his arms. "What's it gonna be? A fight with Isaiah, or a lifetime without Nazra—because let's face it, you won't manage to repair things with her if you go ahead with a duel."

Zaire's eyes snapped open, pinning Tate with a glare.

"And bear in mind that if you lose Nazra, you'll lose your position of Alpha as well," Havana tacked on. "Then giving up Quinley will have been for nothing."

And that … *that* seemed to get through. Because Zaire's glare eased, the hardness in his gaze melting away. He spared Quinley's cat another look, his mouth tightening, a long exhale escaping through his nose. He then gave his head another fast shake and sharply pivoted on his heel. Moments later, he was driving out of the cul-de-sac.

Havana turned to Isaiah. "For a minute there, I actually thought he'd choose to challenge you nonetheless."

So had Isaiah. "It was that last comment you made that caused him to reconsider." He looked off in the direction of where the car had headed.

"I doubt his cat will pester him to come back, because that little miss up there"—Deke tipped his chin at Quinley's feline—"made it very clear in how she behaved that she's too committed to you to find anything a threat to your partial bond."

Yeah. And damn if it wasn't a seriously good fucking feeling. "Which is likely why she came out in the open. She knew it would get the message across."

Havana gazed up at her, smiling. "She looks so sweet when she's not standing on my fence giving me a death stare. I admire her guts too much to be mad about it."

Tate snickered. "*And* you don't want to be one of the neighbors who finds creepy little presents on their bed."

"That, too," the devil admitted.

The feline fidgeted, turning her head toward the house, digging her claws into his shoulder just enough to get her wish across.

"We're gonna head inside," Isaiah told the others. "Later." Gently plucking the cat from his shoulder, he held her against the front of his chest as he reentered the house. In the living room, he nuzzled her little face. "Shift for me."

Bones snapped and popped as she changed shape. Then he had a very naked woman in his arms.

Burrowing further into him—likely for warmth—she tilted her head, concern etched into her face. "You okay?"

"I wasn't, because he was pissing me off. But then your cat made an appearance. And realizing she didn't perceive him as an impediment to the development of our bond … that got me." And everything inside him and his feline had relaxed.

"She did want to make a point to him, but she was also anxious to soothe you. For me and my cat, he's just a nuisance. We still don't want him near you, but we have too much faith in our growing bond to think anyone but me, you, and our animals could jack it up."

Which they never would.

"I swear, Lucinda could walk right up to our front door—and yeah, I'd want her gone; I'd ensure she knew that she wasn't to come back. But I wouldn't worry that seeing her would change things for you. Not now. You assured me the day we saw her at the mall that you'd let her go, and I trust that you meant it."

That was yet *another* warm punch to his chest. "Good. Because it would change nothing. You're all I want. All my cat wants." He cocked his head. "How much of the conversation did you hear?"

"A lot, but I don't know how long you'd been talking before my cat snuck over. I heard you mention something about sensing that his bond with Nazra was chipped at the edges." She sucked on the inside of her lower lip. "You were right in believing he wanted to push you into throwing down a gauntlet—it was plain to see."

"He wanted my blood, but he needed an excuse to draw it."

"He wouldn't have felt better for it afterwards. He also would have screwed everything up for himself—and for no good reason at all. Havana shouldn't have had to point that out to him." Quinley idly tugged at Isaiah's collar. "Maybe he'll now go mend his bond with Nazra."

Isaiah couldn't say he wished him luck or anything. The guy was a fucking tool, and he'd let Quinley down one too many times. Not that Isaiah was mad at Zaire for giving her up—he never would be, because she wouldn't otherwise be his—but he was pissed that the male had never tried putting an end to the crap she'd dealt with for years from his peers.

"It surprises me that I appear in his dreams. I mean, he did used to appear in mine when I was younger. But after he claimed Nazra, it stopped for me. I would have thought he could say the same." Her expression turned cautious. "Do you still dream about Lucinda?"

Ah, such a deceptively casual question.

"I won't be upset with you if you do," she hurriedly assured him. "It's not exactly something you can control. I'm just wondering."

He brushed his mouth over hers. "No, baby, I haven't dreamed about her since before I claimed you." Quinley took up too much of his mental space to leave room for anyone else.

Her lips hitched up. "I'm glad you're free of them."

Well, of course she'd be more bothered about how *he'd* be affected by the dreams than how they'd make her feel. *Typical Quinley.* "I dreamt of you before I even met you."

She blinked. "You did?"

He nodded. "The night after we exchanged messages on FindYourMatch.com. I don't remember the dream all that well, but I do remember you were pregnant."

A thoughtful expression slipped over her face. "Do you think it was something to do with Lucinda being pregnant? Like … your mind substituted me for her in the dream as a reflection of how you were moving on?"

"Not sure. All I know is that I woke up feeling good for the first time in a while. It made me more eager to meet you." He slid his hands down to cup her ass. "And when I saw this phenomenal ass right here, I was sold."

She chuckled. "I have noticed you seem to like it."

Considering he'd bitten it, finger-fucked it, claimed it, come inside it, and spanked it hard enough to leave a handprint there … yeah, he wasn't surprised she'd figured that out.

"For me, it was how cool and steady you are that pulled me in. *I'm* not shallow, you see, so I'm not swayed by physical attributes like you clearly are."

He grinned. "Bullshit. You eye-banged me just as I did you."

"Believe what you want."

"I believe what's true."

A little shiver took her. "Now I need to dress, because I'm getting chilly even with your body heat. Also, I want to hunt down a snack or two."

"Naturally," he said, his voice dry. "Before we get down to just enjoying the rest of our day, I want you to know one thing. If Zaire comes back, I may kill him."

She thought about it for a moment. "Oh. Okay."

*Oh. Okay.* Isaiah smiled and hugged her tighter.

# CHAPTER TWENTY-TWO

"Wow," breathed Aspen. "That is one *beast* of a burger."

Isaiah nodded, grimacing as Andaya placed a large platter on the table in front of his mate. On top of it stood a high stack of beef patties that were skewered between two buns. Between each layer were sauces and other toppings such as slices of tomato, cheese, or pickles.

"How many patties are there?" asked Havana.

"At least thirty," Isaiah estimated, scratching his jaw.

The pride had decided to hold the hamburger eat-off in the communal yard behind Alex's apartment building. A table and two chairs had been brought out for him and Quinley. They sat side by side with a person-sized space between them.

The scents of grilled meat, melted cheese, and warm bread drifted through the air, mingling with the smells of pond water, wildflowers, and tree bark.

Isaiah stood reasonably close to the table, a bunch of his pride mates fanned out around him. Though the yard was large, it was cluttered with trees, rockeries, shrubs, and tall grass—thus making it the ultimate playground for pallas cats. Still, there was enough space for the pride to gather around and witness the eat-off. Other spectators hung out of the building's windows, including Elle—who was babysitting a currently-sleeping Aurora.

An identical tower of patties was right then brought out by Valentina, who set it in front of Alex. The male wolverine regarded it with a haughty *Is this it?* expression, as if all he'd been given was a bag of chips.

A low snort popped out of Bree, who then glanced at Isaiah and said, "To be fair, he has a right to all that arrogance."

Maybe so. But the same could be said for Quinley, who was studying her own stack with a cunning eye. She wasn't at all nervous. Isaiah knew it for sure, because the only flickers of emotion he felt breezing along their partial bond were anticipation and hunger.

For the past few days, they'd each been able to feel echoes of the other's emotions. Something which delighted them both, just as it did their inner animals. It illustrated that the imprinting process was still progressing.

With a sigh, Havana turned to him, an awkward expression on her face. "Look, Isaiah," she began carefully, "I know your mate can eat like a fucking dinosaur, but surely she doesn't have enough room in her small body to fit *that* many patties in her."

"Don't underestimate her digestive system." It was like nothing he'd ever before known. "I wouldn't bet against her." His cat felt quite sure she'd win.

"She doesn't seem at all deterred by the size of the burger," Tate noted.

No, she didn't. Her posture was relaxed and confident, her smile easy and casual. Like she was just sitting down to dinner at a restaurant. And it wasn't an act.

"Alex doesn't seem put off either, though," Deke observed, idly playing his fingers through his mate's hair. "He also doesn't look like he has any intention of losing."

Alex was in fact the image of determined, cricking his neck, his gaze focused on the burger with lethal accuracy.

"Well, my guy's very competitive, as you all know," said Bree. "He'll be furious at himself if he loses." She looked at Isaiah. "You think he will, though, don't you?"

"Yep," said Isaiah. He'd allowed his mate to think he wasn't so sure, but only to mess with her. "Wolverines are big eaters mostly because they're greedy. Quinley's not greedy—her metabolism is just freakishly fast. She can eat and eat and eat without ever really getting full. Biology will win over greed." Alex would hit a "wall" at some point. She wouldn't.

"My money's on her," Bailey piped up, leaning into Deke. "But I think Alex will be a close second."

Bree winced. "He won't take that well."

"Just give him a blowjob afterward," advised the mamba. "He'll get over his snit quick enough. It works with Deke."

The enforcer frowned down at her. "I don't get in snits."

"Of course you don't." Bailey gave an exaggerated wink.

With a slow shake of his head, Deke faced forward again. Which was right when Quinley looked their way, a pretty smile gracing her lips, and gave them a little wave.

Isaiah returned the smile, his cat nudging at him to head over to her, not liking the distance between them. The feline was starting to become a clingy little shit. But as Isaiah didn't like being apart from her either, he really couldn't judge.

"Luke would have loved to watch this." Blair sighed, clearly wishing he was here. But he, Farrell, and Camden were absent—all back on the hunt for the Vercetti Pack.

Isaiah had expected to find at least *one* of the pack hanging around. Of course, it wasn't easy to be sure that none were loitering about, because not every pack member's picture had been circulated online. But none of the pride had noticed anyone or anything suspicious.

Bailey caught Blair's eye. "You should take a video for Luke so he can watch it when he gets home."

Her eyes lighting up, Blair whipped out her cell. "That's a great idea."

"I'm full of fabulous ideas," claimed the mamba.

Aspen slid her a sideways, dubious look. "I wouldn't call them 'fabulous.'"

"That's because you're boring," Bailey told her plainly. "I feel so sorry for Camden. No wonder he never smiles. You must make his life so dull. So. Very. Dull."

Deke's eyelids fell shut, a tired sigh easing out of him.

Aspen's face firmed as she angled her body to face the mamba. "My mate is perfectly happy, thank you very much."

Bailey's brow dented. "Why are you thanking me?"

"I'm not—ugh, stop being a pain in my ass."

"Learning new habits is hard," stressed Bailey. "And boring. Like you."

Her face reddening, Aspen made a move toward her.

Havana slammed up her hand. "Leave it."

The bearcat's brows drew together in frustration. "Oh come on, getting slapped around would do her some good."

"It would amuse her, nothing more," stated Havana. "And Deke will only get between you anyway. Let's not make him pay for her sins again."

"Sins?" echoed Bailey. "I'm an honest to God's angel."

Deke actually snorted at that.

Havana cast the mamba a disbelieving look. "They don't call us the unholy trinity for nothing. You are far from angelic. And you really need to stop pushing Aspen's buttons."

"Why?" It appeared to be a genuine query. "And how is pointing out a character flaw triggering for her? We have to know these things or we can't grow as a person."

Havana's eyelid twitched. "Don't play innocent."

"But I like that game."

Deke curved his arm around the mamba's neck. "I think maybe it's time you paused the game, though. The eat-off is about to start anyway."

Bailey brightened, turning her attention back to the table. "Awesome."

Isaiah looked over to see one of their pride mates Archie standing behind Quinley and Alex's chairs. His inner cat slinked closer, not wanting to miss a thing.

The older male clapped to get everyone's attention, nodding in satisfaction when the chatter died down. He cleared his throat. "Okay, contestants, prepare yourselves."

Alex plucked off both the top bun and first patty at once. He squeezed them together as if to make them thinner and then held him near his mouth.

Casually, Quinley removed the top bun but put it to the side of her plate. She grabbed the first patty, along with the toppings splattered on it, and positioned it in front of her lips.

Just then, Isaiah's parents appeared at his side.

"I think I'm more nervous than Quinley," said Andaya, putting a hand to her stomach.

Koen's lips quirked. "I don't think the girl's nervous at all."

She wasn't. She was completely confident that she had this in the bag. And as her gaze leapt to his, Isaiah gave her a slow and encouraging nod.

Archie lifted a finger. "Ready. Set. Go."

Alex stuffed his food in his mouth, eating it in only five bites.

Quinley wasn't quite as savage, but she ate like a beaver in fast-forward. It was fascinating to watch.

"You got this, baby!" Isaiah called out, his cat pacing.

Other voices shouted words of encouragement to one or both parties as the seconds ticked by. Both the wolverine and black-foot broke down the patty tower layer by layer. Occasionally they'd pause to sip from the bottles of water provided, but then they'd go straight back to their food.

The faster eater of the two, Alex fell into the lead. But Quinley didn't appear whatsoever dispirited by that, and no feelings of tension or self-doubt tripped down the partial imprint bond.

Isaiah kept on loudly egging her on, as did his parents. Alex's family were equally as loud and vocal, and there was a touch of smugness in their tone.

A smugness that faded when Alex began to slow, his cheeks stuffed, his mouth chewing hard, his throat bobbing slowly as he swallowed.

The guy had hit a "wall," just as Isaiah had predicted he would.

Quinley, on the other hand, was undergoing no such struggle. She was also catching up fast, able to swallow her food more easily than Alex because she broke them down into smaller bites.

Suddenly, with only four patties left to eat, she stood up. Isaiah frowned, thinking she might be quitting. But then she continued to eat.

"She's making it easier for her belly to expand," Blair realized. "Smart."

It was. Alex didn't mimic her move, but he did begin to recover from his earlier struggle. He went back to scoffing down his food ridiculously fast.

Reaching the last patty and bottom bun, Quinley nabbed both along with the top bun she'd earlier put aside. She then slapped the three layers together, making a conventional burger, and began to eat.

Isaiah understood her strategy, then. Buns were filling. You might have a better chance at fitting lots of meat in your belly if you saved the buns for last. *Clever girl.*

Alex kept on eating *mega* fast, even though he looked a little pale. He snatched the bottom bun from the skewer … just as Quinley was announced the winner.

She beamed, delighted. But clearly not at all surprised.

Isaiah whooped while his cat plopped down on its ass, smug as all hell.

Alex, however, moodily tossed his food on the table, disgusted at having lost.

"Oh, dear," said Bree with an amused wince. "He's a seriously unhappy bunny right now."

While people clapped and cheered, Isaiah and Bree walked straight to their respective mates.

Rounding the table, Quinley proudly notched up her chin. "Told you I'd win. You shouldn't have doubted me."

"I never did, not even for a second." He caught her by her hips. "I just let you think I did."

She gave him a playful, dirty look. "Asshole."

"Yeah." He planted a quick kiss on her mouth.

Quinley looked at her fellow contestant, doing her best to stifle a smile. Alex was leaning back in his chair with his arms sulkily folded, his expression a pure glower. She'd been warned that he was a *terrible* loser, but she had to admit she hadn't quite expected this level of self-directed fury. Bree stood beside him, clearly dying not to laugh.

"You mad?" Quinley asked him, her cat a mixture of perplexed and amused.

The wolverine grunted, stubbornly not meeting her gaze.

"You did really well," she praised. "Almost beat me."

Apparently, that meant nothing to him, because he kept on glowering at thin air.

"It's the taking part that counts."

Alex glared at her. "No, it isn't. All that matters is winning. Only. Winning."

*Ooookay.*

Valentina materialized near Bree. "Son, I have no words. A wolverine does not lose at eating contest. We *invented* eating contests. We always win. Always. This loss defies logic."

"Thought you said you had no words," Alex dryly muttered.

"I am speechless. *Speechless,*" Valentina repeated, a hand to her head. "That is not normal. And I am never without words."

"You're *still* talking."

"Bah." Valentina strode off, muttering about weaknesses.

Alex stood and pointed at Quinley. "You. Me. Rematch. New Year's Eve.

Tavern."

Bree's brow furrowed. "That's when our pride has its annual party."

"It can be part of the entertainment," he stated with a shrug.

Quinley cocked her head at him, curious. "You find it fun for people to watch you lose? That's odd."

Bree started cracking up.

Alex's glare landed on his mate. "What are you laughing about?"

"I'm not laughing." Bree pretty much wheezed out the words.

"I can hear *and* see you." Shaking his head, Alex prowled off.

Quinley exchanged a smile with Isaiah, who then drew her away from the table. Their other prides gathered around to pass on their congratulations. She was honestly surprised that so many people had come to watch the contest. But then, she was used to being part of a pride that had divisions and separate celebrations. The Olympus Pride was different. A huge, tight, supportive family. And she was delighted to be part of it.

When the crowd finally thinned out, Isaiah asked her, "What would you like to do with the rest of our day? I feel like we should celebrate your win somehow."

She gave an easy shrug. "I don't mind what we do."

"We're all planning to go bowling," Havana cut in. "You two should come."

Uncomfortable with going too far from the pride when there was a target on Isaiah's back, Quinley let out an uneasy hum. "I'd rather stay local," she said, to which her mate nodded.

Aspen frowned, her shoulders drooping in disappointment. "Ah, come on, there'll be a huge group of us. What's the worst that could happen?"

Bailey spoke, "Earthquakes. Falling meteorites. Nuclear explosions. The death and destruction of all we hold dear."

Impatience flickering across her face, Aspen sighed. "Ignore her, Quinley. It will make your life so much easier."

"I resent that," said Bailey with a huff.

Aspen gave Quinley a tight smile. "As I said, ignore her."

Bailey grabbed the bearcat's index finger and started prodding Aspen's temple with it. "Stop poking yourself, stop poking yourself, stop poking yourself, stop poking—ow, bitch, that was my nipple!"

"*I don't care!*" Aspen blasted.

Bailey smirked. "Thought you were ignoring me."

That was when the bearcat all but flew at her.

Havana swore. "Aspen, let go of her throat *now!*"

As Deke and the Alpha female worked to pry the females apart, Isaiah looked down at Quinley and said, "I say we skip bowling."

She pursed her lips. "We could go play pool at the Tavern?"

His brows lifting slightly, Isaiah nodded. "That works." His gaze darted to her empty plate and then down to her belly. "Need to vomit first?"

She felt her brows draw together in honest confusion. "Huh?"

Smiling, he gave a shake of his head. "Never mind. Let's go."

# CHAPTER TWENTY-THREE

The chiming of her cell phone snapped Quinley out of her reverie. She'd been staring out of the kitchen window unseeing, caught up in thoughts as to what Isaiah had in store for tonight.

He'd earlier made a passing teasing comment designed to keep her on sexual edge, the shit. And she couldn't pester him for answers because they had visitors in the form of Tate, Luke, Camden, and Deke—all of whom were chilling with Isaiah in the living area, drinking beers and discussing pride issues that needed addressing before the New Year's Eve party tomorrow.

She retrieved her phone from the kitchen island. *Raya.* Smiling, Quinley answered, "Hello?"

"Be smart and alert no one," a male voice said. A voice that was gruff and cold and unfamiliar. "Believe me when I say that the life of your sister depends on it."

Dread curdled in Quinley's belly and caused every muscle in her cat's body to seize up. "Who is this?"

"I think you know."

It could only be one of the Vercetti Pack, couldn't it? *Fuck, fuck, fuck.* Terror snaked around her throat, its hold tight.

She wanted to go to Isaiah, but she didn't trust that—unaware of the danger to Raya—he wouldn't simply snatch the phone once he picked up on Quinley's distress.

She swallowed. "You're one of the Vercetti brothers?"

"We can get the introductions out of the way when we meet. And you're going to want to meet with me if you want your sister and her mate to live."

Her gut rolled. Raya *and* Lori? "How do I know you really have them? Maybe you just stole Raya's phone or cloned it." After all, it wouldn't have been easy to capture *two* black-foots.

A choked female scream sounded in the background and made her cat flinch.

*Oh, God.*

"Still think I might be bluffing?" he taunted.

Maybe not, but she had to consider that … "All I heard was a scream. That could have been anyone."

There was a rustle, and then her caller spoke to someone in the background: "Say hello to your sister."

"Fuck you, asshole," was hissed in response.

Quinley's eyes fell shut. Her cat let out a low, drawn-out yowl of distress. That was definitely Raya.

"Good enough?" he asked.

Her pulse speeding up, Quinley opened her eyes. "Yes."

"What do you say to a trade-off? You for them?" It wasn't really a suggestion. It was a demand.

It also took her by surprise. Quinley had thought they'd ask for her *and* Isaiah in exchange. Then again … that wasn't really the pack's style, was it? They took women and children, not men. And never dominants.

"I won't tell you that you'll walk out of this alive," her caller continued. "That would be a lie. Hale killed someone important to us. Now we'll end the life of someone important to *him* … Or we'll end that of these two bitches here."

Right then, Isaiah rounded the corner of the living room and stalked into the kitchen, his brow furrowed. He'd sensed a flash of her anxiety, she thought.

Quinley slammed up a hand and shook her head, warning him with a wide-eyed gaze to do nothing. She put a finger to her lips, and he stealthily made his way forward.

"I only really meant to take your sister, but she was rarely without her mate so I simply took both," her caller said. "Their stay with us hasn't so far been very comfortable. They're eager to go home. You want that for them, don't you?"

"I do," she said as Isaiah put his ear close to her cell, doing his best to overhear the other side of the conversation.

"Good. Then be outside the phone box near your local train station in an hour. *Alone.* If I see anyone else with you, both your sister and her mate are dead."

Isaiah's gaze shot to hers, blazing with anger.

Her stomach dropping, she took a shaky breath. "I'll be there." As an idea came to her, she added, "Although …"

"What?" her caller prodded.

"I guess I'm just confused about why you wouldn't rather trade them for

Tommaso."

A long pause. "Your pride does not have Tommaso in their custody." The statement held a hint of unsurety.

"My Alphas detained him the night he tried assassinating me," she said, watching as a smile of sly approval pulled at Isaiah's lips. "He's been with us ever since."

Another pensive pause. "Your mate would never have let Tommaso live if he'd tried killing you."

"Isaiah would like to kill him, yes, but he's set on first finding out the location of your pack. Tommaso is the only one who can give us that information. But he hasn't been talkative so far."

A gruff hum sounded. "I'm not sure I believe you. What I'll promise you is this: If you trade yourself for the females I have here, I won't kill you. I'll instead offer your mate the option of exchanging Tommaso for you. If Tommaso *is* alive, you'll get to go free. If he isn't, you die as planned." With that, the line went dead.

The terror that had earlier gripped her throat squeezed, and she grabbed onto Isaiah's arm as if to anchor herself. "The Vercetti Pack has Raya and Lori."

Isaiah pulled her into his arms, calling out, "Tate, we got a situation here!"

She sank against him, trying to get a handle on her breathing—it had turned quick and shallow. Her cat was no better. The animal was freaking the fuck out.

He rocked Quinley from side to side, palming her nape. "I got you."

"What is it?" asked Tate, striding into the kitchen with Luke, Camden, and Deke.

It was Isaiah who explained, "Someone from the Vercetti Pack just called Quinley."

Tate's jaw dropped. "The fuck? How?"

Quinley licked her lips. "They used my sister's phone—that's why I answered; I thought it was her. The pack has both Raya and her mate."

"Bastards," Luke spat.

"Call Havana and Blair," Tate barked to his brother. "They need to hear this."

Anger stomping through his blood, Isaiah pressed a kiss to his mate's hair. A dozen curses hovered on the tip of his tongue, but he held them back. She was expectedly shaken, and she needed him to be calm; needed to feel steadied. If he released his own anger, it would only feed her distress.

His cat—anxious to both soothe their mate and hunt down those who'd dare upset her—pushed against Isaiah's skin to be closer to her. The fuckers *would* pay for this.

He guided her over to a stool and gently propped her butt on it. "Just sit here, Quin." He poured her a glass of water and pushed it into her tremoring hand. So she wouldn't spill her drink, he curved his palm around her hand and helped guide the glass to her mouth.

She tip a sip, visibly striving to pull herself together. "I heard her scream," she said. "He did something, and Raya screamed. It was my fault. I called his bluff, so he hurt her."

Frowning, Isaiah set her glass on the breakfast bar and palmed the sides of her head. "Hey, it was not your fault. If he hurt her, it's because he's an evil fuck—that's it."

Her lips trembled, plucking at his heart. He held her tight again, rubbing his hand up and down her back.

Havana and Blair arrived quickly, accompanied by both Aspen and Bailey.

"What happened?" demanded Havana, her face a mask of unease. "What's going on?"

"Quinley just received a call from a member of the Vercetti Pack," Tate told her.

"*What?*" Bailey burst out.

"They have Raya and Lori," Isaiah added.

Blair gaped. "Are you sure?"

"Positive," Quinley murmured. "I heard my sister's voice. It was definitely her."

Camden's jaw hardened. "Kidnapping people is nothing new for the pack." His gaze settled on Isaiah. "They want you in exchange?"

"No," said Quinley. "Me. They want to kill me to punish Isaiah for Samuele's death."

*Not fucking happening.*

Curses rang throughout the room.

"I wasn't supposed to tell anyone." Her brow creased. "It's weird that he'd be adamant about that, isn't it?"

"What do you mean?" asked Isaiah, brushing a hand over her hair.

"Well, we're mates," she replied. "He has to have known you'd sense my panic; that I wouldn't be able to hide from you that something's wrong."

He shrugged. "Maybe he counted on you to lie about why you were panicking, or maybe he doesn't know we've imprinted on each other enough for me to sense your emotions." He only really felt flickers of said emotions, and not all the time.

"I guess." Quinley rubbed at her throat. "I'm supposed to go to a meet-up location alone. I'm sure that kind of thing works out okay in movies. Real life? Unlikely."

"The pack would kill Raya and Lori even if you did cooperate," Luke told her. "We have a better chance of saving your sister and her mate if we take on the pack as a pride."

"I know. I'm trusting you to save them." Quinley paused. "I tried convincing whoever called me that you have Tommaso in your custody; I put the idea in his head that he could instead trade Raya and Lori for him."

"Clever," praised Bailey. "What did he say?"

"He doubted I was being truthful." Quinley began tapping her foot restlessly on the rung of the stool. "He said he still wants me to come to him but he won't kill me—he'll instead propose to Isaiah that he could hand over Tommaso in exchange for me."

"It was probably Sebastian who made the call," hedged Aspen.

Quinley's brow wrinkled. "I'm not so sure about that."

Isaiah stroked a hand over her hair again. "Why?"

"He never once referred to Tommaso as 'my brother,'" she explained. "He'd say 'your sister' and 'your mate,' but he didn't use similar terminology when talking about Tommaso."

"I suppose it doesn't really matter who made the call," said Deke. "What matters is that we act fast."

Havana nodded, her gaze sliding to Quinley. "Where exactly are you supposed to meet the pack?"

"The local train station in an hour. You need to be careful how you go about this. He said he'll kill them if I don't go alone." Quinley looked at Isaiah, and whatever she saw on his face made her breath hitch. "You're thinking they're already dead," she sensed.

Isaiah clamped his lips shut, not wanting to confirm her assumption. But the fact that he didn't—couldn't—deny it was enough for her face to briefly crumple. He kissed her forehead, silently apologizing for being unable to give her any reassurances.

"What's the plan, then?" Camden asked no one in particular.

Tate twisted his mouth. "We get to the spot well in advance. We scope it out. We try to anticipate where he may wait for Quinley to appear." His attention zipped to her. "You'll stay here."

She tensed. "I'm submissive, but that doesn't mean I can't be of any help here."

"We know that," Isaiah assured her. "This isn't about you not being a dominant. You're the furthest thing from weak that any person can be." She was strong, brave, smart, and cool under pressure. "But I'm not using you as bait."

Her expression went tight. "Isaiah, I can't do nothing."

"Baby, I've been studying how this pack works. I've read up on every job they've ever completed. And what I feel right down to my bones is this: They have no intention of doing any trade."

Her brows flicked together. "What?"

"They took Raya and Lori so they could draw you out into the open and ensure you stay in one spot. They mean to shoot you where you stand; kill you right there and then flee." Just the idea of it made his chest pang and his cat lash out in fury.

Quinley's lips parted. "That's why you think my sister and Lori are probably dead."

He dipped his chin. "If the pack keeps them alive, it'll be with an intention to traffic them—nothing more." He hadn't wanted to confess that, but she was smart enough to figure it out on her own anyway.

She squeezed her eyes shut and ground her teeth. "Shit."

"I get that you want to be part of this, Quinley," Havana cut in, "but it wouldn't help to throw you out there as bait. The pack hasn't evaded capture this long by being careless. They've already messed up their past three attempts at trying to kill members of our pride; they're not going to risk it happening again. That means they won't take the chance that you haven't told us about the phone call."

Camden nodded. "They wouldn't make a grab for you—they wouldn't risk putting themselves out in the open like that. They're more likely to decide on a drive-by shooting."

Quinley let out a long sigh. "Okay."

Tate frowned, seeming surprised she'd backed down. "Okay?"

"Well, you're all right in what you say. So if I wouldn't make good bait, there's no sense in me going. I'm not an enforcer. I don't want to be in the way or take up a car seat that should be given to someone who's trained for this type of situation." Quinley zeroed in on Isaiah again. "I need you to promise me you'll be careful."

Relieved she'd agreed to hang back, Isaiah palmed her neck, giving her a pointed look. "I promise you."

"Do we tell the Crimson Pride Alphas about the kidnapping?" asked Bailey. "I mean, as Raya and Lori's Alphas, they have a right to know. Not that I *care* they have that right, just asking."

"It would be fair to notify them," Tate allowed, "but they wouldn't work *with* us. Especially not Zaire. I honestly wouldn't trust him not to cause problems just to push Isaiah's buttons so they finally end up having that brawl he wants. We don't need those kind of distractions. Raya and Lori don't need them, more to the point."

Everyone murmured their agreement, including Quinley.

Tate's phone rang. He pulled it out of his pocket, peeked at the screen, and then quickly answered, "I was beginning to wonder if you three were still alive … Okay, no need to take that tone … I'm not home, I'm in the house next-door; Isaiah's place … Right." He lowered his cell. "That was Sergei."

Isaiah had figured it was one of Alex's uncles, since Tate had said "you three."

"Have they found the pack?" asked Havana, her hands joined.

"I don't know yet. He hung up before I could ask." Tate pocketed his phone as he left the room. Moments later, the front door hinges squeaked and Tate again spoke, "I called and called. None of you answered your phone."

"We were on hunt," said Sergei, his voice indignant. "We do not use phone when hunting."

The front door slammed shut. "You said you'd keep me updated regularly," Tate griped.

"I did not."

"Yes, you did."

"Then I lied."

Tate reappeared, grumbling something beneath his breath. The uncles came in behind them.

Dimitri immediately went to the fridge as he announced, "We found Vercetti Pack."

"Where?" asked Isaiah, his cat going still.

"Burned-out compound near old textile factory," said Isaak.

Camden cocked his head. "The one that used to house human anti-shifter extremists?"

"Yes." Isaak planted fists on his hips. "It is derelict now."

Camden's mouth tightened. "I searched that area and found nothing."

Dimitri pulled a pear from the fridge. "Of course you found nothing. You are not wolverine."

Quinley leaned into Isaiah. "We have pears?"

Apparently so.

"The pack uses old mine tunnels beneath compound," Sergei told them.

Aspen looked at Camden. "If they're hiding underground, that'll be why you didn't realize they were in that area."

Dimitri scowled. "No, it is because he is not wolverine."

"Right," Aspen drawled. "Anyway, I wouldn't be surprised if whatever humans own the building are aware that the pack's using the mines."

"It is probable," Isaak decided. "I think extremists once used tunnels to traffic weapons. They have done it before in other locations."

Sergei cricked his neck. "Scramblers were used outside to mask scents so no one would pick up trail to follow."

Tate looked at Camden. "That'll be why your nose didn't lead you to them."

Another scowl from Dimitri. "No, it is because he is not—"

"Wolverine," Tate finished. "Whatever." He swept his gaze over everyone. "This changes our plans. I say we invade the mines and rescue Raya and Lori rather than scope out the train station."

"Makes more sense," Havana agreed. "Camden was right that they'll probably choose to do a drive-by shooting, so it'd be hard to catch them anyway."

Deke's gaze bounced from wolverine to wolverine. "How did you find the pack?"

Dimitri gave an easy, arrogant shrug. "It was not so hard."

"Then what took you so long?" Deke challenged, a brow inching up.

Dimitri narrowed his eyes and chucked the rest of the pear in his mouth, core and all. "Do not annoy me, dumb cat. I am too hungry to argue. I would only eat your head, and then you would scream like babe."

"Without a head, I can't scream," Deke calmly pointed out.

"I said, do not annoy me."

Quinley twisted on her stool to better face the uncles. "When were you last at the compound?"

"A few hours ago," Isaak told her. "We came straight here when we were sure it was their hidey hole."

"Did you see the pack take any females inside? They've kidnapped my sister and her mate."

Isaak's eyes rounded. "Ah, I thought those two looked familiar. They were at your party, yes?" He turned to Sergei. "Did I not say we had met them before? I was so sure, but I could not remember where."

Quinley grasped her knees tight. "They're alive?"

"They were," said Isaak. "I do not know if that is still so."

"We'll find out once we're inside the mines," Tate piped up. "On that note …"

His simple prompt had everyone readying themselves to leave.

Isaiah kissed Quinley on the temple. "I won't be long."

She squeezed his lower arm. "You come back to me."

The anxiety in her expression was killing both him and his cat. Neither wanted to leave her, but taking her along was not an option. "Nothing could stop me from coming back to you." His concern was that he wouldn't be able to return with good news about her loved ones. "Raya and Lori—"

"You are *not* to blame if something happens to them. I know you'll do your best to bring them home alive if they're not already dead." She choked on the latter word.

Swallowing, he touched his forehead to hers. "I'll see you soon."

Watching several shifters file out of the house in the cul-de-sac, Sebastian Vercetti smiled from his position in the woods at the rear of it.

"You were right, Seb," said his brother Davide beside him. "She told the others."

"I knew she would." Feeling his upper lip curl, Sebastian rasped a hand over his buzzcut. "You can always count on a submissive to turn to dominants when panicked. They can't handle shit themselves."

Their mother had been the same—a weak, spineless damsel. One who'd cowered from her father, even when the bastard was beating or caning her own sons.

On his left, Wattie noted, "A lot of them are leaving. Why that many?"

Sebastian spared the dark, burly hyena shifter a quick look. "They probably plan to surround the train station and catch us in action." And they'd fail, because there would be none of the pack there for them to find. Just imagining the bastards scratching their heads and chasing their tails made him smirk.

That smirk widened at the sight of the black-foot waving them off from the porch. "There, Hale's left her behind." It had been a given that he would, since a submissive would be no good in a fight. She would be too scared to go along in any case. Probably begged Hale to leave her at home.

The only reason Sebastian and his pack had had trouble with *this* particular submissive was that she was a black-foot. Running one to the ground had its … challenges. That was why they'd shot her sister and the other female with tranquilizers before dragging them from their car.

The pack had originally thought of capturing Hale's black-foot the same way, but none of them could ever get close enough to her for that—the pride's security was too tight, and Hale acted as her guard at all times.

Sebastian had known that if they could somehow draw away several of the strongest members of the pride, they'd have a chance of getting to her.

That chance had arrived.

Their plan had been successful. The Olympus shifters had fallen for it, thinking the pack intended to use Hale's mate as bait. Nah, it was her relatives who were the lure.

Davide turned to him, a glimmer of conflict in the amber eyes they both shared. It was hard to look at him sometimes; made Sebastian's throat ache. Aside from having different colored irises, he bore an uncanny resemblance to the baby brother they'd lost, even down to the scruffy haircut.

"Are you *sure* they won't contact the Crimson Alphas?" asked Davide. "The females we took are under their protection. They'd have the right to know that their pride mates were kidnapped."

"Hale isn't going to include the true mate of the woman he claimed—he'll want to be her hero," Sebastian pointed out with an inner eye roll. Once shifters mated they lost their edge and turned into fucking pussies. "Besides, what does it matter? The involvement of an additional pride won't help them. They'll be looking for us in the wrong place."

Davide didn't appear reassured. "But if the Crimson Alphas *do* hear of it, the Alpha male would probably come straight here to protect her—then he'd find us."

Sebastian shrugged, unconcerned. "Then we'd kill him." Simple.

His brother and Wattie exchanged an uneasy look. Something they did a *lot* lately. Samuele's murder had thrown the entire pack, and it had turned *these* two shifters into fucking fretters who hesitated to take chances. His wolf swiped out a paw, annoyed by their lack of confidence in Sebastian and his plan.

He looked from Davide to Wattie. "Remember: We need to move carefully. The Olympus shifters won't be expecting this, so they won't be prepared for it. But the enforcers who are left will still be on the lookout." The fucking pride seemed to have eyes everywhere.

*But not here.* Because Sebastian had already shot the cat who'd been patrolling the wooded area.

His brow knitted, Davide caught him with a probing gaze. "You don't still mean to kill her, do you? I want Hale to suffer as much as you do, which means I want her to suffer. But if we snuff out her life, we'll never get Tommaso back."

Sebastian licked over his front teeth. He'd known there was a high probability that the pride was somehow responsible for Tommaso's disappearance. So many times his brother had ranted about how someone needed to go blow Hale's brains out. Sebastian had insisted it was too predictable and they needed to proceed carefully.

But whereas Davide and Samuele had always been fairly easy to maneuver and manipulate, Tommaso was too erratic and impulsive to be controlled. So when he'd snuck off and then hadn't returned, the pack had figured it was likely he'd gone after Hale and been subsequently killed. Sebastian had been shocked when their packmate Peter—who'd made the call to the black-foot—notified them that she'd claimed Tommaso was alive and in the pride's possession.

Sebastian was also highly skeptical that Hale would have allowed his brother to keep breathing. He let that skepticism show on his face as he cocked his head at Davide. "The Olympus Pride isn't known for being merciful. You really think they wouldn't have executed him?"

Davide's square jaw firmed. "What I think is that *he'd* never give up on *us*. If he thought there was a chance we were alive, he'd keep looking until he found us or had proof we were goners. And the pride isn't merciful, no, but they might have decided to hold off on killing him until they have our pack's location—they'll be intent on wiping us all out."

True, but … "I'm not convinced he's alive. Hale's mate seemed to know a lot, though. If the pride really has him, she'll know where. She can point us in the right direction. And if she doesn't, or it turns out she lied, I'll just make her death that much more painful."

He wasn't going to make it an easy death. No fucking way. Blood was owed, and it would be taken.

Wattie rubbed at the back of his head, ruffling his tousled dark hair. "Maybe we should just back off."

Sebastian glared at him. "Haven't we been over this already?"

"Yes, but I still say it might be best to cut our losses," said Wattie. "You can't say you don't wish we'd targeted a different pride. We thought it wouldn't be too hard, since the Olympus shifters don't live on a massive stretch of land somewhere. That was a huge miscalculation on our part. These assholes are proving tough to take out."

"We just killed one of their enforcers, didn't we?"

"Yeah. *One.* We also went after several of the pride—a kid, an enforcer, and a black-foot. Every attempt went to shit." Wattie lifted his shoulders. "We could just walk away."

"But we're not going to. Their fucking enforcer *killed* Samuele."

"Maybe we should have listened to him. He had doubts about going after the pride."

With that, Samuele's words flitted through Sebastian's mind ... "*I say we pick another pride to target, Seb. You know their reputation. Pallas cats are crazy motherfuckers. I don't feel like pitting myself against them.*"

Sebastian had waved that off, undeterred. To go after a pride with such a rep would only lead other shifters to fear the pack more. "Are you saying it's *our* fault he's dead?"

"No. I'm saying we made a mistake in dismissing his concerns."

"Stop being a fucking pussy, Wattie. We're not cutting our losses. End of." The days when Sebastian ran from anything were *long* gone. He wasn't that reedy little kid anymore who'd been preyed on by his own grandfather. Sebastian did the preying now.

Once upon a time, he and his brothers had been a mere group of lone shifters—no pack, no land, no other family, no protection from shifter groups. So they'd built their own pack. They'd pulled in other loners, expanding it one by one.

Their pack was what shifter groups *should* be. There was no hierarchy. No ranks. No weak links like submissives or omegas or females.

When they wanted to fuck, they brought in women—shifters, humans, it didn't matter—and had their fun. Then they either killed them or sold them.

Occasionally they'd let a female leave so she could spread the word that the pack was still something to be feared.

Fear was important. It kept people in line. It kept them cooperative. It kept them at bay.

For years they'd been public enemy number one. They liked it that way. No matter what group of shifters they took on, they always came out on top. Always.

This time would be no different. Sure, they'd had a few ... issues here and there. But that would just make their triumph over the Olympus Pride so much sweeter.

Wattie exhaled heavily. "Let's at the very least back off for a little while; let them think it's over. We could come back months from now, when they won't be expecting it. Come on, Davide, you have to agree it's the best option."

"I would agree … but we can't walk away when they might have Tommaso," said Davide. "They know he's missing, so they either have him or they've killed him—just as we'd already suspected. We *have* to know what happened to him."

Wattie swore beneath his breath. "We need to make this quick, then, or we're not going to get out of this alive. As soon as she realizes we're in the house, Hale will know something's up. He'll feel her fear. He might not know what's wrong, but he'll know she needs help."

"He'll only sense that if they're fully imprinted. There's *no way* they're that tightly bonded. They were mere strangers when they mated." Sebastian glanced at his wristwatch. "We'll give the cats time to drive a fair distance away and then we'll head over there. We have questions to ask, a black-foot to kill, and a nice surprise to leave for Hale to find when he gets home."

# CHAPTER TWENTY-FOUR

Slumping onto the sofa, Quinley swore long and hard. All she'd done since Isaiah and the others had left was repeatedly alternate from sitting to pacing. And there'd been cursing. Lots and lots of it.

Stuffing her hands between her thighs, she rocked forward slightly. God, she felt like screaming. She really did. Anxiety crawled over her, making her skin prickle and itch.

It made Quinley feel shitty that she couldn't be relieved to be tucked up in the safety of her own home right now. Isaiah had wanted her to be, to *feel*, safe and therefore at ease. But it was *hard* for a person to be left behind at times like these.

It would absolutely be harder for those driving into danger, yes—*ten times* harder. But it was a kind of torture to be here alone while others risked their lives, especially when one of those people was your mate.

Watching Isaiah go, waving him off, going back inside and doing *nothing* ... She felt useless. Powerless. Useless *to him*.

If she'd been dominant, an enforcer, she could have gone with him. She could have helped, could have had his back and fought at his side. But Quinley was neither of those things, so she would only have been a hindrance to him. That hurt in a huge way, as did the fact that she'd need to trust the others to watch his back. They had their own mates to look out for.

Her inner cat was in no better state, anxiety-wise. She was all knotted up inside, worried for Isaiah and Raya and Lori; annoyed that she wasn't part of the hunt for the Vercetti Pack.

For the feline, it wasn't only about wanting to help, though. It was about answering her craving for vengeance. The animal wanted to savage the bastards who'd shot her and tried to take Isaiah. She knew they wouldn't stop coming until *someone* was dead.

The cat was determined that that "someone" would not be either her or Isaiah. So was Quinley. But here in the house, she wasn't able to do anything to ensure it didn't come about.

Sitting up straight, she took a stabilizing breath. It didn't help much. Impatience, panic, and uncertainty badgered at her.

It felt as if time had slowed down. Every minute felt like an hour. Every five minutes without a call from Isaiah made her stomach bottom out.

The occasional faint vibe of reassurance skipped down their partial bond. It made her heart squeeze that even now, when he had so much to think about, he made sure to take moments to comfort her and set her mind at ease.

But even with that reassurance he offered, her stomach kept rolling and her chest kept tingling and she couldn't shake off the dread. Her mind kept obsessing over what might be happening to Raya and Lori; over whether they were even still breathing.

*Please don't let them be dead.*

Fear for them lived and breathed in her gut. Quinley felt that same fear for every member of her pride who'd gone to the mines. She even feared for the three wolverines.

But most of all, she feared for Isaiah.

As mates went, she couldn't have done better. He was amazing. Everything she could ever have wanted. And if something happened to him at the hands of the Vercetti Pack—

She cut the thought off, her lungs burning at the mere prospect of it.

Even as she told herself not to think about what could happen, corners of her mind conjured up and fixated on worst case scenarios. *None* of which helped calm her cat.

Biting at her lips, Quinley put a hand to her fluttering stomach. He'd be fine. He would. The universe wasn't so cruel as to hand her such a mate and then snatch him away in a matter of weeks.

A floorboard creaked.

Quinley started. Held her breath. Went unnaturally still.

She heard it again. Another creak. *The stairs.* Someone was on the stairs.

A chill raced down her spine, and her cat nervously jumped to her feet.

Her phone. She needed her phone. She quickly glanced around and then remembered that, shit, it was in the kitchen.

She didn't really have time to make a call, though, anyway. Not if she meant to hide. So Quinley called to her cat and shifted.

H is hands clenching on the steering wheel of the SUV, Luke sighed at the wolverine riding shotgun. "I'm just saying that aggressively invading the mines would not be the best way to go."

"Why not?" demanded Isaak, who wouldn't stop whining about the Alpha pair's plan to conceal their presence from the pack as long as possible.

Tate had written off the wolverine's protests before hoping into the other SUV with Havana, her bodyguards, and their mates. The rest of them were riding in this vehicle.

"Once they know we're there, they'll kill Raya and Lori if they haven't already," replied the Beta, a hint of impatience leaking into his voice.

Isaak's brows met in confusion. "Who?"

"Quinley's sister and her mate," Blair reminded him from her seat behind Luke.

"Our aim is to rescue them, not put them at risk," Luke said to him. "So rather than charge into the mines like Viking marauders, we need to do as Tate ordered and move quietly. It's best we pick off their numbers one by one."

Isaak peeled back his upper lip. "Such a hideous plan."

"You mean tedious," Dimitri remarked, sitting beside Isaiah in the rear passenger row.

Isaak twisted his head to peek at his brother. "Is that not same?"

Dimitri pursed his lips. "Well, yes."

Isaiah exhaled heavily, feeling sorry for whatever females mated these crazy fuckers. "Tedious or not, stealth is what we need here."

Dimitri huffed. "Fine. My brothers and I will lead," he declared with the authority of an Alpha.

"You really expect Tate to agree to that?" asked Luke, catching the wolverine's eye in the rearview mirror. "Because he won't."

Dimitri sighed. "Why must you argue? Always you cats want to argue."

Luke's face scrunched up. "That's *you*."

"It is best we lead," Sergei maintained from Dimitri's other side.

"Why?" Isaiah challenged.

Sergei shrugged. "It just is."

Dimitri exchanged an exasperated look with Sergei. "Always they want to argue."

Isaiah stilled as an echo of fear skittered down the partial imprint bond, sharp and cold. A buzz of adrenaline came next, rapidly followed by a sense of "fight or flight."

Unease clutching his throat and raking at his cat's insides, Isaiah whipped out his phone and called Quinley. It rang and rang and rang, but no one answered. *Fuck.*

"Something's wrong." Isaiah shot forward in his seat, his cat anxiously unsheathing his claws. "Luke, stop the SUV. *Now.*"

The Beta frowned. "What?"

"Stop the fucking SUV! Quinley ... I felt her fear. A spike of adrenaline. And now all I'm getting is *pure* pissed-off female."

Cursing, Luke slowed the vehicle. "Call one of the neighbors; have them check on her."

"I don't need to," began Isaiah, speaking through his teeth. "I *feel* that something's wrong. The rest of you should head for the mines—our pride can't afford to be outnumbered—but I'm going back."

"Do you think it's Zaire?" asked Blair, her expression concerned.

"I don't know, but it could be the Vercetti Pack," said Isaiah, talking fast. "It didn't make sense to me that Sebastian would try luring her to the train station—the plan had a low chance of success, so why bother? Maybe all he wanted to do was draw us away. Luke, let me out of this fucking SUV or I *swear ...*"

"I'm stopping, I'm stopping." The Beta pulled up as they reached the emergency lane at the verge of the road.

"I'll call Farrell and have someone pick you up," said Blair, all business, her phone in hand. "Stick to the side of the road while you're running and you'll cross paths with them at some point. I'll also have someone check on Quinley for you—don't worry, they'll move cautiously."

Isaiah ragged open the sliding side door and hopped out. "Do whatever you have to do to save Raya and Lori if they're alive."

Sergei's brow wrinkled. "Who?"

Isaiah gritted his teeth. "Fuck this shit."

"Always such drama with these cats," muttered Dimitri.

Staring down at the puddle of clothes on the living room floor, Sebastian narrowed his eyes. "She must have shifted into her cat form. Probably sensed us."

No matter. They'd find her.

He wasn't surprised that she'd chosen to hide. *Typical submissive.* She was probably trembling in pure terror—a thought that made his mouth curve.

His inner wolf stirred in anticipation of the hunt. He wanted to track and maim the feline. No, *this* kill would be Sebastian's.

Davide glanced around, his brow pinched. "I don't see her anywhere."

"Could she be outside?" asked Wattie.

Sebastian shook his head. "A window or patio door would be open." The cat couldn't have closed them behind her. And if any *were* open, the sound of the wind outside wouldn't be so muffled. "She's here somewhere. Close the living room door so she can't get out. You two find her while I position these explosives."

Sebastian used tape to stick all three against various walls. Satisfied, he activated them with the app on his phone.

Once he and his pack mates were safely away from the house, they'd blow the place using the detonator linked to his cell. But not until Hale was home and had discovered his mate dead—Sebastian wanted him to feel that gut-wrenching pain of losing someone you loved; of *seeing* them dead and bleeding. Only then would Hale die.

Done, Sebastian tracked his pack mates to the kitchen. Both were searching cupboards, muttering curses beneath their breath. He frowned. "You haven't found her yet? Seriously?"

Davide scraped a hand through his hair. "It's like she vanished."

*For God's sake.* "She's just a tiny little cat."

"Which means she's better at hiding than the average shifter," Wattie pointed out before he moodily exited the room.

"It's hard to follow her scent," groused Davide, slamming a cupboard door shut. "It's everywhere and nowhere. There's no actual trail coming from or leading to any place."

Sebastian reached out with his senses, searching for a ribbon of scent to follow. There was none. "So maybe she just didn't come into the kitchen."

Davide gave his head a fast shake. "There's no trail in *any* room. I'd suggest we shift, but our animals would do no better at finding her. They'd also eat her alive if they did, and you're set on snapping her neck yourself."

His frustration mounting, Sebastian kicked a stool, sending it skidding aside. "She has to be here somewhere. She can't have just disappeared."

"Seb?" Wattie called out.

"What?"

"I think … I think she might be sitting in the Christmas tree."

Feeling his brows draw together, Sebastian stalked out of the kitchen and through to the living area.

Wattie pointed to a particular spot. "Look."

Sebastian tracked the hyena's gaze. A tawny, black-striped cat was perched on a tree branch, huddled near the thin trunk, her light-green gaze fixed on his.

His irritation wisping away, Sebastian grinned. "There you are."

She didn't move. Didn't tense. Didn't look in the slightest bit perturbed.

She was either too dumb to sense the very real danger that she was in or she stupidly thought her mate would get here in time to save her.

His wolf snarled, inching closer, hungering to attack. "Come on out," Sebastian coaxed. She wouldn't understand his words, but her human half would; she'd communicate what he wanted to the feline. "We're not going to kill you. Not if you shift back and tell us where Tommaso is."

The cat only blinked. It was a slow, uncaring movement that held a hint of dismissiveness.

His wolf's hackles rose in affront, and Sebastian pressed his lips together.

"It's that, or we butcher you here and now. Imagine how your mate will feel coming home to find your body, dead and bloody and broken."

Another lazy, nonchalant blink.

*Disrespectful little bitch.* Sebastian put his face closer to the tree. "Come out from there right fucking *now.*"

She lunged. Dove at him so damn fast she was a mere blur. Hissing, she clawed rabidly at his face, scraping a claw right down his eyeball.

He staggered backwards as he cried out in pain, reaching up to grab her. That fast, she was gone. Gone. It was like trying to catch smoke.

Putting his fingers to his eye, he backed up and whirled around. He couldn't see her anywhere. His furious wolf let out a loud growl of pure challenge.

"Jesus, are you okay?" asked Davide, wincing.

"No. *Fuck.*" His eye felt like it was on fire. "Where did she go?"

Wattie puffed out a baffled breath. "I don't know. She moved too fast for me to—Shit, Seb, your eye don't look good."

"Of course it doesn't! She scratched my goddamn eyeball! *Find. Her.*"

They searched everywhere, flipping up or knocking over furnishings; emptying cupboards and clearing shelves; ripping open—

A pain-filled curse erupted out of Wattie as one of his legs crumpled, his foot wobbling. The big man went down on one knee, hissing in sheer agony.

His sore eye squeezed shut, Sebastian scowled. "What the hell?"

Wattie bared his teeth. "She got my Achilles heel, the bitch! Darted out of nowhere, fucked up my foot, and then vanished into thin air *again.*"

Growling a curse, Sebastian returned to ransacking the living area. With Davide's help, he did the same to the dining area. Then the kitchen. But—

A bellow of agony burst out of Davide, his back arching, his face scrunching up in pain.

"What?" demanded Sebastian.

"The cat pounced on me from behind," he ground out.

Sebastian examined his brother's back. Claw marks ran down the length of it all the way to the base of his spine. Cloth was torn and skin was shredded. It was like she'd landed on his nape, hooked her claws into his flesh, and then dragged them right through his skin as she skidded downwards.

"She's in here!" Wattie yelled.

Snarling, Sebastian darted back into the living area, his wolf raking at his insides; demanding release so he could savage the cat.

"She ran under the sofa," Wattie told him.

Sebastian whipped out his gun—topped with a silencer so as not to attract unwanted attention from neighbors—and pulled the trigger again and again, peppering the couch with bullets. A hissing yowl of pain rang out.

He smirked, prowling to the sofa. He moved it out of the way … and his smirk faded in an instant. There was nothing. Not even the scent of blood.

He clenched his fist. "That fucking cat is toying with us. I'm gonna blow her head off, *I swear to Christ.*"

# CHAPTER TWENTY-FIVE

S o tense with the sense of urgency thrumming through him, Isaiah almost jumped when his phone rang. Leaning forward in the front passenger seat, he whipped it out of his back pocket. *Farrell.*

Putting the cell on speakerphone so that Evander would be able to hear everything, Isaiah answered with: "Tell me." The words came out hard and fast.

Farrell pulled in a breath. "Sebastian Vercetti is in your house," he reluctantly admitted.

Isaiah hissed out a breath. Rage, powerlessness, torment, anxiety, panic, horror—it all pummeled him like a shower of sharp rocks. His cat went AWOL.

"Jesus Christ," breathed Evander, pressing his foot harder on the pedal.

"Davide is there as well, and another of their pack mates," Farrell went on.

Isaiah gripped the edge of his seat as if it could anchor him. Truth be told, nothing could steady him in that moment. "And Quinley?" The question came out choked. He knew she was alive, because he could *feel* her. But "alive" didn't mean "conscious" or "uninjured."

"Unhurt, by the looks of it. It's hard to tell."

"Round up some pride mates and get inside the—"

"A bunch of us are discreetly surrounding the house," Farrell assured him, "but we can't barge in there."

Isaiah scowled. "Why the hell not?"

A pause. "They've attached explosives to the walls."

Terror spiked through Isaiah's blood and made his gut roll. "*What?*"

"I don't know if they've come ready to die here or if they just intend to blow up the house when they're away from it. Either way, if they think they have no way out, if they feel cornered, they might set off the explosives."

Isaiah squeezed his eyes shut.

"We have to move cautiously," Farrell continued. "Sneaking inside wouldn't be a problem. But if the pack detects our presence, they might press the detonator."

Isaiah rubbed hard at his forehead. "Why are they even there if it's not to kill Quinley?" Were they waiting for him?

"It does seem that their goal is to get rid of her. But, even armed, they're having a difficult time with that. Mostly because they can't find her."

Isaiah's hand dropped to his lap. "They can't find her?"

"She's in her cat form, hiding. She pops out every now and then, deals them a little injury, and then disappears again."

*Jesus.* Isaiah didn't know if he wanted to give her a metaphorical bow for her mercilessness or to shake her for not staying completely out of the pack's sight. His inner feline was leading toward the first. "So she's playing with them."

"She's a black-foot, Isaiah. What did you expect? They don't do well with being targeted. They may run, but they'll circle back and come at you. You personally got some vengeance when you killed Tommaso. She wants her own piece of the vengeance pie. The pack should have expected that, but they have a habit of underestimating females."

Right then, Isaiah was grateful for the latter. The pack hadn't arrived prepared for a struggle. That had given her an advantage. "How did they manage to sneak past Joaquin?"

"They didn't. They found him in the woods and overpowered him, then left him—either thinking he was dead or that he soon would be. We took him to Helena, he's fine now."

"That's a relief at least," muttered Evander.

"Like I said, we have the house surrounded," Farrell went on. "If the pack members try to leave, we'll take them down. But it would be risky for us to try to enter. If you want us to take that chance—"

"No," Isaiah blurted out. "No, we can't risk that they'd decide to go out in a literal blaze of glory." He pinched the bridge of his nose hard. "I don't get why they're so set on catching Quinley. They could just walk out and then press the detonator." He hated to voice that fear aloud, to give it *life*, but he just couldn't understand.

"Sebastian watched his baby brother have his neck snapped, and he'll know there's a high probability that our pride eliminated Tommaso. My guess, considering he hasn't been content with attacking her from a distance? Ending her life with his bare hands is the only thing that'll satisfy his need for vengeance. Plus, well, I'm not even sure a house explosion would actually end a black-foot—they're freakily difficult to kill. He'll want to be sure she's dead before he presses that detonator.”

“He could decide ‘to hell with that’ if he can’t catch her.”

“They’re not trying to hurry, so they must be under the impression that you can’t sense Quinley’s emotions. It means they won’t suspect that you’re on your way home, or that the pride is aware of their presence here. That gives us time.”

Yeah, but would it give them *enough* time? Isaiah hauled in a jagged breath. “Be ready to take them down if they leave.”

“Will do.” The line went dead.

Isaiah clutched his phone tight, tempted to fling it. “I shouldn’t have left her.”

Evander slid him a sideways look of reprimand. “Isaiah—”

“No, I was suspicious of why the pack would try luring her to a train station. I’ve studied Sebastian—he’s a guy who’d expect a submissive to be too afraid to follow such an instruction. I found it odd that the pack would believe she’d truly do it, but I didn’t question it the way I should have.” Self-loathing filled him, slow and slick. “I didn’t think they’d come to the house for Quinley.”

“None of us suspected they’d do something like that.”

“But we should have. They’ve done far worse and far riskier shit. Like they get off on riding that edge between life and death.” Most especially Sebastian, from what Isaiah had gathered.

“This isn’t just risky, it’s reckless. There are all sorts of variables. They can’t *know* that you and Quinley aren’t bonded. They can’t be sure she wouldn’t receive a visitor, who’d then likely spot them. They can’t be certain you wouldn’t return early. Yet, they made this move regardless. They’re never careless, but this? Yeah, this is careless.”

“Careless” was a good word for it. “Arrogant” would be another. As Isaiah saw it, the only people who’d blindly ignore the variables that Evander had mentioned were people who’d be desperate for vengeance. Which brought to mind the surviving Vercetti brothers.

Sebastian seemed to call a lot of the shots, so he was likely the main person behind this plot. For him to take so many risks … it was as if the death of Samuele, the disappearance of Tommaso, and the pack’s subsequent failures to come after the pride had chipped away at his feelings of power and control—things a person with his upbringing might crave; things he’d feel unsteady without—and, thus, somehow destabilized his thought processes or something.

“If they do catch her, they’ll sense the partial imprint bond,” said Isaiah. “They’ll know then that they’re not flying under our pride’s radar.”

“They won’t know *for sure* that we’ll be aware she’s in danger, because a partial bond means you don’t feel everything your mate is feeling,” Evander pointed out. “What do you plan to do once we get to your house?”

The only thing that Isaiah really could do. "Walk in there like I don't know she has company."

Evander flicked him a sharp look as his brows snapped together. "They could shoot you dead the second you enter."

"No, I don't think they'll do that. They'd want me to first watch Quinley die."

"You could be wrong."

Isaiah raised his shoulders. "What other choice do I have? Someone needs to be able to get into that house to help her. If the pack sees others, they'll fire without hesitation and maybe panic that their game is up. Me? They'd like that I was there." And neither he nor his cat were prepared to sit safely outside the house while their mate was inside without backup.

It struck him then just how difficult it must have been for Quinley to agree to stay home while he and the others waltzed into a dangerous situation. If only he'd taken her along, or if he'd just *stayed* with her …

Evander sighed. "Maybe don't go in alone, then. Maybe take just one person with you. Three against three is better odds." He paused. "It'd need to be someone as hard to kill as a black-foot."

Isaiah twisted his lips. "I can think of someone."

"I say we just leave," declared Davide, his face lined with pain.

Sebastian stiffened. "What?"

His brother sighed, his shoulders drooping. "Seb, my back is shredded. So is Wattie's Achilles tendon. The scratches on your face are deep, and your eye needs seeing to."

As if Sebastian needed the latter reminder. His eyeball still blazed like someone had shoved a boiling hot chunk of coal in the socket. His vision was *fucked*.

No way was he leaving without doing what he'd come to do, though. Besides, he owed that little bitch. He was going to stab her eye with his goddamn claw before he killed her. "We can go to a healer once we're finished here."

"Let's consider the job done," Davide pushed. "The place is wired to blow. She won't survive the explosion."

Sebastian cast him a hard glare. "Wasn't it you who earlier insisted it would take more than that to wipe out a black-foot?"

Davide spluttered. "Yes but, on second thought, I'm pretty sure I'm wrong."

*Lying asshole.* "You want to admit defeat to a goddamn tabby?"

"What else are we supposed to do? None of us can catch her. She's too fast. The longer we're here, the more we risk detection. Let's just do what Wattie suggested earlier and cut our losses."

"I vote for that," said the hyena from the armchair.

Ignoring that, Sebastian arched a brow at Davide. "Thought you wanted Hale to suffer?"

"I do, but we wouldn't be letting him get away with what he did to Samuele," said Davide. "We'd just be putting a pin in it. We can come back at another time when he won't be expecting it."

"And what about Tommaso? I thought you wanted answers about our brother."

"Again, *I do*. But he wouldn't blame us for regrouping if it meant we survived. As I said, we could return later. We can kidnap a random pride member and demand Tommaso in exchange for their life. What we clearly can't do is *catch that bastard cat*."

"You really want to flee from *her*? A submissive, female, teensy weensy cat?"

Wattie grunted as he shifted position on the armchair, his face pale. "Seb, it don't matter that she's tiny or a submissive or a woman—it doesn't change that we can't get a grip on her. We can't even get a *bullet* in her. What else are we supposed to do?"

Sebastian felt his lips flatten. This was what he got for bringing pack members who thought it their place to question him. "We're not leaving until she's dead. You hear me? Bitch and moan all you want, but we're not moving from this house until she's a goner."

Both males sagged, anger washing over their features and mingling with the pain there.

Sebastian's wolf sneered, disgusted by their weakness. "Now, for God's sake, let's nab this damn cat."

Unable to properly walk, Wattie remained seated as Sebastian and Davide searched high and low for the black-foot. It was like trying to search for oxygen—you knew it was there, you just couldn't damn see it.

Sebastian kicked a half-smashed vase across the floor, making more pieces of it break away. "How can it be possible for her not to stand out? She doesn't exactly blend in with the décor."

Davide gave a clueless shrug. "I don't know. I still say we should—"

"*Don't.* I told you already, we're not leaving until …" Sebastian trailed off as something outside caught his eye through the window. His pulse jumped, and his wolf went still. "Hale's home."

Wattie sat up straighter, his eyes widening. "What?"

"He's walking up the driveway as we speak," said Sebastian, his hand flexing around his gun. "He isn't with the others. Just one male—I haven't seen this one before." In which case, the guy couldn't be an enforcer or anyone important. "We can take them both easy."

"*Or*," began Davide, "we could just walk out—"

Sebastian growled at his brother. "Stop being a bitch. Get out your guns, both of you."

Red staining his cheeks, Davide begrudgingly pulled out his gun. From the armchair, Wattie did the same.

Not trusting that either of the Olympus Pride males wouldn't scent Sebastian or his pack mates, he didn't wait there. He pulled open the living room door and aimed his weapon just right.

Both Hale and the other male casually strolled inside. Hale froze as his gaze landed on Sebastian. A gaze that bounced from him to the gun and back again. Behind him, his companion went rigid.

"If either one of you runs back out that door the other takes a bullet to the heart," Sebastian warned, the dark promise heavy in every syllable.

Neither male tried to run. They both pinned their gazes on Sebastian, their expressions hardening.

He smirked. "Hale, stay right where you are. Other Guy, shut the door. Then both of you put your hands up."

The Olympus shifters moved stiffly as they followed his orders, every movement begrudging.

"Thanks." Sebastian shot Other Guy in the chest.

The male reared back, hit the wall, and slid down to the floor as blood poured from the wound. Seconds later, he went limp.

Hale hissed, clearly eager to help his friend, but he remained still like he'd been told.

"How nice of you to drop by," Sebastian quipped.

Looking at the motherfucker, it was hard not to pull the trigger. Images flashed in his mind. *Hale diving at Samuele. Hands gripping his brother's head. Those same hands wrenching hard, snapping Samuele's neck.*

"Where's my mate?" Hale predictably demanded.

"Somewhere," Sebastian fudged. He held up his cell phone. "See this? It's a detonator for the explosives I've put around the house. Make a wrong move and I press it."

Hale clenched his jaw tight.

"Now, we're going to go into the living area. It's cozier that way." With every step Sebastian took back, Hale took one forward until they were fully in the room.

The pallas cat's gaze darted around, taking in everything—Davide, Wattie, the weapons, the explosives.

"You know, I wasn't sure you'd really leave her alone here," said Sebastian. "A smarter man would have realized it was a trap. Did you really think I'd actually rely on a submissive to put herself in danger?"

A muscle in Hale's jaw ticked. "I thought maybe you believed she'd rush to the aid of her family regardless."

*Idiot.* "You thought wrong, as you can see." Sebastian tightened his grip on his weapon. "Where's Tommaso?"

"The place we put all our captives," Hale vaguely replied.

"Which is where?"

"Put down your weapons and I'll tell you."

Sebastian felt his mouth curve into a mocking smile. "No, I don't think so." Knowing there was only one way to make the asshole talk, he called out, "Kitty cat, you need to come out now. I swear to God I will put a bullet in your mate's brain if you don't."

Moments later, she appeared from … Sebastian didn't even know where. She just materialized a few feet away like magic. It was downright eerie, but he'd never admit it aloud.

Noticing Hale's muscles bunch as if he might make a grab for her, Sebastian flicked up a brow. "Careful. There are bombs planted all over, remember? One push of this button on my cell and *boom*."

"You'd be killing yourselves," said Hale, clearly doubting his word. He shouldn't.

"You think any of us are afraid to die? We've been tempting Death for a long time—he hasn't come for us yet." Sebastian took sideways steps over to the armchair on which his pack mate sat. "Wattie, take the phone."

Obediently, Wattie carefully took it and hovered his thumb threateningly over the screen.

"Davide, keep your gun aimed at the son of a bitch. He moves, shoot him." Sebastian bent over and roughly grabbed the cat by the scruff of her neck. He immediately jammed the barrel of his gun against the side of her head. She didn't even have the downright decency to hiss in pain.

Hale tensed, his fists clenching as he visibly wrestled with the urge to rush to her rescue … just as Sebastian had once wrestled with the urge to retrieve his baby brother's body before driving off. God knew what the pride had done with it.

"Where's Tommaso?" he asked Hale. "Either you tell me where he is, or I shoot her."

Hale's nostrils flared in outrage, every muscle in his body rigid. "You shoot her, you'll never know his location. I'll be on you before you can fucking blink."

Sebastian held back a snort. "Davide."

His brother fired a bullet into each of Isaiah's kneecaps, making the son of a bitch drop like a stone.

"Not now you won't," said Sebastian. He almost laughed as a rumbly growl of fury slid out of the cat in his grip. Who knew she had that in her?

Davide spit at Hale. "That's for Samuele. Unless you want more bullets in you, *talk*."

Propped up on one elbow, Hale slammed hateful, agony-filled eyes on Sebastian. Blood stained the legs of his jeans, and the smell delighted Sebastian's wolf.

"Let her go, and I'll tell you whatever you want to know," Hale swore, pain coating every syllable.

Sebastian hummed, pretending to consider it. "I don't think so. She's the only thing keeping you cooperative."

"Fuck," muttered Davide.

Sebastian spared his brother the briefest look. "What?"

"I just saw someone sneak by the window," Davide clipped. "We've been spotted."

Sebastian inwardly cursed. The pallas cat on the floor didn't look the least bit surprised. "Did you already know we were here when you arrived?" It was possible. Maybe he was bonded to the black-foot after all.

"Does it matter?" Hale tossed out, lines of agony etching themselves deep into his face.

"No, I don't suppose it does." What *did* matter was that the house was likely surrounded by pride members. That meant that neither Sebastian nor his brother nor Wattie were going to get out of this alive.

Fury zipped through Sebastian, heating his blood, making a tremor run through the hand still jamming the barrel of his gun into the black-foot's head. If he and his pack mates were going to die, they were going to take Hale and his little bitch with them.

Sebastian shot her point blank. Hale's head jerked as he felt a ghostly impact of the bullet sinking into her brain. Huh. So they *were* bonded after all.

The animal sound of pained rage that tore out of Hale was quite something.

Smirking, Sebastian tossed her lifeless body aside like it was trash. The look Hale gave him ... oh, he would have *flung* himself at Sebastian if he could have.

Hale looked as if he'd army-crawl toward her, so Sebastian shot at the hardwood floor in front of him. The pallas cat stilled, his eyes flashing cat.

"You don't have siblings," Sebastian gritted out, "so you can't know what it's like to lose a brother. But now you know what it's like to lose a mate. So there's that. *Why* shifters are stupid enough to claim mates, I don't know. Nothing good comes of it. They weaken us. Case in point. And now you—"

"Seb?" Davide interrupted.

Sebastian pressed his lips together. He *loathed* being interrupted. "What?"

"She's, uh, she's still moving."

Sebastian glanced down. The feline was writhing on the floor, though she made not one sound. *Freaky little shit.*

He fired two bullets into her flank, satisfied when her body went limp; loving that each one made Hale flinch.

Davide sneered. "Doesn't feel good losing someone you love, does it? Oh, we know that pain well. Don't we, Seb?"

"We do." Sebastian took a lurching step closer to Hale. "I would have snapped her neck like you did Samuele's. That was my original plan. But I'm nothing if not adaptable. You know, it's funny, but if you hadn't—" He stopped talking when his peripheral vision caught sight of her wriggling once more. "What the fuck is *with* this cat?"

He fired. Again. This time, he aimed at her neck.

As her body sagged, he turned back to Hale. "Now where was I? Oh yes, you were about to tell me where Tommaso is." Sebastian paused. "Is he alive?"

Hale glared up at him. "Yes. And I already told you where he is."

"I want the exact location, and I want it now." Sebastian narrowed his eyes as something occurred to him. "Or are you stalling for time, thinking your pride mates have any chance of helping you?" He couldn't help but smile at the ridiculous idea. "That's not going to happen. All of us here are going to die today."

"Then what do you care where Tommaso is?"

"I want his location so I can notify my other pack mates where to find him." Something flashed in the enforcer's eyes. It was there and gone in a heartbeat, but it made Sebastian's gut seize. "What have you done?"

"I haven't done anything. As for my pride mates? Well, they could have gotten up to all kinds of things while down in the mines."

Davide swore, and Wattie growled.

As for Sebastian … rage surged through him, singeing his lungs so every breath hurt. "You motherfucker!"

"Uh, Seb?" Wattie warily cut in.

*For the love of God.* "What now?"

"She's gone."

# CHAPTER TWENTY-SIX

Isaiah hid a feral smile. It was amazing that he could *want* to smile when such stomach-roiling pain racked his blown-out knees, leaving him at honest risk of vomiting.

Sebastian's brows flew together. "What do you mean *she's gone?*"

"I mean she was there and now she's not," snapped Wattie.

Isaiah hadn't noticed his mate slink away, but he had known she wasn't dead—which was the only thing that had kept him from launching himself at Sebastian; the only thing preventing his cat from forcing the shift in pure rage. Instead, the animal paced and snarled and whipped his tail, his sanity anchored by their mate's pulse, strong and even, skipping along their imprint bond—a bond that had snapped fully into place when Sebastian had put that gun to her head.

It was in that moment, when Isaiah had feared neither of them would make it, that he'd also realized he felt no surprise at the idea that she'd be taken from him somehow.

He'd known right then what had been blocking the bond and preventing it from fully forming: The expectation that he would lose her. His fear of it happening had been so all-encompassing that—scared to feel secure in the knowledge that she wouldn't be stolen from him—he'd braced himself for it to happen. In doing so, he'd held back slightly from their mating without even realizing it. And he couldn't be more infuriated with himself for it.

"She can't have gone far," clipped Sebastian, his gaze darting around.

Davide's mouth thinned. "There's no blood trail, so I don't even know what direction she went in. Seriously, fucking black-foots are too weird to exist, they ... Shit, the big guy Hale brought with him is gone as well."

Not a surprise. A single bullet to the chest was never going to be enough to put down one of Alex's kind. If the pack had known he was a wolverine, they would have taken more care to ensure that he was dead. Isaiah had been banking on them *not* knowing.

Sebastian pulled in a breath … and Isaiah saw it on his face; saw the wolf's realization that everything had gone to shit and could only get worse from here. Resignation flitting over his features, Sebastian turned to his pack mate. "Wattie, just press—"

A blur of tawny fur sprung at Wattie, snatched the cell phone from his hand, and sprinted away.

The guy jerked in the chair. "Fuck!"

Everything that happened next seemed to move at hyper speed. Alex's wolverine charged into the room with a roar. Bullets whizzed out of guns. People burst into the house from both the front and back. Isaiah awkwardly flung himself at Sebastian's legs, knocking him down flat and sending such mind-numbing agony through his injured knees that his vision went black around the edges.

Only able to reach as high as the wolf's stomach, Isaiah plowed his fist into his gut over and over just before a bunch of his pride came over in their animal form.

Propping himself up on his elbows, Isaiah surveyed the scene with grim satisfaction. Pallas cats were swarming the intruders. Literally. They wrapped their furry bodies around faces, arms, and legs; mercilessly tore strips of flesh from scalps and bone; made weapons fall from hands and clatter to the floor. And so the sounds of gunfire quickly stopped, rapidly replaced by curses, screams, growls, hisses, and snarls.

Feeling assured that the threats had been neutralized and the pack members were going nowhere, he caved to his cat's demands that they call for their mate. "Quinley!" He could feel her pain and fatigue—both arrowed down their bond in sharp, hot pulses.

Right then, Vinnie crouched beside him, his brows lowering. "Jesus, Isaiah." He turned to another of their pride mates. "Get Helena."

"Don't let them kill Sebastian," Isaiah told him, his tone clipped. "That fucker is *mine*."

"They wouldn't dream of robbing you of that pleasure."

Mollified, Isaiah nodded. Movement from his left caught his attention. He looked to see Quinley's little cat padding over to him. *Thank fuck*. His inner animal sagged in relief, though a growl eased out of him when he saw the patches of blood matting her fur. Isaiah felt his back teeth lock as anger zipped through him at the sight.

"Her kind really is tough to take out," Vinnie marveled, watching her approach.

Sniffing Isaiah, she carefully clambered onto his stomach, her light-green eyes tired.

"Hey there, sweetheart," he said, his voice soft. He wanted to cuddle, nuzzle, and surround her protectively. But he didn't dare even touch her until she'd been healed, not wanting to accidentally aggravate any of her wounds.

His cat glided up to writhe just beneath Isaiah's skin, anxious to comfort her. He hated the scent of her pain; hated the fatigue dragging at her bones.

As a strange energy ever so slowly began to ease into his body, Isaiah glared at her. "No, do *not* use up any of your strength relieving my pain." But it was too late; the energy gradually chipped away at the agony tearing through him.

The cat didn't look one bit sorry. She met his gaze evenly, a *Whatcha gonna do about it?* challenge there.

Vinnie let out a soft snicker. "She could no more ignore your pain than you could ignore hers. You know that."

Helena materialized at their side, wincing. "Oh, hell."

"Heal Quinley's cat first," Isaiah told her.

Kneeling beside him, Helena rested a hand over the little black-foot.

Isaiah felt a faint echo of healing energy sizzle through his mate; felt her pain lessen and lessen until finally it disappeared. Helena gave him the same aid, and he felt his injuries right themselves.

"Thank you," Isaiah said to the healer, gathering his mate into his arms as he sat upright. "Alex took a bullet to the chest, just in case you didn't know."

"I'll see to him," said Helena. "If someone can convince him to shift back, that is—he's presently having way too much fun mauling the wolf over there."

"Typical of Alex's wolverine," muttered Vinnie, standing. He and Helena then melted away.

Isaiah nuzzled his mate, who gave his jaw a quick lick. "You had them idiots running around chasing their asses, didn't you?" He was proud of her even as he wanted to shake her for not simply remaining out of sight. "Let me look at you."

Even as he intellectually knew she was healed, he needed to *see* for himself that her wounds were all gone. He carefully checked, skating his fingers through her fur; earning himself the occasional yowl of complaint when he accidentally plucked at the matted strands.

"Sorry," he said, cuddling her close. "I'm done now."

His own cat—still in full-on protective mode—wanted to take her upstairs, lick the blood from her coat, and tuck her away someplace safe and comfortable so she could rest. A place where no one else would know where she was.

Isaiah was certainly behind the cleaning-and-cosseting-her plan. He wouldn't even mind hiding her away from the world. But there was something he needed to do first.

He gently bumped her nose with his own. "You stay here," he began, a deadly intent creeping into his voice, "while I go murder the living fuck out of the bastard who tried to take you from me."

He rose to his feet and carefully set her down on the upturned sofa. "I'll be back in a minute." He purposefully strode over to where Sebastian lay, flailing and crying out.

The wolf was still covered head to toe in pallas cats, all of whom were delighting in introducing him to a new level of pain. The scent of his blood was sharp in the air.

"Back up," Isaiah barked out.

The cats reluctantly did so, though they didn't retreat completely. They kept the wolf's limbs pinned to the floor with their weight.

Sebastian stared up at him, his gaze glazed over with pain, anger, and powerlessness. He looked … pitiful. A mess.

Claw marks crisscrossed over his face, many of which sliced through his lips, eyelids, nose, and eyebrows. Strips had been torn from his scalp. His clothes were ripped enough that Isaiah could see the many puncture wounds and rake marks littering his body.

Isaiah towered over him, both he and his cat admittedly liking the sight of all those injuries. The wolf deserved every single one of them—not only for what he'd done since targeting the pride but all the crimes he'd committed before then.

"You should never have come here." Isaiah sliced out his claws. "Which I suppose you've already figured out by now."

Sebastian gifted him a sneer. "What kind of dominant male shifter needs their pride mates to hold down another before they'll strike? Let us fight one-to-one."

"I would. If you were worth it. But you're not. I don't duel with those I don't respect. I just kill them."

The wolf's attention cut to the side as Quinley's cat flounced over, twitching her tail.

Isaiah silently sighed. Well, of course she hadn't stayed put.

He had to battle the instinct to bare his teeth at her. Like his feline, he didn't want her near this fucker. But while his cat hissed to chase her away, Isaiah didn't. He respected that, all things considered, she'd want to watch Sebastian die. Isaiah wouldn't have hung back either.

The wolf glared at her, loathing and scorn rippling over his face. In return, she regarded him with an aloof, clinical detachment. The pallas cats around them, however, rumbled warning growls at him, protective of her.

"You were brought down by what you consider weak, Vercetti," Isaiah taunted. "Almost poetic, really."

Sebastian's hateful gaze cut back to him. "At least tell me if Tommaso is dead before you kill me."

It would be a decent thing to do, but … "No." Isaiah bent down and stabbed his claws right into the asshole's throat. He didn't remove them as Sebastian spluttered and choked. He kept his claws buried deep, staring the wolf right in the eye until the glimmer of *life* there dimmed out.

Only then did Isaiah withdraw his claws and straighten. His cat sniffed down in disdain at the dead shifter whose demise had been long overdue. He'd died too easily, really, but at least he'd suffered some before he did.

Quinley's cat moved forward and sniffed at him, as if wanting to ensure he was dead. Their pride mates, no longer needed to restrain the wolf, backed off.

Isaiah wiped his bloody claws on his jeans. "Pretty sure I told you to wait over there, little cat."

She looked up at him and did a long, slow blink. Then yawned.

"Minx." Isaiah glanced around to see that things were presently calmer. Pallas cats no longer crawled over the other two Vercetti Pack members. Both were as dead as Sebastian. Alex was now back in his human form and seemingly healed.

Isaiah sheathed his claws just as Quinley's cat scrambled up his body and settled on his shoulder. "Quick question: Are you going to shift back any time soon?"

She only stared at him.

"I'd like to cuddle your human half too," he explained.

The staring continued.

A sigh eased out of Isaiah. "Which is my problem, not yours. Right. Gotcha." His feline would have snorted if he could have.

Isaiah suspected that the female cat wouldn't want to shift back until the corpses were gone and the house was empty of visitors. He could feel through their bond that she was still a little on edge from adrenaline.

Vinnie crossed to them. "We need Sebastian's phone so we can deactivate the explosives. Then we'll take them down." He cast a quick look at the black-foot. "Think you can convince her to pass it over, Isaiah?"

"Sure. First, though, are the others still at the mines?"

"I presume so. I haven't heard from Tate yet, and he always calls me after any kind of battle so I know he's safe and well. He's gonna be furious when he realizes that Sebastian not only came for your mate but managed to fool you all the way he did."

Oh, for certain. "And Joaquin? How is he?"

"Alive. Helena got to him in time to save him. Which means the Vercetti bastards in here caused no casualties. Let's hope our pride mates in the mines can claim the same about the pack members there."

I t was another half hour before Tate called. Isaiah had to assume he'd spoken to either Vinnie or some other pride mates beforehand, because the Alpha's first words to him were: "I heard there was all kinds of action we missed while in the mines." He did *not* sound happy about it.

Lying flat on his back in bed, Isaiah met his mate's eyes. They were filled with wariness, her body stiff as a board as she awaited news of her relatives' fate.

He used his grip on her ass to draw her closer to his side. The house was now free of explosives, corpses, and pride mates. But the first level was still a wreck after being ransacked, so he and Quinley had retreated upstairs.

It hadn't been easy to get her cat to subside. A few people had stopped by, including his parents. Quinley's cat had stared at them the entire time, ready to lash out in his defense if they stepped a foot wrong. It had been cute as hell.

Once Quinley had finally resurfaced, they'd showered, pulled on sweats, and—in her case—snacked on some candy she'd stashed in her nightstand. Honestly, she had snacks hidden away in every room.

"I'm sure that goes both ways," he said to Tate, the call on speakerphone. "Raya and Lori?"

"They're fine, albeit pissed that they were kidnapped. They're now on their way home."

Quinley melted into his side as a mound of air seemed to gust out of her in relief.

Isaiah curled his arm tighter around her and dropped a kiss on her head. "Since you don't sound murderous, I'm assuming no lives were lost on our side."

"None," Tate confirmed. "Many of us came away with injuries, but no one was on death's door. The pack put up one hell of a fight, but they all met their end."

Tension trickled out of Isaiah's system. "So it's over."

"It's over. But I'm pretty damn pissed at myself right now." Tate exhaled a rough breath. "I should have been prepared for Sebastian to pull something. I should have left guards with Quinley just to be on the safe side."

Isaiah stifled a smile at how his mate stilled in annoyance, her nails pricking his chest. "I'd pass on an apology from you to her, but then she'd growl at me again."

"Growl at you?"

"I've already received a stern lecture for feeling bad that I hadn't guessed what Sebastian had planned."

"Well, we *should* have guessed."

She groaned, rolling her eyes. "Oh, my God. Dominant males and their god complexes. I can't take it."

Isaiah chuckled, rubbing her hip. His cat sniffed, not understanding her issue, feeling that both his and Tate's feelings were only to be expected.

"Thank you, Tate, for helping to save Raya and Lori," she said.

"No thanks necessary," Tate told her. "Just so you know, I recommended that they inform their Alphas of the kidnapping—I wouldn't expect them to keep such a secret—so I imagine I'll hear from the Alpha pair at some point tonight to complain."

Quinley's nose wrinkled. "Sorry in advance if they're assholes."

"There's no need for you to apologize on their behalf. And don't go worrying that they'll start trouble—they know better. And they don't really have the grounds to do so anyway, since we saved their pride mates' lives." He paused. "I hear your cat gave Sebastian, Davide, and their pack mate a hard time."

Quinley sniffed. "It was insulting that they thought I'd be an easy mark. But I'm glad they weren't prepared for the struggle my cat put up."

"They weren't prepared to be discovered in the mines either. There was no strategy in how they fought back; no escape plan. They flapped when they realized we were there."

"Arrogance," she drawled.

"Yes. And because of that arrogance, the Vercetti Pack is now officially a thing of the past."

That they were, and Quinley couldn't be more glad of it. There was no longer a target on her mate's back. Things could go back to normal. And they could start the new year on a much better note, all the Vercetti bullshit firmly in the past.

The same relief she felt had rooted itself firmly in Isaiah—she could feel it. Like a pleasant hum in her bones. That they were now fully bonded delighted both her and her cat.

It had been a shock when the connection abruptly snapped into place earlier. Despite that there had been a gun to her cat's head and that two weapons were aimed at him, sheer joy had coursed through her.

Content to just snuggle into her mate as he smoothed his hand up and down her side, she mostly stayed quiet as he and Tate passed on details of what they'd each missed earlier.

Once the conversation was over, Isaiah placed his phone on the nightstand and then looked at Quinley. "Feel better now, baby?"

"I'm so relieved that Raya and Lori are okay. I told myself they would be, but ..." A shaky breath left her. "I'll call Raya in a little while just to check in."

Rolling into her, Isaiah pressed a kiss to her forehead. "She won't be mad at you."

Quinley felt her brow furrow. "What?"

"You're worried she'll be upset with you because she and Lori got dragged into our mess," he correctly sensed. "Don't. Neither of them will be angry with you, only with the Vercetti Pack. Though they might be annoyed with themselves for getting caught."

"That's possible." Raya hated when anyone managed to take her off-guard, and Lori got all pissy whenever she wasn't able to save Raya from any kind of upset.

"Then stop worrying."

"I have stopped."

"No, you haven't."

Totally true. Quinley's lips thinned. "I'm not going to get away with much now that you can sense my emotions so strongly, am I?"

"Nope." Isaiah looped her hair around her ear. "I didn't realize I was blocking the bond," he said, a note of apology in his tone.

She frowned. "Of course you hadn't realized. You would have done something about it if you had. So don't dare say you're sorry as if you did it on purpose."

He grunted. "You're in a bossy mood tonight. My cat finds it cute."

She felt one brow shoot up. "Cute?"

"Yeah. Considering how the day went, he should still be seething. But he's so content that we're finally all-the-way mated that he's reasonably chill."

She felt her lips tip up. "My cat is the same." The feline was pressing close to be near him. "She's also feeling pretty pleased with herself after tormenting the pack earlier."

"I can't say I like that she didn't just stay hidden to protect herself, but I am nonetheless proud of you both."

That pride streamed down their bond ... but another emotion joined it, making her lips tighten. "Stop feeling guilty for not being here to protect me."

"I shouldn't have left you alone."

She bit his arm.

His brows flicked together. "Ow, what was that for?"

"I can't tell you just how done I am with you taking on blame that doesn't belong to you." It was honestly maddening.

"No need to bring your teeth into it."

Her cat twitched her tail, amused. "Oh hush, you like when I bite you."

His lips curving, he cuddled her closer. "You know, for such a small person—"

"Hey!" she griped. There was no need to bring height into it.

"—you pack a punch."

"What, physically? When have I ever punched you?"

He chuckled beneath his breath. "I mean the impact you have. You're everything I need all bundled into the prettiest package. I never stood a chance. Fell for you so easily it's almost embarrassing."

Her heart went ahead and melted. "Is that your way of saying you love me?"

"Yeah, I love you," he readily admitted, his voice warm and soft. "Which is good, because you love me too."

She smiled so wide her cheeks hurt a little. "I do." More than she'd thought possible. "And I'll never stop."

"Never, ever?"

"Never, ever."

"Neither will I, baby. Neither will I."

# CHAPTER TWENTY-SEVEN

So this was how she'd die. Death by orgasm. What a way to fucking go. Seriously, Quinley wasn't sure she'd survive the insanely electric pleasure building in her belly. It was *his* fault. He'd repeatedly pushed her to the edge but then backed off, knowing it would make her eventual implosion so much more intense.

She'd been rinsing bits of toothpaste from her brush when a naked Isaiah came up behind her. He'd roughly kicked her legs apart, startling her into dropping the objects she'd held, and shoved up her long tee. After treating her to a minimal amount of finger-fucking, he'd plopped her butt on the vanity, gripped her hips tight, and then crammed every inch of his cock in her pussy—with not one word spoken.

And now he was powering into her, grunting against her neck. There was no sensual finesse, no caressing or sweet words. This was *fucking*. Savage and basic and aggressive.

Her cat reveled in it.

Quinley clung to him with every limb, her eyes closed in pure euphoria. Her body was in full-swing—chemicals racing, hormones dancing, nerve-endings blazing.

Orgasm approaching.

A drawn-out snarl vibrated against her neck. "Hold it," he ordered, sheer assertiveness buried in his words.

She'd just *known* he was going to say that. "Not fair," she whined, opening her eyes. "Don't wanna."

Slowing his pace, he lifted his head to look down at her, the sheen of *such need* in his gaze. "I didn't ask you what you want, did I?"

"Dick."

*"Hold. It."*

Whimpering, she bit down on her bottom lip.

"That's it," Isaiah praised, sensing her beat back her release. "My perfect little fuck doll."

He went back to plowing into her, his grip on her thighs bruising. Damn if he wasn't addicted to this woman. Her taste, heat, scent, softness—it all called to him. Everything about her did.

His cat pushed at him to fuck her harder, knowing she could take it. Isaiah upped his pace, wishing he'd whipped off her tee so he had a view of all the brands he'd left on her. He had a map of her body memorized in his head; knew the location of every brand, dip, freckle, hollow, scar.

There was no part of her he hadn't touched or tasted. No part he hadn't made *his*.

Echoes of everything she was feeling—bliss, frustration, a winding tension—skittered along their bond. It all fed the coiling force inside him that pushed him toward his own release.

"Let me come," she rasped, tipping her head to the side, offering him her throat; anticipating what he'd ask of her.

Isaiah latched onto her neck with his teeth and jutted his hips harder and faster, slamming deep each time. He slipped a hand between them, rolled her clit with his thumb, and rumbled, "Come."

He felt an echo of a white-hot onslaught of pleasure raid her body, surging and crackling through her. The sensation gripped his balls and triggered his own release, making him explode inside her with a hoarse groan.

She sagged forward, resting her cheek on his shoulder, her breaths coming as fast and heavy as his. "Well. Though my butt isn't keen on this cold marble, I thoroughly enjoyed that."

A smile warmed his chest. "You said it was sore after last night," he pointed out, going for innocent.

She raised her head, her eyes narrowing. "Oh, so you were just benevolently attempting to soothe it?" A mocking question.

He shrugged. "I couldn't just ignore that your ass is tender, could I?"

She snorted. "You could stop *making* it tender."

"Why would I do that when you like having my cock up there just as much as I do?"

"It was just a thought."

"It'll have to remain a thought." Nuzzling her temple, he curled his arms around her. "Now kiss me."

She delved her fingers into the back of his hair as she touched her mouth to his. The kiss was soft and lazy and drugging. "Don't rev my engines again—we have a full schedule today, and we're already a little behind since we slept in."

"Are you looking forward to the party later?"

"I am." She doodled a circle over the claiming brand on his shoulder. "I'm also looking forward to seeing Raya and Lori. And the rest of my family, obviously. But I need to know my sis and her mate are okay after what happened."

Her whole family were coming to visit in an hour or so—something she and Raya had arranged last night. As he'd predicted, neither Quinley's sister nor her mate whatsoever blamed anyone for their kidnapping other than the Vercetti Pack. In fact, her relatives considered the Olympus shifters "their heroes."

"I haven't told them yet that we're fully imprinted," she said. "I want them to have the surprise."

He personally didn't think they'd be all that surprised. None of his pride mates were—and yes, they'd all heard about it. They'd apparently all anticipated that the imprinting process would happen fast for him and Quinley. His parents were on cloud nine.

He brushed a kiss over her forehead. "I like feeling you through our bond. I particularly like feeling you come."

She hummed, linking her fingers behind his nape. "It sure does enhance the sex stuff. But when I'm having a casual conversation with your mom and suddenly feel a buzz of arousal spurt down our bond? That gets awkward. She wants to know why I look all flushed. And you oh so innocently sit there acting clueless."

He felt his lips tip up. "Would you prefer I tell my mother I'm imagining doing seriously wicked things to you?"

"No, it would just be best if you didn't have such imaginings unless we're alone."

"I'm not that well-behaved."

"Don't I know it," she mumbled.

His softening cock slipping out of her, he kissed her little pout. "Told you we wouldn't be one of those couples who has to wait a long time before they fully imprint."

One unimpressed brow inched up. "You're really going to gloat?"

"Yup."

"No one likes a smug bastard."

"I got a lot of reasons to be smug, baby," he said, drifting his fingers through her hair. "It's been that way since I first found you."

Her face went all soft. "Dude, you can be super sweet sometimes."

"Seems stupid for me to hold in the words when you know how I feel." Their bond was as emotionally invasive as expected, but he found he didn't mind. It meant she'd never have any doubts about what he felt for her, and it meant he could keep a mental eye on her emotional wellbeing.

She planted a kiss on his throat. "Me and my cat are pretty smug, too, if I'm honest. We can't imagine that anyone would have suited us better than you."

His father had once said the same of his mother, but Isaiah hadn't seen how that could really be possible. Now, he got it. Strong connections could form with or without a true mate bond. It was about the couple, about how they fit, not if they were predestined.

Quinley *felt* like she was meant for him. What he felt for her was just *that* deep and true, and he couldn't envision himself ever feeling that way for anybody else. She meant more to him than he'd ever imagined that anyone could.

"Sorry to ruin the moment, but I'm about to start leaking, so …"

He chuckled. "Then I'd better get you in the shower and clean you up, hadn't I?"

"It would be best."

He peeled off her tee, scooped her up, and carried her into the shower stall.

"Are you going to sulk all night?" Quinley asked, raising her voice to be heard over the chatter bouncing off the Tavern walls.

Slanting her a frown, Alex asserted, "I'm not sulking."

"Brooding, then."

"I'm not brooding either."

"Of course you're not," Bree cut in from beside his chair, gently patting his shoulder. She sliced her gaze to Quinley and mouthed, "He's totally brooding."

"I heard that, Bree," he said without even looking at her.

Quinley silently chuckled. She hadn't thought he was serious about having another hamburger eat-off at the New Year's Eve party, but at one point the music had cut off and Valentina had bid the contestants to come forward.

Quinley had merely shrugged at Isaiah and then made her way to the chairs that were placed on the stage, along with a table. Patty towers identical to those that she and Alex had eaten last week were brought out and, yeah, she'd won again. Her cat didn't understand why he was so surprised. Or why Valentina—once more "speechless" but not really—had strode off.

Isaiah took her hand and gently pulled her out of the chair. "Well done. Not that I doubted you for a second."

Alex rose to his feet. "We're having another rematch," he told her.

She pursed her lips, lifting her shoulders. "Hey, if you want me to keep publicly humiliating you, that's fine. I don't mind. But I would have thought you'd be—"

"How could you, Aleksandr?" demanded Isaak, clambering onto the stage with his brothers.

Alex sighed. "Don't."

"Wolverines never pretend to lose," Isaak clipped. "Never. Always we win."

Quinley felt her brow crease, her cat bristling. "Hey, I won fair and square."

Sergei gave her a pitying look. "That is what Aleksandr wants you to think. Not true. He lost on purpose."

Alex shook his head. "Much as I hate to say it, she won."

Dimitri glowered at him. "Why you lie to protect her feelings? It is good for people to lose sometimes. Builds character."

"If she cries, she cries," said Isaak dispassionately. "But she will learn from mistakes. You do her no favors by letting her win."

Dimitri gave a hard nod. "People need to learn to lose."

Quinley offered the three brothers a meaningful look as she said, "Yes, they do."

Isaak spoke to Alex as he flapped a hand her way. "See, even she agrees."

So *that* comment had seemingly gone right over their heads.

Sidling up to Bree with baby Aurora in his arms, James rolled his eyes. "Will you just accept that she won? It isn't a huge deal."

Isaak tensed, his brows flicking together. "No one asked for your opinion, dumb cat. Give us our Galina. You should not be touching her."

James held the infant tighter. "Stop calling her that. Instead of trying to hog *Aurora*, why don't you instead go gatecrash someone else's party?"

Dimitri bristled. "We were invited."

James arched a dubious brow. "Yeah? By who?"

Dimitri hesitated. "I owe you no explanations."

"Ignore him," Sergei advised his brother. "He is not worth energy. Why our Valentina does not see that I have no idea."

"You know," began James, glancing at all three wolverines, "most shifters in your shoes would have just accepted by now that I'm not going anywhere. They wouldn't persist in being assholes, hoping it would scare me off. They wouldn't keep trying to talk their sister into leaving me. They would also stop making attempts on my life and just—"

"So much unnecessary information." Isaak sniffed. "I do not care."

Amused despite herself, Quinley turned to Isaiah, stepping into his arms. "Aren't you glad my family likes you?"

Isaiah hummed and curved his arms around her. "I am. Much as I'm glad my parents adore you the way they do. You're easy to love, so it's not surprising." He gave her a quick kiss and then guided her off the stage as their pride mates began to move the chairs and table.

The Tavern was as packed tonight as it had been for their own party. Similar decorations were hung around. Plenty of food was spread over the buffet table. Drinks were flowing at the free bar. There was singing and laughter and dancing and lots of photos being snapped.

It wasn't really just the coming of the new year that the pride was celebrating, it was the demise of the Vercetti Pack. News of it had spread far and wide. The Olympus Pride was now incredibly popular among shifters everywhere, so the Alphas had received a lot of gift food-baskets.

Quinley had charitably offered to take some off their hands, of course— as had the wolverines, including the three uncles.

Their pride's newly retired police officer, River, had managed to uncover exactly which anti-shifter extremist owned the compound that the Vercetti Pack had used to hide. Quinley wouldn't be surprised if the wolverines paid said extremist a visit.

"I'd ask if you need to vomit those patties back up," began Isaiah, "but that would be a silly question, wouldn't it?"

"Of course."

His lips twitched. "You having fun?"

Music started to blast, and then one of their pride members was singing on the karaoke completely out of tune.

"Well, I *was*."

Isaiah guided her away from the speaker but, yeah, there was no sparing her the horror. His cat pricked his ears, backing away from the noise.

Their mate smiled, saying, "I love knowing my family will be here next year."

He pressed a kiss to her temple. "And every year after that."

When she'd earlier invited them to attend the party, they hadn't turned it down for a *bad* reason. It was that they wanted to attend what they planned to be their last party on Crimson Pride territory. It would also serve as a goodbye-event for them.

They hadn't mentioned it to Quinley until this morning but, now certain she wouldn't be leaving the Olympus Pride, they'd enquired about a transfer. They wanted to live near their baby sister, and they liked how differently those without status were treated here.

Though Havana and Tate had told them they'd be welcome to join, Adaline and Raya had held off on telling Quinley, meaning for it to be a sort of "Happy New Year!" surprise. But Lori had accidentally spilled the beans. Quinley had let out a low squeal of delight on hearing the news.

Isaiah was happy for her, knowing how close she and her sisters were bonded. What had initially made the black-foots hesitate to transfer was that they'd no longer be permitted to work at Blue Harbor. But, as Isaiah had pointed out, there was no reason they couldn't open their own version of such a beauty salon.

When Quinley mentioned the prospect to Havana a few hours ago, the devil shifter had confirmed that it would be doable. She and Tate had apparently already talked about it, anticipating Quinley would make such a request, and there was a vacant premise near the pride's coffeehouse that could be turned into a salon.

Isaiah liked that idea, preferring that she wouldn't have to travel far for work. It would give both him and his cat some peace of mind to know that she'd be surrounded by pride mates. The Vercetti Pack were no longer an issue, but the world of shifters was rarely without danger.

Since he no longer needed to act as her guard, Isaiah had gone back to acting as Tate's bodyguard as well as an enforcer. Though it wasn't as hard to be physically apart from her now, he still wasn't a fan of it. He'd worried at first that his change in hours might upset her, but she'd made it clear that those worries were senseless. Quinley was completely fine with being left to her own devices.

Not that she *was* left alone. He often returned home to find that she had visitors. Sometimes it was Elle, sometimes it was the unholy trinity, sometimes it was his mother or even Valentina. People just liked to be around Quinley.

Brushing past a cluster of their pride mates, he heard Aspen whine, "Get a room."

He looked to see Bailey pull back from making out with Deke, who she'd all but melted into.

"A room for what?" the mamba asked Aspen.

The bearcat's lips thinned. "The rest of us would rather not see you sticking your tongue down Deke's throat and feeling him up."

"Then they need not watch," snarked Bailey.

"I'm just asking that you have some sense of decorum."

"Why? So that I'll argue with you? Are you bored? Well, now you know how Camden feels every day."

Deke closed his eyes, muttering something too low to be heard.

Before Aspen could advance on the mamba, Camden stepped between them and said, "We're not going to do this here and now. It's New Year's Eve. The countdown will begin soon. I'd rather you weren't starting the new year covered in cuts and bruises from an unnecessary fight," he told Aspen.

Sighing, Deke took his mate's arm. "Come on, trouble, we're gonna go stand over there."

"Why?" asked Bailey, sounding genuinely baffled as she allowed him to lead her away.

Quinley leaned into Isaiah as they kept walking, her mouth quirking. "Raya and Lori think Bailey is hilarious. I happen to agree."

The main reason the two female black-foots adored the snake shifter was that she'd effortlessly picked the locks that held them captive—something they'd told Quinley and Isaiah all about when they visited earlier that day.

As expected, Zaire and Nazra *had* been furious that they weren't given the chance to be involved after Raya and Lori were kidnapped—something they'd expressed to Tate and Havana by phone. The Olympus Alphas had given the pair some spiel about how it had been necessary to move quickly and that they hadn't been so sure Nazra and Zaire would care all that much about two unranked members anyway. The Crimson Alphas eventually dropped it.

Zaire had apparently quizzed Raya later, though, wanting every detail. Isaiah had *not* been happy on hearing that the male black-foot made a point of asking if Quinley was okay and if she'd been touched by the pack at all. Just the same, his cat didn't like that the Alpha still showed an interest in Quinley.

Neither Raya nor Lori had informed him of what happened to her, claiming ignorance and suggesting he contact Tate if he had questions.

Zaire hadn't.

Nor had he returned to the cul-de-sac or showed at any of the pride's stores, which was good. Considering the Crimson Alpha pair were still together, they were presumably working on their issues. Isaiah couldn't give a shit so long as they kept their distance from his mate.

"How cute is that?" said Quinley, gesturing at his parents, who were dancing all slow and graceful despite that the song playing was upbeat. "They're so adorable."

Isaiah squeezed her hip. "Just so you know, I'm not good at slow dancing."

"Oh, thank God."

"What?"

"You're just so amazing at everything that I was beginning to get a complex. It's good to know there's at least *one* thing you're not great at."

"Glad it pleases you," he deadpanned.

Quinley couldn't help but chuckle. She wasn't joking, though. He was just so competent and capable it was kind of intimidating.

Two enforcers materialized and were quick to congratulate them on fully imprinting. It had happened several times throughout the night. She didn't bother playing down just how delighted she was.

Catching something in her peripheral vision, she looked to see Elle huddled in a corner. As Isaiah and the enforcers fell into conversation, she detached herself from him—laughing at his frown of complaint—and crossed to the redhead. "Are you ... are you hiding?"

"No," Elle denied, folding her arms.

"Oh. Okay."

The redhead exhaled heavily, clearly annoyed. "*You're not being pushy.*"

Quinley stifled a smile. "Elle, you're definitely hiding. Tell me why."

"All right, all right—don't get hysterical. I'm avoiding Joaquin. I mean, not *completely*. Just taking breaks here and there."

Ah. "It can't be nice that he expects you two to carry on like you never crossed the friends line."

"That's exactly it," said Elle. "We promised we wouldn't let the fling ruin our friendship—I'm *all* for that. But I don't know how to act like it never happened. Especially when I want things he doesn't."

"Have you suggested maybe having a little space?"

"No, because it'd be like passive-aggressively striking out at him for what he *doesn't* feel for me."

Quinley hadn't thought of it that way before. "Ah, yeah, I get that. It wouldn't be unreasonable of you to want a little distance, though. I mean, it's not like he doesn't know that you want more. He's expecting you to both go on as if that's not the case. Life isn't that simple."

Elle smiled. "I like having you around, Quinley. You have this thing where you say stuff that's very validating."

"I'm here for you." Quinley hugged her tight, sensing she needed it.

Elle growled. "Goddamn submissives."

This time, Quinley didn't fight her smile, knowing the redhead secretly lapped up the comfort. "Suck it up and deal."

"Fine. But I'm allowing this under protest."

"Noted."

Isaiah joined them, his brow pinched. "Everything okay?"

"She's forcing a hug on me," Elle complained. "I don't know how to detach her from me without hurting her feelings."

His mouth tilted up. "I see."

Quinley lifted her head from Elle's shoulder as she noticed something. "Joaquin's spotted you, and he's on his way over. Not sure if you wanna—"

That fast, Elle was gone. Like magic.

Isaiah sighed. "She's still struggling with the Joaquin thing, I'm guessing."

"It has to be hard for someone you have non-platonic feelings for to want to spend a lot of time with you 'as friends.' If you were angling for that, well, I'd want you in my life. But I'd also want to punch you in the throat on occasion if you weren't giving me space when I needed it."

Draping an arm around her shoulders, Isaiah drew her out of the corner. "You're my best friend for sure, but what I feel for you is far from platonic."

Aw, he said the best stuff. "If someone had told me a month ago that I'd be *this* happy in just four weeks' time, well, I wouldn't have believed them. Which is sad. But here we are."

"It seems crazy that I didn't know you existed last month. It feels like you've been around for years. You're so much a part of me that it's weird to think of when we weren't bonded."

She knew exactly what he meant, because she felt the same way. Part of it was the imprint bond, but part of it was just how seamlessly they'd *clicked*. Sometimes, you could meet a person, slot into their lives, and feel like you'd known them for years. It had been that way with them. "When are we having our mating ceremony?"

"Whenever you want, providing I don't have to wait long."

"Maybe next weekend, then."

"Works for me."

They halted as Aspen stumbled their way with Bailey on her back. The mamba had her arm curved around the bearcat's throat, trying to choke her out.

Deke swore long and hard as he and Camden caught up with them. "What is *wrong* with you two?"

"She needs sleep, that's all," Bailey told him. "Say 'night, 'night, Aspen."

Deke plucked the mamba from Aspen's back.

Camden hauled his coughing mate to him. "I turn my back for thirty fucking seconds ..."

"Let's just keep them apart for the rest of the night," Deke proposed.

"The rest of their lives sounds better." Camden guided Aspen away, rolling his eyes as she began hurling insults at Bailey—who only laughed.

Right then, the music cut off and the DJ announced that the countdown would start very soon.

"I don't know how Deke and Camden cope with those two," said Isaiah, "I really don't."

"They're a riot," said Quinley.

"Yeah, but I could never have someone like that as a mate. Someone who I'd worry would destroy the world if I didn't have my eye on them twenty-four/seven."

"You need someone more low-maintenance," she agreed.

He turned her to face him. "I need *you*."

She went pliant against him. "You have me."

"I know. And I'm never letting you go."

"I'll never want you to." She planted her hands on his chest. "And if you try getting rid of me, you're gonna find all sorts of wonderful delights on your pillow every day." She wasn't joking. He'd pay for it until the end of time.

"Won't happen," he stated. "You're stuck with me now."

She smiled. "I can think of worse things."

The DJ cleared his throat. "And now it starts. Ten, nine, eight, seven ..."

Isaiah pulled her closer and brushed his nose against hers. "Love you, Quin."

"Love you, too. God, we can be so soppy, can't we?"

"I can live with that."

"Same here."

Cheers rang out and party poppers went off.

His mouth curved. "Happy New Year, baby."

She kissed him hard. "Happy New Year."

# ACKNOWLEDGEMENTS

As always, a major thanks must go to my family - when their wife/mother is someone who has people in her head running around with scissors and setting stuff on fire, their days are going to be trying at times.

Thank you so much to my son for designing the book cover, I envy your ease with editing software.

A humungous thanks to everyone who gave this series a chance, whether it was to read just one book or all of them. I appreciate every one of you.

Take care

S :)

# ABOUT THE AUTHOR

Suzanne Wright lives in England with her husband, two children, and two Bengal cats. When she's not spending time with her family, she's writing, reading, or doing her version of housework—sweeping the house with a look.

## TITLES BY SUZANNE WRIGHT

*The Deep in Your Veins Series*
Here Be Sexist Vampires
The Bite That Binds
Taste of Torment
Consumed
Fractured
Captivated
Touch of Rapture

*The Phoenix Pack Series*
Feral Sins
Wicked Cravings
Carnal Secrets
Dark Instincts
Savage Urges
Fierce Obsessions
Wild Hunger
Untamed Delights

*The Dark in You Series*
Burn
Blaze
Ashes
Embers
Shadows
Omens
Fallen
Reaper
Hunted


*The Mercury Pack Series*
Spiral of Need
Force of Temptation
Lure of Oblivion
Echoes of Fire
Shards of Frost


*The Olympus Pride Series*
When He's Dark
When He's an Alpha
When He's Sinful
When He's Ruthless
When He's Torn
When He Dares


*The Devil's Cradle Series*
The Wicked in Me
The Nightmare in Him
The Monsters We Are (coming 2025)


*Standalones*
From Rags
Shiver
The Favor
The Pact
Wear Something Red – An Anthology

Printed in Great Britain
by Amazon

39685460R00145